One of the best books I've read this year. Scott A. Jones tells this hopeful and heartbreaking story of love and scars and fresh starts with graceful prose and a beautiful appreciation for the complication of both place and the human condition.

—Anne Hillerman, best selling author of *A Cave Of Bones*

The supporting characters throughout Bec's story ring with authenticity. From the ex-teacher who's become the town lush to the hash slinger with a heart of gold to a gaggle of wacky women and a squad of broken soldiers, the author depicts them all as real folk with their own crosses to bear and, therefore, worthy of compassion.

Jones is a writer whose words often make emotions explode in silence, such as when he describes a marriage slowly crumbling. He writes, "They lay apart, a full twelve inches of separation. The space between them cut a thousand yards deep, a ditch of human suffering." His insights also bite with the sting of truth, as when he's describing Bec and her husband (in uniform) strolling through a crowded airport. "From the curb, through the door and to the counter, William received nods, friendly expressions, small waves. Everyone could be thankful for his service, as long as they didn't have to serve. Or send their children."

Jones is an author working at the top of his game. You appreciate getting to know the people he creates. You love the sound of his voice on the page. Perhaps best of all, when you reach the end of his novel, you know that your time has been profoundly well spent. RECOMMENDED by the US Review

— *US Review Of Books*

Some readers may be unnerved by Jones' unflinching descriptions of the physical realities of cancer treatment ... In her struggle for survival, Bec lives on a razor's edge, and Jones subtly charts her progress and psychological shifts—which, the author points out, are also affected by medication ... As the story progresses, readers will be drawn ever closer to Bec—they'll gain a profound understanding of the challenges she faces, and be awed by her spirit of survival. But there are also feelings of joy in this harrowing novel, as Bec's newfound conception of self arises from her sense of loss and despair. Overall, this novel offers a nuanced and thoroughly believable portrait of a cancer patient's everyday life that offers hope and sadness in equal measure.

A deeply affecting and fearlessly descriptive story that charts the complexities of life with a potentially fatal illness.

— *Kirkus Reviews* (A starred review)

This poignant novel is stylish and poetic as it travels through the troubled seasons of a woman's life...

Scott Archer Jones's emotional and dramatic novel *And Throw Away the Skins* follows the unpredictable and often painful twists of a woman's life ...

And Throw Away the Skins is a poignant novel that isn't afraid to throw curveballs at its characters.

— Delia Stanley, *Foreword Reviews*

And Throw Away the Skins by Scott Archer Jones is the story of Rebecca, known as Bec, whom we meet on the tail end of her fight with breast cancer. The book is set in 2008 and 2009, and her husband is sent off to the middle east as an Army chaplain. Even prior to his departure, their marriage is strained, Bec noticing a palpable relief on both of their ends once the physical separation occurs. Due to finances, and with a desire to spend time alone to recuperate after her disease, Bec moves up to a remote mountain cabin on her family's land in New Mexico....

The writing style is poignant but succinct, and at times the short paragraphs read almost like a poem. Much of the story was almost hinted-at by brief flashbacks into Bec's past, or by the things that were left unsaid in conversations, which took some getting used-to but also contributed to the overall minimalistic tone. I was particularly moved by the author's descriptions of the fictional town and surrounding landscape, which set a very specific mood that hung through the entirety of the book. It was almost as if the town into which Bec had moved had a spirit of its own, one that permeated the actions and choices of all the residents that settled there...

I would recommend it highly to those who appreciate raw and emotional stories with complex and nuanced characters. I rate this book 4 out of 4 stars.

— Online Bookclub Inc

And Throw Away The Skins

Scott Archer Jones

Fomite

Burlington, VT

ISBN-13: 978-1-944388-61-4
Library of Congress Control Number: 2018959645
Fomite
58 Peru Street
Burlington, VT 05401
www.fomitepress.com

I dedicate this book to a chocolate half-lab named Siena. She accompanied me through the four years the book demanded: she sacked out on my feet until they went to sleep, nudged the laptop to get some attention. She shared the writing down of these people, these New Mexico places. I wish she had lasted long enough to see that first box of books arrive. But – she would have preferred a treat.

Acknowledgements

I acknowledge that Santa Eulalia de Mérida is a fictional village and that other physical details of the world have been modified to fit the book's needs.

I wish to thank the VA National Cemetery Administration for the day's briefing I received from the Commandant of the Santa Fe National Cemetery.

I want to thank the usual cast of scoundrels, low-lifes, and writers who nudged this book closer to the finish line – especially Sandra Hornback Jones, Phaedra Greenwood, and John Dufresne.

There is a wilderness we walk alone / However well-companioned"
Stephen Vincent Benét, *Western Star*

"Sometimes we want what we want even if we know it's going to kill us."
Donna Tartt, *The Goldfinch*

CONTENTS

William's Fragment

   Chapter One – Prayed Over   3

   Chapter Two – Northwest   12

   Chapter Three – Drama   24

   Chapter Four – Distance   33

   Chapter Five – Sordid Past   41

   Chapter Six – Tough   52

   Chapter Seven – Quitter   60

   Chapter Eight – At the Edge   70

   Chapter Nine – Such Babies   78

   Chapter Ten – Help In Any Way   91

   Chapter Eleven – Hunkered   103

   Chapter Twelve – Steeled   112

   Chapter Thirteen – Caught Stealing Pie   123

   Chapter Fourteen – Nursery   131

   Chapter Fifteen – Separate   140

Michael's Plague

   Chapter Sixteen – Long Time   153

   Chapter Seventeen – Cheer   167

   Chapter Eighteen – Step   176

   Chapter Nineteen – Groping   183

   Chapter Twenty – Control   193

   Chapter Twenty-One – Quiet   200

   Chapter Twenty-Two – Other Planet   212

   Chapter Twenty-Three – Quaver   226

   Chapter Twenty-Four – In Common   234

   Chapter Twenty-Five – Married to the Army   247

   Chapter Twenty-Six – The Hell Away   255

   Chapter Twenty-Seven – Clockworks   264

   Chapter Twenty-Eight – Dreaming a Good Dream   274

Bec's Storm

   Chapter Twenty-Nine – Snow   289

WILLIAM'S FRAGMENT

CHAPTER ONE – PRAYED OVER

S PRING 1977.

Out under the hedge apple tree, nine-year-old Rebecca squatted. Mud caked the knees of her coveralls. She had scooped a pond in the dust, now turned to a red paste, and assembled pebbles in a long fence line that surrounded her play farm. The two stick ponies Uncle Howie had whittled craned their necks over the fence, strained for the grass on the other side. Just like real horses.

She twisted around to scoop up a willow stick – the fence needed a gate, an arch to welcome visitors. Startled, she gaped at shoes planted in the dust. White leather on top under the laces, surrounded by tan cowhide with tiny punched holes. The brown cuffs crumpled over the laces and legs rose as twin pillars, soaring up to form the giant towering quiet, so close. She flinched when she saw those shoes, heard that voice from above. She hunched her shoulders and shrank herself small.

Held close under the tree, the deep rich tones suffocated her. "Your father said I'd find you here." He hunkered down beside Rebecca, dropped a hand like a slab of fatback on her shoulder. He said, "It's time, Rebecca, you're grown up enough."

Rebecca didn't feel grown. "What do you mean, Reverend?"

"Most of your classmates have re-dedicated themselves to the Church. You haven't even been going to Sunday School. You're, what, ten?"

"Nine."

"You should reflect upon our Savior Jesus Christ and his part in your life. You should contemplate our very own Church of Christ's Witness. I'll pray now, pray you welcome Him into your heart. Kneel with me." He picked her up, folded her legs so she'd end on her knees, set her down in the mud puddle, on her fence. With a heavy grunt, he dropped onto one knee beside her.

She glanced at him, a darting flick. His face was pink where he had shaved his jowls close. His temples dripped beads of sweat; the hat brim stained brown from previous redemptions soaked the droplets off his forehead.

He kissed the top of her head. His left hand kneaded her shoulder as he ducked his head, and she thought her bones would break.

He thrust his right palm to the sky, the slanting sun behind it a fireball. He began. "Lord, let Rebecca be surrounded by the Church, enfolded in its loving arms, protected forever and ever –"

Her head buzzed, like a fly droning against window glass.

—⁓—

March 2008.

Bec leaned against the doorjamb and watched her husband – not because it was a casual thing he did or because she didn't want to help. She propped herself up because she felt lightheaded and death was in the room.

William shuffled from the dresser to the duffel on the bed – packing every T-shirt and pair of briefs he owned. After two years in the Army, he had established a system. The duffel concealed two rolls of toilet paper to bridge him over to a tougher, less-coddled butt. He crammed in spare boots, camouflage, the miniature e-reader that displayed three versions

4

of the Bible and, she knew, the Qur'an. Nothing about him, his duffel, his uniform smelled of death. It all carried salvation, for everyone but her.

—∿—

Waiting, Bec perched at the breakfast bar, a half-finished cup of tea at her elbow. She had steeped chamomile with ginger for the nausea, but truth be told, the smell that wafted up unsettled her. William's latest crossword puzzle book lay open in front of her. With a pencil, she worked on what she called a psychological crossword – she ignored the clues and wove her own tapestry. Number 4 across, four letters – *lies*. Number 4 down, four letters – love. That gave her an *e* for Number 6 across, three letters – *sex*. Number 39 down, seven letters. Might be *Passion*. *N* started Number 42 across. *Nurse*. Number 23 down – *hospital*. Number 41 down intersected 42 across – *cancer*. The page revealed small islands of meaning. Memory, prophecy. She nudged the puzzle away. The sores in her mouth stung, unappeased by the tea.

Ten minutes before the taxi arrived, she could hear him rooms away, pacing the house. Fiddling with his packing at this, the last minute. She knew what was up. Dig out the LED flashlight, slip it back in, fill a small pocket with cough drops, remember two hundred Q-tips just in time. And why only two hundred?

—∿—

She wobbled across the living room – his room, not hers – wobbled behind William as she carried his puzzle book. This room resonated with the meltdown, the quarrels that led them to this crux. Now another goodbye, and they could only hint around at what had changed their lives. He wouldn't speak of it, even if she pressed.

She caught at the back of the chintz-covered couch. His duffle with roller wheels scored long, deep tracks in the benign carpet, like scars without the staple marks. From behind he struck her as a massive truck that dragged a small trailer. She pictured him for a second with tail lights.

His Army Class A's spread tight across his shoulders in the familiar green, the color that constituted his favorite joke: "I dripped spaghetti sauce all over my pickle suit. Is my pickle suit back from the cleaners? I'm the Pickle Pastor." She hated that joke.

He threw open the front door with its leaded glass to let in the Dallas spring. He shouted over his shoulder. "Cab's here. Are we ready?"

She jerked to a stop in the long hallway. A familiar rush of queasiness crested clear into her sinuses, the metallic taste of bile in her mouth. She flapped a hand at him, pointed out through the open front door. As she whirled to the half bath beneath the stairs, she said, "Be right there."

She crashed to her knees on the tile and flipped the lid back. Perversely, the leaping in her stomach and esophagus died away. She clutched the bowl's rim and gawked at her fingers, the chipped polish, the dirt under the fingernail where she had pried up a weed outside the kitchen. She should dig out that dirt later in the taxi. Her nails hadn't turned black from the drugs, not yet. She waited for the jerking spasms to cycle back. Nothing. Two weeks since she had received the first jolt of chemo – maybe the days of retching had run their course. She rested her head on the cool porcelain and waited for the hot pulsing of blood to dissipate. In a moment, she groaned to her feet, unsure if the episode had dispersed. She murmured, "That was much ado about nothing." A weak grin. In the mirror, a bald head waited for the scarf.

—w—

He hovered on the sidewalk by the back of the cab, his eyebrows clamped together with that deep furrow between – the wrinkled face he wore when things needed fixing. The driver had already heaved the duffle in the trunk and shut the lid. William called up to her, "Everything okay?"

6

She nodded and the world didn't stagger. Dizziness held at bay, she locked the door and plodded down the sidewalk.

—⁓—

William leaned over the seat and ordered the driver, "DFW. United Airlines."

She could smell turmeric and cumin, and a background odor of perspiration and deodorant. The taxi breathed life, maybe more than she. Maybe even now she carried tiny cancer seeds in her. Possibly they waited in her chest, or had broken out into her body.

Solicitous, William loomed over her in the back seat. "We could have brought your car, Rebecca. More comfortable for you. I could have driven."

She squashed her amusement. As usual, he focused on the wrong thing. "But I'd have to plod all the way into the parking garage and drive myself home. No, this works out fine." Her hands were cramped in knots, again. She glanced into the cabbie's rear-view mirror – it flashed a glimpse of her face. *Pallid* described the ashen skin. She twitched the red scarf that shrouded her skull, checked it camouflaged her, at least from the ignorant. The damned silk slipped again.

He shifted away – he had given up, she could tell, on how they should have handled the journey. He cradled her hand – for miles the weight of that moist paw distracted her. As he peered out the window, he said, "There's DFW." He leaned to the driver "United. It's Terminal B."

He slumped back into his seat. She contemplated him, memorized everything about his size, his shape, his color. Memory might be all she'd have. Two hundred pounds, thirty of it fat. He kept his hair cut short; naked on top, a quarter-inch brush right in front. In the duffel in back hid the uniform he preferred, the combat uniform; his chaplain's badge velcroed on the right above his name tape, his lieutenant bar on the placket in the center of his chest. Here in his Class A's and at his age, he

7

appeared unsuccessful, incidental. The lowly rank, the few patches and meager ribbons – he had joined up so late. An open, warm face, burnt dark with red undertones. Dark tanned wrinkles cored in white, like threads, raced back from his temple and out of the corner of his mouth.

—⁓—

From the curb through the door and to the counter, William received nods, friendly expressions, small waves. Everyone could be thankful for his service, as long as they didn't have to serve. Or send their children.

DFW, the size of the military-industrial complex itself, stretched out across the Texas plain, its square concrete tubes filled with bustling travelers. In front of check-in, all those people and their aberrant paths reminded her of ant swarms. Another stomach leap, a hand wave to nausea. Boarding pass in hand, he shepherded her to where a row of chairs turned their backs to the Dallas sun.

They settled in, tenuous, quiet; he stole her hand. He said, "I have to watch the time – it eats up more than a few minutes to clear security. Do you want anything, Rebecca? Water? Tea?"

Her mouth caught a teaser of bile, a hiccup before it burst. "No, I'm fine. I'll just sit with you until it's time." She classed the sour taste in her mouth as the color green. All taste had color, or colors.

Their stretch of seats, a good distance from any other flyers, kept them wrapped in a gauze of quiet. In his eyes that far-away gaze; in all likelihood flashing forward, onboard the final flight – the one that would wing him from Kabul into Kandahar. Bec sorted through what the next few days would be for her. Not much else but the poison, but now everything was so hard. Exhausting.

He glanced at his watch time after time. Bec counted the seconds between his checks, her soothing monotone at the edge of actual speech. "One thousand and one. One thousand and two."

The minute hand reached the secret goal he had set. He leaped up,

8

ready to sprint away from the silence. He scooped up his messenger bag. "You don't have to hike down to Security with me. It's a long way."

Mute, she held out her arms. He gathered her into his grasp, hovered over her. His hug didn't progress beyond tenuous, delicate. His fear he would hurt her.

She set him free, rocked back a step, felt his relief well up. "Call me when you arrive at the base."

"I'll call you from McGuire, from the passenger terminal. Again when I hit Kabul. And from the base too."

She should try harder, keep the conventions up. She nuzzled her face into his breast bone, rested her head. "I love you."

"You're not crying onto my tie, are you?"

She muttered. She wanted William. Just not *this* William.

"What?"

"I said, I don't want you to go." She had believed she didn't want him at home. Did she need him tiptoeing around in the background? Easier alone. Strange, detachment filled her, even as her chest ached with the moment.

His voice rumbled above her. "Rebecca, I am so sorry. I should have requested more time."

More time, so he could hover over her and pat her shoulder. "We couldn't know, William. I've never had cancer before. We didn't know what to expect. I guess I'll have to brew my own tea and do my own laundry."

He brushed her head, shifted the silk scarf across her skull. "How will you handle the chemotherapy visits?" Worry-wart mode.

She should ask, How will you handle being shot at? "William, we talked about this before. The Bible-study ladies from our old church will pick me up and drop me back at the house, every other day. It's okay. The first two weeks weren't that bad."

He let out a shaky breath. "No? I'd hate to see really awful."

"Awful is war."

9

"Yes, but war has rules, doesn't it?"

"Does it? I have rules too."

"Name one." He must think this was some form of teasing.

"Accept life a day at a time. Thank God for being alive."

"Yes, let's thank Him."

His quiet words blurred as he prayed over her as if she were a parishioner he visited in the hospital. Her old hypocrisy twinged, but she closed her eyes out of duty. Like God would notice.

He twitched his arm to glance at the wristwatch again. "It's time. I love you, Rebecca." He gave a final gentle squeeze, dropped his arms, He pivoted, strode across the acre of tile and back into a resolute, codified life. Much less messy. More frightening – to those who stayed home.

She dropped back into the chrome and vinyl chair. To catch her breath. Acid tears etched into her eyes – she dug for the Kleenex in her handbag.

He could die out in that wasteland, and it would be her fault. She had shoved, prodded at their unhappiness like she picked at a scab, until he'd do anything to stop it.

—᠁—

Some fights you never forgot, even after years, after cancer. William had shrunk into the chintz sofa corner as if it rendered him invisible. Bec strode back and forth in front of him – she burned and it drove her to her feet.

In her bones she knew she had to say it. "Why do you deny how miserable you are?"

"But I'm not. I have good days and bad days."

"Ten bad days out of the last two weeks."

His eyes stretched round as a startled cat, a bit buggy. "You're keeping score now?"

She held out her hands with her palms facing him and fingers flared.

10

"Ten. Count them."

"Bec, don't do this. I don't want to talk about this. There's a church finance meeting in an hour."

Her jaw hurt, she bit down so hard. She rubbed her cheek. "Never the right time."

"What? I'm sorry, I didn't hear."

No, he wouldn't. "Fine. Go to your meeting."

—⁂—

But she couldn't hang around in an airport terminal forever, hitting the rewind button.

Once on her feet, she trekked outside to the cab rank. On the sidewalk in the Dallas heat, she queued for a taxi.

Tiredness oozed through her like molasses. The bandages over her breasts, or where the breasts had been, itched with the persistence of fire ant bites. Lord, she wished she could have a drink. Gin and tonic on top of anti-nausea drugs – not a ghost's chance.

Every time he left, he had to pray. But this hadn't been the worst time she'd been prayed over.

CHAPTER TWO – NORTHWEST

JULY 2008.

Eighteen weeks of living alone. Really alone. No more church services for Bec. No Food Bank. No crisis phone calls from her old parishioners, distraught with their imperfect lives.

She heard only from the professional hand-holders. Everyone else was embarrassed by disease, turned off by its aftermath. Maybe she preferred the silence – she was the hero in her own play.

In the bathroom, Bec angled in towards the floor length mirror with a shuffle – she sneaked up on herself. Her body-double poised on the other side of the looking glass. Voyeuristic, Bec scanned her form. Her eyes swept up, contemplated the whole picture. She flinched.

Blue eyes, a fuzzy scalp – her emaciation painted her as a child. Or a Stone Age mummy. Tribal marks, two slices of purple thread ruled out in straight horizontal lines below her chest. The body-double slid her forefinger across her ribs, traced the left breast's scar, far less puckered than a few weeks before. At least they had left the muscles underneath, so she didn't have craters. Her finger touched the welt, a mere sixteenth of an inch high, from one side to the other, cut straight across in defiance of human shape and curve. Pagan ceremony. Cut away hunks of her body to fend off death, to propitiate the old, blood-soaked gods. Her finger returned again to search for what she had lost, traced out the violence. "Ghost woman, who talks to herself. Blame the chemotherapy." Sometimes she wanted something to blame, someone to scream at.

Boy-thin, small-assed, now flat chested, she shrugged on a robe. She wandered downstairs and into the wide hall, headed for a cup of tea. In the chilled humidity of the air-conditioned house, her bare feet left damp tracks on black-stained pine planking and led her past the kitchen. In the front hall, bundles of cardboard waited to be turned into boxes. A carton of strapping tape squatted on the floor, its top a gaping hole. Her hand traced a frail curve across a roll of packing paper. Soon. Maybe today.

—◊—

Tea mug in hand, she stalled at the foot of the bed. It sprawled out in bland immensity, a landing field. William preferred large beds; she'd rather sleep secure. Over on one side, her side, she left the covers turned back to reveal the foot-and-a-half of her domain. She set the mug on the bedside table and scooped her panties from the bed. She spread the band of elastic, stepped into the white cotton. Her hands tugged the fabric bottom down over her flat butt. Up front, the cotton concealed all but the navel. Only proper. Jeans, a wrinkled oxford shirt, direct from the dryer. She waited on the edge of the bed and toyed with the cover. The sheets sighed, hushed. The air conditioning kicked on and droned. She clambered under the covers, turned her back to the sunlit window. Her hair, its first stubble sprung from her scalp, scratched into the pillow. She tucked in her chin and closed her eyes, her hands folded under her chin, her knees bent. That warning voice in her head, "Now, don't you cry."

—◊—

Spring 1975.

Seven-year-old Rebecca had been bad. Late for chores. Her pa had collected the eggs, not her.

13

She peered at her father's feet, clutched her hands in front of her. Where was her mother? He wore brown boots, scuffed, the laces repaired with knots. She tried to wish him away. Blue jeans frayed at the bottom. He let out a long and weighty sigh. "What will I do with you, Rebecca? I just don't know."

"Yessir. No sir." Already her bottom stung.

He grunted his way out of the chair on the porch. "Wait here."

He thumped down the steps and out to the willow tree at the yard edge. With a jackknife fished out of his pocket, he cut a long branch and doubled it back to hold the fat butt and the skinny end together. Slow as molasses, he clumped back across the yard and mounted the steps to the wooden porch. He dropped into the wicker chair like a tree crashing to the floor of the woods.

"Get over here. Drop your jeans."

Her hands fumbled at the button, slid the zipper down. She sniffled.

He seized her by the wrist and jerked her forward.

The shock of the switch on that first stroke raised her off his lap and she howled. Pain raced out in a wave, crested in her neck and her heels. It ricocheted into her skinny buttocks. He slapped his hand hard into the small of her back, pinned her against his coveralls. "One." She let out another wail as the second fell.

"Two. Don't cry, Rebecca." She tried to catch the wail in her throat, strangle it against her lips, the back of her teeth and gums.

"Three." She imagined blood that spurted out and stained her panties.

"Four. Only bad girls cry, Rebecca." She sobbed, in spite of herself. How many?

"Cry, will you? Then I'll give you something to cry about." He raised his switch again, and again. "Nine. Good girls don't tell, Rebecca."

He was right, he was right. She would never tell. Momma would never know she had been bad. Let it end!

14

"Ten." His voice slid up a pitch – she could hear it through her yowling.

—⋙—

July 2008.

Four days before the move, the abandonment of Texas. Packing the living room ate up two days. Shattered by cartons, paper, stacks of possessions, the room rendered itself down and crept into boxes. Bec christened each carton – "BOOKS" – "PICTURE FRAMES" – "ART GLASS." She slid each one she completed across the waxed floor, stacked it against a wall that ran the room's length. On her knees, she rolled up the rug, taped it so it couldn't uncoil itself and restore any comfort to the room. All of this amounted to the final tithe for the Church, a purchase price out of slavery. She sealed her own two boxes shut in front of the fireplace, boxes where photos hid divorced from their frames and a keepsake or two loitered, half ashamed.

—⋙—

Tuesday. Ninety percent done, and she hurtled towards an apogee.

Of course the Church had been on stage, its helping hand thrust out. The deacons had driven back and forth Saturday and Sunday afternoon, carted away furniture and carpets to the church resale shop. By Monday evening most cartons had disappeared. The house bounced back her footsteps, echoed the squeak of her sneakers. Now that Bec had pressed through the bulk of the packing, she could breathe. She hummed, a nonsense song from childhood. The house felt happier. It foresaw a time without her and William.

Last Thursday she had carted all her medical records up to his office, to the pastor's sanctuary. The shredder swallowed them, all the drug bills, the lists of procedures with their fake price tags, the surgery, the months of follow-up poison sessions in their own pink folder.

She had already scheduled the next step, the final medical agony.

15

In Santa Fe, after her relocation to New Mexico, they would render unto her a last procedure, a portacath removal. After, live or die, she'd be free of the plastic invader that lay beneath her skin and punched down into a blood vessel.

The shredder ate all of it, spewed out bits of confetti, details eradicated. Maybe the system held her digital records somewhere, maybe they had her trapped like a fly on sticky paper. But at least she wouldn't know it.

She wouldn't miss this office. They had fought here.

—⁓—

Even after three years, that argument throbbed, like the ache of a new bruise. Speaking her mind – that had been inadvisable. She had slipped around his chair to the window and stared out between the wooden slats. She said, "Try not to be so whiny."

"Fine. Now I'm whiny." His pink face, a child's color, turned ruddy. She watched his mouth stretch thin, back towards his jaw – like a surgical incision.

"William, you're so unhappy. And it poisons me. It poisons everything." She opened the plantation blinds, let the Dallas sun into the office. They couldn't go on this way.

He leaned back in the chair, rared up like a prophet. The chair complained with a dismal creak. "God gives us all challenges. I'm lucky to have this church. You may think I'm a complainer, but not many other ministers could have ended up here. In such a large church. It buys you all of the good things. So I think you'd tolerate my moods once in a while."

"Like I care about about cars, about the house. I care about you, and what this church is doing to both of us."

"Both of us?"

A tremor ran up her neck. He was so selfish sometimes. "In case you hadn't noticed, a minister's wife has a full time job. Your job, but my work too."

"Whiny." He grunted his way to his feet, shuffled files on the desk. "I left my briefcase downstairs." If a man could huff out of a room, he huffed.

She glanced down, picked out the briefcase in the desk kneehole. Right. This office was his prison, and their boxing ring. But then, they had fought in most rooms.

—⁄⁄⁄—

Across the bed her hanging clothes scattered, shrouded in plastic, destined to lie on top of all the boxes in the truck to slide about, fall in the fissures. The doorbell. William's brother Ted had arrived. The bouncing, boyish Ted. She eased down the stairs, slid a hand along the bannister in case a ripple of dizziness attacked. Onto the planks, the tiles at the front door. Through the leaded glass she picked out a collage of Beach-Boy fragments, a kaleidoscope bust-up of blond bangs, sunglasses shoved back, white-white teeth. As she tugged the door open, she exposed the full image just as he rang the bell again. Ted lurched back. He eyed her. "Jeez, Bec. You're like that stubble-headed Irish singer." He wagged his finger at her. "Hot new look."

She grinned at him – what else could she do? "Thanks for coming, Ted. Thanks for the compliment – I think." She didn't bother to tell him she had shaved her own head months ago and kept it shaved all through the chemo.

"Hey, what's a brother-in-law for?" That struck the right mood – he beamed, so pleased with himself.

She stepped back and gestured into the house. "Can I brew you up some tea, or coffee? William left a can of coffee in the cupboard. No, wait – I gave away the coffee maker."

He trailed her into the house, closed the door. "You what? The man's coffee master?"

"Mistake, huh?"

He leaned down, gave her a hug, scrubbed her fuzzy head like an

17

indulgent grandpa. Next he patted her on the ass. His hand covered one entire buttock.

She twitched and stepped sideways. She knew he'd try again, but it was nice to know she still had a good ass.

His face was bland, a denial it had happened. "How's the packing thing going?"

"Well-organized chaos."

"You should have called me sooner."

She twitched her head. "You're here now and I'm thankful."

"William would never forgive me if I didn't. I don't know why you packed all this yourself." He had habitually been the protective one – and the brother-in-law with a thing for her.

She flashed the grin at him, the one that blew him off. "Call it therapy. Or call it a goodbye. I left the greasy part for you, though."

"Gee, thanks. What greasy part?"

"I left all of William's tools scattered around the garage. Up on the mountain I might need them. Better pack it all."

He grinned. "You're enjoying this."

"Not guilty. It's like a twister flattened the house." More like running away from home.

He handed her a sheaf of paper. "I've been looking forward to the road trip. I rented the truck and the trailer for your pickup. I stuffed my bag behind the seat in the cab. You owe me six hundred and change."

She stepped out onto the porch beside him. "I'm good for it. Drop the trailer and back the U-Haul up the drive. After that you can box up the garage."

He stepped closer to her. Her senses registered his sheer size, the smooth, musky cologne. Hair tousled to charm, skin buffed by a dermatologist. Cargo shorts, a knit shirt. Ted played the yuppie around her – he thought that's what it took. She believed he'd been raised in a locker room in an all-boys school.

18

She punched him on the bicep. "Come on. You only have five days off, you said, and we have a lot to do. I'll carry my clothes down – they're light. Next I'll drag out the kitchen boxes." She pivoted away, peeked over her shoulder as she hobbled up the stairs, two halting steps to each shiny wooden tread.

He snapped to attention. "Yes ma'am, sergeant ma'am. Truck up the drive, tools into the back. Await further orders."

—⚯—

The truck, a big orange and white box scarred by a hard life, towed a trailer with a pickup strapped on it like a mummy on a board. The bench seat pretended to be buckets, with some contouring to suggest a nonexistent comfort. Stiff springs jogged them up and down. A phantom sensation tickled in her brain: her missing breasts bounced on her chest. She rubbed her hand across the missing nipples, chased the itch away.

She had hesitated on the curb, stared at the house already lost to her. Its big bluff face, the eighteen shutters so foreign to her – she couldn't envisage that she had actually lived there, behind those windows. She swung up into the cab.

Mockingbird Lane to the Carpenter Freeway, clear the town, and northwest on 287. Dallas fell behind and kept the keys she had dropped in the mail. The vultures at the foreclosure company – screw them. Laughter bubbled up. Odd. She had expected to be sad.

—⚯—

The miles rolled out; the parched yellow grass burnt by drought gave way to Potter County's desert weeds, punctuated by vast irrigation circles. The western sun poured into their laps. They had given up on the melancholy air-conditioning, so the wind roared in the open windows.

Ted said, "Are you sure? Motel 6? That's what you chose?"

"You may not be broke, but I am."

He let go of the steering wheel to wave both hands. "But we need to keep ourselves strong and fit. Three hundred miles today, four hundred tomorrow. All at fifty-five frickin' miles an hour."

"You expected room service? A cart with a starched white tablecloth?"

"And a bucket of ice with a bottle in it."

She cracked up. "Sorry, I can't drink yet. You'll have to settle for the Burger Barn, and the Waffle House for breakfast."

"Bullshit. We'll use some of my hard-earned commissions and splurge on a steak. Amarillo is bound to have a steak house. After, we can prowl around searching for ice cream." The wind ruffled his hair, made him appear young and carefree. He could have been a commercial.

"No doubt." She slid sideways into it. "Have you heard from William lately?"

"Email a couple of days ago. I told him I was hanging around the house, helping out. He told me to keep my hands in my pockets."

She jerked her head around and cocked her eye at him. "Really?"

He snickered. "Naah. That's just me trying to make him sound interesting."

"Your brother isn't interesting?"

"That's not the adverb I'd think of. Dull, dependable, predictable. I never understood why you chose him over me – you grew up with me too."

She had picked William because he was safe. She could never pick this boy who drove the truck. "I think you meant 'adjective,' not 'adverb.' "

"Whatever." Ted didn't like to be needled about his skin-deep literacy.

She scratched her nose, gazed out at the view. "Did you say anything about the move?"

"Naah again. I want to shock him with how great a brother I am."

"Um, that's good. That you didn't mention it. William doesn't know." She squinted at him, to gauge the reaction.

"Know you're moving?" His voice jacked up an octave.

"Know we lost the house to the bank."

He stared at her like her shirt had caught fire. "Shit, Bec! He doesn't know? How can that be?"

"I didn't worry him with how fast the money bled away. Maybe I misled him a bit."

"Misled? Lied?"

"William was never good with money. He can't even balance a checkbook. Besides, in military families, the spouse at home handles the finances."

"Why'd he buy it?"

"I told him what he wanted to hear. I told him his investments were doing fine."

Ted's mouth wrinkled like a prune. He'd been bankrupt twice, but he disapproved. "And he believed it. What happened?"

"The investments dwindled away. You might have detected the death of the market?"

"For Christ's sake, you drive a Lexus. And he's in a Rover. There must be money."

She laughed, dry and tight. "Drove a Lexus. We've been a couple of years on a lieutenant's pay. Hardly the big bucks we made as Minister of the Thousand Pew Church." She bit her lip, peered out at the motels and car lots as they rolled by. "William had a calling and it wasn't from a giant church. He needed the Army."

"Are you sure that's fair? To keep him in the dark?"

A bead of sweat, cold like ice, coursed down her ribs to her waist. "He doesn't need the guilt and I don't want the house." Or the church's iron grip either.

Ted grumped. "He'll think he needs both his house and your guilt."

She caught his frown and shrugged. "William forgets I'm a farm girl. I grew up with tractors, not granite countertops. Skinny-dipping, not vacations in Florida."

He grinned, glanced sideways at her from under his blond eyebrows. "Yeah, yeah. You harp on that farm-girl stuff a lot. Petticoat Junction, huh? Which daughter were you? The perky one or the feisty one?"

"The smart one."

Two exits trundled by before he started in again. "Okay, smart one. What's the plan?"

"Motel 6 here in Amarillo and in Albuquerque. We drop the trailer off and I drive the pickup in the rest of the way. You'll be right behind me with the van."

"God, you're relentless, you are."

"I want to drive myself to my great-granddad's place. Momma always drove us up in our pickup."

"Sentimental? I wouldn't have imagined – not you."

She snorted – she wasn't sentimental. "We unload at the cabin. You dump the U-Haul back in Albuquerque and fly home."

"Getting rid of me that quick? Maybe I need the vacation. You didn't tell me much about your granddad's place."

"Great-granddad. It's a cabin on the mountain."

"I thought your family were all dirt-kickers and flat-landers."

Distracted, she flapped a hand of denial at him. "The cabin descends from my momma's side. Paw-Paw was an insurance guy. He built the cabin as a vacation spot and it stayed in the family."

"Ski-lodge type thing?"

He'd like a ski lodge. "Here's your exit."

—⁓—

Bec alone in the pickup. Past Española the road climbed through road cuts lined with crumbling sandstones, filagreed with dark shale bands and capped with massive dusty rock. Cooped up in a truck cab with Ted, harmless as he was, or solitary? This was so much better.

She left behind the Rio Chama languishing in its slow oxbows – a thin streak in a wide bed of khaki sand. She turned right, up the Prado valley. A sharp piñon smell blew in through the vents as she crested onto the plateau, headed towards El Rito. Bec rolled down her window. From here the road still tracked through desert, but the mountain shaped it. She propped an elbow on the windowsill. The wind crowded its way into the cab. The clinking rattles behind the dash and under the seat shuddered with the bumps in the road. Not bad. She closed in on home at fifty-five miles an hour. Tinny C&W spilled out of the radio – life could be worse. Her breasts didn't define her anymore. It could be worse. She touched the port under her collarbone, the chemo-door, her fingers like a breath so she wouldn't wake cancer's beast.

She hesitated on the shoulder, kept watch in the rearview mirror. The U-Haul labored up the slope behind, crawled up to the flat. "He's out of his depth. That's not a BMW, and he's not on the Interstate." Soon, the real climb. She turned off the main road at the ranger station in El Rito onto 110, a skinny blacktop. She paused so Ted would spot the turn and then bumped on up into Carson National Forest. The scrubby cedar and sagebrush gave way to pines.

The sky shone white from heat, graded down to the horizon ahead in a deep blue. Twisted old juniper huddled under the pines that dominated the crests, yellow stalks of bloom choked the road's ditch. Gangling, mangy sunflowers and tight bushes of periwinkle blue. "Must have rained."

She'd like to be the low sprawling juniper or fragrant cedar – tough, twisted, ugly, here a hundred years. Wait patiently for the next rain – not just wait for the next onslaught.

She drove northwest.

CHAPTER THREE – DRAMA

THE NATIONAL FOREST OFFERED PINE, fir, and spruce, and a swath where fire had left blackened snags. New pine sprang up as acid-green saplings out of ash. Cold washed over Bec's left arm, crowded into the front seat, bit through her cotton shirt. She rolled up the window, slid on the heat, cranked up her own manic grin. The crest of a pass and she left the National Forest – her white truck led on – the U-Haul lagged behind. She swung into the switchbacks down to the valley. A brief rain shower, a thrumming on the roof. She tested the wipers – good. Hardly a streak and most bugs scrubbed away.

The village of Santa Eulalia de Mérida began as a series of abandoned tumble-downs, punctuated by single-wide trailers, and fields fenced in behind old adobes that hugged the road's shoulder. Next the two '30s government buildings. Through the village, past the diner, the gas station, the closed and shuttered school, and the Mini-Mart.

Santa Eulalia was more a history of failures than a town. For two hundred years it had draped across a small valley, a flattened diminutive canyon scoured out by a beneficent glacier. For two hundred years the village had tried to become something. It was proud to be a small market for the Indians and the Spanish with their Genezaros, their stolen Indian slaves. It grew into a stop on the stage line, with stables and barns that had long since burned down, with only an old stone well left behind.

The early whites, Texas ranchers, closed the chapter on the sheep and the sheepherders.

Northwest of Santa Eulalia, she wound along on the road gone to dirt and gravel. Hapless Ted in his U-Haul truck – "Close up the gap, Teddy."

The gate waited, much the same gate as she had always known. Now its green had mostly vanished and the dark brick color of rust had captured most of the pipe. She tugged the gate back, drove forward onto the two-track, crept along as she skirted the ruts and sags of a home-made road. In the rearview she checked out the U-Haul as it swayed, danced with the hollows and the dips. City boy driver. The road broke out of the firs and spruce into a cup of sunlit grass, green beneath a thatch of last year's yellow. The old pasture laid out the size of a football field, with its holes and bumps, strewn with rocks half hidden. Mountain bluebirds cut the air in front of the pickup, teased the truck's clumsiness with acrobatics.

Her grandfather's cabin, tucked into the trees, nestled in on the far side of the meadow. She spotted the chimney first, and the gray galvanized roof, and vertical log walls covered in bark. The windows, small squares rimmed in turquoise, were nailed in from behind, set back like eyes in a skull. The cabin capped a tall foundation and the porch hung proud off the front, visible from halfway across the pasture. Up close, the cabin revealed itself as more ramshackle than she had remembered. The poor old dear needed some repair. "Not the only one." At least the cabin had her now, full-time.

She hopped down from the pickup seat and waved to Ted. As she waggled her hands, she cajoled him out into the field and back to the porch. The luckless dunce ignored her gestures and reversed the truck into the roof edge, bent the corrugated tin. What a landing. At least they had arrived safe, alive.

He hesitated in the knee-high grass, glanced away, rueful. "Shit! Sorry. But I didn't scratch the truck."

Unfailingly an excuse, a rationalization. "It's happened before and will happen again. See how wavy the edge is, where we've bent it back up? Open the truck. I'll unlock the door." She held up the tarnished brass key. Her momma had unlocked this door the same way, with the same key, until her death and the passing of the key to Bec.

She paused inside the door – and he bumped into her, muttering, "Sorry."

Murky light from the south and east windows spilled dim mystery across the room. The dust floated up and charged the air with an electric, dead smell. Under that, the taint of something rotten. The echo of her voice waded across the close-shrouded air. "One big room in front – the kitchen and the living room. In the back, two bedrooms. That's two, Ted."

He shuffled forward in the half-dark. "We won't be bunking together?"

She snorted. He couldn't leave it alone, even after the accident with the roof.

Ted waved at a home-made pole ladder. "Where's the ladder go?"

"Up to a children's bedroom, about six feet high at the peak. We grandkids used to sleep up there in bunkbeds."

"Bathroom?"

He wouldn't be able to spot her grin in the dusk of the room. "Out back, over a hole in the ground. We call it an outhouse."

He gave an audible shudder. "Washer-dryer?"

"Galvanized tubs on the back porch."

"Maybe electricity?"

She flipped on the light. "Arrived about ten years ago. Cost us three thousand to run it in from the county road, can you believe?"

Ted wobbled his head no. "Couldn't you stay in Dallas and rent an apartment near Uni?"

"You don't understand the beauty of this. The cabin is entirely free."

26

"How broke are you?"

She burst out in a laugh. "Not that broke. You just haven't figured it out yet."

"I prefer a condo with a tennis court and a swimming pool."

She inclined her head. "And that's what you've got. So we're both happy."

He peered at the kitchen table. "Well, what you've got is mice."

"Hmm. Clean first, I think, and bait the traps. That's for me." Better not tell him about Hantavirus.

"And what are my orders?"

"First, fetch me a dust mask and the bleach from the supplies in the truck. Then you can stack the boxes for the house on the porch and store the tools in the barn behind the cabin."

He didn't show signs of being as happy as he had starting.

—◊—

Bec couldn't remember a more exhausting day. She and Ted perched on the porch edge, dangled their feet. Darting pain across her chest and into her ribcage – she had strained something, tugged too hard on the scar tissue. Too much in one day, but they had emptied the truck. Boxes full of bedding hunkered on the foot of both beds.

As twilight rolled over them, dragged darkness from east to west, they ate stale Subway sandwiches and over-salted potato chips flavored like vinegar. She sneaked out a Tramadol, slipped it into her mouth and chased it with a gulp of orange soda. The bread tasted good, but the meat and cheese knotted her stomach. She offered him her chips.

He scrubbed his mouth with a paper towel, asked, "Now what?"

"The sun goes down, you go to bed."

His mouth oxbowed down, sadness personified. "And I was hoping for ESPN."

"Long, long day today. And a long one tomorrow."

27

"What about breakfast?"

"I bought you some cinnamon rolls. And I'll make coffee."

"And showers?" His voice sounded whiny, little-boy.

"It's in the back hall. We installed a boiler that heats water and a tank over our heads. I've already turned the valves back on and lit the pilot."

"Is there at least a shower stall?"

She enjoyed this more and more. "No, just a drain in the floor and two hallway doors you can close. The shower head works on gravity."

"Anything here from the twenty-first century?"

She flapped her hand. "Not even you, dear one."

—m—

Ted had finished all his jobs and now his city attitudes irritated her. Relief trickled through her as she leaned on the porch column and watched her wastrel brother-in-law pitch and bump down the lane across the pasture. Bec waved until he disappeared into the trees. With a profound weariness, she shuffled back inside.

Boxes were strewn throughout her domain, their maws agape. All the surfaces in the kitchen were piled with grocery sacks and unboxed kitchen objects. She shambled back into the bedroom, fell back on the bed. If she died here, they wouldn't find her until she was a skeleton.

The board walls were painted an aging turquoise. The furniture scratched castoffs from other houses. She gazed at the ceiling and said, "Cheated death again. Maybe." When she had dragged the chenille bedspread over her, she slid sideways from consciousness into a six-hour sleep, not even aware her eyes had closed. Just before they snapped open, she dreamt of her momma, dead these nine years. She dreamt of the second time Momma brought her here – when she was old enough to remember.

—m—

Early summer, 1973.

Five-year-old Rebecca curled up on the bench seat of the truck, nestled in against her momma's side, her momma's elbow resting on her arm. The cab beat like a drum – the wind roared in the windows, rocketed around to smack the windscreen, stirred her momma's short-cut hair into a dancing storm.

Rebecca lay below the tornado, free of the wind's buffets. She dreamt, of oddly shaped balloons, of riding her own horse, of sneaking out of her pa's house. Of crouching in the dark, all alone, hidden by the trees near the smokehouse.

She wanted to wake up, but the swim all the way to the surface was so hard. She had to jerk herself awake.

The air smelled different, sharp and sweet at the same time. She popped upright in the seat, rubbed hard at her eyes. Her sight caught inky green pine trees, not the dusty oaks and sycamores of home. A river bed, wide and shallow, snaked through the plain below the road. Brown mud houses, flat-roofed, squatted by the highway, each protected by its cars and trucks, stacks of firewood, gray wooden buildings scattered about. Every house showed off a huge cottonwood that shaded its front door.

Her momma nudged her. "Are you awake? I began to believe you'd sleep the whole way." Momma's voice was sweet and slow, not all twangy like her father's.

Rebecca dipped her head, grinned up at her mother's profile. She slid across the seat to the door, propped her feet up on the cooler's white lid.

"It won't be long, honey. Do you need to pee? Should I look for a stop?"

Rebecca shook her head.

"You could just tell me what you want, you know. What's in your head, little girl?"

Through the windshield Rebecca gazed out on the two-lane road that crawled uphill. Black dulled tar stretched out to the next sweeping bend, bordered by dusky gray where the asphalt held shining chips of gravel.

"Why don't you fish us out an RC? And there's a banana on top – grab that too."

Rebecca curled her feet up onto the seat, wrestled with the cooler's lid. The bottle rattled up out of the ice – a torrent of drips cascaded onto the cooler and the floorboards. But she knew enough not to shake the water off. The pop could spew out like a gushing water hose.

Up and up, then into the village her momma said was Santa Ooo-la-lia. It dozed in the afternoon. Rebecca gazed at the tan-colored walls, the green metal roofs – wondered why houses were so different here. The cattle in their pens, the barns and sheds, some of them about to tumble down. The church, with its square box of a tower and tall thin windows rolled past. Its mud, painted white under the gray roof overhang, faded to a sand color at the bottom. The grocery store was newer – it had big sheet-glass windows covered in white paper with food prices in red paint. Like her finger paints.

The road wove back and forth, crawled up a steep hill, the steepest hill she had ever seen. The truck worked, and her stomach jumped from all the swaying back and forth. They rumbled across a cattle guard – they had those at home too – and packed hard dirt, a road that led to the gate. She had climbed on that gate last year, but now she waited on the vinyl seat while her momma jumped down and swung it open.

They thumped across the field – the truck wheels bounced underneath and banged them up off the bench seat. Ahead a fold-out travel trailer spread its wings and crowded three other tents into the cabin's shadow. Cars were scattered about, abandoned where people had jumped out and wandered away. Her cousins clustered beyond the cabin, in the barn door, a couple of them rolling together in the dust. Her mother jabbed the brake. The truck lurched to a stop.

They both jerked at the door handles, tumbled out onto their feet in sweet green grass. Her momma called her, "Come with me, Rebecca. They'll all want to hug you."

She thrust her hand into her mother's. The afternoon sun lit her so her clothes shone golden.

"Look, Rebecca, it's your Paw-Paw, climbing down off the porch."

Rebecca held up her hand to block the sun. Her great-grandfather hobbled down the steps. His hair was white, his ears the size of saucers. His shoulders leaned forward, curved his back, and his shirt hung outside of his shorts, shorts with a red and white plaid. He revealed all his teeth in a grin that tickled her as he rocked along on his feet as fast as he could. He leaned over her. "Give your Paw-Paw a hug! How's my best girl?" He dropped down on one knee and drew her close. She picked up a sniff of old person smell, with that spicy aftershave too. She breathed in deep.

His head swiveled up to her momma. "I don't 'spoze she's started talking yet? I mean, you would have called?"

Rebecca didn't want to talk. Maybe not ever.

—⚘—

July 2008.

Two days slipped away into the clouds that streamed past, while Bec nested in her bed. Paperback books surrounded her, a cup of Chinese green tea rested on the nightstand, its astringency an affront. Cotton flannel hung loose off her shoulders, lay soft across her chest, pooled in her lap. Exhaustion hung off her, a miasma of despondency.

As she lay in bed, she tried to suss out whether this would be the house of hope or of the dead. The old wooden headboard, for so long a pale yellow, showed off scuff marks on the big round balls that topped the posts, marks that flaunted a deep hidden red. A bead of light that ran clear down the window frame's edge, a shining crack that let in sweet air and would bleed through winter's cold. A water stain filled one ceiling corner – was the roof so gossamer-thin that the rain seeped in?

She left the cabin only to visit the outhouse, shuffled out in her

31

Crocs and back in relief. Sleep consumed days and smoothed out the aches and pains of moving. Sleep spread out the shock of traveling, arriving, unloading.

In mid afternoon the sun spilled into the room, warmed her in her sleep. She dreamt she was the ceiling – contemplated the woman in the bed below. What did she observe? A queen-sized bed crouched below, solid on four wooden posts, shrouded in white sheets – the Mexican color of death. An emaciated figure pinned to the bed by gravity or reluctance, disguised by a red and white striped night gown. The ceiling studied a small angular skull, softened by the returning black stubble, now with a streak of gray. Those boards, silent witnesses, wondered if they watched a corpse. She snapped awake.

She blamed the painkillers for the dream, but it was something else too. She knew what the ceiling would perceive, if it had watched her wake. Striking blue eyes, big in the small face, eyes once described by a horny conniving boy as "luminous." She had liked that.

The ceiling discerned an ordinary face, a mouth too thin, a chin with a funny point, a nose small, neat, workman-like. Bird face, damaged. A face that, alone in this room, fell open like a secret book, jittery, fearful. Evinced an inward counting, a sorting through the body for that first flicker of returning cancer. The ceiling gazed down at an imitation of a santa del retablo. But she wasn't a saint, or Catholic. She grinned – what a drama queen.

CHAPTER FOUR – DISTANCE

BEFORE DAWN ON THE THIRD day, Bec's bladder forced her to leave the warm bed and trek into the dark behind the cabin. As she gazed up, she discovered the night sky again, something Dallas had stolen from her. Stars shone out with hard jewel light, unwavering in the chill New Mexico air. Back inside, overwhelmed, she closed the back door, shut out the spectacle.

Why not unpack? She marched into the living room. As she turned on a light, she gazed at the clutter, the boxes everywhere, stacked against the walls. She peered down into a box and fished inside. Flatware, a crockpot, two flour canisters. She carried the box to the kitchen table, reached in and lifted out the contents, crowded them onto the tabletop. She pivoted to the cabinets, scratched her sharp chin, considered where the first kitchen implement should go.

At noon, she quit. The unpacking could go on forever, but at least she hadn't slipped back into bed. The porch steps lay warm and inviting. She retired into the sun with a cup of floral tea, leaned against a porch post, content to contemplate the process of nesting. Birds, mice, and Bec extended the nest through tiny defiant acts. She owned the kitchen and soon the living room would succumb. Alone, she could fold the cabin around her like a quilt. Maybe tomorrow, the village, and confronting her fear.

—⁓—

When the groceries bought on the drive through Santa Fe had

disappeared she said, "The invalid's day has passed. Time to drive into the village." As she held up her hand, she gave herself benediction, a joke for a lapsed Christian.

What was it time for? Time to tell William.

—◊◊◊—

Bec parked in the canyon head, right at the edge, to gaze down on the village below, to contemplate this map of her youth with grown-up eyes.

Logging had ratcheted up during the two world wars, but the sawmill closed when the market disappeared. The sawdust burner, Santa Eulalia's skyscraper, nestled behind the village. Logging left that fat nipple and a field of wood scrap that moldered into artificial ridges and hills through the years. Bec gazed down on the sawdust burner. One more nipple than she owned.

The sixties arrived with a shock and their own commune set in the hills. For a while, a bakery-tea shop squatted in Santa Eulalia with a book in the window that promoted its own theft, and organic whole wheat muffins that tasted like cattle feed. A macramé web in the window sheltered the shop's denizens from local scorn but not from infighting in the commune, and the hippies trickled away in pairs and threesomes.

How had the village changed since her childhood? Economic depression settled in during the eighties. Two bars made their owners a living out of neighbors' misery. When a few vacation homes and their city owners arrived, the village, amused, turned its Hispaño farmers into plumbers and carpenters. Now they could lay tile and install Corian countertops. They would grab the work as long as it lasted and afterwards fall back on what they had done for two hundred years. To keep up their poverty skills, they lived on beans, tortillas, Navajo bread, and in the fall, poached elk and deer from the National Forest.

Even with the out-of-town money, the village still created the impression it could moulder right into the ground. Bec memorized its contours

34

and swept up its clutter. Six stubby side streets teed off the highway, led to two-hundred-year-old houses and new trailers. The school and the old supermarket presented black flat roofs, but most else sheltered under forest-green or silver tin roofs. Pickups and fat American sedans squatted close to each dwelling.

"My town now. From here to the end." She shifted the truck into gear.

—∽—

Four plastic bags of groceries from the Mini-Mart cut deep into her fingers – she stowed them in the floorboard on the passenger side. Scanning the street, she decided to head to the café for tea and to check out Wi-Fi, if it had such a thing. "No Wi-Fi means I can delay telling him. One more day."

The café didn't show off too proud from outside. Sheets of plate glass flanked the door, a neon sign in the window shouted "Open." The front had once owned an awning, but it had fallen away. Above the door, a scar, an old sign painted over. She could read its contours and bleed-through color. "Bobo's Wash-O-Mat."

Settled on a stool in the window, a cup of Lipton astringent cotton-mouth tea at her elbow, she nerved herself up to talk to William, to the blowup she was about to provoke. Like other disasters in the past. When the real Bec and real talk had broken free.

—∽—

Never stage a fight in traffic. She had been driving William down to that godawful Dallas church because his Rover was holed up in the shop. It ate away at her, right into her forebrain. "Why don't you quit? Type out a letter and hand it over to the nearest board member."

He shrank, nearly balled up. "Why in the world would I do that?"

Stop here, or keep going? "You hate it. It's started to show. They talk about the Pastor's 'moods.'"

"I don't hate it. *You* hate it."

Why force it back on her?

He turned a red face to her. "It's because that flyer arrived in the mail for you today. The conference for counselors. Summer retreat, lake breezes. A mutual admiration society."

"You shouldn't distract the driver." She punched the accelerator, rocketed forward until traffic slowed her down. Childish.

He spit out a giant "Huh" and tugged at his seatbelt. "This is all about your old job. What you sacrificed. How you loved being a counselor."

"No, that's over. I locked that away in the closet years ago. It's about you and how you hate this church. How I hate it and hate the minister's wife I've become."

"You admit it's about you then."

She jerked her head up and stared at the headliner. "Yes, William. It's all about my disappointments. I'm sorry I brought it up. God strike me down if I mention it again."

—⚌—

Of course, Bec had mentioned it again, and he'd finally joined the Army. She flipped open the laptop. She could pick out that smell of burned sugar-waffle hanging in the café air, a sweet tang that hurt her teeth. Moment of reckoning.

She logged into Skype and sent her video call rocketing around the earth, routed into Kandahar. The ringing on her end signaled the alarm on William's laptop. She waited. One thousand and one, one thousand and two ... one thousand and twelve. She pictured him clicking the pad, capturing the call before it could slip away down the net. Maybe he wouldn't be there, and – a chime and the screen flashed. "William, honey, how are you?"

His forehead was wrinkled as tree bark and his mouth turned down in an oxbow. "Nervous as a cat, thank you. I haven't heard from you for five days, and that was a text. I called the house and the phone was out of order. So I'm glad you Skyped me." The sound kept up for a half second after his mouth slapped shut into a frown.

"I'm sorry I was out of touch. I've been on the road and didn't have good Internet."

His eyebrows shot up. "On the road? You're kidding me. Did you have to drive down to Houston to that clinic? Tell me someone else drove you."

"No no no, not at all. I've got big news, both good and bad. The good news is I've handled the bad news. I'm in a coffee shop in New Mexico, close to my momma's old family cabin. I've relocated out here because it's the cheapest place in all America that I – we – can live."

"Wait. That sounds like the bad news. Just out of surgery, my wife moves from Texas to New Mexico without telling me!" His voice slid up the scale through the mini speaker, like a cartoon character's.

"The real bad news is we're broke. After trying to sell the house for a year, I had to let the mortgage company take it. All your personal things are in storage in Dallas. Ted helped me with the relocation, so it wasn't too bad."

His eyes shone like round silver quarters. "We lost the house?"

"It's no big thing, William."

"No big thing?"

She said, "Three bedrooms, an office, and a three-car garage? Nobody like us needed all that. We're liable to spend the rest of your professional life either here in New Mexico while you're deployed, or in base housing when you're stateside."

He flushed – hot pink muddied his tan. "The bank took it?"

His mindless echoing grated on her. She let out a long ragged breath. "You're focused on something else right now – staying alive. Remember?" Even she didn't believe that.

"You could have told me. At least we could have talked about it when I was home for your... surgery." His face lost its hard edges. She bet he had just remembered her cancer, her struggle with death. Still, he kept it up. "It's plain thoughtlessness." Now he sounded like a child.

"William, be fair. If you'd considered it at all – how much did we earn in Dallas?"

"One ten a year." A note of pride rang through his words.

She asked, "And how much do you make now?"

He dropped his head. "Thirty-seven a year."

"And how much did we pay the mortgage company?"

"Just under four thousand a month."

She asked, "And that adds up to what?"

Instead of cluing in, he burnished up a bright pink. "We own investments. We saved some all our married life. You could have cashed those in."

"Country's in a full-blown recession, William. The investments –"

"The Army gives us allowances. Housing pays nine hundred a month, subsistence and family separation allowances add up to another five hundred."

She smiled and patted the side of the screen, a sweet gesture they had both used before. She didn't mean it this time. "Believe me, William. I know the numbers. We bring in forty-five to fifty thousand less a year than four years ago. And I for one don't care. Let the house go – I sure did."

His mouth opened, closed, flapped twice more. "You lost the house." He was puffed up like a red balloon.

"If I could have prevented us going broke, I would have."

"You threw it all away! And you kept me in the dark."

He was right about that. The first important thing he'd said.

"I'm so angry, I don't know what to say. I can't talk right now."

It sounded like barking to her. "I know it's a shock, William."

38

"Christ on a crutch, Rebecca!"

She had expected cold anger, not histrionics. "You're right. I should have let you know. But this isn't getting us anywhere. I'll call in a couple of days. William.... "

"Yes." The "s" sound drew out in a hiss.

"Everything is okay here and I love you. You don't have to worry about me."

He turned from the screen, slapped the lid down on his side. The call flicked to black.

She eased the computer lid shut. "God A-mighty. God damn it." She clenched her fists beside the black PC case. Tears flushed into her eyes and burned like coals. He didn't even know yet that she had sold both their cars and kept only his truck.

"Excuse me."

Bec swiveled towards the sound of the voice. A tubby dark woman in a food-stained apron. A pug nose, slabs for cheeks, epicanthic eyes. She held out another cup and saucer, steam rising from it, a biscochito perched on the rim. "You're drinking Lipton tea, right?"

Bec dropped her head to hide her wet eyes. "Yes, thank you." She reached for the saucer.

"We couldn't help but overhear." The woman waved her hand over the café.

Bec's head snapped around, scanned the restaurant. A half dozen people rubbernecked at her as if she was a monkey in a zoo. Eyes fixed on her! "Shit!"

"He'll come around. Men always do – if you wait long enough. Especially when he realizes you pulled his bacon out of the fire. Name's Chuma. I own this place and do all the chef'ing."

Make the best of it, of the humiliation. She should have anticipated she would attract attention. Bec thrust her hand out at the woman, "Mine's Bec. Short for Rebecca."

Chuma shook her hand, her face unreadable. "Well, Bec, if you need anything, let me know. You won some people over to your side today." The woman turned, floated off for the kitchen, light-footed in spite of her weight. At the swinging door she paused, glanced back, said, "Tea's on the house. Good luck on that marriage thing."

—⁘—

Dark and tannic on the tongue, Lipton fit in with brooding. Marriage? It hadn't occurred to her until the café owner mentioned it. William would never divorce her. No, at the worst, it would be like her parents, grown far apart but locked into the same life for so long. They had lived in separate rooms in their old farmhouse; their lives had intersected only at meals. Her momma did all the farm-wife things. She dug a garden, put up preserves, fed the family, drove off to church by herself. A dull old Methodist church. Once a year, she and Bec, Rebecca back then, traveled to New Mexico to Rebecca's great-grandfather's summer place.

Bec's father, Pa Grassic, planted, fought the weeds, harvested. He killed deer and turkey every year. Pa slept in the upstairs bedroom, the bedroom that had been his when he was a boy. He, not her momma, attended the school functions with her. He carried her off to his church, three times a week. A shouting church, full of dripping brimstone and the claws of salvation.

Would distance like that grow between her and William? He hadn't coped with her surgery. The sheer physicality – pain, drugs, drains that seeped out blood and pus. He was scared of her broken body, of breaking it further. "Like he could hurt me." And she had thrown away his symbols of success. William needed a success; a soul saved, a soldier he had talked out of despair, something his.

Otherwise, he might lock her out. Divorce by distance. She muttered, "Either way, Bec, get used to living alone." She reveled in "alone," but the uncertainty could eat away at someone.

40

CHAPTER FIVE – SORDID PAST

WHEN BEC WAVERED OUT OF the café, she jerked up short. Settled in her passenger seat – an old man. She stepped to the hood and gawked through the windshield at him. A sheen of glare on the glass played tricks with her, but a couple of details bled through the dazzle. A brown, tweedy sports coat, a white shirt without a collar, and hunched narrow shoulders. She knocked on the hood. The figure lifted a hand and dropped it back into his lap. What on God's earth?

Bec marched round to the passenger's side, popped the door open. "Why the hell are you in my truck?"

With one hand, he mussed his thick white hair – hair that stuck out in clumps. The coat was threadbare, tweed blown out at the elbow. A dirty neck, a neckline stained. He must weigh only a hundred pounds.

Composed as a judge, he gave her a crooked simper. "Why, I awaited your return. What happened to your hair?"

A seedy bum in her truck. "Get out of my truck." As she glanced down, she spotted his old boots on top of her groceries. Worse and worse.

"I need to head up the valley. You're going that way, sooner or later. I spotted you as you drove down."

"Get out of my truck!"

"Perhaps I can trade you something for the ride."

She tugged at his tweed. He shrank back. With a small heave, she levered him out of the seat and watched him topple clear to the ground. "Shit!"

From the jumble of limbs, he raised a boney hand. "Not to worry. I am not irreparably maimed."

She stooped over him, thrust her hands under his arms, and hauled him to his feet. He was heavier than he looked. A darting pain ripped from her left pec to the side of her neck. She winced. "Sorry. But it's your own fault." Now that he was on his feet again, what should she do with him? She man-handled his limp frame to the curb and over it, wrapped his arms around a light pole, and stepped away. He teetered back towards her. She wedged her hand in the curve of his spine and propped him forward. "Hold on till you get your balance. There. You're okay. Gotta run."

As she backed the truck away from him, he called out, "Since you asked, my name is Marcus. A true pleasure to meet you."

Sarcasm, or the words of a loony?

—⁂—

At the post office she eyed a queue of one, a garrulous older woman who leaned over the counter to buy a money order from a female employee, the Postmistress. Five minutes burned up in that simple transaction, while Bec eavesdropped about the woman's grandchild, now a cashier in a bank in Santa Fe, and the Postmistress' cousin – just out of rehab and back home with his mother.

The Postmistress' body shot upward and outward in an inverse pyramid from tiny hips to large breasts and shoulders like an ax handle. She cut her hair in a gray mullet and wore half glasses. As Bec filled out the paperwork to rent a box, the woman interrupted continuously. "Always glad to see someone new in town. I hope you stay. Most folks move in all excited, then drift off after a year or two."

"My name's Rebecca Robertson."

"I know. I read it upside down. I'm known around here as Miss Junie."

"I go by Bec."

42

"Good name. A bunch of us eat lunch at the café on Sunday after church. Be glad to have you join us."

Bec murmured non-committal noises. Another person chewing away at her solitude.

Miss Junie said, "I'll fetch your key." She clopped off into the back with Bec's paperwork.

Bec wrapped her arms tight around herself, leaned sideways on the counter, and tried not to brood about that old man. She had never been good with new people and hated it when they forced themselves on her. Except William, long ago.

—ᴍ—

Summer 1981.

Rebecca and William first met when she was thirteen and he was fifteen, on the hillside behind the school. But on that day, she began alone.

It was an ice cream social, an annual blight on the happiness of her solitary summers. Against the cool blue color of the grass at dusk, Rebecca smoothed out the muslin fabric of her dress, teased the folds until they splayed out around her skinny legs like a fan. Far away, down at the end of her ankles, the black shoes bought for church twitched back and forth, metronomes set at different speeds. The grasses, five varieties that she counted so far based on the tassels and seed heads around her, swayed themselves gentle. The wind had gusted out of the south all day, but now veered around. It bore sound up from below. No need to wander back down to the school to join the others. The giggling, the hoarse shouts filtered up to her. The screams as the boys chased the girls back and forth. The girls would let themselves be caught. Better to listen from the grass on the hill. A voice behind her. "Hey."

Rebecca nearly jumped clear off the ground. She twisted around and glared. A boy, a big lunk of a boy hovered on the slope above her, cross-legged in the ankle-deep grass. Black hair bristled off his forehead

43

like a hedge and stuck out in most directions around his skull. He had pinned a stalk of grass between his front teeth – it shot out of his face like a green wand. She narrowed her eyes. "Hey yourself."

He jerked the stalk out of his teeth, stared down into the grass.

She said, "You know.... "

"What?"

"You scared me."

"Sorry. I didn't even know you were here at first." He ducked his head. She scowled. "Well I am."

"What's your name?"

"Why should I tell my name to someone who's spying on me?"

He turned his head, gazed off sideways. "Not spying."

Was he embarrassed? She said, "Feels like you were." He gazed off anywhere but at her. His face was soft, unformed. After a moment he said, "Sorry. My name is William."

She turned her back to him pretended to watch the school below. "You're the new kid?"

"Uh-huh. Got here in June." His voice floated down the hill past her, pleasant enough, even now high-pitched. Not broken and scattered like some of the older boys.

"I'd hate that, being the new kid."

He dipped his head. Is that what he did, stare off into space and duck his head? "You're Rebecca."

Rebecca let a beat go by. "So you already knew my name?"

"Maybe."

"Maybe nothing. You know my name."

"Sure. I asked somebody. I thought, sometime we could get a Coke. Together."

A pushy boy. "I don't think so, William." She dragged the name out long as a tease. "See you around." Rebecca leapt up and waltzed down the hill. Her dress fanned and flared with every step.

44

—⁂—

July 2008.

When Bec popped out the post office door as the proud owner of a minus-cule brass key, she hoped the old man had wandered away. He hadn't. He plodded uphill, up the ditch only a block from the café, but past where the sidewalk ended. Not making good time. She drove past him, jammed on the brakes. Backed up.

The old man staggered from the ditch into the road, grasped at the right side view mirror. He opened the door and with a groan like child-birth, clambered in.

She traipsed around to the passenger side, opened the door.

The whites of his eyes blazed out, his mouth hung open. He resembled an opossum in the headlights. "You wouldn't evict me again, would you?"

"No. I want to fish my groceries out from under your feet. I don't need my eggs broken." She grabbed two bags and dangled them into the back of the truck. The reach over the edge to the bed stretched her from belly to wrist. The skin tightened across her chest, stabbed again.

"Here, let me help." He shoveled two more plastic bags into her hands and whipped his door shut as she stepped back.

With a snort she jumped into her seat. She slapped her hands onto the steering wheel and cocked her head to stare at him. He hadn't shaved in several days. He hadn't bathed in at least a week. She rolled down her window, adverse to the funk. "What's your name again?"

"Marcus." He shrugged, gazed at his kneecaps. "People insist on calling me Mark. I'm the local madman. Can we go?"

She leaned over to him. As well as the stink of old perspiration, the tang of sweet wine hung on him.

"You have observed my condition. Yes, I am intoxicated. I assure you – it is not a frequent condition."

She grinned. "I have to start locking my truck. Where to?"

45

"I'll tell you when I spot it."

She drove back through town, up the canyon towards the pass.

"Stop!" he shouted.

She whipped over to the side. "What?"

"You nearly passed Mannie's place. I'll be right back." He hopped out, wove across the highway, and slipped into one of the town's two bars.

She grasped the steering wheel and stared at her knuckles. What temporary insanity had trapped her into this?

In a minute he ambled out with a brown paper sack. He crossed in front of the truck and labored to climb back into his seat. "All right, we can go."

"Why, thank you."

"I like you. What's your name?"

"Bec."

"What kind of name is Bec?"

She shoved the truck in gear. "What kind of name's Marcus?"

He dipped his head. "Point taken."

One lapel on his coat stuck out, as if someone had grasped him, jerked at him. Marcus didn't have many friends, did he?

They drove up the canyon, within sight of the top. "You sure you live around here?" she asked.

"Just ahead." He pointed out a cabin. The porch had collapsed and been dragged to the side – it left a scar across the front. The roof sported a good-sized hole and the chimney was afflicted by a chewed-off corner.

"Looks like a fixer-upper."

"It's not mine," he said. "I am house-sitting for wealthy friends."

She jerked the truck to a stop. "Right."

"I'm sure your vacation home is equally nice. Where is it? Perhaps you'll drive past here often, and I could catch a ride."

She wasn't about to tell him anything.

He swung his legs out, dropped to the ground, and stumped over to the step. He fiddled with the door latch and disappeared inside. She hung on the wheel, watched the cabin. Her fingers tapped on the plastic. She kicked her door open, tramped to the back of the pickup, and crawled into the bed. Her knees ached on the metal as she dug in the plastic grocery bags.

The step was made of creosote railroad ties. Marcus answered the door and she caught sight of a dusty table. Firewood racked itself inside, all along one wall. Gray and half-rotten.

"Here," she said. "You need this more than I do." She handed him two yogurts, a loaf of bread, and a can of soup. And fled.

On the way up the hill, she caught sight of the mine tailings. Coal mining had come and gone in their valley, the grimy men with their dungarees and mules discouraged by the coal, the insipid flame it cast, the stench of sulfur and toxic metals it released. The village's hinterlands had also been ravaged by gold miners for two years, but they had no way to channel the meagre streams up to the seams to blast away the cliffs with water. The ranchers liked that fine, not in favor of the ugly scarring. They preferred the sweep of open grazing and a savannah of cows.

—ɷ—

Bec entered her cabin, hung the keys on the hook by the door. As she plunked her plastic bags on the kitchen table, she spotted the mouse turds scattered about. With an angry mutter she swept the table and scrubbed it off with a soapy dish towel. "Little bastard. You'll rue the day you crossed Bec Robertson."

In the bedroom she changed from boots to Crocs, but kept her fleece on – July night-time temps ran in the mid forties here. Her only heat radiated from the stove in the living room. She stoked it, lit the tinder, and threw in an old stub of a candle for good measure. She marked a worrisome backdraft of smoke, but tried not to obsess about a clogged flue. She draped a comforter over her shoulders, folded up in a cross-legged crone-shape on the couch. Leaned into the fire's reach. On the shelf behind the stove, a photo of William in his class A's, the service uniform. A shrine, complete with a cross and a card he had sent for their anniversary. Her momma's old clock crowded up beside William. Its brass pendulum ticked back and forth.

She regarded the photo. "So you believe I botched this one? Maybe. But it's not the end of the world. Bec Grassic can show little Billie Robertson how to live the simple life. Mouse turds and all."

Yes, she could show him how to live. That's how she had bullied him into joining the Army.

—⁓—

The tipping point, the breaking argument, had been three years ago. William had collapsed in that damn chaise on the patio for an hour. It must have been the Special Events Committee. Either that or the elders had rebelled again. He could sink into a quagmire of depression. He could be drowning for a week, turning her life to shit again.

She charged out the French doors, wheeled to a halt in front of him. She grasped her arms, hunched around herself. That damn bent bra hook cut into her back. "William, you've got to stop this. This church is killing you."

He gazed up at her, his eyes empty, indifferent. "Not again."

"Yes, again. See how it's sucked you under, for the millionth time."

He rolled up out of the chaise, plodded off into the house.

She trailed after him, her voice cranked back to normal, maybe even rational. "Let's talk it through. What other direction in life would make you feel better?"

He huddled into the chintz couch – the one she hated and he adored. His mother had had a couch like that. His spherical eyes goggled at her. "Life isn't about feeling good. Life is about persevering."

48

"Bullshit."

His fists balled up, but not in a threat, not like it would have been with her father. Even so, she experienced that old surge of fear and hate. He said, "I have a calling here."

She couldn't temper herself. "If your calling is here, why are you always going dewy-eyed about a mission in Peru or a soup kitchen somewhere or becoming a chaplain. For Christ's sake, William, pick one!"

He sucked in a huge breath. Next he levered himself out of the couch, bled the breath back out. He peered unfocused into the empty fireplace, switched his gaze back to her. "Maybe you're right, but I don't have to suffer this abuse. Why is this so important to you?"

He had never talked to her this way. Maybe she had shoved him too far. "Because I love you."

"You have a funny way of showing it." He stopped in the door, his back to her. "I'll think it over. Pray over it. I'll let you know what I decide."

That's how she hooked him into the Army.

—◊—

Cafés are meant for loitering. The smell of baking bread lulled Bec into foolish vulnerability. A warm room, great smells. Comfort.

Chuma's eyes opened wide. "He told you what?"

Bec recoiled, surprised by Chuma's reaction. A fake-wood table separated them – Chuma's immense bosom parked on it.

Bec said, her voice careful and flat, "He told me he preferred to be called Marcus."

Chuma's mouth dropped full-open in a bray. "Too rich, too rich! That old coot is named Emmet, not Marcus, and boy, has he built a reputation. Mrs. Martinez insists he's the one who kills her chickens and leaves only the feet. She says he does voodoo with the chickens, but I believe he eats them. Hopefully he boils them first on that old wood stove of his."

49

Bec twitched her head no. "He said 'Marcus' and he said he was the local loony."

"Pain-in-the-butt more likely, making the old sympathy play. Emmet is our drunk, not our village idiot."

"I admit he smelled of booze. And we stopped at Mannie's."

"You made a wine run for the old bastard? This gets better and better."

"You aren't going to tell anyone, are you?"

"Oh, hell yes. But seriously. Emmet might be dangerous. Not to me – I'd smack him down. But a sawed-off thing like you? You're pretty reckless, taking up with him."

Bec frowned. "What makes you suppose he's dangerous?"

"Drifted into town five years ago. Lives alone. No past, no future, nothing to lose. Nobody knows what he keeps in that cabin or where his few bucks come from."

Bec tapped the back of Chuma's hand with her finger. "That could be me. Except I've been here only three weeks."

Chuma snorted, then conceded with a twitch of her head. "You're right. An old souse like him might steal something off your porch, but he probably wouldn't do you any harm."

Bec nibbled at her chocolate chip cookie. "I believe I'll keep an eye out for him, even if his name is Emmet. First snow will show in only four or five months."

"Better think about yourself first, sweetie. You ain't seen no winter here. You're in for a shock, even if you're ready in time. And another thing – about your pet project, the loon. Don't bring Emmet in here unless he scrubs off some of the stink. Business is slow enough as it is." Chuma attacked her tart with a fork.

"Chuma?"

She grunted – her jaws worked.

"How did you end up here?"

Chuma grinned, sly as a fox. "Why should I tell you my sordid past?"

"You do know a fair amount about me."

She dumped the fork onto the plate with a clatter. "Only because you fight with your old man in my restaurant. Okay, here's the short version. I moved off the Rez to wash dishes in Vegas. The one in Nevada.

"Was that better than the reservation?"

"Hell no. Next they let me chop Romaine for salads and grate Parmesan. I graduated to onions because nobody likes mincing onion. After a while, I worked up to head chef at a small place, but it didn't last. They hired a hotshot with a culinary degree."

Bec let out a delicate cough. "How did you end up here?"

"Dunno. It had something to do with a cowboy and a bottle and a long drive."

"You made that up."

Chuma whinnied again. "Of course. I ain't goin' to tell any white person all the truth."

CHAPTER SIX – TOUGH

EARLY AUGUST 2008 – LATE in the rainy season.

An idea had lodged in Bec's mind – her scar tissue would seize as hard as a rock and leave immovable bands threaded through her muscle and skin. She perched on the edge of her bed in the morning chill.

Two days before the Santa Fe appointment for the chemo-port removal, Bec massaged the scars, shirt unbuttoned and goosebumps chasing across her skin from the damp air in the bedroom. With some distaste, she worked the incisions, hopefully into suppleness. Plunked on the edge of the bed, ten fingers kneading.

And she located a lump. Pea sized, it nestled in behind the spot where her right nipple had been.

She jammed her hands into her armpits and hunched over. Aloud she rang words out across the tiny bedroom, "Shit! Ahh! I can't believe it!" Her fingers crept back to the spot. Yes, definitely. A hard ball of death, beneath the skin. She vented out a wail, a keening straight from her gut up through her vocal cords, a fountain out of her throat into the echoing room. The humid air held all that sound while she hollowed herself out and wheezed in a shaky breath. She let in all the fear. A hot tangle of thread sewn into her chest, death and fear. Death was unimpressed.

Whispers – all she dared. "I'm in for it now." The idea to relocate to

New Mexico, a fool's choice. Four miles out of town, buried in the woods, no phone, no friends nearby. A warrior husband in a desert far away. A disease that lurked inside her.

Chilled from the core out, she hugged herself in the iron bands of her arms. Until the shaking began. She crawled under the quilts. A long cry didn't compel the knot to disappear. A two-day wait didn't numb the fear.

—⋙—

The Santa Fee appointment had been scheduled for nine in the morning, so Bec left before daybreak. She wore a fleece as she ran out to the truck to warm it up. Down in the mid-forties, the temperature would continue dropping until an hour after sunup. In a minute she locked her front door, carried her go-mug of rose-hip tea to the truck, along with a small bag of cosmetics and extra underwear. She might unlock the door tonight, slump back through it into her life. She might not.

The heater huffed out an uneven warmth – the sifting air chilled the backs of her hands. She drove over her field to the gate and the highway, navigated by intuition in a thick fog. As she bumped along the mist eddied, drifted her along. The damp cold cascaded downhill into her village and she drove with it, wrapped in gray. She gripped the wheel, knuckles luminescent in the dashboard light and her shoulders pinched together, hard. Sudden twitches raced through her back muscles. It must be the cold.

—⋙—

They also cranked the temperature down in the examination room. Frigid, and the gloves tacky, like a fly's feet. The Doctor palpated her skin, her scars, her thin pads of pectoral muscle. At least his hands didn't feel warm or human. She couldn't have tolerated that, warm groping hands.

He leaned back, stripped off the nitrile. "I would guess it's a cyst. Nothing to worry about."

"That's what they said the first time."

He grinned, uneasy. Patients weren't supposed to challenge the almighty doctor. "Well then, we'll make sure. Sonograms can tell the difference between a cyst and a cancerous lump. I'll have Betty here trot you down the hall to our tech and we'll take a little ol' look-see. After that, if all things are okay, I'll remove the port."

Her jaw throbbed with the tension. It felt unbearable. If he had said "cancer," then at least she would know and transition on to the next bit of misery. The nurse helped her hitch the examining gown back over her shoulders and tie it across her waist front to back. Bec asked, "What if the sonogram can't tell because of the scar?"

"Then a biopsy." The Doctor grinned from ear to ear – why shouldn't he? "I'm sure it's fine. If it wasn't for that itty-bitty lump, everything would be great. You've healed nicely, with minimum scarring." He dropped his hand on her shoulder, nudged her towards the door. "Cysts aren't unusual, you know. There was a lot of damage caused by the mastectomy. Just a side effect, I'm sure."

Right. A lot of damage, when they cut out her breasts. An aide herded her down the hall, a sheep in a gown. Another aide parked Bec in a room with an exam table and carts of equipment. They helped her onto the paper-clad bench, where she squinted into the fluorescent overhead.

The technician had wandered off on break, so Bec waited. The aide draped a blanket over her. She closed her eyes. Her calf muscles jumped and cramped, as if she wanted to run.

Behind her eyelids she played out a movie she'd already watched before, many times. The big operation. That time they had strapped her into a gurney, wheeled her down a mile of corridor. Why strapped down? Did they expect her to flee the scene? The drip in her arm had sneaked in an extra jolt – some alien in scrubs and a white mask had injected clear fluid into the saline. What did the mask conceal?

"Something to help you relax till the team turns up, honey." She

54

was a "honey." But that wasn't quite right. She was a sacrifice. A lamb. She lay on the altar as the Eucharist. It was the biggest event she had ever attended, and she cringed on the offering block. What God do we do this for? Sacrifice the hand, the leg, to save yourself from death. But they wouldn't hack off her hand, or her leg, would they? Her breasts. They intended to peel her skin back and remove her humanity, leave her forlorn, unlovable.

—w—

"Okay, sweetie." A voice jolted her back into this Santa Fe room, away from a memory like hot fire. "We have to pluck back the blanket and unbutton your gown again. This jelly's at room temp but it may feel cold." A woman in scrubs and a mask leaned over her, but with her hair and ears exposed, bare forearms. A recognizable human being. The technician consulted the chart again. "Now let's see, right breast, possible cyst." The gel chilled the patch of goose-bump skin. Bec flinched, like she flinched away from the specter of cancer. What would she do?

Not everyone could face it. Her Uncle Howie had chosen the fast way out.

—w—

Christmas 1974.

Six-year-old Rebecca, strapped into the passenger seat, watched the miles roll away. Her momma perched behind the truck steering wheel, hummed to herself. Just audible over the road noise. Jammed between them her mother had parked a grocery sack full of presents. Rebecca held the cake in her lap. Her job today, to protect the cake. Her lap heated the space between her and the plate. Her hands reached clear around the plate and grasped the edges, and she was careful to keep her forearms away from the white frosting. Momma didn't bake many cakes, but she did for Uncle Howie.

As they left, her father had handed her the cake, dropped it onto her lap. He leaned across her and said, "Tell my atheist brother Season's Greetings. Tell him Christ died for his sins too." He slammed the truck door. Rebecca knew what the word atheist meant. It meant "not good enough."

Uncle Howie lived only forty-five miles away, but it might as well be all the way to Dallas. He was her favorite, even counting her momma's people, but he never drove over to visit. She asked, "Momma, why doesn't Pa like Uncle Howie?"

Her mother turned her head, cocked it to the side. She didn't speak for a moment: Rebecca felt her measuring gaze. Sometimes grownups treated you like you were grown up. "Well, baby girl, even though they're brothers, your father has a lot of reasons. But the main one is that your father and Howie are very different. Howie sees the world as a happy place and your father perceives it as a struggle."

"Happy place?"

"Maybe not this year. Your uncle has had some trouble in his town. There's a reason he never married and people think they know why. And he's been sick."

Her face turned back to the road, and Rebecca watched her. Her momma's hair, braided and clubbed up in back, showed off light brown lights and a wisp of gray. Her face, tan from summer's sun, had a brown spot about the size of a dime, right between her ear and her cheekbone. Her hair, so bound in back, flew loose in a couple of strands over her forehead. Rebecca wondered what it would have been like, a different life. "Momma, what if you had married Uncle Howie instead of Pa?"

"Then you couldn't call him Uncle Howie." Her momma twitched out a smile.

"That's silly, Momma. Why can't we visit Uncle Howie more? I liked the time I stayed with him."

"Right, when I was in the hospital. We're tied down with the farm,

56

Rebecca, and Howie is busy in his own town. He hasn't forgotten you — he calls on your birthday every year."

"Uncle Howie's fun. We went to a movie. And also to a carnival. And he read to me a lot."

Rebecca turned off the highway at the stoplight. "Rebecca, he did take the whole week off for you. It wouldn't be that way all the time."

"And we didn't have to go to church. We played golf. I drove the cart."

They rattled along through the town, turned at the Dairy Queen and crossed railroad tracks. Uncle Howie's place was located in a neighborhood with houses like his, separated from the street by a grass-lined ditch and a half-naked lawn. New compared to the house on the farm, his house exhibited brick on the bottom half and siding on the top. Long skinny windows like squinting eyes ran across the front. Uncle Howie had a carport instead of a barn. "I want to live in a house like Uncle Howie's someday."

Rebecca's mother parked behind Howie's car and reached across for the cake. "You can get the door for me, Rebecca."

Rebecca pried the storm door open against the tug of the hydraulic piston and reached for the knob. It turned under her hand — no one ever locked doors. Her momma brushed past her and Bec strung along behind. The washer and the dryer squatted right against the wall, and Rebecca slowed down to gaze at the groceries and newspapers piled up on the machines. She ran smack into her mother's back.

Her momma whispered, "Oh Dear God!" Then louder, "Dear God!"

Rebecca peered around her mother, clutched at her leg. Uncle Howie humped up in a chair at the kitchen table. His head lay on the table top and his eyes, big and motionless behind his glasses, goggled straight at her. His face had a waxy gray color to it. The blood had dripped off the table and dried in a big puddle on the Linoleum floor.

Rebecca's brain didn't know what to think — she froze, waited to understand something, anything. She had never seen a real pistol before.

So cold and motionless, by his hand, but it could leap up, turn on them. Shoot her mother, and her.

Her momma sobbed. She dropped the cake. Shoving at Rebecca, she forced them both out into the carport. Rebecca's nightmare for years – the few seconds with Uncle Howie that last time. The kitchen, the blood.

—⚏—

August 2008.

William couldn't figure it out. Bec asked him, "Please, William. There are other people here. Could you hold your voice down?" She stabbed at the volume button. She glanced around Chuma's diner; a hot flush burned her face.

He jabbed his finger at his screen, at her. "You drove down to Santa Fe by yourself, sure you had cancer and you might die? And you did this alone?"

"Be fair. I couldn't ask Chuma to close the café for two days."

"I could have flown in from Afghanistan. I could have been with you."

"I only knew about the lump two days before. I had an appointment anyway, for the chemo catheter. And it turned out a false alarm – only a cyst, and it's already gone. The Doctor drained the fluid right out. And anyway, you just burned a bunch of compassionate leave."

"You drove down early in the morning, spent all day in the medicos' hands and dragged yourself back up the mountain in the dead of night?"

"No, I didn't. I stayed on at a La Quinta and drove back the next day."

"If you had been in Dallas you would have had a support group."

Lord, he churned out the objections today. "You mean the Church. Yes, they would have helped. But then, I can't afford to live in Dallas."

"What about a church in New Mexico?"

"The village church is Catholic. I'm not comfortable with that." What is this, twenty questions, a trial?

Red as the sunrise, his face wrinkled up. Was he about to cry? "I

58

just hate it. You're in trouble and I can't do a thing about it." He was crying, his face flushed, his eyes scrunched up.

"But I handled it. Don't I get some credit for that?"

He snuffled, seized his nose, and in an all too familiar gesture, honked into his palm. "Yes. Handled it without me. Makes me feel like chopped liver." The crying had clogged his nose with mucus and he sounded like he had a cold.

"I don't think you're chopped liver. I love you for being so protective, but it's not really necessary."

"Alone and afraid you had cancer."

Distract him, wave something trivial at him. "Darling, I had a bad three days, but it's behind me. I've moved on to the next problem and you should too."

He echoed. "Nex' pah'bem?"

"Problems. The roof leaks some. And I need firewood. Enough for the full winter, and I'm not sure I have enough time."

"Fie-a wood. Jus' buy de darn logs."

Not now, William. "Not practical, honey. Up here it's two hundred a cord, and I guess four cords for the winter. I've got to go – Chuma has set my sandwich out for me. I love you – stay safe!" After she lied to force the conversation's shutdown, she clicked offline. Head down, she carried the empty tea cup back to the cash register to pay. Were more people in here than when she called him?

Bec said, "Here, Chuma, here's seventy-five cents for the tea."

Chuma snorted. "Not staying for lunch? I thought not. The tea is on the house – the show was worth it. Made the big guy cry, huh?"

"He felt helpless, out of the loop."

"Made him cry. Damn, you're tougher than you look."

59

CHAPTER SEVEN – QUITTER

AFTER BEC HAD PINPOINTED HER leak inside the attic, she surveyed the roof from on top. A sheet of tin was turned up on one edge and water had slipped its traitorous way in, rotted a hole through the thin plank boards of the ancient roof. Now dressed in her grungiest clothes, she inched her way up a home-made ladder from the barn, earned a couple of splinters in her hand, and commenced a second perilous traverse to where a winter storm had flayed open her cabin. She eased the open bucket onto the roof, but it was full. A sticky mess sloshed back, onto her shoulder, her arm, her cheek.

Already hammered back down, the sheet of corrugated roofing ran in a rippled scar up the slope away from her. She should start at the top. She shoved the can of black tar ahead of her as she spread her weight. Spidered out, she grounded any handy part of her body she could to the metal. She winced as the roof creaked below her. The roof wasn't about to collapse, was it? Near the ridge, she fished the brush out of her back pocket and began to dab the black goo onto the tin scar as she worked her way back down towards the life-saving ladder. Good and thick. No desire to ever crawl back up here again.

—⚍—

Bec had been burning her way through the four-year-old firewood stacked close to the cabin, some of it so punk it smoldered for a day before it died down into a mountain of ash. She needed cords of new wood, but balked at the price from the local woodcutters.

She chose a location for timbering that kickstarted her chain of problems. The trees on her field's east side cast long shadows across the cabin in the early morning. To capture that precious first warmth, she resolved to cut back the woods where they began a hundred yards from her front porch. A mistake, but not one she realized at first.

She attacked an old monster fir with the pathetic suburban chainsaw she had brought from Dallas – her second blunder. Two hundred dollars later, she had a reconditioned Stihl and three tempered chains.

Cancer wasn't the only hunter. More than one way in the world to die – the first tree taught her that. Her number one monster fell at right angles to the direction she expected. It frightened her out of its all-crushing path like a scampering field mouse.

And to cut it up! The fir top worked out for her. She de-limbed it and stacked the slash as she worked, chopped the tree into foot-and-a-half lengths. Sawdust clogged her boots. In an hour, she edged down the trunk to cut logs she couldn't even roll after she cut them. She would have to split them in place, with a hydraulic splitter she hadn't even bought yet. And how could she hoist them up on the splitter?

Worn out, whipped, she slumped on the cabin's porch and studied the hundred yards out where she had abandoned the saw and the pickup – and the beast of a tree down on the ground. There had to be a way to manage this. A big tree counted for a quarter or maybe a half of a cord, all at once. But she could handle the smaller trees if not the giants.

She counted aloud. "I touch each piece of wood how many times? Once to drop the tree, once to de-limb and cut to length. Once to split. That's three. Once to chunk into the truck. Once to throw out of the truck, once to stack. That's four, five, six. I tote it in, stack it in the firebox, park it in the stove, burn it, and carry the ash out to sweeten the outhouse. Ten? Eleven? Is it all doable?"

"Tomorrow, let's buy the splitter, and after that bust the tree down to girl-size pieces in a hurry. This year, small trees. Maybe I'll work up to the monsters next year." It could be a deal-breaker.

"And – Bec? You better stop talking to yourself."

"Uh-huh," she answered.

—⚏—

Like all the backwoods pioneer types on the mountain, Bec drove to Santa Fe or Albuquerque to shop for big-ticket items. She and all the fiercely independent people in these rural places traveled down to the big-box stores – stores full of things shipped from overseas and sold at the lowest cost. Her log splitter, diminutive when hitched behind the truck, carried a sticker that rated it for thirty tons, whatever that meant. This and the chainsaw had set her back for the month – she was perilously broke until William's paycheck arrived.

Limited to forty-five miles an hour, the trip back lasted an eternity. Not ready to try backing a trailer when she stopped at Chuma's, she parked out on the road where she could drive straight out.

She shoved open the heavy glass door and stepped inside. The sleigh bells cascaded from their rattling ring back into a muttering silence. Chuma was nowhere in sight, but Bec spotted a dozen patrons dug in across the restaurant. They claimed tables and booths – settled in. Unmoving except for a nod here, a hand raised there to acknowledge her entrance. The yellow enamel walls soared up to a ceiling covered in stamped tin, lit by fluorescent lights suspended on chains. Cobwebs, not many, trailed from the ceiling and nested in the chains. Summer flies better beware.

She perched on a stool in the window front on the street. With all due care she rested the laptop on the slab of a shelf.

No answer on Skype. An email in the queue from brother-in-law Ted. She wasn't sure whether to lump him into the ass-hole slot or the scamp category.

She read, "Hi Sis, Wanted to tell you what a great time I had in New

Mexico chowing down Subway take-out and sleeping with the spiders. Back in Dallas, I sold 6 Beamers in the first week, made money hand-over-fist. BTW I met a girl named Mara who doesn't care anything about money at all – at least that's what she says. She's Irish – the white-skinned red-haired-beauty Irish type, and she's doing a sabbatical at U of Texas Austin. This relationship will torch and burn, but we'll have fun for a while. Be sure and let me know if you need anything from civilization. And don't forget, it's only the idea of driving William crazy when I talk about your cute butt that keeps me coming back. Your Teddy."

Bec typed back, "Hello back, Teddy. Glad you're emerging from your hermit's shell and venturing out into the world. Thanks again for all your help. I'll certainly think of you if I need sushi or a new pair of designer sunglasses. Yr sister-in-law, Bec. P.S. Mara sounds interesting. Treat this one right for a change."

She deleted several junk emails – opened a long one from William. He'd shipped it to her two days earlier. She dove into the text, unfolded the story. Not something for casual conversation.

"Dearest Rebecca,

Right now it's full dark in your end of the world and burning daylight here. I've meant to talk to you about what I do – not the blah blah that any preacher or officer does here, but the real work. The reason I joined up. I've just finished a session with one of my young soldiers and it troubled me enough to tell you about it.

We're all in camouflage, you know. The combat uniform that masks the edges of our bodies and at best turns us invisible and at worst makes us fuzzy targets. It's an analogy because each of us here wears camouflage of a different sort. Camouflage of the soul.

The Military teaches us we are hunting animals, carnivores, the ultimate killers. Of course it knows we are fallible humans, afraid, vulnerable to our inner selves. That's why the Army deploys chaplains, why men like me are on the ground.

63

It's not that I represent Protestants or Jews or Catholics or Muslims, which you well understand. But what I do provide is a set of ears. I listen in the deep shade under the awning or the dusk of evening after chow. Non-judgmental listening – that's about all I can offer.

Like I said, this email was prompted by a young soldier. She's having a rough time of it – nightmares, flashes of distrust for her comrades, moments of panic. As a woman, she isn't even recognized by the Army as a combatant, but here she is in a forward base. More than a few ugly things have happened to her that distress her. It doesn't help she has killed once that she knows of – when she first sat down with me, it was about her indifference to the killing. Now it haunts her, what she did in the line of duty. Like many of us here, she carries around an additional complication – her private life. Her mom in Georgia is raising her daughter.

This soldier fears she is suicidal. She says she has been raped once, of course by fellow soldiers. Also that it's hard for her to recognize the enemy. She is profoundly depressed."

Bec stared out into the street. Two pickups rolled by, but she couldn't focus on them for the tears that blurred her eyes. With a sniffle loud enough to surprise herself, she read on.

"Many of them, the men and the few women, are like this. They are afraid, and to admit that you're afraid turns you into a risk to the unit. They're terrified of letting their fellow soldiers down. They're usually angry.

The ones I worry most about don't show any of these things. Mostly the soldiers on third or fourth tours – they're numb, armored. Maybe they have become military in a way no one can understand, least of all them. I worry about what they are capable of.

We have the wounded also – and what the trauma of blood and pain does to them. If they are wounded badly enough, I never set eyes on them. They're choppered in from wherever they were shot or blown up into the medical compound, stabilized or pronounced dead and lifted out to Kabul. If it's not life-threatening, they may be here long enough for me to visit. I get as much out of those visits as they do.

Last year early I spent time with a newly-promoted sergeant, a young man named Tony who had lost his hand. Nothing 'life-threatening,' just something that will change his life forever. He was pretty loopy on morphine, but he joked about it. He tells me, 'One minute I was daydreaming about Sausalito and the next I possessed only five fingers, not ten. It hardly bled. The IED burned my stump, so I was cauterized.' Then he said, 'I lost my college ring. I loved that ring. Maybe I can buy another on eBay. For the other hand, of course.' Such courage humbles me.

So that's why I'm here. I know you've heard this before."

No, she hadn't. She had just filled in the blanks.

"That's the call to Christ I heard, and while all the details are different than I expected, this is the service I want.

Miss you. Love, Your forty-six year-old 1rst Looie."

Bec jumped when the saucer clattered beside the keyboard. "Here go," said Chuma. "Your tea. Darjeeling. You're the only one that drinks this crap, but I'll stock it for you."

"God, you scared me half to death!"

"Indian girl sneak up on white chick."

Bec glanced at the screen. "I suppose you read my mail."

"Nice note, what I saw. Maybe I'll have to cut the guy some slack. What you been up to?"

"Piling up firewood for the winter."

"How's that going?"

"Small trees this year. I've heaped up some logs, where I cut them. I have to split the wood, truck it, and stack it."

"Can you do all that?"

"I better, or I have to pay my neighbor Rubio for wood. Rumor is he sells light cords."

Chuma frowned and jabbed at Bec's arm with a finger. "Everything about you is reckless. Your friends, your logging, your living alone. I think you're taking this spunky stuff way too far. What happens when you're a fat old woman like me and you've set all these high-flown expectations?"

"We can rent a house together and you can wait on me hand and foot."

Chuma hooted. "We'll be known in town as the Two Old Broads."

Bec said, "We can plant a garden."

"We can collect a dozen cats."

Bec flourished her hand. "And a dog named Franklin."

"Screw that. Needs a Zuni name."

"In that case we'll acquire two dogs."

Chuma hee-hawed. "The only males allowed in the house. And even then I insist they're neutered. Chop those balls off." She shouted this last across the room as she glided away.

Bec turned to discover Miss Junie bearing down on her. June tacked across the room, her broad shoulders like sails. "Bec, you remember me? From the post office. I invited you to join us here after church, but you missed it last Sunday."

Good lord, had it been an appointment? "Umm, sorry. I've been fighting trees and equipment to stockpile firewood for winter."

"Surely, girl, if you're going to live out on the mountain, you'll at least hire a strong back or two and get it done right. Buy it and have it delivered. Here," Miss Junie said, "Let me give you a couple of names."

Bec surveyed the woman's head as she wrote with a Bic on a napkin, shredding minuscule tufts up from the paper. Miss Junie suffered from thinning hair, and the part in her mullet was a half-inch wide, hidden in a moused pelt.

She stabbed the napkin at Bec like serving a subpoena. "Here you go. Use these guys, not that old pirate Rubio."

Bec liked Rubio, not that she fully trusted him. His wife was charming, his fifty-year-old son worn down, with sad, kind eyes.

Junie capped it all. "Now we expect to see you next Sunday."

Bec turned back to the keyboard to reply to William.

—⋙—

The way Bec grasped it, a splitter could save a life with wood for the winter, or crush a hand. She bent and picked up the heavy log. A promise of warmth in every pound. Toiled four steps to the splitter – later on that would be a dozen steps, unless she learned how to back the splitter up without driving off at unintended angles. She heaved the log onto the cradle, held it in place without planting a finger or thumb in the way. Bec cursed it, "You big lovely bastard. You're not going to mangle my hand. Damn loud, you are. I need ear plugs." Shoved the handle forward. The wedge crushed into the log end. It split! Fell off onto the ground – of course. She hoisted up the nearest half, dropped it on the cradle, split that. The log exploded off in both directions with a loud cracking noise. "You bastard, right into my ribs." She chalked the bruise up to experience.

She lifted the four pieces of firewood one at a time and threw each into the back of the pickup. When the truck bed was mounded high, she drove them around the back of the cabin, twenty feet from the back porch. She laid out a linear stack at the base of a tree, pointed across the cabin width.

—⋙—

Three hours of bending, carrying, worry about where her hands were – and where the splitter's threatening wedge moved. That pretty much did her in. She stumped up the back steps, feet like lead. Fir sap mottled across her hands and two fingers stuck together. Her thumb throbbed with a deep splinter buried in it. Gloves, she needed gloves. She boiled Ramen noodles, carried them off to bed to eat. After a long nap, she'd

67

figure out if she could manage another two hours. She had strained something in her right shoulder, a dull ache that flared at random times into a searing lance into her lower back. Of course, something else she didn't need. She would never finish in time. She couldn't finish even if William was here to help. Not that he would have been any good at this.

The voice in her head said, "A quitter, huh?" She had quit once before.

—ᴨᴠ—

Summer 1983.

Rebecca could deal with the devil. Only the devil unfailingly won. For ten dollars spending money all her own, fifteen-year-old Rebecca would do nearly anything. Her father kicked the door frame, made it ring like a drum. He said, "You tear this chicken coop down, stack it neat, roll up the wire, and cover it all with the roof tin – I'll give you ten dollars. You have to do all your chores and no money comes with them. But for this special project, you deserve something."

Three days when she had believed it could only eat up two. First she jerked staples from all the posts to release the chicken wire. She rolled it and stabbed her hands several times, the needle ends driving into her palms. No gloves.

Freeing the tin off the top meant advancing along the roof edge with a screwdriver and hammer, prying up each roofing nail of the first sheet, shifting the ladder across the coop's interior to work the next sheet and the next. The chicken shit rose in a cloud that surrounded the ladder and floated up to cover her hair, her bare arms, her face. She hammered apart the boards and dropped the sides to the ground – more dust, and the last-to-go-down scratched her arm to the blood. Hammering back and crowbarring out the nails ate up another half day. She was nearly finished, close enough to grasp the ten ones in her hand, when she stepped on a rusty nail. It drove through her shoe into her foot.

68

Her father discovered her flopped in the dirt, hunched over her bloody naked foot. He inspected her and said, "Quitting early today?" He wandered over and kicked a board. He picked it up. As he stacked boards in the coarse meadow grass, boards that would lay untouched for years, he allowed, "You did most of it, but not all. I'll pay you, but both of us know you quit."

Her momma drove her into town for the tetanus shot and her father docked her eight dollars for the medical bill. She needed a real job, in town, not the devil's deals.

CHAPTER EIGHT – AT THE EDGE

L ATE AUGUST 2008.
Bec set eyes on the bobcat the day before the village women invaded.

The cabin's front porch had granted Bec hours of counseling, but no revelation. Sorting through, digging up her life with William resolved nothing – just ended in a quiet view into the meadow's world. A world that needed no marriage, no answers, no humanity. She promised on her momma's grave she would stop obsessing and listen to the meadow's cue. Just be.

In the first light of morning when sleep denied her, she waited on the front porch, wrapped in a jacket, binoculars in her hand. She scanned the sky and trees for birds. Out of the corner of her eye – the bobcat swung round the cabin to her left, allowed a wide berth but otherwise ignored her scent. Bec froze stock-still.

The bobcat's gait glided through a mystifying slink, physical but unreal. All the musculature rippling under the fur of the shoulders, in the hind flanks. Clockwork intent. Bec couldn't understand how mere bones and tendon, muscle and blood could articulate like that.

Parting the grass with silence, the cat disappeared into the tall green of the field. Bec brought the binoculars to her eyes. Her breath returned as a mere tease. Somewhere out there, not far at all. The grass swayed, a curving track flickered. A pattern, searching the meadow. A full stop. A silent moment.

The cat exploded out of the green, up four feet, and dove claws-first into the tall grass. Bec heard the scream, a sharp bleating. The field swayed, formed a wide wake that swept toward her. The cat popped out onto the drive. It toted a sack of fur in its mouth. Rabbit. Bec could distinguish the wet neck that drooped to one side, the bloody wound where the head had once connected. The cat, scornful of her presence, trotted past her, towards the tree line.

It wasn't Dallas.

—⚞—

Sunday's early afternoon light cut across the meadow, so hard it felt cruel. The trees stood out as white stripes and black shadows, the birds in the sky darkling silhouettes. Again she dawdled on her porch, and this time civilization closed in on her. The first car, a new metallic-gold-colored Impala, shone as a rising star on the meadow's horizon. The second, an old black Cougar, crept its way along behind, muted into a specter of evening, lurking behind, sneaking along. Bec linked the echo of this to her bobcat's hunt. She took exception to the visit, and the claustrophobia that had kicked in.

Miss Junie unfolded from the Impala, the first out. The woman resembled a full clipper sailing across the grass and up onto the porch. Bec's hand was seized in an iron grip, and the half glasses bobbed towards her scalp. Miss Junie said, "I hope you forgive us, Missus Robertson. We decided you needed a visit. You must be going crazy out here by yourself."

At her elbow, another woman, a short soft blimp, glided on the boards. "We haven't met. I'm June's sister Karen. She said you would be attending our Sunday lunch, but when you didn't show all month, we decided to bring it to you. I've fetched coffee." Karen thrust out a thermos wrapped in a kitchen towel.

"And I've brought the cookies." A third woman stumped up the

71

steps, one riser at a time – she led with her good foot and thrust up off her knee with a hand. "Where shall I set them, dear?"

Bec heard her voice trickle out. "Living room. Come in."

The woman on the step said, "Name's Eugenia. I'm a schoolteacher during the week, south at Abiquiu Elementary." She twisted around on the step and shouted at the autos. "Girls, shag your butts out of the cars. She doesn't bite." Eugenia opened the screen door and marched herself into the cabin.

Meek as the rabbits in the pasture, Bec trailed her into her own house. A moment later she fished out coffee cups and Miss Junie rousted out plates and forks for the cake. Six women piled into her chairs and couch. They vibrated the old ceiling boards above with their voices – dust trickled out of the cracks into the living room air. By the wood stove, Bec settled quiet and hunched over in a kitchen chair.

An immense woman, twice the size of Chuma, leaned across and patted her knee. "We're the DIVAS, dearie. That's our initials, see. We're Daring, Intoxicated, Vulgar, And Sexy."

Bec eked out a grin. An organization built on outrageousness – why wasn't she more intrigued?

"And what's your story? Are you Catholic, or do you drive to Española for church? Check out this picture here, is that your husband? He's in uniform. That why he's gone?" The DIVA left no room for an answer.

Two or three ongoing conversations had driven out from town and poured themselves into this small space. Bec bet even Mannie's Cantina in town wasn't this loud.

Miss Junie slapped her hands together. The chorus died down. "Okay girls, let me introduce Bec. Bec is short for Rebecca." She dipped her head to Bec. "Correct me if I deliver any of your bio wrong. She's moved up from Texas, and this place has been in her family for years – you might know the Staffords, married to the Grassics. Her husband is off in Afghanistan keeping us safe. They don't have any kids, her momma and daddy passed away, and distant cousins lurk in the background. She's a minister's wife, so watch those four-letter words."

Bec shrank back in her chair. How did Miss Junie know all this?

The round-robin of introductions began. "Karen, like I said before." She was a chubby partridge of a woman, with a major scar on her chin buried beneath pancake makeup.

"Eugenia." Eugenia the schoolteacher was a Norteña, jet black hair that might be dyed, a mass of wrinkles engraved across her brown, unadorned face.

"Marcella. I'm a part-timer, live in Miami during the winter." A stork, a narrow shouldered crane bowing into the circle.

Already Bec had lost the thread – the names slipped away.

"Linda. Nice place." Linda was the torrent of questions, a hundred dollar red haircut with blonde highlights, orb-shaped face, and three chins.

"Glory. I'm the artist." A thick braid of gray hair, bib overalls, clear eyes, reading glasses hung around her creased, thin neck.

Linda leaned across Bec, addressed the woman on the other side, a lady whose name was? Bec had already forgotten. "That odious little man will destroy Santa Eulalia."

The answer bounced back, "He's our mayor. He's run the town for decades."

"Only because it's Santa Eulalia. That's hardly the big time. Sammie Maduro lost us the big supermarket and he and the School Board gave up the high school. We wouldn't have any school at all if it wasn't for Catholic primary."

On the other side of the room, out of the depths of the couch – "So drunk she tripped and fell right off the steps into a snow drift." Wild cackling from half the circle.

Miss Junie responded. "Now, Glory, don't be cruel. She does catch ear infections and lose her balance."

"Ninety proof infections."

If the DIVAS had arrived and filled the place like a whirlpool, they streamed out like a riptide. In the aftermath of the afternoon coffee, Bec was wedged between Miss Junie and Karen on the couch. Karen said, "Now the fun can kick off." She reached into her capacious tote and fished out a bottle of silver rum.

Miss Junie asked, "Do you have any fruit juice or lemonade, dear?"

Bec stared at the bottle. "I believe I have a can of powdered lemonade in the kitchen."

Miss Junie said, "To the left of the sink, I think?"

"I'll whip us up a batch," said Karen.

"We should warn you right up front, dear. My sister and I either drink far too much, or not enough."

—⚹—

The bottle waited, mute but confident on the coffee table between them. Two large glasses full of lemonade and rum were cradled in the sisters' hands. Junie had set herself to home with her white walking shoes up on the table – Bec was huddled back in the couch with her second drink untouched on the table in front of her. Karen's story filled the room. "Yeah, I'm a feminist. Men run most things and screw them up. Of course, I recognize women in power sometimes go astray, Indira Gandhi for instance – genocide on a quiet scale, year after year. How like a man. I taught in Texas at Austin for years, Women's and Gender Studies, but they were totally unwilling to grant tenure. Then I ended up in Ann Arbor – also no tenure – and after that a Montessori school in Albuquerque. Catch 'em young."

Junie leaned into Bec's ear, sotto voce. "Boy, have I heard this a few times."

The rum ran around in her blood, a racetrack of hot dizziness. She replied, "Umm."

Karen scrutinized William's miniature shrine on the shelf behind the stove. Bec felt peculiar about it. The stare crowded her, like someone who leaned in too close to you or popped into the bathroom unannounced. The mantel clock ticked like thunder. The ice in her glass fell with a shuddering clink.

Karen's head swiveled; she gazed at Bec with crystal clear blue eyes. She turned back to William's photo.

Bec cleared her throat, asked Junie. "Have you always worked for the post office?"

Miss Junie rolled up on her hip on the couch so she could turn an eye on Bec. " No, not at all. I worked for a Texas Congressman in Washington for years."

Karen grunted. "He was a conservative. A fascist, actually. Watch June like a hawk. She never outgrew the experience."

Bec said, "Are you sure you two are sisters?"

Miss Junie allowed, "Different fathers." Her voice pitched barely above the clock ticking.

"Now you're the Postmistress?"

"I'm no one's mistress, honey. I'm the Postmaster."

—◆◆◆—

Bec wavered into the living room on her way back from the outhouse. She studied the two women on the couch. The bottle squatted within reach, as empty as the overcast night sky outside. With a sigh, Bec said, "Do you want to stay for dinner? I can whip up a salad and I have soup – chicken vegetable. It's organic."

June said, "That would be sweet."

Karen added, "Great. We can add wine – we have some in the car. Think I'll sneak a little nap."

Junie rose to her feet, a graceful tower. "I'll help with dinner. Karen snores."

They journeyed the whole eight feet into the kitchen. Bec figured the snoring would reach them all the same.

Junie's big rangy body sat at attention at the kitchen table. She chopped vegetables for the salad while Bec stirred the saucepan's contents – an organic soup she couldn't afford and shouldn't have bought. Junie had morphed for Bec, from federal supervisor to partying single. Bec picked up on the curling corners of the woman's mouth. The incandescent light streaming down on them highlighted two wrinkles between the eyebrows, the frown lines, the mole that cast a shadow onto the upper lip. Junie said, "Having trouble figuring us out? I ought to warn you. Both Karen and I have a different sexual orientation. Not to dance around about it – we're lesbians."

Bec's eyebrows flew up towards the ceiling. "I see."

"I don't like to make too big a thing about it. Karen though, she can get in your face."

"Isn't that a bit difficult in the village?"

"We're old enough people figure we're not active, you know, no longer dating. We're kind of forgiven because we're ancient."

"But – that is.... You do date even now?" She sketched the double quote marks with her fingers, and felt ludicrous. Who did that anymore?

"Sure. The sex drive doesn't die off – that's a hetero myth."

What could she say to that?

"I expect Karen will hit on you before we wander out of here. She's the aggressive one."

A flush ran up the back of her neck. "Thanks for the warning."

Junie rose from the table with a paper towel full of vegetable scraps. She scuffed over to the plastic trashcan and dumped it. After, she slid down the counter to the sink, a half step from Bec. She rested her hand on Bec's shoulder. "You know, I'm sure. These things can be awkward otherwise. If you say yes, that's fine, and no is fine too. But if Karen isn't your type, I wouldn't mind."

Mind? She had stumbled into something like this before. "I don't think so. I'm married." Her heartbeat ran way up – because she was afraid? Because she had a fondness for the statuesque woman who hovered over her? Not likely.

"Chaplain Robertson doesn't have to know. Been this way for centuries, the women together while the men are off hunting."

The moment hung on the knife edge. Her body tingled, but for flight? She wobbled back a step. Junie leaned back – a grin twitched her mouth.

Bec said, "Thanks for not pushing." That sounded an echo in memory.

—w—

Fall 1982.

Rebecca lay on the cool earth under the porch of her great-grandpa's cabin with a dog she had borrowed from a relative. Bars of summer light streamed in dusty beams down between the boards. Both dog and fourteen-year-old girl drifted in and out, drowsy from the unusual heat. She murmured to the dog, "Good boy, Happy, good boy." She scratched his ear in a desultory way. She knew that word, desultory.

The cabin door creaked open and sandals flip-flopped across the boards. Two pair of legs dangled over the porch edge. Women's legs. Bare and pale, backlit by the huge sun. Voices murmured. One was her momma's.

They droned on and on, like bees. Sleep stole her thoughts, shuttered her eyes. The voices fell silent. Grasshoppers in the field spun out a huge quiet. A whirring blanket of nothing. Rebecca hung at the edge of waking and dream. But her mother's voice cut through, alarmed, high.

"Please don't. I don't like that."

CHAPTER NINE – SUCH BABIES

OCTOBER 2008.

Bec could smell smoke from the wood stove in the living room. She couldn't escape facts – something wasn't right with the flue. She stabbed at a mouse turd up against the baseboard, tried to worry its minute ellipsoid out with a ratty-ended broom. For eighty years the cabin had lived here in the meadow, dreamt away summer and hunkered down in the winter. It had both sheltered family members and watched them dry up and blow away. Great-Grandpa willed it to Grandma. Grandma was Paw-Paw's favorite and a firestorm swept the family when he bequeathed it to her rather than parcel it out in shares. Only a promise of an open door and unlimited access restored the fabric of family peace. Her own momma inherited the place at the death of her mother, as she turned thirty. After her momma passed, Bec repeated the same promise of open-doors to the cousins.

But the cabin had perpetually oozed dirt. A true cabin, a rude construct, a site-built edifice of pinned-together planks and logs. Bec imagined minute, untraceable crumbling that seeped down onto the floor and jelled, thickened, dried into flecks, grains, even miniature balls of mud. Every three days, no matter what the season, she rousted the place, tried to approximate cleanliness, and disturbed the ghosts.

Her momma must have been one of the ghosts. "Farmers need to spend time somewhere they don't have to farm," she had said. New

Mexico was the only place her mother had ever felt happy, and maybe been in love. The only place she wasn't on edge. "You're safe here, Rebecca girl. Breath easy."

Her momma died nine years ago, in a dreary hospital in Lubbock. Bec knew her soul wasn't trapped in that complex of blond brick structures and not out on the Grassic family farm. Besides, the Arbulls next door had bought the farm for the taxes, and most everything at the farm sale too.

Bec couldn't believe in heaven, maybe because heaven's promise would justify the persistent level of horror on earth. She derived joy in the thought of each person, each fleck and grain of humanity turned into light or energy and returned to the universal pool of effervescence. She preferred to think of her momma's sparkle haunting the old cabin.

At the table, a table that had been surrounded by so many Grassics and Staffords, she worked her way through another psycho-puzzle, a book of the New York Times toughest. Especially the way she did them.

Number 12 down – nine letters, "sheltered." That gave her an E to start Number 21 across – six letters, escape. Number 16 across – alone. Number 33 down – expire. Over from the left, Number 34 across, five letters and the third had to be a p – empty.

The tea slid across her tongue cold and bitter. Funny, how the same themes popped back up, even here in New Mexico.

—ᴡ—

Linda, the DIVA with a mouth like a torrent, arrived in time for poppy seed rolls and English Breakfast tea. A bit reckless, she powered down the lane through the meadow, her silver GMC SUV rocking. From the window, Bec watched the figure inside the truck seesaw, cling to the wheel. Linda stopped at the steps, rolled down the window. "Can we talk please?"

Inside on the couch and chair, they faced each other. Bec clued in – her memory leapt back to eavesdropping in the Post Office – Linda was related to Miss Junie, and it was her son who regarded drug treatment centers as a revolving door. What did Linda want? Why was this happening to Bec?

In the dim room, Bec snapped on the light by the chair. She crossed her legs, leaned forward, clasped her hands on her knees. She had learned this pose in Dallas as she counseled church members unhappy with their moneyed existence. "What do you need to talk about, Linda?"

Outside the crystalline day waited, the New Mexico light at its clearest, a quality of sensation that shocked the eyes into perceiving the world. Inside Bec folded herself up into shades of dimness, lamented that she wasn't out in her meadow. She watched the sun daub its way through the window, paint the floor, paint the hair of the woman before her. Blonde streaked through Linda's red hair, cut in a bubble, and the sun lit the two tufts of gray the woman allowed at her temples. Linda's face in repose showed the smooth, plumped-out skin of a baby, tiny pores, curves all swooping and gentle. In anxiety Linda revealed a cant to her mouth as if she might break into a wail. "I would have called, but you don't have a phone."

"Hmm."

Now that she had settled herself in, Linda demonstrated a great reluctance to begin. She picked at the pattern in her immense sundress. "I thought."

A four-beat while nothing happened. "Thought what, Linda?" God, old habits die hard.

"You seem a sympathetic person."

Bec dipped her head. "Thank you."

"I mean, everyone says nice things about you." Linda fluttered a hand up to her throat, as if she waved off heat stroke.

"That's good, I guess."

Linda turned her eyes into the corner — Bec wondered what she glimpsed there.

"Linda?"

"The thing is. No one ever says anything nice about Alex."

That rang a bell. But best to let her tell it.

"Alex is my son. He's my ex's son too. I believe divorce gives rise to problems, don't you? Alex is eighteen and lives with me during the summers but goes to school in Chicago where his father lives. He may not graduate, because of the – you know – all the drugs, and he's already a year behind. We want the best for him, but he's always had trouble in school and now he's behind his regular class, and he says he doesn't go to school much even though his father says he does. I'm just, well – I've got my back to the wall, and he's disappeared, been gone a week, and he'll come back, but he may have sold his car for drugs and he'll be in terrible shape. What do I do? Open the front door and invite him in?"

"Linda, I don't know your son, so how could I give advice?"

Linda jerked on the fingers of her right hand, popped her way through each knuckle, a castanet of worry. "You have seen something like this before?"

Unfortunately. "Is it meth?"

"No, thank God. It's just pills."

Synthetic heroin, that's what it was. Oxy and all the rest. "Then it's not the worst."

Linda narrated a three year ordeal where her own anguish figured highly. Bec didn't believe Linda could serve as much of an advocate for sobriety – she could imagine the young man rolling his eyes, making promises that kept the status quo going, killing time until the next binge of pills.

Awful to hear. Linda's tale wound to a close, ended in a minor key with a flourish of tears. "So what do you think?"

Bec unfolded, crossed her legs, linked her hands. "I'm not a counselor anymore, Linda. But you have a couple of choices. You can assume Alex hasn't figured out what he wants, for himself and for his life. If that's the case, you can try to shock him straight with a program like Outward Bound. He'll be where he can't buy drugs and where they wear his ass off running up and down mountains. It works for some kids. Maybe one out of ten."

Linda's face folded like a towel dropped on the floor. "I don't know. That sounds awfully rough. He used to like the outdoors, when he was a small boy, but not now. Not really."

"You could ask him what he likes, besides Vicodin."

"Yes. I suppose. Two choices? What's the other?"

"Hmm. You can drop the hammer. If he uses and you catch him, you can throw him out. Even if you don't, he'll track along a standard pattern. After he's stolen from you, humiliated himself and his family in public, lived on the street and used every drug he can score, he'll hit bottom. Then he has to decide if he wants to live or die. Maybe after that you can step back into his life. Rehab might work then if he wants it, although he'll always be a recovering addict."

Linda popped all her knuckles with one great wrench. "Gawd! That's awful. How could you say something like that?"

"It's how these things work out. I've seen it a lot."

"You're not helping me, saying I should write my son off."

"I'm just trying to prepare you. I can even say you should seek out some help for yourself. But where do you believe things stand?"

Linda's eyes drowned with tears. She shoved her glasses up on her forehead, swabbed at her eyes, and smeared her eye makeup. "Not good. Going wrong. He does steal from me. And he lies about everything. And it's worse every month."

Bec shifted out of the chair to cradle the woman in her arms. "Alex is already making that second choice, where he'll leave home. Let's at least try the first choice."

—⚭—

January 2009.

She snapped her eyes open, fell out of a dream into confusion. Full

82

of soldiers who had been burned. How much of that had been dream, how much a jigsaw from her life and William's emails? She rose from the bed and paced barefoot through her cabin. Before one of her small windows, she gazed out into her field. Skirls of snow obscured the treeline across the way. Each gust hid and revealed the conifers black spires. Bishops all, they cast a beneficence across the meadow. The tall yellow grass spiked up out of the thin white cover. Not much snow yet, only about a foot. If the forecast turned out right, she'd soon witness the grass disappear from view, perhaps until April. That close to the window she could feel the cold seeping in, and she hugged her bathrobe tighter.

"Soon I'll light the fire, throw together a meal, crack open a book. When the weather breaks, Rubio will show up to plow out my lane. Till then I am me by myself, and the snow is the whole world." She twirled away from the leaky window, performed a three step towards the kitchen. Her bare feet fluttered over the black-stained boards. "Welcome the solitude, Bec. Yogurt and whole wheat toast for breakfast. Christmas behind us, thank God. And in March, we go meet William in Croatia." Croatia was dirt cheap, and the boy wanted somewhere cold after the Middle East.

She put the kettle on, dashed into the bedroom to don pants, the rough old coat, the black stocking cap. She'd set light to the fire, march out for a quick pee, and pack some wood back in. She lit the tinder in the stove on her way, wiggled through the backdoor into the wings of snow that brushed her.

As she stepped from the outhouse zipping her coat, the thick orange flame rose above her cabin a magnificent twenty feet, cast its brightness like a beacon across the packed snow, through the eddies of new crystals. Her chimney was on fire.

—⁓—

February 2009.

Chuma's was so hot inside that beads of condensed water ran down through the fog on the inside of the windows. Bec sidled through a line at the counter. She dodged around the bakery case and the young boy who scribbled orders and made change. In back, Chuma squared up before the two-foot by two-foot griddle – her hand shimmied a spatula that stirred scrambled eggs, and fried bacon and sausage. She waved the blunt aluminum blade towards Bec. "They never get tired of breakfast burritos. I sure as hell do, but they'll eat the same damn thing every day. What's my white chicken up to?"

"Wanted to escape the mountain and do some shopping while the roads are clear. And warm up. The chimney guys out of Española are just getting around to replacing my flue. I've been frozen for weeks, even with a Walmart space heater."

Chuma snapped her gum. "I told you that you could bunk at my place. What's the damage gonna set you back?"

"Too much. A couple of rafters, a patch for the decking, and new pipe. I'm broke again."

Chuma handed her a burrito, with a sly grin. "At least you're saving some of that firewood you bought from Rubio."

"Don't remind me." She bit into the burrito.

Chuma rapped the spatula edge hard on the sheet of stainless. "By the way, that Glory woman left you a letter, 'cause you don't own a damn phone. I'm turning into the community bulletin board. How do you know her?"

Bec nibbled on the tortilla, worked her way into the heart of the burrito from the end. Chuma's burritos were long on egg and salsa and short on potatoes. "She's an artist I met through Miss Junie and Karen. I like her – she's somehow weird, but in a nice way. Where's the message?"

Chuma turned around, peeled a magnet off the side of her walk-in cooler, handed over a folded square of paper. "Of course she wants you to do something for her."

"How do you know?"

Chuma snorted. "I read the note now, didn't I?"

Bec unfolded the scrap, read aloud. "Bec, that so-and-so Sam Maduro is killing any chance we have to re-use the grocery store. Can you come to a meeting with me on the afternoon of the fifth? I have some ideas about a senior center, a place for art classes in the summer, and maybe an organic garden in the back for the kids."

Chuma said, "Better call her on my phone. She left that four days ago. Today's the fifth, and she'll maybe hit the road to your place at any minute to kidnap you."

—◦◦◦—

Glory's wry scratchy voice had directed Bec to her studio out on the end of the smallest side street in Santa Eulalia. The dirt road hadn't been graded since summer, so the pickup heaved as Bec rocked through the snow-covered ruts around the biggest holes. She hopped out and hiked up to the studio – an oversized garden shed. The entire front face was patched together out of salvaged windows of various sizes – Glory popped through one that had been converted to a narrow short door. "Come in, come in. I was sure we'd miss each other and you'd skip the meeting." Glory scowled, as if Bec had failed her and let her down.

They perched on stools beside an old fashioned stove that roared with flame and kept the drafty shop nearly warm. Glory slung her silver braid back behind her and lit a cigarette "How's it going with our two old lezzies?"

Old? Glory must be as old as Junie. "It's going great. They keep their hands to themselves and they're good friends."

Polite, Glory blew her smoke back over her shoulder away from Bec. "They're biding their time, sure you'll capitulate."

Bec rejected that. "They know I'm hopelessly heterosexual. Not to mention married."

"Hah! That ain't the vibe you give off, girlie."

A draft from somewhere slipped up the back hem of Bec's coat. She shivered. "I like them. They're fun to run around with."

Glory snickered. "But you had to drive them back from Taos when dinner turned a bit wild."

When they were both drunk on their asses. "I have advantages as a friend. I'm the natural designated driver. But that's not why I'm sitting here as frozen as a popsicle, is it?" She hugged her arms around herself.

"No. I wanted moral support. I'm about to go to war with the Council."

Glory believed peace unnatural. "Why me?"

"You're a preacher's wife. That's a lot better than a wild-eyed, flaky artist. Here's the deal. Mayor Maduro won't assume any Village liability for the old grocery store. The company that shut it down owns it outright and they'll let us use it for a write-off or a deduction or something. But, maintenance and utilities would be our responsibility. They've asked for a one year lease for only a dollar. But Sammie, that scaredy cat, prefers to let the building cave in rather than risk any expense."

"Maybe he doesn't have any money."

Glory drew her mouth in a hard cut across her face. "He doesn't have any balls, that's what he doesn't have."

"Maybe, just maybe he's right."

"Goddamn it! Whose side are you on?"

Bec figured it out – Glory's way or temporary enmity. "Yours, of course."

"The space is perfect. We could build movable walls and shift the space around anyway we want. The old folks could play bingo. The young kids could do crafts."

Glory was right, the building could work for the Village. Or it could be a huge sink of time and effort. Bec cocked her head. "If you want widespread support, you need something for everyone."

Glory held her hands out as if she presented the twelve apostles. "No problem. Dances for the teenagers. A flea market a couple of times a year. Meeting space for anyone needing a temporary office. Something for everyone but the drunks in the bars. But AA could hold meetings."

"More than enough. Write up a list, read it off to the Council."

"But Sam won't go for it and he'll block the Council. We need a few hundred dollars a year to sweeten them."

Bec tugged at her lower lip, leaned closer to Glory and the stove. "Why don't you form a nonprofit and do it with grant money?"

Glory squinted up one eye. "Who would write the grants?"

Bec took it upon herself to feed the fire – a log, the metal door opened, a roar of naked flame before she slammed it shut again. "Damn, it's cold in here."

"Try standing around with a paint brush. Then tell me about cold."

Bec bet Glory liked the cold, and liked complaining about it. "As for grant writing, I've done it before. Not for William's church of course, but for Big Brothers and Big Sisters. I can show you how."

"That would be great. Who hands out grants?"

Bec shrugged. "The Feds. The State. Family foundations. The County."

Maybe Glory realized this was more effort than a simple shouting match. Her face fell slack, frowned. "Sounds like a lot of work."

Damn! Why was she having to convince Glory? Bec dropped her hands onto her knees, leaned forward. "To set up, the first year. After that it's cookie-cutter. But you can look all this up."

Glory's voice spooled out flat. "Like where?"

"The Santa Fe Public Library."

Glory jumped up, wandered twice around the stove and Bec. She scratched the back of her neck, glanced at Bec. "Good. We'll go together."

Worse than handholding Linda. Bec had just been sucker-punched. William would be snorting that smug laugh if he could see her now.

Afternoon at the Village Hall. The Council room housed a table for eight, with six chairs shoved against the wall for the public. Somebody had nailed up dark cheap paneling from the eighties. Carpet runs shot here and there across the space, and only one window fought the gloom at the far end. Purgatory could be no worse, and time could crawl no slower.

Bec felt sorry for the Mayor. No wonder he didn't want a new financial commitment. The old plastic chair dug into her spine – where she needed to straighten up, it curved forward. She listened, focused on the meeting as it crawled to order with only four present. Council members straggled in until eight in all clustered round. All men. Mixed race. Same bland, nebulous age. They shuffled paper, leaned over to each other for side conversations, and paid a limited amount of attention to the startup. Including the Pledge of Allegiance, during which two of them texted away on their phones.

Bec hadn't encountered Sammie Maduro before.

Maduro stacked up about five-nine, a Hispanic fireplug of a man with an unexpected tenor voice. His best feature, silver hair, bristled short on the sides and tried to fake another two inches of stature in a vertical thatch. Bec could tell Sam's nose had been to the wars. Bent, shot through with veins and deep craters. He wore his shirttail out to hide his belly and a lime green sports coat over that. He appeared indistinguishable from the basic Sun City retiree, down to that slight wobble from the first heart attack or stroke. He stopped in each chunk of business to interject, and to instruct. Master and servants, a king who could bully only the serfs.

The Council rushed past the budget shortfall – an amount that left Bec open-mouthed. They hung up in a discussion about the State Fire Marshall's visit. Sammie asked, "What will we show him?"

For two minutes, the fire chief advanced ideas and retracted them.

This opened it up so the Council could help. Each board member stepped up to the task, and another thirty minutes slipped away.

The meeting dragged on and on, plodded through agenda points in "Old Business" more and more slowly. Glory leaned over and whispered, "I think they hope we'll give up and go away."

Finally! "New Business. Any new agenda points."

Glory jumped up as if the chair launched her. "Mr. Mayor?"

Sammie scanned around the room for someone else to call on. Finally he dipped his eyes to Glory, breathed deep. "Go ahead."

"Mr. Mayor, would the Council entertain a discussion on the old supermarket? Mrs. Robertson and I have a proposal that can be decided today."

The free-for-all played out as Glory predicted, a turmoil of unspoken agendas, sly insults, avoidance. Bec scrutinized the Board, the interplay, until she discovered the weak link. She leaned forward to Glory and whispered in her ear, "Tell that sad little guy on the end we have time before the Mayor signs the lease to win a grant.

Glory addressed her remark at the mole-like white man. "Teddy, you understand we'll secure the money before you sign the lease? The grocery people said they'd give us until June."

Teddy bobbed his head. He glanced at his notes. He committed a political sin and betrayed his mayor. "Didn't catch that." He coughed into his hand. "It seems to me that the Council can pass a resolution of support for grants. Basically, the writing of a grant, and then maybe... Well, we table signing the lease. Until the last council meeting in May, and, ahh. Our ass isn't hanging out, pardon my French." Teddy peered down the table at the other counselors. They goggled back.

Sammie tried to glare him down into a damp spot in the chair.

Another councilman said, "It's no skin off my nose. They do all the work, right? And they run the center if it takes off, right?"

The fire chief said, "I'd give it a shot, not that I have a vote."

A chorus of agreement circled round the table, even as Sammie jumped to his feet and flapped his hands in shooing motions – like the councilmen were puppies headed the wrong way. With a high piping voice, he shouted, "Who runs it?"

"Glory can run it for us, if she don't mind doing it all-volunteer."

Sammie said, "But who writes the grant?"

Glory held out her hand to Bec. "Mrs. Robertson said she'd do it – she's a professional grant writer."

Bec tasted bile in her mouth. But they came across as such babies. Bigger amateurs than the Texas church. As long as she didn't have to attend the meetings.

CHAPTER TEN – HELP IN ANY WAY

M ID MARCH 2009.
    Bec was slapped with winter's insult four days before her flight to Europe.

Inside in the hushed cabin air, it was a god-awful crash, a rending thunderclap that jerked her out of bed onto her feet. The cabin roof cracked, popped, banged like gunfire. From the outside in the snow-storm, it must have appeared like a dance, like the ballet swan folding its wings and sinking with muffled flutters to the stage floor. She scooted into the hallway in time to witness the collapse, angular as an origami bird, through the ceiling and into the second bedroom, bringing the eighty-year-old tongue-and-groove down like quills and coverts to rest snow-covered across aged furniture and boxes of summer clothes.

—⚏—

From the ground Rubio supervised his cousins, a swarm on the roof, mostly in their shirtsleeves. "Not much snow load. Surprised it collapsed. Que, this place is older than dirt."

He was entitled to say it, since the cabin had been framed up ten years before his birth. "What happens now?"

"Not much, till Spring. The chicos, they know what to do. We'll hammer in some two-by fours across the hole on the outside, tarp her up, and nail that down. Shouldn't cost much."

"How much?"

"Oh, four hundred. Plus material."

The wind on her face was no colder than the bitterness inside. "Can I pay you next month?"

"Chure. Pues, I know where you live." He sniggered, ate at his mustache with his lower teeth. "We fix her good in the spring."

"What does that mean?"

"We strip her down, like shearing a sheep, lo ves? Throw away all that old decking but keep most of the tin. After, we repair the rafters, sister them up with new boards where they rotted. Then we start over."

She would be eating macaroni and cheese for the rest of her life.

—m—

"Surrealism!" Bec wandered through the International Sunport in Albuquerque – she suffered a giddy dislocation. International travel on a March snow day. She had driven out of the white high country and into the warmth of a Rio Grande Valley afternoon. An Interstate dry as the valley's desert and busy with traffic brought her south to the Sunport, a trendy almost-international airport. Into the conspicuously SouthWest-style main hall.

Caught a peek at the woman across the way, in shorts and flip-flops. Bec wished her legs were that tan, that she owned those sunglasses. People swarmed like ants. Her brain was about to burst.

She stopped at the coffee bar for a tea and had to settle for Constant Comment. "That will pickle your tongue."

The barista appeared confused. "What? Something wrong?"

"Sorry, talking to myself."

—m—

The flight to Dallas, a short jump, lasted less time than her drive to ABQ. She tucked one leg under her, dreamed about William the whole flight. His soft hands, his gliding touch, how he always did for her before she could do for him.

92

She had chosen the flights for the lowest airfare, settled for a collection strung around the globe with plenty of stop-and-go. Five in the afternoon – Dallas to Atlanta, Atlanta to London, London to Zagreb, Zagreb to Dubrovnik – thirty-nine hours. Time lost out to the power of flying, blew away in the sky as contrails spun out behind her. Locked up with two hundred people in the aluminum bottle – they all suffered from some inflammation of the soul. She watched a couple, each three times her size, struggle out of their seats to the restroom and return, to compress themselves again into seats designed for hundred-pound humans. The man in particular wore a woebegone face, knees against the seat in front of him, the tray table an inch from his buttons. Bigger than William by seventy pounds.

Her chaplain. Why was he so strange on Skype and in his last emails? Good for them to be together, to see and touch and talk face-to-face. She could discover what troubled him. The house or her?

Content for once with her own size, with plenty of space, Bec stretched out her back. She reached both arms over her head, flexed. She hid under the lint-textured blanket. If she kept her eyes closed, the presence of all those other people faded out.

Midway over the Atlantic, the thin atmosphere scrubbed the plane's skin – the muted roar blanked out everything. She fell asleep for six hours. As they descended into Heathrow, she woke to a mid-day glare. Adrift, sticky, she de-planed with the others. She wandered Terminal One until – a miracle – she located the gate for her next flight. She suffered through a six hour layover where she struggled for sleep in an unforgiving chair.

In Zagreb she had a fifteen hour layover and checked into the Royal Airport Hotel. Eighty dollars bought her a double bed and token sleep.

Feeling a hundred years old, she waved her boarding pass, shambled onto the tarmac and up the stairs. She sank into a seat, clasped her arms. Don't even think it. It crawled out of her head as soon as she crossed over from tired to exhausted, a reptile of an idea. What if he and she… what if the sex was no good?

—⁓—

Dubrovnik had settled in at twenty degrees Celsius under blue skies. William's winter vacation – no desert here. She queued for a taxi. After the driver plonked her suitcase in the trunk, she pointed and pointed again at the itinerary with the hotel name, cocked her eyebrows to ask if he understood.

Her pantomime pissed off the driver. "I speak English good. All taxi all over world speak English. On way in, I show you my city, tell all, after drive the motorway."

Their hotel – red brick banded by white stone. Orange tile roofs and palms all about. William waited in the modern lobby, a made-over Renaissance rising up around him to dusty pale bowls of lights. He rushed forward and stooped to hug her, smushed her head to his chest. Her cheekbone was jammed deep into his sternum. "I was worried. Why didn't you call? I had my mobile turned on."

"William darling, I don't own a cell anymore."

"No matter, no matter. This place is great. Dubrovnik is great – you're going to love it."

"Can I nap for an hour or two? I'm really dragging."

"Sure, sure!" He grabbed her bag.

—⁓—

First he dragged her to drinks down the block in a basement bistro. "What do you want? Local wine? An aperitif? Even a beer? Great beer in Croatia."

"Sorry, I'm still not drinking. I'll order a bitter lemon."

"Oh."

He had bought tickets to an early performance in a magic lantern theatre. Scrims and flies projected a ghostly medieval city for the audience.

Language didn't count, as actors tumbled in and out through the screen, sang, and disappeared as if by a magician's trick. She nodded off twice and woke with a guilty jerk each time.

Dinner in a palace. They spent a half hour in the bar before being paraded to a table. Waiters rolled out a five course prix fixe, with wine for him. Skewers, roasted pork, a stew. The waiters brought gnocchi, spelled with strange vowels and a "z." A cottage cheese pie with winter squash.

She watched the waiters circle in with plates, like vultures that flapped down. "I don't believe we can afford this."

"Don't worry. We'll eat in small places later. This is your chance to sample the spectrum. Don't you like the dessert? You've hardly touched it."

Of course she hadn't touched it. Bec tried to grin at him, but the smile fell from her face in despair. She prayed for a long nap snuggled into sheets, against his warm back, maybe after slow, dreamy sex. Not an evening out. She would give anything to close her eyes, just for five minutes. She ached for sleep, for him.

Back out on the sidewalk, he wasn't done. "We could catch a cab and tour around the city. Or ride the cable car up Mount Srd and gaze at the lights."

Her eyes – they pinballed about, collect flecks of the city like flash photos. Gray stone, polished brass railing across the front of windows above her, marble-paved pedestrian streets. A middle-aged couple in dumpy overcoats – they held the hands of a blonde-headed girl child between them. Glue for a marriage. "William, can we please go back to the room? I'm dying to sleep."

Silence hung like a curtain between them during the trek back. She stifled yawns; she kept an eye on his face – the pinched furrow between his eyebrows a shadow.

—◊◊—

William left the door to the bathroom ajar and the light on as he shuffled to bed. Bec lay naked on her back, peering up in the dimness. She listened to his breathing draw close. He shifted up beside her from the foot of the bed, the thin mattress bent under his weight. His fingers traced her chin. The kiss, lingering. He craned his neck, kissed both her eyes. His hand ghosted across her hip. Both her hands on his chest. His head froze over her, poised. His breath guttural. She reached for him, discovered he wasn't ready. She could fix that. She ventured the most personal of massages.

No. It was going all wrong. Adrenalin was soaking into her brain, her heart. She could smell his sweat, the wax on the furniture. Now the light was far too stark, burning her eyes.

She hitched up onto her knees. "William, come here." Hands on his shoulders she tugged him until he faced her kneeling. The mattress formed craters around his knees and she slid down the cotton surface towards him. "You have to do this. You can get used to it. It's not horrible or anything."

She reached out and caught his wrists, tightened her grip. She drew his hands towards her chest, and the fingernails of one of his hands grazed over her belly as she tugged. Palms out, his hands faced her. Like a cop stops traffic. He held her off, suspended four inches away from their reunion, their reconciliation – fought her yearning. "William, darling." He locked up like a wooden statue, rigid.

"I. Can't." He dropped his hands, heaved himself off the bed. Fled to the bathroom and closed the door. On her knees she gazed across the murk of the room at the crack of light around the door. In a moment, a racking sob trickled out from behind the door.

She snapped on a lamp. Like a silent, vacant body she slipped down on her side into the fresh white sheets, folded her hands into her chest. With a small light gesture, she traced the edge of her scar with her finger. Her eyes remained wide open, stared at the faint pink slash across her chest.

Holiday. They call it "Holiday" in Europe, and the sun obliged. William and Bec marched around Dubrovnik on dutiful day trips, tour books in hand. Their marriage shambled along behind them, tried to keep up, all clawed and ramshackle. Four days, tramping about, strained words at the table, making small talk in their room. At night, he parked himself on an sleek leather sofa watching Croatian TV until she slept, or pretended to.

The cathedral. Medieval fortifications. Days in museums, poised in front of art, appraising technique, insights galore. She fell onto a bench while he poked his finger towards what might have been a Tintoretto.

She muttered, "He's trying to impress me with how much he knows. How did we become so pathetic?" She watched him consulting the guide in his hand. "I wish it would rain – the sunshine is such a lie."

All things on earth, good and bad, last only a little while. His leave, five days plus travel – his flight back booked by the Army. At breakfast in the hotel dining room, they placed themselves across from each other, separated by white starched linen. The smell of coffee and burnt sugar hung in the air – nausea rose up slow in her chest. The room slow-cooked her, and a springing flush of perspiration made her sweater unbearable. His knee jiggling, a friction against the table leg that created ripplets in his water glass. He was working up to something. Something he was nervous about.

"Rebecca, it's been over a year since the surgery. Have you considered when you might think about – consult with them about the, ahh... breast reconstruction?"

"If I need radiology again, the fake breasts could interfere with it."

She watched the sheen on his upper lip. He scrubbed his face with his napkin – he was burning with the heat, the embarrassment too. "But they've been checking you each month, with no sign of the cancer."

"Every three months now. It might be behind us. Might not."

The waiter appeared bearing two white plates edged in cobalt blue. William signaled for the potato and onion patties he had ordered. The waiter set a boiled egg and a crumpet in front of her, lost on the large platter.

William waited until the waiter had bustled away, asked, "Best to be positive about these things, don't you think?"

"Yes. Each day, one at a time."

"We could go ahead? Shouldn't we schedule – I have leave in the bank I can use."

"I don't know, William. I think it's too soon."

His face puckered up, peevish. All the effort to bring it up and now he was stymied. Frustrated. "But I can be with you to help. I need to know so I can arrange things.... Travel."

She jammed her hands into the table cloth, wrinkling it towards him. "Do you know how it works? They cut into me and insert expanders behind my muscles. Next they pump me up time after time with saline, to stretch me out and tear loose the muscle. Finally they cut out the expanders and give me implants."

"But everybody does it." He picked at his potato cake with a fork.

"Maybe you'd prefer real tissue in the breasts." She flared. "They could cut off pieces of my butt and do a swap job. It's called flap reconstruction. Maybe that would be more suitable?"

His mouth drew into a hard thin line. "Easy now. I'm trying to be helpful."

"For which one of us?"

He shook his head like a dog throws off water. "Why do you always pick a fight in a restaurant?"

"Not fair and you know it. Chuma's café is where I can log into Skype. And you picked the fight this time."

"What I'm hearing is that you're not interested in breast reconstruction." He glanced at a couple who edged by between the tables. He jerked his eyes down – he was ashamed.

"Look at me, William. This is me now. Sure, we could buy me fake breasts so you can touch me again. It won't erase the fact I'm repulsive to you right now. Can you imagine how that hurts me? To know I was two milk machines you wanted to paw?"

"Now who's unfair? I can't help the way I feel, what my subconscious does to me."

"The way you should feel is to love me, in sickness or in health."

"I do love you. I just have this hang-up."

"I'm not going back on the surgery table so you can feel better about yourself." She jerked to her feet, threw her napkin on the table. "I need to pack. If you don't mind, give me a few minutes alone."

His face, a ghastly mask, cracked like it would crumble off. He was about to cry again.

She strode off, through the elegant room – she left behind a flushed, fragmented man. Let him work it out. Let him say he's sorry. Let him go to hell.

—⋘—

They were going different ways – him first. Numb, she scuffed at the shiny roll-out vinyl in the airport. She clenched her hands. Her bag hung over her shoulder, an enormous scarf shrouded her torso. Body armor.

He scooped up her hands in his. "I am so sorry, Rebecca. I don't want to leave it this way. I promise I'll try harder." He bent to kiss her cheek. She smacked a kiss into the air, left it at that.

He straightened up, dropped her hands. "Security sucks up a long time. I have to go. Promise me you'll let me know when you're home safe." He stooped for his bag, turned. Hesitant, he turned back. She lifted a hand, forced a small wave. He trudged off, glanced back twice. He turned the corner and disappeared back into the Army. Into his life.

She glanced at her hands – they were hooked like a bird's talons. Rigid, like her heart. Cold and hard.

—◊◊◊—

August 1987.

Rebecca's momma loitered in the doorway of Rebecca's room, leaned against the jam. She folded her arms and rested her head on the frame. "You have to talk to your father before you leave for college. At least say goodbye."

Rebecca's gaze swept around the room, searched for a way out. The pale blue walls, an old antique mirror, surrounded by a chipped, ornamented frame with flaking gold paint. She scooted away from her mom on the bed and hugged her knees. "Just because he's sick doesn't mean he's a different person."

Her mother gave her that tender look, the one that said, We know how it is, even if we can't do anything about it.

Rebecca rejected that. "He made it clear long ago we're here to do his bidding. Talking to him won't help. He'll never change."

Momma unfolded her arms, turned in the doorway. She glanced back. "It's not about who he is. It's about who you are."

"I'm nineteen. I can do what I want." What she wanted was to please her momma, not her pa.

—◊◊◊—

Rebecca knocked at his bedroom door and elbowed it open. Even in the blistering heat of a Texas summer, he had turned off the window air conditioner and opened the sash. In a few seconds her pupils dilated and she could pick out the details. The bed, sheets wrinkled and heaved in a unmoving wave. The easy chair, carried up from the living room months ago and now a cradle for his frame. The monster himself, diminished,

100

sunk into the cushions. He held a wadded tissue in his hand, brought it to his lips, emitted a liquid hawking noise. He said in an unadorned way, "I thought you might not bother."

She dragged the ottoman away from him and perched on it. "Mom will drive me over to San Antonio tomorrow and drop me off at the Robertsons. Fall classes kick off in three days."

His voice creaked out flat, colorless. "Three days. In a hurry?"

"I don't work this weekend – finished up at the hardware store. No sense in hanging around."

His head swung up – his eyes huge in that fleshless skull. "That's right, go running off and have fun. Leave me here, sick and alone... "

Rebecca jerked back, said to him in as wooden a voice as she could summon, "I'm going to school."

He held a hand out to her, as if she should lean forward and grasp it. "There was a time when you would have stayed."

Somewhere in the back of her throat, a rage craved to leap out. "I have always wanted to get out of this house. I would never have stayed."

His eyes glinted. What was he thinking? "You're like your mother. Ungrateful."

The manipulative bastard. Her scream spilled out into the hot air. "You beat me. You beat Mom. You even beat the dog!"

He dropped his bony hand, his emaciated arm. "Your mind's already set. You won't have anything to do with me. Even though the cancer has me."

Twisted her gut. She jumped up, edged away from him. Even now she didn't want to turn her back on him. "I'm here to say goodbye. I'll be home either at the end of the term or for the funeral."

His mouth opened, soundless, and his head retracted like a turtle's. He muffled a deep liquid cough with his palm. "Maybe, you could forgive me. Give me a hug and tell me you forgive me. Let me die knowing that." Tears glissando'd in his eyes, shining lights.

She said, "I'll give you credit for one thing. You taught me that to survive this life, you have to be hard." She backed through the door, yanked it closed with a bang.

—⚬—

March 2009.

Inbound and an hour out of Detroit, packed into the cabin with hundreds of passengers, Bec twisted her hands. She'd crammed the paperback into the seat pocket in front of her, already dog-eared, already abandoned. Sharp breaths. Was this a panic attack? She released the seatbelt, jumped up, crawled over the two passengers between her and the aisle. "Excuse me. Sorry. Excuse me."

Jogged down the aisle and into the restroom. She slammed the lock over, flopped onto the toilet lid. She peered over the sink into her own eyes. She dropped her head in her hands. With no transition or warning, she began bawling. Tears burned her face, great wheezing breaths ratcheted in and out of her mouth. Her face screwed shut on itself, hot, clinched.

A trio of knocks on the door. Interfering bitch of a flight attendant. "Hello, are you all right in there? Can I help in any way?"

CHAPTER ELEVEN – HUNKERED

THE LAST WEEK OF MARCH 2009.
Bec stood spraddle-legged a foot deep in snow and burned her slash pile. Not much of a heap, since all the firewood work was abandoned when Rubio brought split logs to her. The gray sky lay draped like a cloak on Bec's shoulders. Flakes appeared out of the cloud, sifted down, and disappeared in the universe of snow piled around her. The lacerating cold bit at her, an earned cold, a confirmation. The fire crackled in front of her, the white super-heated smoke rose straight past her face into the frozen atmosphere. A tower of heat in the middle of a bloodless white field.

Sorel boots and insulated coveralls under a parka, with a ragged black wool stocking cap drawn down around her ears – they kept her on the edge of warm. Not everywhere though. The air teased at her face and stung her with cold. It struck through her wet gloves until her fingers ached. She held her hands out to the fire, but could not feel the flames.

"This is okay, Bec. Tough, but no tougher than it needs to be. This is your time. Alone in the snow, huh? A perfect day in the life of a perfect woman. Perfect except you talk to yourself." She prodded at the fire with a branch – it lit, alarmed her at how fast the fire twined up it. She flipped the branch into the pile and yielded it to fate. What would it be like to share slash day with William? Probably shitty.

"Time for a cup of tea. If this fire escapes the meadow and burns up New Mexico, there's no justice in the world." She turned toward the cabin, struggled up her trail with a plastic gas can. Her breath rasped in and out as she fought through wet snow. "Damn! I need some snowshoes." Drowned in her oversize parka, she stumbled out of the snow into the plowed-out lane, breathless, sweat beading up on her. As she plodded along in the stout boots, she hummed to herself. Here's to another forty years of snowstorms, white winters, solitude in a small cabin.

It would be perfect, if she only had Internet. And if she could afford the new roof. And if her village women would drive out to her more often.

And what about William? Would he ever really join her here? He hated working with his hands, and he would complain. She didn't wish him here, not right now.

—⁂—

Bec jerked the truck to a halt in front of Chuma's. She whipped the café door open enough to slip in and bang it closed against the howling wind. She scanned the room.

Linda's three chins wobbled as she yakked at Glory at a table by the door. Bec tried on the inquisitive face, eyebrow up and question on her lips. Linda held up a thumb, waggled it at Bec. Never slowing, she drowned Glory in words. What the hell did the thumbs-up mean – son Alex had quit drugs, or was climbing mountains, or had been thrown out?

Bec's gaze swept deeper into the room. The usual suspects, but Emmet roosted in the back with another man, a big guy. A strong hand squeezed her elbow.

Chuma grumbled into her ear. "Damn it, girl! I wish you had a phone out on the mountain. I needed to contact you."

"What's up, Chuma? And why did you let Emmet in here?"

"Not because he brought me a stolen chicken! Check out the guy that's with him. Emmet says he's looking for you. They've been holed up

104

back there for a couple of hours. The new guy has been buying Emmet chicken soup. Emmet is stinking up the place." Chuma was unsettled.

"What do you want me to do about it?"

"Get your ass back there and find out what they want."

"I can do that."

Bec wove her way through the tables. "Emmet, how are you? Winter treating you okay?"

"Bec!" Emmet creaked to his feet. "I want you to meet a new friend of mine. Bec, this is Tony Gibbon."

Her first impression rang out "soldier." Muscled up, sunburned. Her second impression contradicted the first: Tony needed a haircut – his brown hair splashed across his collar and soared in wings off the tops of his ears. Jeans and a golf shirt, in the winter. A weedy green parka hung over a nearby chair. He knew how to flatter women – he stared into her eyes, focused on her.

"Mrs. Robertson. I know your husband." He thrust out his hand. "I'm Tony, like Emmet said." He grasped her fingers in his right hand and pumped, crunched her knuckles.

She massaged her hand.

"I know your husband, Chaplain Robertson. He told me if I was ever in the neighborhood I should drop by. So here I am!"

Great, just what she needed. Another soldier full of surprises. She gave a feeble grin. "And how do you know my husband?"

"I'm one of his basket cases. He cheered me up for a few hours before they evac'd me out. After I blew my hand off. Small world, huh?"

She studied his left hand on the chair back.

"You caught sight of my false paw. At least it's not a hook, but the plastic weirds people out." He waved his left hand, a pink, false-flesh color.

"Did you lose your college ring that day?"

"How could you know that?" He beamed, like her knowledge made them instant friends.

105

"William told me. You're a sergeant?"

"Not anymore. I did six months getting retooled at Fort Gordon in Georgia. Afterwards, I copped a medical discharge. After phys therapy and three months on my mom's couch, I set out to see the world. Gonna be a writer, do my memoir."

"That's great. A whole new life, a big adventure." But how could he type?

"The Chaplain said you lived way out here, but he ran short on details. I planned to swing by and say hello to you and the kids. Maybe stay a week or two. But Emmet says you don't have kids. And you don't live in town, you live out on the mountain. I guess staying with you is out of the question."

"Damn straight it is," said Chuma behind Bec's shoulder. "Mind if I sit down?"

"Why don't you both take a load off." Tony let Chuma drag a chair over, heaved one out for Bec.

Chuma ended up on the corner, next to Emmet. She wrinkled her nose and brought the full pressure of disapproval to bear. "Damn, man. Don't you ever shower?"

Emmet gazed down his nose at her. "Bathing is unhealthy. It leads to marriage. Or hives, I forget which."

Tony leaned so far towards Bec she thought he was about to kiss her. His breath smelled like sauerkraut – he must have ordered the Reuben.

He was all smiles. "Isn't this great? I make friends everywhere, but here I find one already on station. How's the Chaplain?

"Still in Afghanistan."

"I know that, 'cause he's stayed in touch. I meant how's he holding up? He takes it all too personal, you know."

"He's fine, considering where he is and what he does." And considering he's estranged from his wife.

"He was the best. In spite of the fact he's squeamish, he spent that day with me. Helped the medico change the dressings. I thought the Chaplain would faint or puke, but he hung in there."

"Good for him." Bec shot a glance at Chuma, turned back to Tony. "When did you pull into town?"

Tony glanced at the watch strapped to his false wrist – a watch with a simple round face, a canvas web band. "Thirteen hundred hours, so just over three hours ago. I met Emmet at Mannie's. Brought him down here to feed him – he said he hadn't eaten in a couple of weeks."

Emmet said, "My young friend exaggerates." With a graceful incline of his head, he winked at Chuma. "Glorious chicken soup, madam."

Tony said, "Emmet's teeth hurt him. Soup is best." Tony propped both arms on the table, as if he was ready to crawl over it.

She leaned back to acquire some space. "Where have you been so far on this big adventure?"

"Once I was a civilian, I checked through the VA in Miami. Years of dry heat in the Sandbox and I choose Miami's wet heat. My folks live in Tallahassee, so it worked out. A couple of months more of physical therapy and my Dad helped me buy a car. Since that time I've been working my way across the South towards California. Was lost for a month in Texas, but everybody does that."

"They do?"

"Sure. Barbecue ribs, big city bars, loud friendly people."

"And you're driving on through to Arizona?"

"Not right away. The Nissan broke down, near Abiquiu. I left it on the side of the road and hitched on up here."

Chuma cracked out a "Tchaa! In the winter? Don't you know it's not safe?"

Tony grinned. "Why? IEDs buried under the roads here too? Anyway, a fellow I met at Mannie's owns a flatbed. He's hauling me and the car to Santa Fe tomorrow."

Bec had to ask. "What happens tonight? Do you have a place to stay?"

Tony jerked his head at Emmet. "I'll stay with my friend here. Now I've met you, we're back to his place to fix a hole in his roof."

Hole in the roof. Bec sighed, a lingering surrender. "Give me five minutes and I'll drive you. I have an email or two to send." She carried her laptop over to the window table.

She typed, "William, your friend Sergeant Tony Gibbon surprised us all when he turned up here. Did you know he'd consider your offer for a visit seriously? You might have mentioned it. He's a nice guy. His car is giving him some trouble, but he should be on his way to California in a day or two. Tony sends his best." She hesitated on the stool, one foot on a rung, the other already poised to leave. She typed, "Your loving wife, Bec." She backspaced over it, and pressed send.

—␣␣—

Outside the snow kicked up again, one of those late-winter freak storms. They stepped out into a squall that jerked at them, whipped Bec's scarf into Emmet's face. He flapped in alarm, tried to fend off the savage beast. Bec urged him towards her truck. "Jump in! Jump in!"

In the cab it was all too close for comfort. Tony had dropped his soldier's duffle in the pickup bed, but even so the three of them locked shoulders. She jammed in behind the wheel while Emmet hugged the right door. Tony, even larger now than in the café, covered the entire center console, his head cocked against the headliner.

Emmet coughed. "Any chance for a quick stop at Mannie's, to achieve a small purchase?"

Tony patted Emmet's knee. "It's okay, partner. My duffle is hiding a bottle as we speak."

A cheery grin lit Emmet's face – a black gap where a tooth had disappeared. "A bottle of what?"

"Like you care? Let's jump on fixing that roof before your house fills with snow."

108

Emmet's face turned mournful. "Ahh. It may be a bit late, for at least one room."

"Is that it, up ahead? Nice cabin. I'll have it in tip-top shape for you by spring."

Bec asked, "Spring?"

—ꝏ—

May Day 2009.

Bec was no closer to hoarding up money for a new roof than the Afghan war was to finishing. Glorious spring, yet the temperature dipped below the freeze line at night, even as the buds crept out of the red elderberry bush into unfurling purple-tinged leaves. They resembled the most elegant of all winged insects emerged from the chrysalis, unfolded from stiff paper umbrellas into ravaged new greenery. The spruces, darkened by winter, switched on growth spurts and cast out a powder blue candle at the end of every branch. The recent rain added to the snowmelt and that meant raging creeks. Canyons were choked with shattered branches carried down from above. Mud painted everything, even the blacktop.

Her pickup became two-tone, white on top and milk-chocolate on the bottom. Dried shards of brown fell to the ground when she slammed the door. Mud formed ruts that had only been vague stripes in the snow weeks before. She would remember, much later on, how happy she had been and how the stranger's footprints caught her so unprepared.

Bec had chosen a flat spot to the south of the cabin last fall. She had covered it with newspapers purloined from Chuma's and with tarps. Now she hauled the plastic back to reveal the rotted paper, the dead grass. She ordered a load of topsoil from Rubio. Unlike his firewood, the topsoil was low-quality. Scant dirt, the color of bark from a dead tree. From the dump-truck mound, she trundled dirt forth in a rusty wheelbarrow loaned by Emmet and Tony. Shovel by shovel, she shifted the topsoil into raised beds, long mounds. She mixed in the winter's tea leaves and eggshells as she worked the beds, and she picked out the thousands of middling rocks Rubio delivered with his dirt. As she worked the pitiful soil, she mulled over her unlikely friends.

Emmet had not yet revealed his story, and the alias "Marcus" was a mystery. Tony was all about the future, not the past – but he wasn't shy about his personal history. "Football ain't War, or vice versa. I've participated in both, and these battle phrases in sports, that's all bullshit." He had trained as a body builder, but not for competitions. "I just like walking around without my shirt, showing off." He turned out a great soldier, if he said so himself. But now, onward.

He visualized himself as a writer, with a best-selling memoir. He announced to the café he was gay and that he named the memoir Gay Warrior, One Hand Clapping. Short brown men and women in the café inspected the table tops, but kept their Catholic mouths shut. Anglos muttered, and sometimes thanked him for his service.

After she'd sprinkled fertilizer across the mounds and topped all with bags of moss, she needed a garden fork to turn it, as deep as her muscles could dig. Off to the barn.

And the shock of the year. Muddy footprints, unnamed, strange, trailed across the ground from the barn to the house. Her shoulders seized so tight that when she turned her head, it was like a lightning strike. Bright lights behind her eyelids.

Who'd been in her yard? What neighbor had dropped by, and why? She spotted the huge boot prints, right by the back steps. Waffle tread. Fairly recent – one print showed water pooled in it. And a third trail. This set of tracks led to her bedroom window, faced the sill, shuffled from side to side, peered into her house!

As far as she could tell, he hadn't broken in – yet. The stranger's boots had flattened the new damp grass as he slipped back into the woods.

She skirted wide of the barn's corner, shied away from the tree line. She worked in the new garden, out in the open. That would be enough to protect her during daylight, wouldn't it? All the while, as she built the bones of her future garden, she could sense the eyes. Someone spied on her from the forest edge, hunkered under a tree.

Chapter Twelve – Steeled

AT DUSK BEC LOCKED THE windows, shut away the clean, reincarnated air of spring. She carried a kitchen knife to the bedroom, located it with care on the bedside table.

She lay in the dark at midnight, tense – the threat palpable, looming in a miasma of fear.

Her subconscious knew what to do – scare her half to death as soon as she dropped her guard. It spun out an earthquake of a dream. Waking in a panic, she pawed at the bedside table, knocked the knife onto the floor. She slid out of the bed. Swept her hands about until she brushed across it. She crouched in the dark, both hands on the wooden grip. Listening so hard – the floor boards creaked in the quiet as they shrank with cold. No one else, not in the bedroom, not in the cabin.

Her sweat cooled and her heart slowed. But the images roiled in her mind, vivid. "Not me. It's not going to be me." But it could be.

Who was he? She needed to know something, anything.

—⚏—

A simple idea surfaced in the hour before first light. Even the bobcats used game trails and slipped down their frequent paths, recognizable and open to her when she searched. The stalker's patterns – his highways and byways were mapped around her cabin. Bec made up her mind.

After sunrise when the dawn flared into redbird displays of scarlet and carmine, she slipped out. From the back of the house she crossed the drive to the barn, its open gaps between boards showering east light into the dark interior. The stalker left no sign inside, but yesterday's footprints at the door led back into the trees.

She trailed the occasional scuffs of his feet to where a game trail, an elk path led up the hill and over the top. Half the time she was sure she had lost the way. Doubtful, she would pick the easiest step next, until she spotted caked mud, his trace again. She hunched her shoulders tight and snapped her gaze back and forth, nauseated with tension.

Here and there, dead limbs snapped off at eye level. On the downhill side, after the ridge top, she threaded her way, sometimes over deadfall, seldom able to stumble across a straight stretch. She picked up another elk trail. Other traces joined it and it splayed out wider, a stream that flowed down to the valley. Near the bottom, his dried boot mark, a message.

The woods broke open. Elk beds lay in the first tall-grass, oblong wallows where the beasts settled in at night. She spotted the trailer humped up on the brow of a small lumpish hill below her. With a bent back, crouched, she eased down the slope, used the saplings in the meadow for what cover they could give. She stopped a hundred yards from the trailer, knelt in the clump grass.

With a slight tremor, she wondered if William's troops knelt this way, surveyed dusty swales below through binoculars, checked for their own or the enemy. She carried binoculars too, but not William's holy cross. She scanned the site for her stalker.

The trailer was hooked to power – a sad line dragged down off a leaning post to the meter on the wall. A dish for satellite TV perched on the south wall, screwed to the metal side. A truck, an antique in good shape, parked by the trailer. She committed the license plate's six digits to memory. No sound, no activity spotted through the small windows. A degenerate living in the middle of nowhere. Alone.

She muttered, "Now what? I can't stroll in on a peeping Tom. Or a rapist."

Retreat. Scheme. Get help.

—⁓—

On her drive to the village, Bec scrambled through options. The café waited empty except for Emmet and Tony. The banging of industrial-sized pans in back rang out – Chuma. She worried about how to open the conversation.

"Emmet, Tony... how are you?"

Tony said, "Grumpy. It's a lovely spring day and I'm stuck inside with Emmet. How's that wheelbarrow working out?"

She eased into a chair. "Fine. Thanks for the loan." Bec regarded her hands, folded in her lap.

"And the cold frames?"

She hadn't sought them out to talk about cold frames. "Not embarked on yet."

"And the seeds?"

She opened her mouth and let it happen. "Somebody is stalking me." Way too loud, not the calm woman she wanted.

Emmet and Tony dropped their chins to show their teeth, glanced at each other. Predictable.

They probably thought she sounded hysterical. She leaned forward, lowered her voice. "What should I do? Call the cops?"

Emmet held up an imperious hand. "If you could pause a moment." He rose, shambled to the kitchen pass-through, and stuck his head in. "Miss Chuma. Something requires your attention out here."

She burst through the swinging door like a horse out of the gate, wove through the chairs, and plunked down. "Make it quick – a pan of lasagna has my name on it in back. What's up?"

They all fell silent. Bec could smell tomato sauce. She was so clear-headed. Salt was spilled across the table, Emmet hadn't shaved in a week, Tony's red T-shirt showed through a hole in his zipped-up green parka. She could hear her own breath.

Tony pointed at Bec, a motor in his hand humming as three fingers curled. "Bec's acquired a stalker."

"So? Shoot him." Chuma rose out of her chair.

Bec said, "I don't have a gun."

Chuma glanced over, handed it off. "Have Tony shoot him."

Tony hated that idea. "I'm done with killing people."

Chuma collapsed back in her chair with a grunt. "Now we have us a problem. Tell Aunt Chuma everything."

"Someone is spying me from the woods. He may just be a peeping Tom – but he's also a trespasser – his boot marks are scuffed in all around my place. He lives on the other side of the ridge to the north."

"How do you know?" asked Tony.

"I trailed him over the ridge from my place. And I haven't seen him yet. Just his trailer and his truck."

Emmet harrumphed. "This spying on you, how long has it been going on?"

Bec said, "How could I possibly know that?"

"Has he threatened you, left messages or any disturbing artifacts?"

"He's sneaking around my house, for Christ's sake!"

"Yes. Most intimidating. But nevertheless an unknown quantity."

Tony slapped the table. "I know! Call the police. They'll handle it – I hear it's what they do."

Chuma said, "No need to go all sarcastic."

Emmet wobbled his head no, his forehead wrinkled, his mouth drawn down. "The local law enforcement may not be as accommodating as you expect. I for one have been disappointed in their competence. Their lack of support for the local community."

Chuma said, "Local community meaning you. What was the charge, drunk and disorderly?"

115

The calmest of the four, Tony reasoned, "I like the deputies. They drop in here most times they patrol through."

Bec flushed with anger. "Will you please take this seriously?"

Even Chuma flicked her eyes down. "Sorry."

Bec felt the quizzical wrinkled look on her face – she had been teased by William about that face. "Will they believe I've tracked down the right guy?"

Emmet cocked his head, "Have you? We'll have to inspect his boots."

Chuma said, "It's him."

Emmet didn't yet believe. "Some tracks around your house, a man who happens to live in the next valley over? And mayhap his last name will be the same as the Sheriff's. It's a small world up here."

Chuma said, "You need to trap him, tie him up. Run over him twice."

Bec said, "That's not helpful, Chuma. I better visit the Sheriff instead."

Chuma said, "Okay. But if that doesn't work, we'll all load up and go call on this guy. Bec, slip up here to the counter. I want to show you something."

At the register, Bec asked, "What?"

Chuma fished under the counter, handed her a rolled-up dishtowel. "Here. Don't let the others know. Keep it until all this is done."

Bec unwrapped a small revolver, the bluing on the barrel faded, the plastic grip cracked. A box of shells. "Thanks, I think."

"Can you shoot?"

"No problem with rifles. I grew up on a farm. But never pistols." She flashed on Uncle Howie's gun.

"Jeez, kill a couple of cans or a milk carton. Even the noise could scare him off."

"But why don't you want them to see it?"

"I may have to use it someday on that evil old Emmet. No sense in giving him any warning."

The federalist County Seat in Tierra Amarilla didn't house the Sheriff's Office – that was a hundred yards away, a small stuccoed building practically brand new. Behind the station, a church soared up bright cream-colored against a baby-blue sky. The Sheriff's front door faced across the street to a block-sized crumbling building, yellow and desolate. If Tierra Amarilla hadn't housed the County government, it would have had little indeed.

Inside, two stools hid behind a counter surmounted by a glass partition, presumably bullet-proof. The space behind that held two desks for the civilian workers and a ill-proportioned copier with a giant scoop on its side. Bec jittered in the lobby chair for forty minutes before the desk staff let her into the hall beside the counter. The dispatcher, an Angla in a plaid shirt and a Taos-style long skirt, marched her the ten feet back to the office. The furniture had cost little a decade ago; the move into the building had been punishing. The paint a pale sage green, the desk covered in mounds of paper. The office waited empty.

The Sheriff arrived three minutes later. A Norteño, short, balding and full of energy, he trotted rather than walked. He wore a mustache like the bumper of a car. "Hi, I'm Sheriff Martinez." He stuck out his hand, pumped hers once, hard, and dropped it.

He waved a hand. "Sit, please. They briefed me on the radio – you're the woman with a peeping Tom? Tell me about it."

She perched on the edge of a short chair. When he plunked down behind his desk, she couldn't spot the bottom half of his face behind the stacks of paper. While she spoke, he tapped a pencil on the desk, a drumroll counterpoint to her story.

"Sí, sí. Not an unusual problem, sadly. Here's my take – you're a white woman who lives in the middle of nowhere – a mujer blanca and a good looking one at that. Somebody's taken an interest in you. It could be dangerous, but even if it's not, it's scary. We have wackos all over the county and this could be one of them. I advise you to buy a gun and a dog."

She had Chuma's gun on loan. But a dog? Allergies.

"In the meantime, I'll send my deputy by to check this neighbor out. You have no phone out there? Pity." The Sheriff stabbed a button on his big beige phone, leaned into the speaker. "Carla, Jerry here in the office?"

The speaker let out a crackling sound the Sheriff could interpret. He shouted through the door. "Right. Send him back."

Jerry, unaffected by the hustle that gripped the Sheriff, sauntered through the door. "Yeah, Jefe?"

The Sheriff pointed his finger at the two of them. "Rebecca Robertson – Deputy Sheriff Jerry Block. Mrs. Robertson here has a probable stalker. Write down her statement, have her show you where her place is on the map, and the place where she believes the guy lives."

Bec said, "I copied down his license plate number." Her voice shook.

The Sheriff shone like a proud parent. "Even better. Jerry, check the number. Find out if we know the guy, drive out and check him out. If he stinks, lay the fear of God on him, porqué no? Even if he checks out okay, let him know we got our eye on him."

He wrinkled his grand mustache, the confident defender of women and children. "Ms. Robinson, call us in a few days and we'll tell you where we stand. Pues? Bueno." He sprang to his feet, reached across the desk through the paper. "I'm late for something else." He squashed her hand, charged out into the hallway as he shouted. "Jerry, hazlo ya!" At the door he yelled back, "Carla, I'm back to Española after lunch."

—⋙—

Two days, that should be long enough to wait. She punched numbers on Chuma's phone, perched on a stool back by the range. The dispatcher, her voice as flat as the color gray, read her a message. "The suspect does

118

not appear to be a problem, but has been warned to keep his distance. Please let us know if there are any further developments."

"You're Carla, right? Can you tell me the suspect's name?"

"No ma'am, I'm sorry. Policy says we don't give out that information." Her voice dropped a third, smoothed out like butter. "Besides, Jerry didn't detail it in the memo. Otherwise I might have let it slip. But he did write in the margin. It says 'Harmless. We know this guy.'"

Bec's fear dropped to a murmur, but not into silence. Until two days later — a new footprint on her back porch. She gawped at the sandy brown mud, caked and dry in the waffle shape of a tread. Her heart galloped into a thunderous pace. The world wobbled. She skittered inside, sought out the revolver, dropped it into her coat pocket.

She collapsed at her kitchen table. "So you're back." She willed the storm in her head to slow down. Words spoken aloud calmed her. "Even though the police warned you, you couldn't keep away. Is it lust? Are you murderous?"

Tea was the thing. Tea could help with any problem. She spooned Ceylon loose leaf into a tea egg, boiled the water. "I could go back to the police — and leave a target on my back. Or I could round up Tony and Emmet and pay a visit. And see my friends hurt." She poured hot water into the cup. "Or I could handle it myself, be the tough character I think I am." Only, tough characters didn't talk to themselves all the time.

—❧—

Bec held the paper plate against the barn wall with her wrist, set the brad, and nailed it in. She smashed her thumb and finger with the hammer in the process. Sucking on her thumb, she dropped the tool, retreated eight feet, fished the revolver out of her pocket. Back far enough. The metal was warm in her hand from the pocket. The checking on the grip felt slick — she wiped sweat off her hand and dropped back into the stance. Classic A frame, her shoulders square to the target, both arms straight ahead, her left hand cradling her right. She thumbed the hammer back, stared down the barrel. Both eyes open. Squeeze.

The light gun jumped in her hand like a bird bursting into flight. The high cracking sound bored into her ears. Her left hand failed to hold her right, fell away. Both eyes slapped shut and she waited for it to be over – but it already was. The bullet hole was four inches to the right of the nail and a touch low.

She brought her arms and hands back into place. This time she didn't cock the hammer back, she squeezed the trigger. It was a long haul to raise the hammer – the gun fired again. A loud pop – the gun rammed into her hands and rang her ears like gongs. She had held the recoil – within reason. The plate displayed another hole, high on its edge. Burned cordite tickled into her nose. Shift the feet, brace herself, squeeze again. Faster. The air split, the barn shuddered.

Bec smiled, rather grim. She'd been on the verge of killing before. Killing her pa.

—◊◊—

Early Spring 1985.

Seventeen-year-old Rebecca hid in the field's margin, between the barbed wire fence and an ancient pile of rocks overgrown with grass. Here on the old Cutbert quarter section, common starlings and grackles trailed behind the tractor, hopped in the tracks after the insects her father stirred up. The tractor crawled left and right across her view, edged closer with every turn at the ends of the field. He rode hunched over, gripped the wheel, perched high above the green box of the tractor between the immense wheels. The plow cut and turned the sod, laid out ribbons of red, and turfed up the bugs. More birds swarmed in the air, circled the equipment and the man, a soaring confusion of tight cuts and darting turns.

The wheeling birds didn't distract Rebecca. She focused on

her father. She cradled the two-two-three in her arms, a bullet in the chamber. It would have to be a head shot, but she was good at this. She swept the barrel up and centered it. Through the cheap scope she could perceive the details of his face. His mouth hung open and slack, his gaze steady on the field ahead of him, his eyes squinted against the bright magic of spring's light. She could do it if she didn't catch sight of those eyes. Too bad she had his blue eyes, not her momma's soft brown eyes – she hated that.

The crosshairs claimed him; the barrel arced as slow as a telescope tracks a star as he drove across her field of fire. She aimed right in front of his ear, dead on target except for minor tractor lurches that bumped him up and down. She had waited in deep cover to let the prey circle in close. Ready for the kill.

As he rode downfield, she lined up on the skull behind his ear. There – but her finger wouldn't squeeze. Her heart thudded heavy and quick, her eyes full of tears. Her finger slipped off the trigger. She crushed her eyes shut, hard. The ringing of her pulse in her ears. The man in the khaki shirt rode across the field, oblivious to her murderous intent. Her weakness.

She had crept into the field to stop it all with death, but she couldn't. As she gave him his ugly life back, she lowered the gun and twisted around. She wriggled under the fence and into the windbreak trees. Another time. Maybe another way.

—⋙—

May 2009.

Not at all like the spring day she had hunted her father. Today the sky hung low and oppressive, turned everything gray and mute. She steeled herself for it. When her nerves steadied and her shaking hands stilled, she slipped the revolver into the pocket of her coat and picked up the square white box. She tramped out into the woods. Her woods. She glided through the trees now that she knew the way. In fifteen minutes she topped the ridge and dropped into the valley below. No truck waited by the trailer. She hiked straight down and occupied her place on the steps below the door.

CHAPTER THIRTEEN – CAUGHT STEALING PIE

WHEN BEC'S STALKER DROVE UP, he turned out as immense as in her dream, but all soft fat. He lumbered out of his truck and stopped short when he spotted her. He twisted away, as if he would jump back in and drive off. She froze as motionless as a stalking cat.

He dropped his shoulders and stumped towards his trailer. He appeared weak, formless to her. But a round face with a feeble chin could deceive. She popped up on her feet. Only six feet away from him – his moon face hung there, his feet shuffled. His mouth worked, jaws twitched. His lips pasted across his face, moist and puffy, like maggots.

The gun weighed down her right pocket. The Lady, or the Tiger. Keep the voice flat, even. "I'm your neighbor over the hill. I've been wanting to talk to you for a while. My name's Bec. I brought scones."

She watched him work it through, fleeting changes in his face. He swayed on his big feet, lurched to the side to skirt around her, doubled back to the truck.

Idiot. Where would he go? She said, "Invite me in. It's the polite thing to do."

That rang a bell inside his round head. He blinked, edged past her, led the way inside, grunting as each big leg propelled him up the steps.

The trailer, for all its exterior squalor, was squeaky clean inside. Everything bore the wear marks of long use. The dinette table displayed long tan streaks where the fake wood grain had worn away, but no dirt caked around the aluminum rim. Apparently he had even ironed the plaid drapes, so they hung as crisp sentinels in the windows.

He gave a stiff wave towards the banquette seat and she slipped in. Her right hand remained secret in her jacket pocket; her left slid the pastry box onto the table. He leaned back against the trailer door. Maybe ready to bolt. Or was she boxed in?

His eyebrows drew together into a blackbird silhouette, his jaw muscles tight under the flabby cheeks. Dear Christ, how long would he just stare?

His eyes flickered. "What flavor?"

"Lemon curd and also blueberry."

His breath wheezed in and out. The quiet in the trailer dragged on. She started again. "Would you like one?"

He shuffled the one step forward that carried him into his kitchen. "I'll fetch forks and plates."

She watched him open the drawer, hoped he didn't seize some butcher knife and strike. He brought out tarnished dinner forks, small things in his big fist.

"Do you want a Coke? Or I could stir up some lemonade."

Lemonade? Who was this guy? "Lemonade, please."

He opened a cupboard and brought out a canister, stirred powder into two glasses of water. He placed a glass within her reach. He eased himself into his chair, bracing against the table that creaked under his bulk. She opened the white box one-handed, kept a grip on the revolver in her pocket. "I bought them at the café in town." The paper rustled – two scones had crumbled as she had tramped through the woods, but two were unbroken.

He chose a blueberry. It lay neglected on his plate as he inspected her. "Bec. That's a funny name."

She kept an eye on him. Brighter than he seemed? "It's short for Rebecca. I never liked the long version – it doesn't fit me. What's your name?"

"Arthur. But most people call me Tank. Only my mother called me Arthur." He handed her a fork.

"I'll call you Arthur if you call me Bec."

He cut off a quarter of the scone and threw it into his mouth. "Okay. Bec." The decision chased across his face. "How did you get here? I didn't see any car."

"I trailed you by your tracks. From under my window to your door." Asshole.

He winced.

"Arthur, why have you been hanging around my place?"

His face crunched up. Even while he flushed, his jaws kept working. He swallowed, gazed at his styrofoam plate. "I meant to stop, honest. After the deputy talked to me."

"But you didn't."

He forked in more scone, dropped his head again.

"There must have been a reason. Can you tell me?"

He dipped his head. "You do things. First you cut trees. And burned slash. Now you're digging up that field."

"You mean the garden. I keep busy."

He leaned back, waved his hand at the trailer. "I'm not busy. Nothing happens here. It's the same every day."

"But you drive into town. When you're not peeking in my window."

"Shopping. I don't really talk to anyone in town. You have friends. I've spotted you with them, at the café." He gazed at the plastic napkin holder. Tears gleamed in his lashes.

What a basket case. She slid her right hand out of her pocket. "Arthur, how long have you lived here?"

"They let me out when my mother died and the money ran out."

"Was that a long time ago?"

"They let me out on June 19, 2001. Today is May 7, 2009."

Eight years, alone. "And do you have a counselor or medical help?"

125

He shrugged, a slow roll of flab. "The County Nurse visits once a year to talk to me."

"And you have some money?"

"A check shows up in the mail every month. Bernie at the Mini-Mart cashes it for me. I buy my food and gas at the Mini-Mart, and comic books. I collect comic books." He pointed at two shelves, neat but jammed full.

Bec leaned across the table towards Arthur. "It sounds like things are okay, except you don't have any friends."

"I had friends in the Home. I miss them. Even though I thought I wouldn't."

Bec gazed around the trailer again. An exceptional life, played out within narrow rules. Success made from what little he was handed. "You've been watching me because...."

"It was something new. You're a new neighbor. I hoped you might be a friend someday."

"You spied on me. I understand you're lonely. And bored. But I'm so mad at you."

He recoiled, like she had bit him. "Yes'm."

"I could have shot you. And I will, if I ever catch you peeking in my window again."

His mouth hung open.

She banged the table with both hands. "My husband is a soldier in Afghanistan. What do you think he would do?"

Big bulbous eyes in a spherical head. "Hurt me?"

She may have gone far enough. "Damn straight."

His hands swam at the table edge, like they mirrored his desire to escape. "I promise. No looking."

"Maybe we can be friends. We have to have some rules. Absolutely no spying on me. I don't want to spot your footprints under my window."

126

He nodded. The way he dropped his head – she had shamed him.

"And we visit each other when I say. I like being alone most of the time."

"Okay."

"And we're just friends. No boy-friend girl-friend thing."

His eyebrows shot up, his mouth fell open. "I never meant that."

Bec grinned, but hid it behind her folded hand. His eyes wide, his mouth folded in dolefulness. This could work. "You know what?"

He glanced at her from under his soft brow. "What."

"We're kind-of alike. We both need jobs." It was true.

—⁂—

Late June 2009:

Bec balanced on the front step – she sucked on a stem of grass and watched a red-tailed hawk.

The hawk pinwheeled, lost altitude, soared, cut back towards her. Grace and sweep, calligraphy in the sky. She waited for the plunge into the grass, the sharp struggle. It crashed into the weeds, flapped off into the sky, a gray wad of fur dangled in its claws. The bottlebrush tail hung limp below the carcass. The hawk headed for a tree to tear and shred the squirrel. It flew above a car creeping its way to her cabin.

A clapped out Nissan with deep-tinted windows negotiated the bumps and holes along her road. As if it believed it might not reach the cabin, it crawled its way across the pasture, yard by yard. Now she had to stand, stretch, be polite to guests. "Busts the day. Damn!" The Nissan labored its way to the porch. It scraped the hump between the two tracks. "They never built that car for up here."

The car shuddered to a halt, rang out a spark knock that faded off. A door flew open and Tony emerged with a grin like he had won the Presidential nomination. The passenger door juddered its way open with a groaning sound of deforming metal. Emmet clambered out head first, plopped one hand on the ground and scrambled when his knees wouldn't straighten.

"Boys." She had never invited anyone to the cabin, not even the DIVAS. They just showed up.

Tony planted his hands on his hips, rotated his shoulders back and forth, and gazed about, "What a great day!"

She grinned. Irrepressible. "Yes, and a quiet one too, until you drove up here. What brings you out?"

"We haven't heard from you in a week. Emmet got worried. So worried he hit the bottle this morning instead of this afternoon."

"Thank you, Emmet, for your concern."

He called across the car roof, "You're welcome." He wove his way around the car, wobbled up beside Tony. "The door of that automobile has something desperately wrong with it. Pardon me, Bec. Can you direct me to the facilities?"

"Behind the cabin, Emmet. Help yourself."

"Thank you, good lady." He paced away stiff-legged, tripped only once before he rounded the corner.

She turned back to Tony. "I don't have any lawn chairs, so why don't you perch on the step." She plunked herself back down.

Tony joined her. "I'm here for another reason."

"Do tell."

"I have an offer."

"Hmm."

He half turned toward her and waved both arms in the air. "But I have to tell it right. If I'm a writer, I have to master the art of storytelling." He cleared his throat. "It was a dark and stormy night at Emmet's, and he'd finished another improbable version of his life."

Bec grinned at the "dark and stormy."

"He gave credit to this county for saving his fragile sanity, for healing him of modern society's afflictions. That's pretty much a quote."

She inclined her head. "Continue."

"And I puzzled over it, this wild claim of his. You may not know it, but I'm not cheerful all the time. You know, the happy-go-lucky guy with a nifty mechanical hand. I was depressed — maybe I should have stayed in the Service. They let us gimps stay now if we want. I considered the aimless roaming around I did before I pitched up here. But I felt pretty good about living in the village with Emmet in his pocket-sized squatter cabin."

"I sense you're headed somewhere here, Tony, but correct me if I am wrong."

"This state, this village, why this mountain could be great for wounded vets who need a quiet soul-cleansing before they have to drop back into the real world."

The hairs on the back of her neck prickled. Tony was working an angle.

"I can tell you're thinking 'What a brilliant idea!' I stewed over it for a couple of months during snow season and I recruited some help. I found a librarian in Chama named Myrna — a real expert at grant writing. And scuffed up a retired guy named Celestino in Abiquiu who practiced law. And an ex-banker named Roland in Tierra Amarilla who knows how to create a business plan."

"You're kicking off a business? Good for you, Tony."

"No, I'm thinking bigger than a fast buck. I'm going to build a summer camp for Vets in Need. That's what I call it — V I N. Or maybe something else. New Mexico Retreat for Veterans?"

Bec asked, "Where do you acquire your veterans — who decides who comes and who can't?"

Tony rubbed his hands. "I have the most brilliant idea on that. I want it to be a surprise. You'll love it."

"Why do I have a feeling you're hiding something else?"

Tony cleared his throat, swung his gaze from her to the end of the cabin. "Where's Emmet? Think he fell in?"

She reached over and gave his ear a tug. "Come on, out with it, or I'll pinch." She clasped the lobe and gripped hard.

She may as well have been a dog hanging on an elephant's harness – he only grinned. "The lawyer incorporated us, the banker created lies for the plan, and Myrna helped me write a killer grant. The Feds accepted it. New Mexico's Veteran Services will administer the money."

He'd buried his angle somewhere in all this story. "Congratulations."

"It's for one-hundred-thousand dollars. Isn't that killer?"

"And?"

"If I don't abide by the business plan, I have to give the money back. And my other grants depend on my keeping this grant."

"And? You're here because why?"

"I need somewhere to build my Retreat. We can't buy land with the money because I told them we'd already locked that in – it was our grant match. I thought at the time I had ID'd a possible."

"Good thing you didn't tell them about this property."

Tony squirmed.

"You did tell them." Bec scrutinized him. Her place.

"There. It's out in the open. I feel better." He grinned like a small boy.

He wanted to plant a retreat full of people right in her lap. She picked herself up, stared down at him. "Better search out someplace else, Tony. New Mexico is full of empty places."

He shrugged. "I've asked around for a couple of weeks. Nobody wants to give up their land. Or have a bunch of whacked-out vets next door."

"No." Did he have any idea what he was asking?

He threw glances at her. The smile quavered. "Think about it."

"No." Even to her, her voice sounded gritty.

He ducked his head, like a small boy who had been caught stealing pie. "Think about it for a while. I'm on a deadline here – I have to have a site by the first of August. You can even run it if you want."

She kicked him in the thigh. "I may have to kill you."

CHAPTER FOURTEEN – NURSERY

As Bec gathered the wash in off the line in the back the next morning, a racket on the front porch – an irregular thwacking sound. She sprinted through the house and peered out. A red-tailed hawk flapped its way across the boards, one wing far out to the side. The other wing beat like a drum. For a moment she watched the frenzy, her mind in a panic like the bird's, a bundle of neurons that fired at the speed of light.

Hurt bad. In agony. It would die – nothing for it. She'd learned this lesson before.

—ɯ—

Winter 1976.

Eight-year-old Rebecca perched on the windowsill and watched the clouds break, the blackness of a blue norther fade away and the sun crawl out from behind God's winter. The kitchen lay behind her, cold and gray. It waited for her momma to arrive back from her job in town to give it some warmth and happiness. Her father stomped into the room. She gazed back over her shoulder. His rubber boots tracked cow doo-doo into her mother's clean kitchen. Even eight-year-olds knew that landed you in trouble.

"Where's your coat? I want to show you something in the west field. One of the herd is down."

She dropped off the sill, leaked out a heavy sigh.

"I'll have none of your backchat, girl. Grab your boots, your coat. Right now."

With heavy steps she shuffled onto the screened porch. The coat chilled her shoulders. The boots refused to be tugged on, so frozen that the rubber resisted bending. Just like her.

—⁓—

He stopped the truck with a jerk. As he reached behind the seat for the rifle, he said, "We hike from here. The ground hasn't yet froze underneath all that sleet."

The ice cracked like breaking bones; her white shredded breath chased out of her into the wind, ran away like she wanted to do. She stumbled along behind him in the furrows.

He stopped so quick she bumped full into him. A hard wall she bounced off. He pointed an ominous finger. "Here. See?"

A year-old heifer lay on her side. Her eyes rolled wild with terror. She thrashed as they stepped up to her, then froze.

He said, "I spotted her from the barn and knew right away she was in trouble. It's her front leg. Don't think it's broke. Dislocated, more like."

Bec stared at the heifer, reached out her hand. She rubbed the hard flat bone between the heifer's eyes. "She fell on the ice." She gaped at the leg where it stuck out of the heifer's shoulder. A big round bulge rolled under the skin and the leg pointed off in the wrong direction.

"Stupid animal – to fall even with four legs. I'll put her down. We'll fetch the carcass back to the barn with the loader. You can help me butcher her out."

"Pa?" She scaled her voice all the way down to tiny. "What if we fixed her. Can't we stick her leg back in?"

"I've tried that before. Needs a lot of strength and you have to jam and roll it just right. Not likely to work."

"We could try. I'll help."

132

He snickered.

"Maybe Dr. Jim?"

Her father spit on the ice. "Vet costs would be near as much as the animal is worth. Better we kill her for meat."

The animal lay unmoving. Rebecca knelt at the heifer's head, scratched her ears.

"Step back, Rebecca. Animal's finished. Thin the herd – leave only the healthy." His hand in the rawhide glove grabbed at her shoulder. He jerked her back; she spilled over on the ice. He planted the muzzle on the heifer's head. The shot rang out like the winter day had split apart.

—॰॰॰—

July 2009.

Bec knelt on the boards, watched the hawk in its desperation. It might be her hawk, the one that hunted the meadow. The hawk wouldn't know a broken wing meant death. She knelt on the porch a good distance away – the hawk huddled against the rough bark wall, its injured wing against Bec's empty boots.

Bec pinched at her lip, considered. With a sigh she eased onto her feet. Natural process be damned. She dashed into the kitchen and inspected her traps – beneath the sink she had caught the first mouse of the day, a big one. She ripped off a paper towel and dumped the mouse on it. She reached down a prescription bottle from the cupboard. After she shook out one of her Tramadols, she cut a third off one end. Using the knife butt, she ground it – small pieces shot away, refused to crumble, but she did create some powder. She sprinkled a big pinch over the mouse.

She spilled the mouse out of the paper towel onto the boards, nudged it over to the hawk. Its yellow eyes glared at her, its good wing beat, its beak darted forward at her finger. She froze.

133

The hawk spotted the mouse. It dipped its head and seized the rodent. The talons pinned the corpse to the porch and the beak ripped and tore. Cross-legged, Bec waited fifteen minutes. The head of that fierce predator drooped. Out cold. She stretched the bird out on the planks and worked the wing, from the shoulder to the tip. Felt the feathers, the bone beneath the wires of muscle, the hidden leather of skin. Nothing broken as far as she could tell. Maybe the hawk had torn a muscle, or a ligament.

She had caught a lightning bolt, fallen maimed from the sky, crashed onto her porch. Like lightning, life could discharge. The bird would die if left to nature. This most beautiful of predators lying outstretched in the grasses, its soft tissues eaten away by scavengers. She imagined the eye sockets full of insects converting shreds of tissue back into fuel. She could choose – between the way the world worked and the way she wanted her world to be.

She smoothed the feathers across the slow-moving breast. Bec was nature too.

Inside, she dumped the kindling out of a hundred-year-old beer crate onto the floor by the wood stove. She grabbed a tea towel and lined the box.

With hollow bones, the bird was light but filled both her hands. She nestled the hawk in and closed the lid. Every ten minutes she returned, to check if her hawk had died of overdose or had shaken off the narcotic. The hawk shifted, its head pivoted around to glare at her. She dumped two more mouse carcasses under the lid and set a large rock on it.

—⁂—

In the post office parking lot, Emmet shifted from one foot to the other, knee bent, like a crane but wobbly. Bec whipped over to him, rolled down her passenger window. "Emmet. Checking your balance?"

"Evening, Bec. How goes your quest for a job?"

134

"On hold for today."

Emmet straightened the labels of his tweed blazer. "Can I solicit a ride? Tony charged off to roam about the country and I need to return to my domicile."

"I've already filled the front seat, Emmet."

He propped his forearms on the windowsill. "What does the box hold?"

"It's a hawk." She patted the wood case beside her. "I've been over to Raptor Haven, trying to save it."

Emmet jerked back his fingers. "I hope it won't break free. What ails your hawk?"

"She ripped the muscle where the wing meets the shoulder."

"Still dangerous, no doubt. Why didn't Raptor Haven accept the bird?"

"They're full up and they told me I could cope with it. I just have to keep it from flying until the wing heals. They gave me a hood and gloves, and a chain to tether the bird." She held them up, the gloves stiff and thick, swept back into full gauntlets.

"Marcus Aurelius kept hawks and eagles, but didn't hunt with them. What shall you feed your creature?"

"Mice, dead and alive. Also stew meat, if the traps are empty."

Emmet grunted. "Quite similar to my diet, before New Mexico.

"You ate mice?"

"I boiled them in a tin can. Is there no room for me?"

"Do you mind riding in the back?" Emmet shuffled to the back of the truck, and with a piteous groan, crawled his way over the tailgate. When they reached the cabin, he reversed the painful process and approached her window. Tentative, shy, he said, "The sunset arrives soon. Would you like to take a seat at the door? I have a couple of stumps we use for chaise lounges." His fingers picked at the edge of her side view mirror.

"I'm afraid not, Emmet. I need to get home and feed my hawk."

"Maybe another time."

"We'll do that. Give Tony a message for me, okay? When he shows, tell him he's crazy. I won't give up my home for his center."

Emmet rocked back on his heels. "Why do I have to tell him?"

—⚏—

Bec's Monday afternoon territory began and ended on the card table, right by the hydraulic doors where once grocery carts had trundled out to the cars. She imagined them, hustled along by Indians, Norteños, Anglos – carts full of Wonder Bread, lard, eggs, pork chops, Little Debbies. The carts had disappeared with the grocery store, but the sliding doors had been repaired: asthmatic, they worked again, a gate between the Community Center and a parking lot now cracked and weedy. She gazed around – the Center didn't shape up half bad. Sure, a few tiles had gone missing from the ceiling and one fluorescent light fell last week, but even so. The rolling partitions, six-feet tall and covered in cloth, worked well. The tables had been gathered from across the county, and looked it. The polite thing to say about the amalgamation of thrift-store kitchen chairs – they kept everyone's butt off the gray-smudged tile floor.

From behind the partitions filtered childish screaming. Not her job – she suffered no illusions. Children were unformed animals en route to some bounds of human civilization.

She ran check-in. That was better than playing warden in back. The week the Center had opened, they both received and removed their first interior graffiti – a spray-painted swath of illegible art on the west interior wall. Since that decorative moment, the Center ran on a sign-in / sign-out basis. Glory had conned her out of one afternoon a week on the desk. Besides that, Bec helped with the Thursday potluck lunch and had agreed to run Bingo twice. Dawdling behind this table

136

turned out worse than the deacon meetings in the old Texas days. She dug a hole in her yellow pad with her Bic pen. By spinning it she could drill down into the pad six sheets. Her own fault. She leaned to the floor to fetch her crossword puzzle book. Another psycho puzzle. Number 1 down, five letters – women. Number 4 across, six letters – matron. Number 3 down, three letters working off the n – fun. Number 3 across, six letters with an f – friend. Number 8 down – desperate. Number 11 across needed an e – lesbians. Number 10 down needed an n – insane. What corner had she painted herself into? She contemplated the six letters of insane and the blank squares, but no intersecting word popped into her mind.

The doors wheezed open and Miss Junie charged in.

"June, I was thinking about you."

Miss Junie swept up beside the table. "Crossword puzzles. Good for the brain. Prevents Alzheimers."

Bec's eyes dropped to the puzzle, flashed on the word "lesbians." She shifted the yellow legal tablet over on top. "The afternoons do drag on."

June inclined her Roman nose, dipped her mullet towards Bec. "No worse than the post office. We caught sight of your truck outside, thought we'd dash in."

"We?"

"Karen is climbing out of the car. It takes her five minutes."

Bec grinned. "We know the chargers, and the laggards." Bec admitted to a certain guilty pleasure in her judgment.

June planted both hands on the table, leaned over Bec. "Here's the deal. An early dinner at our house, before you drive back up the mountain. Hors d'oeuvres, a salad, home-made pizza. I believe we bought sherbet."

"I'm sorry, I –"

"We're not asking, we're telling. You'll pay for it anyway, since

137

Karen wants something from you. Probably communistic." Miss Junie pivoted on her toe and rushed out brushing her round, inbound sister as she crossed the threshold.

Karen shot back over her shoulder at her departing sister, "Well, how rude!"

Bec masked the laugh with her hand, sneaked the crossword puzzle book onto the floor.

Karen advanced, nudged her plump thighs into the card table, rocked it. "Bec, how fine you look today."

With her uncut mop of hair and no makeup? "June spilled the beans. I know you want me to volunteer for something."

Karen hissed a breath out of her nose. "She displays no tact, does she? After all that time in public service."

"She did invite me to dinner."

"She did? That's good. A third person at the table for a change." Karen traced the table's edge with her fingertips.

Bec glanced at the fingernails. Karen had them painted like the American flag, with the Egyptian symbol for Female on the blue field. Probably stick-ons. "Volunteer for what?"

"Some of us want to establish a babysitting co-op. The Valley has a lot of working mothers. A share-and-share-alike would give them some time back for themselves."

"Nice idea. Self-supporting, I would think."

"Not quite. We could host it here, so we have the building and utilities, but.... "

"But?"

"We need cribs, and carpet, and some pads for nap time, and a small refrigerator for fruit juice. We need toys and a blackboard."

"That's a lot of needs."

"Bec, dear, could you write us a grant?"

An ex-University professor who couldn't write a grant? "Karen, I don't know if I can spare the time. I'm searching for a real job. How about I coach you on grant writing?"

"But you see, we need to win the grant, no ifs-ands-or-buts. Glory says you're a professional at this."

She could jump up and sprint for the door, roar out of the parking lot and back up the mountain. "That's an exaggeration."

"Please?"

What could be the harm? "I suppose. Just this once."

Karen's face sparked like a poker player who had bluffed her opponent out of the last dollar. "Wonderful, wonderful! And when we set up the Co-op, could you maybe help?"

Karen waited while Bec considered this. Bec cocked her head. "Piece of cake. When I was sixteen I picked up my first job – I ran the church nursery. I can lay out the program, coach the moms on the etiquette of other people's kids, set up a visible schedule. But after that – it's theirs. Kids and me – that's an uneasy truce."

"As long as you can be around to hand-hold the moms."

Uh-oh.

CHAPTER FIFTEEN – SEPARATE

Mᴵᴰ Jᴜʟʏ 2009.
William slung his duffel into the back of the truck. Two alone, Bec and her first lieutenant wedged in the narrow space between the pickup and a Infiniti. In the coolness of the airport parking garage, she could smell the cement and under that, the bite of Albuquerque desert waiting for them. She said, "The passenger door sticks. Let me show you."

She slid past him, tugged on the handle, opened the door with a creak. They both hesitated in the V of the door. Maybe this wouldn't be like Dubrovnik.

"Let me look at you," he said. His big hands lay on her shoulders and he peered into her face. The foreign sun had burned him dark. His teeth flashed out, white and glowing. He kissed her eyelids, her forehead. A tentative brush across her lips.

She seized him, drew herself into his bulk. "William."

"I know. We shouldn't have left it that way, broken between us. Not for so long." He released her, swept her up in another hug.

"Can I drive?" he asked. "I've hardly driven in ten months."

"Sure." She handed him the keys. She hopped into the passenger side: he churned around to the other door.

Out of the airport he turned right off Sunport Boulevard, merged into Interstate 25 traffic. "My God, look at all of this!"

"The traffic? It's not bad this time of day."

"We're zipping along! And everyone's so well behaved! Kabul traffic is a real demolition derby. Packed tight too, cheek to jowl, and slow."

"No on-ramps, I bet."

"And look at the city – so clean, so spread out!" They passed Avenida Cesar Chavez, a tough neighborhood. "Richer than Afghanistan, that's for sure."

"Are you hungry? I like a place on Rio Grande called Flying Star. They have a great patio."

"Sure, that would be fine!"

Bec nodded to his enthusiasm. A certain wryness tickled the corner of her mouth. William was infected with vacation euphoria, in full honeymoon mode. She patted the back of his hand as it gripped the steering wheel.

—⁓—

He ordered food that the Army didn't provide. "Of course they serve salad in Kandahar. But not Asian salad! And maybe you can share my sweet potato fries. And green chili stew! Wow, really?"

She parked across from him in shorts – the wire garden chair pressed waffle marks into the backs of her thighs. "I'm so pleased you like it."

"Is your friend Chuma's place as good?"

"Yes, but different. Much more down-home."

"I'm going to enjoy meeting your friends."

This month was her's, and his, not a round of visits with her friends. "All nine or ten of them? Fair warning, William. They're not the church ladies."

"That would be a kick... I think."

"More important than the ladies is my hawk – I've got a convalescent at the cabin."

"A hawk – you have a pet?"

"Hardly a pet – an injured bird that would as soon tear your finger off. Another four weeks for its wing to heal."

141

"Charming." William wouldn't even watch the National Geographic channel.

She bent over and dug in her purse on the pebbled concrete. "Speaking of kicks – I received a post card from Ted. Picked it up at the post office on the way out of town."

He rared back in his seat. "My brother wrote?"

"Someone forced him to do it – you know about Mara? Listen to this: 'Sis, in Montreal with Mara. She wanted to practice her French and check out an exhibit on Celtic artifacts from Austria. CRAPPY OLD GRAVE THINGS and one bronze brooch. She's filling out post cards and she made me do one. Ted. – P.S. This girl may be a keeper.' "

"Wow. He really said that?"

"Your brother Ted never ceases to amaze."

—⚏—

As they headed towards Española, the sun beat in the windshield, roasted their laps. William twitched into his Army-issue sunglasses and disappeared into the persona of anonymous soldier. Camo cap, invisible eyes.

He said, "We don't have as much time as I wanted. I signed up for training in Maryland and Washington, back-to-back. After that I might spend a week helping out at one of the bases in the area. I'm redeploying August fifteenth."

At the word "redeploy" her head snapped around. "So soon? And all this state-side travel?" Shit. The first smell of trouble.

His head swiveled to check the sideview mirrors. He tugged on his nose. "Yes, well. I suddenly caught some ambition. I'd like a promotion to Captain and up to Major, and I'm already forty-five, forty-six next month. Combat tours are the route up in rank, and rightly so. The highest service to the troops, after all. And the training – why, that's part of it. I have to get my ticket punched."

"How high can you go?"

"The top of the line in the Army for chaplains is Colonel. But I'd be insanely lucky to reach Lieutenant Colonel."

She scrunched around to wedge her back to the door. That way she could watch this stranger. "You could have told me. I expected we'd have more time together." Even to her, her voice sounded thin, a bit petulant.

"I know, I know. But I believed it would be better to deliver the bad news in person."

She allowed him that. "Probably." He was right. About ambition, about telling her in person. It didn't mean she had to like how it ate into their time. Their second chance.

"We do that a lot in Kandahar, you know. If it's good news, you can leave a note on a soldier's cot. Bad news, like a phone call or a family notification from the States – that's in person. The Top Kicks like me to sit in on bad news."

This tangent, on purpose or not, had distracted her. She tracked back. "Just the same, all the time we've spent apart, and you have to run off so quick."

"But that's the beauty part. You can run around the country with me. Temp housing on base."

"Oh."

He adjusted the rear view mirror for the fourth time. "I'm not detecting huge enthusiasm."

"You surprised me. You made a big decision on your own, and now I'm supposed to pack a bag and travel along with you?"

"Why shouldn't I make a decision? You moved up here without asking me."

That was true. "I can't just pick up and run off."

"Why not?" His voice tightened up. The sound of frustration.

"The garden. The garden will die if I'm not here. And Amelia – the hawk."

He flared his fingers around the steering wheel. "Surely you can find a workaround for that."

She bobbed her head. Of course he was right.

"So what's the solution?"

"I could ask Arthur to watch things for me. He doesn't know much about plants, but he'd be conscientious. Probably drown them. And overfeed Amelia."

"Arthur. He's the one who's mentally challenged?"

"Don't you dare say that in front of him. And besides the garden, you should know about a big decision in front of us – and if the answer is yes, I have to be here in New Mexico." Not really, not yet. But she didn't want to schlep around from base to base.

"Big decision?"

"A charity wants to build a veterans recuperation center on my property. On our property. They can't make it fly without our land. I might want to do it. I've thought hard about it."

"Huh? A rehab clinic?"

That had distracted him. "No, recuperation. It's like a retreat."

"And what is this charity?"

"I admit, it's not what as much as who. Tony Gibbon, your sergeant, is behind it all. He's hung around town long enough to go native and now he's won some grants for this project of his. He's up to a quarter million, but he needs a commitment in just a few days."

His snort rumbled through the cab. "And he's qualified for this how?"

"By his optimism and ego, I believe. He does have a couple of medical corpsmen who want in, if we can pay them. Tony is the organizer, not the expert."

"How big would this place be?"

"Open with eight vets, grow to fifty."

William turned his face to her, his sunglasses black. "Can he pull it off?"

144

"I think so. He knows everybody in two counties and he's formed a Board with some good people on it." It sounded so half baked. William would crush it.

The highway ferried them northwest – trees angled shade into the cab. He stripped off the sunglasses, tucked them in his shirt pocket. "I think it's great. If you're for it, I'm for it too. It's your mom's place. You should be able to do what you want with it." He glanced over at her and grinned.

She didn't even know this guy. "Big decision. They could eventually eat up the entire pasture. A lot of people underfoot. I'd lose my solitude."

William flicked a glance from the road towards her. "I thought, after Dallas, that was what you wanted, to be alone. Not all swarmed up with people."

"I don't know what I want. It felt right, but now.... "

"Now?"

"Things change. Old habits creep back."

He drummed on the steering wheel. "Would you still want to live in the cabin?"

"I'd be Manager, a paying job. What, you believe Tony could run it?"

"Why not?"

"I need him out there raising money. Besides, he hasn't planned this through. We need specialized medical support, and a mental health professional."

"Confess, Rebecca, you've already decided."

"Maybe. I've told him 'no' about six times."

He flaunted that minute superior grin. "You're going to do it. I know you better than yourself."

No, he didn't. And now he was ruining it.

"My wife, manager of a military summer camp. That'll keep you busy." He chuckled.

145

She wasn't laughing. If she did this, it wouldn't be a damn hobby.

—ന—

Night coming on. William and Bec balanced side by side on the queen bed edge, held hands. She said, "I hope this isn't too small for you. Not like the king we had in Dallas."

"I've been living on military cots. I can sleep in something less than six foot long and twenty inches wide."

She gave him a minuscule grin, allowed it to waver. "I've thought a lot about you, here. In this room, with me."

He bowed his head, his face pensive, unsure. "And so have I."

She leaned sideways and settled her head on his upper arm. "That's sweet. You're quiet."

"It's hard to begin, isn't it?"

"You mean, being intimate?" Her hand ran gentle down his leg, paused on his knee.

"I know you haven't gone through the reconstructive surgery. Your emails never said anything and you never talked about it on Skype. You're so stubborn. And when I hugged you.... "

Melancholy rose through her like a sister of despair. "No, William. I haven't faced up to the surgery. I would have told you if I had."

"That's okay. I mean, really all right. I hadn't counted on it."

The room hung so mute, her heartbeat was audible.

"Can you explain why again?"

"I never had big boobs to show off in the first place, did I? And I don't miss them, not any more."

"But the scars. And no nipples."

"The nipples were cancerous. The scars aren't so terrible. Very thin, and pink instead of purple."

"Still...."

Her jaw clamped hard. She stared at him like the force of her gaze

146

could budge him. "It's who I am. I survived cancer and those scars saved my life. That's what I did and who I became. Just to live."

"But you did live. The cancer is gone."

She laughed. In her ears it sounded bitter. "We hope to God it's done with, for good. To have to do it all again.... "

"More surgery is hard for both of us to consider."

Again with this, so difficult for him? "I shudder when I think about it. Right or wrong, those doctors are death itself to me. To go back in, lie on the table, have that mask pump away my consciousness. That would demand a lot more nerve than I have."

Tears muddled his eyes. "Even for reconstruction?"

"Maybe someday. As long as you don't push me."

"Rebecca, I did tell you I would try harder. Well I am."

"I know."

"I didn't mean this – this talk. I meant I'm consulting somebody, real professional help. I've got a shrink."

She couldn't have been more surprised if the cabin had collapsed again. "Where, in Kandahar?"

"Uh-huh. More and more mental distress in the Service. They deploy psychologists and psychiatrists now to where the problems start. Rather than wait for the problem to ship back stateside."

"How's it going, you and this shrink?"

"Slow. Good and bad. I see him a couple times a month. Mostly I say aloud what I already know deep inside. And after I spell it out, the Doctor agrees with me."

"And what do you say?"

He glanced through the window, tallied up the evening. This must cut deep for him. "That I can't endure injuries. Never could. That lost limbs and disfigurement frighten me, make me sick. I have a ton of guilt... but I'm repulsed. An automatic reaction."

"So you see me as maimed?"

147

He turned to her, swiveled away. He peered at something, up in the corner of the room. "Yes. Incomplete." His voice sounded thick, full of spit.

"If you would touch it once. Explore it once. You'd be okay."

"Rebecca, I'm not ready. It would be, I don't know. Like caressing a dead person. Only not dead. Sick and hurt."

"William. Poor, poor William." Poor Bec.

Now she couldn't touch him. She slipped the flannel grandma nightgown out of the dresser and removed her clothes facing away. Slipped into bed. They lay apart, a full twelve inches of separation. The space between them cut a thousand yards deep, a ditch of human suffering.

He whispered. "Maybe tomorrow."

—∿—

All the sounds of preparation inside the cabin echoed out the front door. Alone on the porch, her knees drawn up under her chin, she heard the dresser drawer bang, the scrubbing on the doorframe where the duffle brushed, the screen door slap shut. The bag dropped out of his hand to hit the porch boards. He grunted as he folded to the step beside her. They gazed out over the meadow, but they didn't set eyes on the same landscape.

He said, "When will they fix the roof?"

"Before the snow of course. But I want to save ahead on the money. Each month, we're right on the line of being broke."

"Huh. Kind of ramshackle isn't it?"

"My plan, or the cabin?"

"That's not what I meant. I just don't want your life to be hard."

Stall. "It's all right that I drop you in Española?" For a week, a week of silences and false cheer, she had known she would speak. She could touch that moment, but held it at arm's length from her. Any second now, she might tell him she couldn't stand it, couldn't stand him.

He clasped her hand. "Sure. It's not like I'm right back overseas, just to the plane and off to Maryland."

She tugged her hand back, out of his grasp.

His forehead wrinkled. Did he sense it coming?

She said, "We have to talk, before you leave. You have to know how I feel."

He slumped, a tiny lurch. "I do know. You're afraid of surgery."

"Ahhh. That's not it. You have so much to learn about me, the new me. And we're out of time."

His eyes flared like something dangerous. A grenade, a bomb lay on the porch between them. "That sounds bad."

She said, as slow and quiet as a prayer, "I don't want to be married to you anymore. I'm not who you need. And you're not who I need."

"I don't understand how you can say that." Clear irritation in his voice.

"William, I've tried like hell to do my share to bring you around."

"I told you I was getting help."

"No, you told me that you talked occasionally to a shrink so you could feel better about not changing."

"That's not fair."

"You can't love me, not really love me if you let this thing come between us." She began to weep, after she had promised herself she wouldn't. "And I've stopped loving you. Either you aren't who I believed you were, or you've changed. I need you to be strong, not weak. Loving, not disgusted." Maybe, maybe he did love her, but this way was killing her.

He set his jaw; his voice rang flat. "My fault, huh." Anger choked back in his throat, a thickness like a slurring. "Have the darn surgery. It's nothing compared to what we've been through."

"Has this been hard on you?"

"Show me you understand. Show me that you love me!"

"I want a divorce." A salty tear ran down her cheek – she swabbed at it with her sleeve. Now the words were out there.

"A divorce. After all we've been and done? Are you out of your mind?"

149

Of course. Ministers didn't divorce. "I've been considering it since Dubrovnik. I'm sure."

He gritted his words out. "Are you seeing someone else? Is that it?" A real male response, finally.

"How could there be? I live here like a hermit in this cabin. How can you accuse me of that?"

His head, his neck, his shoulders were rigid, like he counted numbers up in his mind, or tallied grievances. He leapt to his feet, stomped away ten feet. She glared at his back, too angry to care if she had hurt him. Across the meadow, two crows fought raucously over some scrap they had hit on. Hands on his hips, he watched them, to pick out how the avian squabble would end.

No way back. And she didn't want it anyway. "William."

His shoulders were set, his anger a wall. The smaller crow seized the morsel of food and bulleted off. William kicked the dirt and turned. He marched up to her, reached past, grabbed the strap of his duffle. He glared at her. "All right. I'll give you a trial separation. Maybe we can talk this out. Now, drive me down to the bus so I can make the airport."

"Separation?"

"Yes, that's all. No divorce, not till we talk it out."

The idiot. Didn't he know they had already been separated, by the war, by the Army, by her scars?

MICHAEL'S PLAGUE

CHAPTER SIXTEEN – LONG TIME

A ugust 2009.

The black Nissan baked in the sun in front of Bec's cabin. Its windows down, its trunk yawned open. Bec didn't listen as much as she watched. Across the pasture, Emmet and Arthur, just short of the trees, toiled away. The grass had yellowed in the summer drought; it waved knee high and hid their feet. They floated through the grass as they roamed about. Emmet picked up one board and shifted it from one stack to another, his complaining voice a thin thread in the distance. Arthur pounded in a two-by-four stake with a hand sledge – his vast shoulders worked in the sunshine.

Beside Bec, Tony lay back on the porch, cocked up on his elbows and in the shade. He said, "Wow, this place would be perfect if it boasted any nightlife."

Her eyebrow soared. She hoped she looked sardonic. "My pasture?"

"No, silly. Santa Eulalia."

"We have Mannie's."

"Right. Drink with people twice and three times my age."

Bec pointed at Emmet, across the way. "You drink with your roommate."

Tony, impatient, rejected that. "That's different. I meant someone my own age, and I didn't mean just drinking. Gay or straight, a twenty-six year old needs someone to date."

When she flashed her eyes onto him, he appeared relaxed,

matter-of-fact. Of course, she had signed her pasture away, so his crisis was resolved. "How did you get away with being gay in the Army?"

He dropped off the porch, paced back and forth. "At first I kept my mouth shut, all through Boot. Came out after we deployed, to the sound of fistfights. I had to suffer through a couple of beatings and give out a couple. After we saw some action, swept a village or two, it didn't matter. We were brothers and they could depend on me."

"You're pretty open about it now."

"I can kick any civilian's butt that gives me a hard time, easy. Lonely out here in the boonies, though."

She pinched her lips. Some revelation was about to drop – something she maybe didn't want to know.

Tony flared his eyes. "Once a week I blast down to Santa Fe. I've discovered a bar called the Blue Dragon. I drive back the next day."

"Thanks for sharing."

"Come on, Bec. You're not that churchy." He dumped back down on the porch.

She wasn't churchy at all.

Tony pointed. "Damn. He's hurt himself." Across the pasture, Emmet hopped up and down, bent over his hand. Arthur rushed up to him and flapped his arms.

Tony shrugged. "They'll shout if it's serious. I plan to build the Retreat with volunteer labor, our first clients in fact." He kicked his left foot out, swinging it like a kid.

"Huh? Your veterans? Isn't that kind of – exploitive?"

"Not really. Great therapy. I should know – I've worked through therapy." He grinned at some insider joke.

"But your guys will be amateurs. Professional soldiers, but not builders."

"I'll be the general contractor. We'll use a local builder – probably Rubio – as our main sub, and a couple of his regular guys, but they'll be side-by-side with my soldiers."

She watched the two across the field. Emmet held his hand out to Arthur for inspection. Incredulous, she asked. "And when does this begin?"

"Next month. I plan to pour the foundations and frame up a dorm before the first freeze. If we're lucky, we close it in and we have winter accommodations."

"Just so we're clear, your veterans can't stay with me in the meantime. How will you handle housing?"

"No problem. I've dug up an outfitter who's loaned me a canvas tent and cook gear. It's more than adequate until first snow. Even after first snow."

She shifted her gaze from the two working men to Tony. He'd drawn his hair back in a ponytail and trimmed up a blond goatee, the color offset by his brown hair. The local style, that layer of scruffiness, was a patina over the bulk and posture of a professional soldier. One with a disarming grin. She wondered how big a swath he cut through the mysterious Blue Dragon.

He rubbed his hands together, beamed out over the pasture at his minions. "Going well. At least I believe it is."

"All the same, feels like a dream to me. Especially when I think of Emmet being on your team."

Tony cupped his hands, held them out, and in spite of herself, she glanced to check what he held. Nothing. He said, "You told me to keep an eye on the old guy. He's in the hands of gentle mercy and I got my kindly eye on him."

Her mouth twitched and clamped back the grin. "And Arthur?"

"Boredom was killing him. And he's surprised me. He knows more than you think." Tony tapped his forehead with his finger. "Good with a hammer. A blueprint – not so much."

"Shouldn't you be supervising them, way over there?"

"I had to okay it with you first."

She stared him down. That had taken it a bit far.

155

Tony grinned. He strode off, a bounce in his step, to check on the batter-board layout.

She said aloud, "He ended up with what he wanted, didn't he? Local buy-in that he'll ignore later." She stumped up the steps onto her porch and through her door. A cup of green tea. Maybe later, drive into the village and make the rounds again. She needed a job.

—m—

Friday evening brought another guest. Knocking rattled the screen door, like hoofs on the porch boards. Bec leapt off the couch, dropped a Tom Robbins novel on the floor. The rat-tat-tat hadn't frightened her, though her heart beat faster.

The light from the living room shone past her onto the dried-up woman on the porch. Black hair, a light chocolate color to the skin, glasses shoved up onto her forehead. Eugenia, one of the DIVAS, with a bag in her hand. "Bec, querida, can I use your extra room?"

Bec rocked back a step. A step that Eugenia interpreted as an invitation.

Eugenia jerked the screen door open and limped past Bec. Down the hall she clumped. Her voice floated out from the second bedroom. "I've run away from home for a couple of days. George has misbehaved and I need to scare him." She rushed back into the living room and handed Bec a bag of Kirkland jelly beans. "Here. I never brought you a housewarming gift." She threw herself into the couch. "You haven't fixed the roof over the bedroom, but that's fine – like camping."

Bec, loitering near the front door, closed and latched it, hesitated for that extra second to scan the dry wood grain. She turned, forced out a smile. "What did George do?"

"He drinks way too much, and he dared to turn insolent this evening. Asked me why I wasn't as thin as I used to be. I'm the skinniest woman in the village, besides you. That beer-bellied old man – who does he think he is?"

"I'm sure I don't know."

Eugenia kicked off her flats and stuck her bad leg up on the coffee table. "So I disappear for a day or two and he panics. Three and he calls my sister in Phoenix and cries on the phone. Let him simmer for a week. After that punishment I let him track me down at the café and beg my forgiveness."

A week. "Wow. You've figured it all out."

"Sure. Happened before. But he knows all my old hiding places. He won't have a clue about this cabin. Out in the middle of nowhere – might as well be Alaska. You're a jewel to let me stay. Have we had dinner yet?"

—⁓—

The last of August and the nights were already cool, in the mid forties. Early mornings that shook in the wind. Bec ambled past the barn to the shriek of power saws, her morning consultation with the swallows cupped up under the roof destroyed by banshee howling. With a tightness across the back of her shoulders and a clenched mouth, she caught sight of Eugenia on the back porch, eating an orange and dropping the peel on the boards. Eugenia shouted out, "How about I do carne adobada for dinner?" A pity Eugenia had retired from schoolteaching.

Bec fluttered her hand and detoured around the house, trap in hand, onto her front porch. In the rafters waited the hawk, her hawk. She dipped the trap to the boards and shook it out. "Small rat this time, Amelia."

The bird dropped to the porch like a rock, flared her wings only at the last second. With a hop, she seized the rodent in her beak and launched off the porch with two powerful wing beats. She pumped twice more and glided in an arc to the treeline north of the house. Bec shouted after her, "Tomorrow."

The air compressor kicked on and the nail gun barked out its first kachunk kachunk of the day. She decided to slip away, down into Santa Eulalia. A plaid wool against the chill, a swap from Crocs to boots, and she jumped in the truck. Rain, blessed rain sifted out of the sky as she drew abreast of the construction site. A mere spatter. The wind picked up, its own fierce message – she rolled up the window.

—⋙—

Now that the Fall had kicked in, mud trails crisscrossed the blacktop all through town – tire prints like lazy tracery. She dodged in the café door, paused in the entrance to breathe in the smells. Bacon, coffee, toast. And of course, a damp humanity. Men and women in wet fleeces, muddy boots, stocking caps and baseball hats wolfed breakfast burritos and huevos rancheros. Bare walls and the menu boards bounced the clamor around, set the air trembling. She had picked this over the job site.

She dumped her laptop on the smallest table, the one wriggled into the back corner. After she dived behind the counter, she tapped a cup of hot water out of the Bunn machine, fished out her box of Oolong from her pocket. She prepared to out-wait the breakfast rush.

At ten, Chuma collapsed in the chair across from her, after all those breakfast burritos and go-cups of coffee. Only three customers remained. Bec gazed at Chuma, in a strangely clean apron, the face broad and square, folds around the eyes. Chuma could appear happy or sad, but never worried.

"Second day you've set up shop in my place," Chuma said.

"I know. Kind of crowded at home."

"What's happening out on the meadow?"

Bec shrugged. "Besides another two weeks of Eugenia? Tony drove up Monday with what he calls a bobtail and four guys – his first veterans. The bobtail was crammed full of camping gear and some lumber. They spent a day to set up a village. Next day, Tony drives up with what he calls a crew trailer. Holds all the tools. On Wednesday he heads off

158

to Española to collect another load of lumber with two of his vets and strands the other two – leaves them to build sawhorses out of scrap, that type of thing."

"Hustle and bustle. A whole army." Chuma wasn't listening – her eyes shifted away, scanned the restaurant.

"Now it's power-tool city. They're at it all day long. It's like living next to a furniture factory."

Chuma rolled her eyes. "What the hell did you expect? You gave them the lease, out of some hasty impulse. You watched them pour the foundations."

"Easy enough to forget about the foundations when they're out in the weeds."

"It's not like you sleep late, girl. You'll get used to it."

Bec twitched her head no, frowned. Hard to come up with any sympathy here.

Chuma humphed. "I bet that's not the crap that's knocked you off kilter. Maybe all those men so close? Lock the doors, carry a hatchet."

Bec dismissed this with a hand wave. "You believe every male turns out dangerous."

Chuma spun her empty coffee cup around in its saucer. "Pitiful, more likely. Tell me about the guys."

Bec leaned forward, propped her forearms on the table edge. "Yes ma'am. Let's see – they're our hard military men, young and muscled, hair cut short, ready to go. Trouble is…. "

"Uh-huh. Tell Momma Chuma."

"They're all missing something. The one named Kevin lost his right hand. The one named Michael suffered the loss of his legs. Jason has only one eye and needs some reconstructive surgery to his jaw and the side of his face. The fourth, Davy, is vague. Probably a head injury."

Chuma snorted, reached back to fiddle with her braided hair. "Jeez, Bec. You talk about them as injuries, not as guys."

Bec bit back her protest – a clear confession. "I'm stuck there right now. Maybe later, after I know them better. I shouldn't say it…. "

Chuma tapped on the table with her spoon, and with her head tilted down, glanced at Bec. "You need to tell someone or you wouldn't be here."

"I'm a touch creeped out. Kevin's mechanical hand doesn't even pretend to be real – he's black, I mean black, and the hand is muddy brown. About your color."

Chuma objected. "Hey! Don't get racist."

"And Michael, he has these plastic knees and aluminum bones that run down out of his shorts into his boots. Like a robot in people clothes."

"What about the guy with the blind eye and the scars?"

"I'm good with scars. No trouble there."

"Four guys, a tent, a campout. Robot hands and legs. A crazy-ass scheme to build a summer camp. Sounds perfectly normal to me."

"You know Tony. Nothing is impossible and no idea is too out there."

"Why'd you ditch your place and show up again today?"

Bec leaned back, crossed her arms. "The racket. Besides, the licensed contractor is supposed to start today and I didn't want to get roped into that."

"Who's the contractor?"

"God, you're nosy. My neighbor Rubio. You know, the guy who brought me topsoil. The one who plows me out after a snow."

Chuma snorted. "Rubio plows your road? The man is seventy years old."

"But he's a contractor with a hundred relatives, all of whom can do something on a house site."

"Hell, they all probably built your cabin. That could explain a lot." Chuma wrinkled an eyebrow, threw her a glance. "And you feel sorry for yourself because – ?"

"My mountain is changing forever. Hard to picture what it'll turn into, but right now it's a wreck. Kind of sad."

"You need something to keep you busy. What about that garden of yours."

"You can't garden eight hours a day. Besides Eugenia's bored and wants to help. I love her, but.... "

Chuma banged her hand down on the table – her fork jumped. She grunted her way onto her feet. "You always throw out an excuse. I better get back to it. You can hide out here as long as you want, do your video call to William, whatever. Some of the rest of us have to work for a living."

"Believe me, talking to William these days is work."

"Huh."

"Maybe I shouldn't bother. Maybe it's his turn to patch things up."

—⁓—

Bec considered the pasture. Even with a double-walled tent the cold was bound to creep in at night. The only facility a porta-john. She could imagine sponge baths in the evening, frosty breath in the air. They lived on camp food. She should invite them all over for dinner. Lasagna? By the time she decided, the laptop chimed and William flashed on the line. His face was set like rock. Thinner, somehow.

"Bec, glad you called." He didn't appear too glad – more wary than anything.

"William, how's it going?" Crap, that sounded lame. He's my husband, not someone I bumped into in the supermarket. "Time to talk?"

"Huh? Sure. I'm half up as it is."

"How are you feeling?"

"Feeling? Sleepy. It's eleven hours later for me. I've settled back into the routine here, but my body clock is all scrambled."

So we're not talking about our emotions. "I miss you." Even if she didn't.

He smiled, really smiled. Like that could be enough. "I miss you too."

161

He was distracted. Or delaying the whole damn thing. "And how is the routine?"

William's laptop threw a peculiar tilt across the picture, as if the room slanted. Behind him leaned a battered metal wardrobe, some shelving nailed together from rough lumber, curving canvas walls. "So-so. We survived a spot inspection of some visiting general. Luckily he didn't quiz me on the Eucharist. Now that's out of the way, we can all get back to normal."

"There's a normal in a fire base?" Her fingernail circled the touch-pad, over and over. Nervous.

"We don't call it a fire base. The proper designation is FOB. Sure we can define normal. We call it boring. The guys get so bored they want to be shot at."

An inverted world. Maybe like sex in marriage, her marriage. "Really?"

He grinned, a big tan block with white teeth. "Not really. But they do love a good firefight."

The front door jangled its sleigh bells as the last customers left. Distracted, she glanced away, jerked back. "What're you up to, today?" Like he was working in the pastor's office, checking his day planner, preparing already for lunch with some church committee.

"Day's over. I counseled a couple of enlisted and I worked on Sunday's sermon. Sunday's crawling closer by the minute. I also checked in supplies this afternoon with Sergeant Grover."

"Is that normal, a Chaplain checking in supplies?" Why were they talking about this?

"It's an excuse to talk to Dan – the sergeant. He flaked out last week, disappeared for two days. His CO buried it, but the guy's in trouble. I want to know what caused it." His voice tailed off like he was thinking about something else.

"I hope you can help him." More likely him than us.

William's mouth stretched into a tight slash across his face. "Me too. I've learned nothing yet – he's buttoned down like rockets are incoming. How's your week going?"

Right. Like they were the Brady Bunch. "Tony's first batch of warriors have arrived. They flew in from all over the States. Davy, the man I believe suffered a brain injury, waited in the airport by himself for four hours."

William pursed his mouth. "What are they like?"

"Beat up. I don't really know yet. They're so busy I think they're avoiding me."

William must have slid something from under his laptop – the picture shook like an earthquake, showed a bare lightbulb hung on a wire. He was probably shuffling files while he talked to her. "Give them time. The military doesn't open up quick to civilians."

So she was a "civi." Or maybe the weird old lady on the other end of the field. "The three credit agencies mailed me a lot of paperwork. I plan to file an appeal, try to get our credit reset." Was she asking some forgiveness? The filing was as much for her as him.

William cleared his throat. It sounded tinny through her laptop. "About that. I wanted you to know. I guess I knew about the house. I just didn't want to think about it. Childish, huh?" His forehead wrinkled up towards his scalp, his eyes opened wide and even sad.

"You're not mad any more?"

"I'm still mad. Just not at you."

But she was. Angry with him.

—⁓—

The knock on the back door gave her a jolt. She strode back and unlatched it. The man at the door owned a striking face, the perfect proportions except for the nose canted over to one side. "Michael?"

"Missus Robertson, I've brought all the laundry over."

163

She beckoned him in. "Leave the laundry on the porch and come in. Let me show you how it works." She tugged open a closet. "Boiler's in here, propane fired. The laundry hose is here at the bottom – I keep it curled up in the overflow pan. You saw the tubs on the back porch?"

"Yes ma'am." He smelled like pine needles – how could that be?

"Let me show you how the wringer works. It looks like it's a hundred years old, but it's electric." She brushed past him on her way to the back porch and stepped on his toe. Or at least she called it a toe.

He trailed behind her. "My grandma owned one of these, stored away in her old smoke house. I've never seen one in action, though."

Between the two of them, they clamped the wringer to the tub side. "Be careful. It's top heavy until some water fills up in the tub. You plug it in back here in the hallway with the extension cord." He crowded in behind her in the dark narrow space. Her heart accelerated.

She bent to plug in the cord and turned her head, spotted his prosthetic legs close for the first time – he wore sandals. Under the sandal straps, tan latex that had toes and bones molded in, like doll feet, disguised the mechanicals. Erupting up out of the fake foot, some joint as complicated as hell, and a metal tube that ran upward. Bullet shaped gray casings cradled the bottom of his legs, what remained of them. The prosthetics didn't pretend to mimic the muscle and flesh of real legs.

He said, "It's okay. You can be curious. Not many of these around." He shuffled back and she straightened. He stepped on the back of his sandal with one foot and peeled out of the shoe and the latex toes. He bumped the foot towards her. The ankle was formed of black and chrome pivots, and two elongate black blades shaped the foot. "Those rubber feet, wrappers really, they're what keep the boots and shoes on. But they do look like horror movie props."

He bent to slide the sandal back on. It dragged on the floor – the feet creaked minutely as he kept his balance with tiny adjustments. She kept her head down, her gaze on the prosthetic. A flush rose in the back of her neck; her scalp prickled. Too private.

"My luck was in – I still have my knees. Those knees have to do the heavy work, but these legs are much cheaper. No batteries or sensors like the above-knee legs. I could even afford a spare set if I wanted – maybe those blade runners. And with all this metal – titanium, aluminum, some steel – I'm guaranteed to set off the metal detectors." Pride in his voice. He laughed, free, easy.

She chuckled also, but her throat bound shut. It sounded fake – change the subject. "Okay, let's do laundry. I'll walk you through the steps. Soap and water first. You'll stir the clothes around with this paddle. The wringer goes forward and backward with this lever on top. The water you squeeze out goes right back into the wash. No, no!" She seized his hand and jerked it back.

"What?" He bumped heads with her, a light knock, and she caught a flash of his blue eyes as she jerked her head back.

"Watch it! The wringers will grab your hand and crush it flat." Even now, she clutched his hand by the wrist.

With his free hand he reached across and patted her fingers. "Okay, I understand. You don't want me to come by another spare part. And this is the rinse tub?"

She glanced at his angular face from the side, the curve of his skull under his Marine Corps buzz, his intense concentration on this simple task. "Yes, and you wring rinsed clothes out backwards. Most of the water goes into the rinse tub, but you heave the clothes out and away."

"The rinse will fill up with soapy water quick."

"I drain it out with this petcock and change out the water."

He straightened, paddle in hand. "You're the only woman I've ever known who can ID a petcock, Missus Robertson."

She flinched. "I may be fifteen years older than you, but if you call me Mrs. Robertson I'll feel forty older. It's Bec." She eased past him. "Any questions? I'll leave you to your laundry then." She rushed inside

165

to the kitchen and parked her hands on the drainboard. Her head hung, and she gaped at the cups and plates. Her breath sawed in as a ragged catch. What was this?

She hadn't had sex in a long time. And William was in Kandahar. And she believed the marriage had fallen apart.

CHAPTER SEVENTEEN – CHEER

FOUR DAYS AFTER EUGENIA FORGAVE George, Emmet leaned on a staff whittled out of cottonwood on Bec's porch, a respectful step back from the door. "Emmet! Good to see you." Bec waved him forward into her cabin, "Come in, come in." She led the way into the kitchen, seated him at the table. "I was thinking about you the other day."

"And I about you. I rode out with Tony this morning, but they don't need an old loony in the way. Besides, I might perspire. Therefore, it behooved me to wander over for a talk."

She rattled the kettle onto the stove, fired the burner. "Tea, then?"

His face dropped. "I suppose."

Bec, her back turned to Emmet, allowed a private grin. "Oolong or Darjeeling?"

"Brown would be fine." She heard the mutter. "Have I fallen so far as to drink tea?"

She set the mug in front of him, with the sugar bowl and a spoon. In her chair with her chin propped on her fists, she asked, "How are the guys? How's the job?"

"I believe it unlikely old Rubio will have much to do – Kevin knows carpentry and the crew hurtles along. They have already erected a wall and done something they refer to as blocking."

"How is Davy on a job site?"

Emmet wobbled his head no. "The lost child. Kevin assigned him as monarch of the boards – tote them here, stack them there. Rather day-dreamy, but what do you expect?"

"And Jason?"

"Hard worker. Do not, I advise, approach him on his blind side."

She smoothed some crystals of sugar across the table into her hand, asked, "And Michael?" Too casual.

Emmet glanced at her. "You have a particular interest in Michael?"

"He's just one of four, Emmet."

"He does well enough. He whizzes around on those metal legs of his. He can swing a hammer. Changeable, though. One minute, he smiles and laughs, the next…. "

She caught sight of her wedding ring, a circle of beat-up gold. "What?"

"Streak of darkness. Something horrendous happened to him."

She rejected that, impatient. "He lost his legs, Emmet."

"No, something else. Something in there, all clamped down. I hope I'm not around when he lets it out."

"Let's hope it's not too bad."

Emmet knocked on the table, glared into her eyes. Like an old-time prophet. "Don't take it lightly, Bec. Don't get too close to Michael. Nor to the others. This is not like bringing Arthur under your wing. These young men have experienced things you and I can't imagine."

She patted the back of his hand. "You sound like an old woman. I'll assume your doom and gloom doesn't extend to dinner. I've decided to provide a feed on Friday evenings. You and Tony should attend."

"This would not be vegetarian, I hope?"

"For the Army and Marine Corps? No, pounds of meat and biscuits with real butter."

Emmet bobbed his head. "I would be honored to attend. Formal attire? Shall I prepare potato salad?"

Bec hooted. "Yes on the formal attire – your best jeans. And I didn't know you could cook."

168

"You don't know many things about me, Bec. Why, I am the village enigma, the mountaintop mirage."

She leaned forward. "Tell me about the enigma. Who is this Emmet who prefers to be called Marcus."

His face walled off like a tomb. "My life would scarcely be interesting."

"Everyone has a story." She cocked her head, waited.

Emmet slurped at the tea, set the cup down. He rubbed the bottom of his nose with his knuckle, scratched the gray stubble. "Are you trying to punish me? First tea, and now the Spanish Inquisition?"

"Convince me I should call you Marcus."

He wheezed out a sigh, a lament, really. "Marcus was the most common name of the Roman Empire, and I was the most common of history and language teachers. Probatur punctum, point proven."

She slapped the table. "I knew you had to be a professor!"

"Indeed I was faculty, but not a decent writer or researcher. I was married back in those days, but I'm afraid when I didn't attain tenure, things rather fell apart. She departed for quarters across campus."

"What was her name?"

"Rosie, a charming and unlikely name."

"She left you for a tenured faculty member?"

He drooped his chin down on his chest. "Dr. Rosie was tenured, and sufficient unto herself. She left me because I drank. After that, I journeyed on. I accepted a couple of adjunct professor jobs. The situation slipped along for a while. I taught classics in a private boys school for four weeks. I participated in a scene the boys enjoyed immensely, and Administration escorted me to the front door."

What scene could cause an instant dismissal? "Painful. Do you speak the classic languages?"

"Why yes. All dead, nothing useful. Archaic Greek, Classic Latin rather than medical Latin, Aramaic instead of Hebrew. I always wanted to absorb Gaelic – it too is worthless."

169

She seized his hand. "Emmet, I'm impressed."

He slipped his hand back, but patted her wrist. "I once could demonstrate great proficiency. Now my talents trickle away."

She refilled his cup with hot water and dropped in a tea bag, even as he trembled in revulsion. "Marcus was also the name of Marcus Aurelius, wasn't it? The philosopher emperor?"

"The last of the good emperors, yes."

She pointed her finger at him. "Here's the deal. You quit drinking and become a stoic rather than a fatalist – I'll call you Marcus. Until that time, you'll just have to be my friend Emmet."

"But after Marcus Aurelius, the Empire descended from gold into iron and rust, you know. Rust. Who knows what would happen to my body without my servitude to Dionysus."

—⁓—

Her first Friday dinner for the Retreat. Eight in all and the kitchen table held only four. Bec had roasted a turkey with stuffing, prepared a bowl of green beans with bacon, and had just drawn biscuits hot out of the oven. Most of the supplies were spirited out of Chuma's refrigerator. Emmet fulfilled his promise with a plastic bowl of German potato salad and Tony strutted in with two of Chuma's pies. William would have been proud, even though he wouldn't have been much help.

The kitchen steamed like hell itself. She forced the window open, let in the relief of a chill night. She slapped one pan of biscuits on the table, gazed around at her quartet. Jason sat at the end with his bad side towards the wall and helped Davy shred his turkey off the bone. Kevin ate like a clockwork man, his head down and the fork locked into the tan hand.

Tony waved a fork and expounded on his new book idea, a modern day Alexander, still gay. "A piece of cake," he said. "I know all about military crap, and all about being gay in 2009, and all about the real Alexander."

Ludicrous. Even if his Alexander ran modern-day Russia, he couldn't go around conquering territory. She should tell him.

She carried the second pan of biscuits into the living room. "Emmet, biscuit?"

He fished out two, balanced one on the leather arm of his chair. "Bread of the gods, dear lady."

"Arthur?"

Arthur's head pumped. He scooped up three, crushed them in his hand. He heaved himself up on his feet. "I need pie."

"Michael?"

He had sunk back into the couch, one of his mechanical legs stretched out on the coffee table. "Yes, please. And to think we ate beans last night."

Emmet added, "Odoriferous."

Michael grinned at Bec as she leaned in to plop a biscuit onto his plate. "Is Emmet always this way?"

Twelve inches of separation. The plate held out between them. "What way?"

"Does he always go for the fart joke?"

The leather in Emmet's chair squeaked as he shifted, only three feet away from them. "Speaking for myself, I am a vulgar old loony. My role and my place, and I play it well, thank you."

Bec said, "At least you're bathing more."

Michael patted the cracked old leather cushion, "Empty place on the couch, if you want." He blinked once, slowly, as he trapped her eyes. She breathed in the air he exhaled.

"Be right back." She skittered into the kitchen. Arthur blocked the space by the oven, forked in pie while he watched Tony declaim. Bec eased around him and scooped a smattering of food onto a plate. She dashed back into the living room and dropped onto the cushions beside Michael. The old couch sagged, tipped her towards him. Her hip slid into his, her knee against the prosthetic casing.

"Is that all you're going to eat?" asked Michael.

She glanced down. The plate held a bit of turkey crackling on the edge and two spoons of potato salad. "I'll go back in a minute." The wood stove poured out heat. She flushed.

Emmet spoke around a mouthful of biscuit, "I shall indulge in seconds myself. Can I bring anyone something?" A rhetorical question – his back turned, he ambled into the kitchen.

Michael asked, "Where are you from? Originally?"

She chuckled. "How do you know I'm not from here?"

He watched her – she was in the spotlight. "I can tell. None of us in this cabin are from around here. The real question – whether any of us are home, or if this is just a stop-over?"

"I believe I'm home. This cabin has been in my family four generations, on my momma's side. But – I moved here from Dallas."

Those blue eyes, flecked in traces of yellow. He said, "Yes. Maybe you're home."

"And you?"

"No home since my folks died. They passed within two weeks of each other. I flew back from Iraq for the funeral, but returned to the Sandbox right away. After that wherever I drop my duffel – that's home."

"No other relatives?"

He dropped into a thousand-yard stare, defocused eyes. "A sister. We don't get along." He fell silent.

She nudged him with her elbow – that was neutral enough. "Hey, where did you go?"

He ducked his head, squinted at her sideways. "Sorry."

"No need to apologize. Want to tell me about your sister?"

"Hell no." He leaned that tiny bit, the small distance that it required, and their shoulders glided together. A shuffle and a cough behind them, and they both jerked away.

Emmet limped into view, eased into his easy chair with some groaning. "Blighted knees." Smiling a gap-toothed grin, he said, "The biscuits have disappeared. It is a mystery bound to puzzle the brightest."

Bec said, dry as dust, "I bet I can guess, though."

"No doubt, but merest conjecture. Now if we only were blessed with a tincture of alcohol to fill a glass."

Bec glanced past the stove, to catch the picture of William leaned up by the clock. Michael shifted back towards her. His fingertips on the back of her hand were dry, rasping. A prickling raced up her arms – she shivered like a chill wind had swept across her. Collecting their empty plates, she leapt up.

After dinner, pie slice-by-slice disappeared off to pie heaven. Dishes done by three jostling vets – the food vanished except for crumbs dusted across the floor and left in the seat cushions in the living room. Around nine, they filed out onto the front porch, paused in the light that fell out the door and windows to paint the boards. They shrugged into their jackets, and one-by-one thanked her for the meal. First off the porch, Michael strode into the starlight and across the pasture to the outfitter tent. She felt – let down.

All seven left on the porch watched his figure. He dimmed into the star flicker, left them behind.

Tony shrugged his shoulder at Michael's retreating back. "Looks like another mood swing on the way. Goodnight, Bec. Thanks again for the hospitality. See you Monday. Coming, Emmet?"

"A moment, Anthony. I shall join you after a word here."

"Sure. Score if you can, big guy. I'll wait in the car."

Bec and Emmet watched Kevin hike off, trailed by Arthur and Jason who held Davy's elbow. She snorted, "Score indeed." Tony could rub her the wrong way.

Emmet replied, "It's all right. He mocks me all the time, but means little by it." He held a finger up before her face.

173

Was she about to hear the lecture? "Emmet, don't say it."

Thinking better of it, he dropped his hand, half-turned. "I believe it would be an unfortunate path to travel, Bec. But I'll say no more. When you want to talk about it, we'll visit. I'll buy you a drink. Thank you, dear Bec, for a magnificent feast."

—ɯ—

September 2009.

What began as a rip in the mountain's fabric soon became the status quo. Each morning, scrubbed, with wet hair, she would saunter out to the barn to fetch a mouse and bring it to the porch for Amelia. After, she'd boil water for tea. The steam from the tea curled up, smelled as green as grass. She stepped onto the porch about the same time Davy fired up the generator. Each day, the saws shrieked and the hammer blows rose like sharp ringing birds into the heaven of morning.

She counted through the vets, separated one from the other. Davy, hands dangling loose at his side, waited instructions. Jason ran the chop saw. Up the ladder, Kevin toenailed two wall segments together – left-handed. Michael, hair bleached in the sun, black glasses, checked the tree line. Michael, a nail gun in his hand.

She had examined the floor plans. The dorm formed a cross shape huddled under a square roof. At each compass point, a bedroom for two. In the middle a living room, utilities, a kitchen. At each roof corner, covered porches. Too complicated. Too many walls that would leak too much heat. A farmer would have done better.

From her distant view, the two-by-fours rose in jumbles, obscured all in a yellow stick forest – but the four vets toured her through it each day at quitting time. They would install trusses soon, throw triangles up above the stick-frame walls. Next they would deck the roof.

Rubio's diesel truck chugged into the pasture and over to the dorm: he'd arrived to earn his contractor's keep. Even now he had the winter

174

plow bolted on the front of his rusty pickup. Too much trouble to change out – snow was only a couple months away. Their contractor hopped down from the high seat and slammed his door. As straight as a rod but propped on a cane, he shouted at Kevin, limped over to the saw stand, shook hands all around.

Rubio had cheated her on the topsoil, but he plowed out her snowy lane twice for free. Hard to figure. Bec popped back into the house for her binoculars and settled on the steps to watch. Rubio strolled through each part of the job with Kevin, and as he proceeded, jabbed his walking stick at this and that. Kevin nodded, dipped his head close to hear the old man. Bec could distinguish Kevin, carpenter pencil in hand, writing on two-by-fours. Michael trailed behind with a stack of short boards, to add blocking where Rubio pointed. He held each cross brace in place, drove in ten-pennies with angry blows. One block split and he ripped it out, threw it to the floor, jerked nails back out of the studs like they were the enemy. Easy, Michael. It's only pine.

Rubio squatted down at the foundation edge and dropped onto his butt. After he dangled his legs over the edge, he eased off the rim onto the ground. He wobbled over the broken ground to the tail of his truck. Jason tagged along beside Rubio – to steady him? No, that wasn't it. Jason handed the old man something, lifted two cases of beer out of the back and into the tent. So that's Rubio's game. He'd brought cheer out to the boys.

Rubio waved to the crew from his running board, lurched inside, and chugged away. That old geezer's only as good as he needs to be. Counts on as much money as he can off this job, I bet. And he'll cash my check this month for the roof.

CHAPTER EIGHTEEN – STEP

SEVEN IN THE EVENING LEFT the sky soft with fading light, and an early bat darted and swooped overhead. Bec imagined the bat squeaks that guided it, right on the edge of her hearing. From across the meadow, a murmur of music. Country and Western. A white ghostly ellipse bobbed towards her; a shattered bright spot of light wavered on the ground before it. A breathless illusion that a ghost jiggled out in the dark, no closer, no further.

The ellipse-shaped phantom transformed into a flashlight, the shattered cone illuminated pacing feet, the feet attached to a body. A man treaded the road ruts, shambled into the arc of the cabin's electric light. Davy hauled off his ball cap, twisted it in his hands. "Mrs. Robertson, they sent me over for – we'd like to invite you for a beer."

Michael would be there. Was it his idea? "Let me grab my coat and I'll be right with you."

Davy guided her steps with the flashlight, worked hard at it. "Don't trip here. Watch that hump of grass. Here's a hole."

He hauled the tent flap back and Bec bobbed inside. The tent was lit with a lantern, like the old days, but this was an LED light run off batteries. The square interior held four spraddle-legged cots, four sleeping bags crumpled on the cots or shoved to the ground. A stove in the center. She had expected a wood-burner like hers, but this ran off an oversize propane bottle. A stovepipe jutted out the top. What remained the same, what had begun a hundred and fifty years ago here on the mountain as miners tents, were the walls of duck canvas, a soft old-linen yellow. Four walls locked the night outside, hung around them like a coat draping on their shoulders. Atavistic, the men faced the fire, huddled in as men had for thousands of years. With a shock, Bec picked out Arthur on one of the cots, his plump face pointed to the tent ceiling. His mouth hung open – he snored.

Two soldiers jumped up for her. Jason hovered closest, hand waving. "Come on in, Miss Bec."

"It's Bec. No need to be formal. Where do I sit?" She glimpsed Michael – as far from the door as the cots allowed, beer cradled in his hands. He glanced over – blazing blue eyes, a frown across his face.

Jason shuffled his feet. "Tank has seized hold of that cot, so you'll have to pick another one. Can I offer you a beer?"

"Sure, why not." Bec perched on the edge of a cot, leaned forward and held her hands out to the heater. "How did Arthur show up here?" Five men in here – Davy was as harmless as Arthur. That left it three-to-one.

Jason said, "Michael spotted him out in the edge of the trees, a lost forest soul. Tank took right to the drinking – I think it was new to him." Jason angled the bad side of his face away from her. He wouldn't be a problem.

Bec said, "Now, you all keep Arthur safe for me. He owns enough troubles." She rubbed her hands hard, flexed them out towards the hot metal. She sneaked a peak at Michael – their eyes met, shied away. "Cold night."

Kevin said, "Now might be the time to take up warm beer. I was deployed with a Brit company in Iraq, but I never developed a taste for their warm beer."

Kevin and Michael were the two to keep an eye on. She asked, "What were they like, the English?"

Kevin grinned. "Most of them were Scottish. Real self-contained,

177

kinda gloomy. Insane when they were on leave in the rear. Crazy mofos, if you don't mind my crudity."

Michael said, his voice like grit, "Don't talk about the war."

Kevin snapped back, "Nothing else to talk about."

She didn't have to worry about these two crowding her.

Jason broke in, spoke to the roof peak. "The English have depended on the Scots to fight their wars for centuries. If I were Scottish, I'd be sorrowful too."

Kevin motioned at Jason. "He's our military historian. Dude holds a perverse belief that the study of war will help you understand it.

Jason gazed at Kevin. "Maybe help us understand what we lived through. Pro'ly not though." His hand crept up and scratched at the scar tissue on his neck.

The C&W music played into the lull, mournful, oblivious to the thing that smoldered between Michael and Kevin.

With a jerk, Jason dug in a cooler. "I forgot your beer."

She popped the top – it foamed and she had to dip and slurp it in. It fizzed in her mouth, tried to burst back out. She gulped. "How long have you been out of the service, Jason?"

"Me, about nine months, after a couple of months in the Wounded Warrior Regiment – the shortest of all of us. Davy here was one of the first casualties from Iraq. Kevin and Michael both served in Afghanistan, out a couple of years now."

She leaned towards him; he twitched his bad side away. "And where were you when ...." Her hand rose to her cheek.

His one eye bored into her. "I wasn't forward deployed. I'm the exception of the four. I was assigned embassy duty in the Green Zone.... "

She asked, "But?"

"A car bomb in a market place caught me unawares."

Michael grunted. "Car bomb. Shit way to get it."

Jason said, "Bad luck – it was a Sunni out to kill Shiites."

Michael's mood scratched at her, dug away. He hung on the outside of the circle like a storm coming. She tried to catch his eye. "And how did you four end up here at the new center?"

They shot each other glances. Jason cleared his throat. "We thought you knew."

Kevin threw his arms out in a pantomime shrug. "Damn. Tony wanted to be the one to tell you."

"Tell me what?"

Kevin shot a glance around the tent, at the reluctant men. "Tony emailed your husband the Chaplain. He used the holy joe network and they recruited us. We're the lost souls the padres worry about."

She flushed. Left out of the loop again. Again. Damn it! "What do you mean, lost souls?"

Michael turned away, yet answered for them. "Mostly no family. Like me and Kevin. But Davy, his folks wanted to dump him in a home. They call it assisted living, but it was warehousing. Jason's story now, it's no happier."

Jason shuffled on the cot. "No need to go into that. This's supposed to be a party."

Something too raw to talk about. Some party. She sipped at the beer. The cold chased into her throat and clinched it shut. She choked on the swallow but refused to cough. She set the can between her feet. "I'm here because it's the cheapest place for me to live. Though I have to admit, the chain saw, the splitter, the gasoline – I hadn't factored those in. And I need to pay for a decent roof on the house."

Jason, ever the host, asked, "Do you regret it?"

A belch tickled at the back of her throat. Be damned if she'd let it slip out. "Not at all. Dallas was – well, Dallas. We lived there because of William's church, but it wasn't where I would choose. Here I wake up each morning and the mountain waits for me. Always the same, always different." They had stopped listening.

—⚶—

One of those evenings when drinkers become overheated. The vets argued, leaned into each other's faces, thumped each other's knees with their fists. Occasionally Kevin shouted, "Hoo-ah!" with Army boisterousness. Michael matched it with a quiet, contemptuous "Bullshit."

She nursed her second beer along. She should soon say goodnight.

In one of those blinks of time, the party flipped. Two vets leapt to their feet, nose to nose. Kevin and Michael, grimacing animals, were about to decide whether violence would sweep through the tent.

Bec jumped up, crowded in to slide between them. "Time for me to go."

Both men, focused on the other guy, ignored her. They watched for that tell-tale flicker around the eyes, or the dilation of the pupils – to know when the other was about to strike.

Do something, Bec! She tapped Kevin on his shoulder. "Kevin, I need to ask a favor. Can you guide Arthur back over the ridge, make sure he reaches his trailer? You're familiar with the path. Arthur widened it out; it'll be no trouble. Can you do that for me, Kevin?"

Kevin gave a bare nod. He interrogated Michael's face, his eyes.

Her hands trembled, her jaw hurt from tightness. She seized Michael's hand. His face frightened her. His lips drawn back, his irises black. Cords in his neck bulged out. "Michael, I need you to escort me home. Davy brought me over and you'll guide me back. Do you have a flashlight? Michael?" Her voice shook.

Like a switch was thrown, his face relaxed, turned blank. Both men's hands loosened from the spade shape of trained fighters into the dangled fingers of men backing out of a fight.

Kevin shifted his false hand up to his collarbone, but only to scratch. They all listened to the Country and Western in the background and waited. The radio sang out, "You don't have to call me darlin, Darlin."

180

Kevin swiveled away. He marched over to Arthur's cot, kicked the leg. "Tank. Tank, big boy. Time to go home."

Michael's grip hurt her knuckles. He hustled her out the door, dressed only in his shirt sleeves and shorts. "We don't need a flashlight – past moonrise – a half moon."

A cruel journey. He strode out so fast over the broken ground that she stumbled again and again. Then he fell. First a stubbed toe. He twisted sideways, hopped once. Flew into the air. He hit on his shoulder. His legs crashed to the ground and banged each other in a metallic rattle.

"Shit!" He rolled onto his back.

She dropped to her knees beside him. "Are you all right?"

"Just winded. I knocked the breath out of myself."

She started to speak: he held up a hand in the moonlight. "Give me a sec." He panted, "Three pivot points where these legs articulate and I never get it right. Son of a bitch!"

She waited.

In a moment, he rolled over on his stomach. "I'm like a goddamn turtle. The tough part is the scramble back onto my feet."

She touched his shoulder.

"No. Don't help me." His voice shredded in anger. He drew one knee up, scuffed the foot under to support himself, like a hurdler about to come off the blocks. His grunts carried over the faint sound of the tent's music. One leg thrusting, a lunge to plant the second foot.

She clutched his elbow, "Maybe we can walk slower from here on out."

"Good idea."

As they crossed the drive, he said, "You must think I'm a jerk. The fight and all. I can't even remember what Kev said."

"He could have hurt you with that steel hand."

"That wimp? I could have kicked him to death with my steel feet. Home safe, Miz Robertson. Sorry – you asked me to call you Bec."

181

She stepped onto the first tread, turned around to face him. He was taller than she, just the same. "Thank you, Michael." She lingered.

He shuffled that half step closer. "A good night kiss, Bec?"

His arm circled round her waist, his body leaned forward. As he dropped toward her, his beery breathe cascaded down. She shoved him hard, both hands against his chest. "Wait. I'm sorry. We can't do this."

He gripped her hips with his hands. She leaned back, away. He released her like throwing a fish back in the water. "Right." His voice filled with a growl. "Good night."

"Michael, I'm sorry. I didn't mean to…. " What, lead him on?

"No, it's only what I deserved. No sweat."

When he was halfway across the meadow, she came so close to crying out his name she frightened herself.

CHAPTER NINETEEN – GROPING

BEC HEADED NORTH TO THE ridge. Arthur would be confused by last night, by the drinking, the befuddlement. She should check on him – and escape the peril of Michael, at least for awhile. Her boots left a wake through wet grass, a low-relief S-shape of darkness where dew had shown silver before. The water weaseled in through the cracks of old leather, soaked into her socks, cold and clammy.

Arthur's animal trail had morphed into a path. As he had hiked it, he snapped off twigs, shifted deadfall aside. He had tended it with a handsaw, cut out saplings to straighten the way. The larger fallen trees still lay there to step over. But, everything one man could do to cut the thicket back and create a garden path, everything Arthur could do to create a byway for her had been done. A stalker mutated into family.

At the top, the basalts had abandoned remnant caps, slabs of congealed rock that held back the grass and trees. She clambered up one, careful not to scrape off any lichen. She plunked on her butt and faced towards her meadow. From above, the destruction of her paradise didn't strike her so viscerally.

One small dorm, after all, Bec. But only the beginning. Maybe if it works, if the dream comes true, carbon-copy dorms will eat up the space and crawl towards the cabin. Maybe they'll build a Rec Center, and an Admin Building. Maybe they'll fence you out.

And if the Center comes true, does your life up here die? That's your problem Bec. First you wanted to hide here on the mountain. The next moment you give Tony the pasture, free and clear, to fill with people. Now, your object of desire turns out to be a chewed-up soldier much younger than you. You've changed since Dallas.

Minute shooting prickles ran through her backside. The rock stuck up rough and unyielding under her skinny rump – she shifted around. Bec interviewed Rebecca. "Do I really want him? Does my heartbeat run faster when I'm close to him? Damn it, Rebecca. Get hold of yourself."

The sun shone hot on her face as she perched on the cap rock. She shrugged her way out of her fleece, folded it, and scooted it underneath her butt. "An infatuation. Chuma would say, either get it out of your system or pass on it, girl."

Why Michael? What shitty luck. It could have been one of the others. Kevin – sensible, sober. Ready to lead. Jason, shredded up and ashamed of the scarring.

"What a waste of energy, Bec. You're not shopping – you're not dating around. And you're married, though that doesn't turn out to stick."

Why Michael indeed. Because scars run through him. Darkness unconfessed. Like her anger towards William.

Two small birds flittered up, landed close by. They searched for insects in the holes of the rock, where the basalt had foamed up dwarfish air pockets as it cooled.

"More than that, you should be afraid, Bec. You've got the hots for him. He's given you that old tingle you haven't enjoyed in a long time. Want to open up to him? Take him in and not let him out?" One of the birds hopped over to her boot. She wagged her foot. Startled, it darted away, swept its mate with it.

She grinned, sardonic, continued aloud. "And what about your scars? Did you stop last night out of fidelity? Or because of the mastectomy? What if he thought you were disgusting? What if Michael couldn't bring himself to touch you? Couldn't understand you were a woman?"

God, how awful. The worst form of irony. Missing two legs and yet wanting a complete woman. Christ, to be humiliated again.

He's young. But he's signaled something wrong in his skull, back behind his eyes. You think you can save him from himself? Not through sex, not that way. Mixes it up with what you want yourself.

Bec, you're screwed.

She dropped a hand on the rock beside her, felt its sharp corrugations. She thrust herself up and, stooping to keep her balance, climbed down the stone. The path to Arthur's lay open, a devotion to friendship.

—⚏—

Arthur's trailer was probably older than he. She wondered, as she knocked on the door, which relative had provided it as the family dumped him out here on the mountain. Spartan or Roman. Abandon the damaged child to the wolves.

Behind the screen door, his delighted look opened his round face like peeling an orange.

"Arthur, I thought I would drop by and see if you were busy. Can I come in?"

He flung the screen door open, missed her by a couple of inches. "Yes, yes, please."

He rattled the kettle onto the range. She slid onto the bench and watched his broad back.

"Is it Wednesday already? I meant to buy a new tea for you, but I forgot. Is English Breakfast okay?"

So easy to be around. "Yes, it's fine, Arthur, and no, it's not Wednesday. Only Sunday.

"Sunday?"

"I dropped by on a whim." While on a fifteen-minute hike.

He set the tea in front of her, fetched a thirty-two ounce Pepsi from his fridge. "I'm glad you didn't come earlier. I just woke up."

"You had a late night last night."

He bobbed his round head. "My first party since I left the Home."

"How did you like it?"

He wiggled into the banquette seat. "The music was nice. They talked about war a lot. I don't know anything about war except what I see on TV."

"Do you like war movies?"

"Not much. I like animal movies. Last night was my first time to drink beer."

She grinned. "How did that go for you?"

His forehead wrinkled in a frown. "Not too good. The first one tasted bitter. The second one made me burp. And after a while, things turned all swimmy, and my tongue wouldn't say what I wanted. So I laid down to wait for the dizziness to go away."

"And this morning?"

"My mouth tasted all funny. I didn't have any spit."

She patted him on the back of the hand. "Promise me you'll remember what you just told me, the next time someone offers you a beer."

He creased his eyebrows into sad miniature tents, gazed at the formica. "You don't want me to drink?"

"I didn't say that. I just want you to remember what can happen."

He lit up. "Okay, I can do that. It wasn't much of a party though. No cake and no meal. Not like Wednesdays when you come here."

She chuckled, a bit smug. She reached across and patted his hand again. "Wednesdays can be pretty good."

"And I get to talk to you. Not about you."

She twitched her hand back. "What do you mean, about me?"

He gazed at the formica again. "I don't know."

"Yes, you do. We're friends and you brought it up, so you have to tell me."

He hemmed. "The guys talk about you. Not only at the party, but

186

other times too. Some of them think you're pretty and others – not so pretty. Davy says you don't eat enough."

"Who else?"

"Jason says you make him sad. He wishes there were no women around at all."

"And anyone else? Kevin?" She paused. "Michael?"

"They say you're hot. That means something besides hot and cold. Hot for an older woman, they say."

"Hot means they find me attractive. For an older woman."

"You're not so old. Are you?"

She rose half up. She leaned across the table, cradled his face in her hands and kissed his forehead. "Thank you, Arthur, for telling me."

—⁓—

Bec strode fast through the woods down Arthur's path, sometimes at a jog. Swerved around obstructions, jumped the logs. A pulse beat in her head – she played an old rock and roll song in her head, an ugly tune. Dirty Deeds. Punish herself. Panted to suck in more breath. She gasped out, "Kevin. Michael. Assholes, both of you. Weighed up like beef! Meat on the hoof, dollars per pound."

She careened into a gulch, hurtled down it, tumbled small rocks in front of her. "We'll fix you, soldier boys. We'll teach you who's in charge."

The branch caught her below her left eye, dug a trench in her skin towards her ear. Shocked, she skidded her boots in the forest floor and juddered to a halt on the slope. She slapped a hand on the wound, held that hand out in front of her. Her fingers were sticky red. The blood killed her anger. She fished in her pockets for a Kleenex. Her breath slowed to normal and a tremor ran through her frame. A hot acid tear coursed down her cheek into the red stained tissue. How bad could it be? Damn it, couldn't she catch a break?

Bec strode in through the grass to the back of the cabin. Two of them at the washtubs on her porch – Davy and Michael with the laundry. Water dripped off the boards. Bec stomped up the steps, angry at what would happen next. As their heads popped up, she pivoted away, hid the Kleenex soaked through, the bloodstain on her hand, the top of her sleeve banded in red. But she didn't fool them.

Michael strode one step toward her, pinched her chin with finger and thumb and with the other hand captured her wrist. He tugged her hand away. "Superficial, minor blood loss. Dirt in the wound of course. You'll need a few stitches."

All Marine. Evaluate, report, command. She jerked back. "It's my face. I don't want a scar."

Michael tilted her head, peered at the wound like inspecting a piece of jewelry, "Just like a woman."

That pissed her off. Davy hung over Michael's shoulder, edged around so he could peer at her face. "Pupils normal. No concussion." A soldier in there, inside that fog.

Michael leaned in close to scrutinize her wound. He hadn't shaved in a while. How hot his breath, like a heater between them. It smelled of sausage, and maybe jelly. "Tony's here so we have a car. We can drive you to urgent care or the hospital in Española, but by the time we arrive it will have spread apart and hardened. They'd have to scrub deep before they staple it back together. And you might already have an infection. If you'll trust me, I can stitch you up right away. No scar in a couple of months, I promise."

Her anger switched off. She nodded, bobbed down into the cup of his hand.

He asked, "Have a first aid kit, or should I grab ours?"

She said, "I own a farmer's kit, fully stocked. I've got antibiotics."

"Then it's a go." He even now held her chin – it hiked up her pulse. How ridiculous.

They broke off the stare – Davy waited close, half forgotten. Michael said, "Davy, you continue with the wash here. I'll take Bec into the kitchen and fix her up." Davy shot a glance at each of them, dropped his gaze to the porch boards. He gripped the clothes paddle.

Michael led the way, turned a chair sideways to the table. He edged her into it and asked, "Where's the first aid kit?"

She pointed at a cabinet, and he fished the kit out, slapped the cabinet door shut.

"Looks good for baby first aid. Nothing like a medic's trauma kit, but after all, this isn't a gunshot." He unpacked items across the table top. "I'll clean it first." He parked himself in front of her, tilted her head back. With gauze and alcohol, he worked the dried blood off her cheek and out of the cut.

It stung like hell. She grimaced with each stroke.

"Sorry. It's bleeding again, of course. Here's a topical anesthesia. Let's work some in." He squeezed white cream out of a tube, skimmed it across her skin and rubbed with tiny grazing gestures till it absorbed.

Better. Her view of him was surreal. She peered up the buttons of his work shirt to his face, all angular, his eyes a hot light blue. Fine wrinkles traced back from the corners of his eyes, frown marks cut out of his mouth.

"The kit's stocked with dissolving sutures, the very fine ones. I'll take five, and use butterflies in between them to keep everything tight. I'll pinch the edges snug, but I won't let them pucker."

"How do you know how to do this?"

He edged in between her knees, bumped them apart with his false legs. It wasn't enough he had tipped her head further back – he nudged it over to the right. "Bad angle for you. It'll probably crick your neck, but it's best for me. What did you ask?"

189

"How did you learn to sew people up?"

His sentences fractured as he concentrated. "Some basics in training. Also from our medic. Not in the field. A guy hit on recon... it's all...
gauze wads packed into the wounds. Tourniquets to... to stop bleed-out.
We did minor repairs like this back at the outpost where Ramon let me
sit in. Let me try my hand."

His fingers swept in with the needle. His delicate pinching thumb
and forefinger blocked her view of his face. His legs edged out, spread
her knees more. This close, she could smell the dust on him, like ozone.

"Here we go. You should sense a minor pressure, but not much else."

Her eye twitched in an uncontrollable tremble, a quick shudder of
blinks. She could indeed detect the poke, the needle go in, slide out, the
stitch tighten and bite. He didn't rush it.

She clutched his hip bones with both hands, steadied them, locked
the two of them into the same frame. Her neck ached from the tilt of her
head.

"Sweet pretty stitches. Only five. I'll snip off the extra thread close
to the skin." He twisted around to the table to fish out scissors. Her hand
dropped off his hip – she planted it back. "Here's the butterfly bandages
going on. I'll swab on some alcohol and we'll slap on a patch to keep the
wound clean."

He swabbed her cheek back to her ear, caressed her with gauze and
alcohol. Her skin prickled cold as the alcohol evaporated.

A quaver ran up her spine. "I want to inspect it. Before you cover it."

"You want to move to a mirror or do I bring one here?"

"A small one hangs on the wall in my bedroom." He turned to go
and tangled up in her leg. She raised it higher across his crotch to let
him out of the V of her body.

He said, "Don't trip the Doc."

The stitching. The same space shared by two bodies. Her mouth had
parched like a desert. Her senses so awake she was dizzy.

He toted the mirror back. "Now I've been in the inner sanctum. I expected more luxury."

"Doesn't matter what you expect. You're not likely to be in there again." Brave words.

He blew it off. "Watch this trick. The Doc knows how to squat." He dropped to her level. He held the mirror beside his face and angled it at her. "Pretty good, huh? Sometimes I fall over." Was he really unaffected by the closeness?

The gouge glowed livid, but the stitches were tight and the butterfly tape helped hide it. Her gaze switched from her image to him. She reached out and touched a white scar running below his Adam's apple. "Where did this come from?"

"Air tube insertion. Lying in a poppy field in Afghanistan."

She slipped her hand onto his knee, felt the heavy silicon beneath the jeans. "When you lost these?"

"No, another time." He glanced down at her hand, twitched his eyes up to hers.

She snatched her hand back. "Sorry." His pupils dilated, left only a narrow band of blue ringing the black.

He straightened, a broad tower once again. "Okay, time to seal her up." He ripped open a packet and slid out a bandage, two by three inches, sticky only around the edges. Careful not to press on the wound, he plastered it onto her cheek. "Done."

The bandage felt like it covered everything from her mouth to her eye. She said, "Thank you, Michael."

He towered above her. A simple gesture and she would be able to lay her face on his stomach. Instead, she said, "I really mean it – thank you. And Michael –" She sucked in a deep breath. "Stop talking about me to the guys like I'm your next one-night-stand."

She shoved the chair back, strode into her bedroom, and slammed the door. In control.

Summer 1984.

The roughness of the car seat pressed against sixteen-year-old Rebecca's arm, scraped her. Teddy Newhousen had installed horse-blanket seat covers – bound to leave waffle marks all across her bare skin. She lay with her head against the door; the handle poked into the back of her skull. She pressed her knees against the seat back, jammed together, so he couldn't lie on top of her, dry-humping himself on her jeans. He might believe he ran things, but she was in charge. He stretched out beside her, his face crowded into her neck. He groaned a bit.

His hand hung on her breast, a hand so large it covered the whole boob. He ground away at it, her nipple erect, tender. It flared to the pain – also the pleasure. Teddy groaned again and she slowed her kneading, the groping of her hand buried in the crotch of his jeans. Underneath her hand, the bulge pulsed – bent in half, it tried to point two directions at once. He was huge but short. She gave him a small twist and backed off. She didn't want it to end too soon.

He shifted beside her, wriggled his face deeper into the curve between neck and shoulder. His hand rubbed down, across her belly, to the top of her thighs. He attempted to wiggle his fingers into that space between, into the V her jeans protected. For one wild moment she wanted to relax her clamped knees, fly open to his clumsy groping. But she tightened all her leg muscles in refusal. She arched her neck and nibbled the top of his ear, before she bit down hard.

Chapter Twenty – Control

EARLY OCTOBER 2009.

On Thursday the skies played deception. At night snow showers hid the full moon but melted as they hit the warm ground. The day sailed virga after virga across the mountains and mesa tops – but the rains were phantoms. Sleet punctuated the morning, a small-time flourish of ill will.

Santa Eulalia appeared more crapulous than usual, dismal in fact. Bec whipped into the diagonal parking in front of the café too fast and thumped the curbing. She jumped out with her laptop and dashed in, spattered by a moment's fleeting hail.

Chuma loitered just inside and gazed out the window at the bedraggled view. "Damn, Bec. I wasn't sure you were going to stop. Neither one of us can afford to replace this storefront."

"I did stop, didn't I?"

"What's eating you?"

"Men's shit attitudes. This damn wound on my face. And I need to talk to William. Duty call."

"Hey white girl. You going to be this irritable, you can use my office in back."

"You mean your supply room with a desk. Thanks." She wove her way back through the kitchen to a Sheetrock cubicle nestled against the bathroom. She opened the laptop, dialed up Skype.

A chime and his face popped in. "Hey, Rebecca. I was waiting for your – what's that on your face?"

"That's where a tree jumped out of nowhere and stabbed me. One of your veterans stitched me up."

"Is it bad?"

She twitched her head no.

"So there are some benefits to having the Army around."

"Marines actually. And let's wait to find out if I contract tetanus before we rejoice."

William leaned back from the screen, held both palms up. "Somebody's experiencing a bad day."

Screw you, William. "Tchaa."

"Okay, this isn't going well. I'll make small talk for a while and then we'll check where we are."

Where "we" are? Don't even fake a smile. "That's our deal. You tell me about your week. I tell you about mine. After that we almost talk about the marriage. Okay, over to you."

Cautious. He came across as cautious and happy, not angry with her mood. "Hmm. Where to begin? You know I've been stuck in the Forward Operating Base?"

"Yeees." Where did this lead?

He grinned so hard his cheeks jacked up under his eyes, scrunched them. "That changed a couple of weeks ago. I racked up enough brownie points to do what I want. Now I ride out to the combat outposts in the convoys, talk to the guys on the front line."

She sucked her lip. "Jeez, William. Maybe it's the right thing to do, but it's not something I feel great about."

"Don't worry so much. I'm in a twenty-ton armored track. The bombs can wipe out the road, but not me."

"Are you sure?"

"Of course. Safe as houses. And I have a captive audience. The

194

guys can't send me back until they unload the meals and the ammo."

Okay, some better. "Sorry. Didn't mean to be negative. Tell me about it." She couldn't help but care, a little.

"Some of these patrol bases have a full platoon in them and some are tiny and have a squad – that's twelve riflemen. Plus other support."

"What are these combat posts like?" Reassure me, big guy. Tell me how safe.

"I rode back in from a COP yesterday. It's an old compound built by a bunch of poppy growers. They were evicted when the Taliban showed up. After the Taliban faded into the villages, we appropriated it."

"Handy."

"The walls are mud, but they're two foot thick and ten feet high. High because thievery is a problem here, even if you're a dope king. The guys sleep in rooms constructed the same way, stuck against the outside wall, maybe four grunts in a ten by ten space. You'll like this part. The team installed machine guns at the four corners, surrounded by bullet-proof glass."

"Wow, sounds like Fort Apache." She felt better in spite of herself.

"Works out great except for RPGs."

"RPGs? Rockets?"

"Grenades launched off a rifle. All that means is we have to wear body armor and the helmets at all times. More or less." His face was dark brown, his forehead a slash of white.

"I don't like it you're on the front line."

"But, Rebecca, it's only ten miles away or so. And that's where I'm needed the most. I'll be careful, I promise."

She snickered at the ridiculous promise. Fooling himself. "William, you were right. My bad day doesn't look to be very bad, or important."

"I might do a patrol or two. I was shot at yesterday – it gave me a huge rush."

"What!" She grabbed the laptop screen as if she would shake his image.

"Guess I shouldn't have blabbed that part. I was just outside the compound's gate. Some of our guys were taking harassing fire out two fields from us. Spent rounds from the natives zipped over my way. Like geysers of dirt. No biggee. But it gave me a taste of what my flock faces all the time." His face was blockier, his jaw more prominent.

"William."

"Yes?"

"Stop having such a good time. It's not a game." Like a kid. Where did this irresponsibility come from?

"Yes, dear."

She flared. "And don't use that tone of voice with me." Was all this adventurism because they were fighting about the marriage?

He held both hands in front of his face, to block her glaring eyes. "Whoo. Change of subject. Why don't you tell me how your recuperation center is coming along?"

She inhaled. What to tell, the truth? That she and Michael swayed perilously on a tightrope? No. "Tony does a wonderful job scavenging materials and tools – he wants to save all the grant money to operate the place once it opens. And my four vets I told you about, they're good guys overall."

"Do you bump into them much?"

"We have dinner at the cabin every Friday night. One big happy family, and you're picking up the tab for it." His mouth crooked over into a lopsided grimace. Now he'll ask what he believes is a tough question. She knew him so well.

"I'm guessing you had reservations. Turning your mother's place over to a charity. Losing some of your privacy. What are your impressions about it now?"

"I feel like I'm talking to my shrink."

"Or your husband."

Irritating. Patronizing. The more he talked, the less she felt married.

196

"Privacy flew out the window awhile back, William, when they built their camp. We do the guys' laundry at the cabin. Men's underwear hangs from the porch to the barn. I park out on the porch in the evening and listen to their music, and most times someone will stroll over to visit. Thank God Tony and Emmet live in town, otherwise the cabin would feel more like the café."

"But the Center. That's what you want?"

What did she want? She glanced at her hands flanking the keyboard, raised her eyes to the camera. "I want someone who can love me." God, she had dropped right to it.

He shifted back and forth, contemplated something off camera. "I love you, Rebecca. It's.... " He cleared his throat. "I'm working on it."

"Are you really? Sounds like you're running all over playing Cowboys and Indians." Even to herself she sounded mean, petty.

"That's not fair. It's my job."

"What do you want, William?" Does he even know?

"I want to be happy, not miserable." A four-count, while they peered at each other's Skype image. She could hear a spatula banging on the grill, a creaking in the ceiling, a dripping tap through the open bathroom door close to her. She could smell cinnamon, and the velvet of hot grease.

He said, "Listen, I need to go. A new squad that just deployed to the Sandbox is here for a day in transit and I want to eat with them in the mess."

"William, be careful. It's not your job to get shot at."

Exasperated – he finally was irritated with her. "Yeah, okay."

"Go talk to your squad. The mess hall must be safe."

"Rebecca, I love you."

She sighed. "I wish you did, William." That was the problem, wasn't it? She gave him no chance and slammed the laptop shut. Marched back to the café's dining room.

—⁓—

The café mostly displayed two conditions, packed and empty. Now the lunch crowd had disappeared. Bec gazed over the stark space, filled with mismatched tables, with white walls scarred by chair backs, and wondered how this echoing place could feel so warm and inviting. Must be the gray sleet that sifted down outside.

At the back table, Chuma peeled potatoes over one bowl and dumped the white spuds in another. Her ample bosom splayed itself across the tabletop and her apron exhibited grease stains. Chuma washed that apron on Monday when the café was closed, whether it needed it or not.

Bec slid into the chair opposite her friend. "It's okay, Chuma. I'm in a better mood. Or at least I'm not so wound up."

"You were shit-storm scary ten minutes ago." Chuma's peeler swiped four, six, twelve times and another potato dropped into the bowl. "Armed and dangerous. How's the husband?"

"Doing okay. Doing things I don't like, cozying up to the war. But it's what he wants."

"Little boys play soldier. Sometimes they grow up, sometimes they don't."

Maybe William wasn't really immature – maybe he was right and the job required all the showing off.

Chuma dug out a potato eye with the peeler tip, peered at it. "And how's Michael?"

"Michael?"

"The new boyfriend. The one you drop hints about."

Bec shot her a glance. "No boyfriend, Chuma. Michael's just one of the guys. I'll keep it that way."

Chuma snorted. "Your brain may say that, but what does your body say?"

"Could we please get less pressure from someone who is, after all, a man-hater."

Chuma shifted her weight, avoided Bec's gaze. "Umm. I ought to explain something. Before you hear it from anyone else."

"Sounds ominous. What?"

"God, I hate to confess this, especially to you. Emmet and I are kind of seeing each other."

Bec's mouth flapped open. "Emmet?"

"Don't sound like that. He cleans up pretty nice. He's been bathing regular and he bought some new clothes at the thrift store."

"Emmet?"

"And I forced him to throw away that ratty old sports coat with all the holes."

"You said kind of seeing each other."

"Mostly we talk, here in the café. But he's making noise about a real date, where we go to Abiquiu to the restaurant on the river and have dinner. Of course, I'll have to drive. And maybe loan him the money."

"Is this serious?"

"Might be. It is for him – he's slowed his drinking way down."

"I'll be damned. Chuma, I'm so pleased for you!"

"I don't know, Bec. I'm still doubtful. At my age, men look for a nurse or a purse. Despite that, he's a lovable old dog. If he only owned more teeth."

"I hope for the best for you." Bec patted her arm.

The bell on the door jangled. Chuma shoved her chair back with a grating reverberation and let her bosoms swing free. "A customer or two have snuck in. If you wanted to peel potatoes till I get back, it wouldn't hurt my feelings any."

Bec chuckled, and Chuma left her at the table. Chuma and Emmet. Was Bec the only celibate in town? Was she the only one who couldn't get her life under control?

CHAPTER TWENTY-ONE – QUIET

MID OCTOBER 2009.

Aloofness didn't work. Instead, Bec's body tormented her first thing in the morning. This running fire must be proof she had beat the cancer. As bad as when she had been seventeen and out of control.

She hadn't had sex since the mastectomy. At first, the steroids drove her crazy and the anticoagulants left her so vulnerable she feared to touch anything. When her desire for intimacy returned, she couldn't find William. Not her William. She had lost him across the world, into the war. She had lost him in that bed in Dubrovnik.

But these new hormones didn't just signal a desire for intimacy. They unsettled, demanded, thrust her in directions she didn't want to go. They flooded through hazy daydreams as she lay in a warm bed – transformed the simplest image into a pornographic catalogue, a full gallery of body parts, of touch, of shining metal legs.

"Ahhh!" She slung her pillow across the room, knocked things left and right off the dresser. "Shit! What is wrong with me! I liked it better when the drugs forced me to pee all the time." At least that gave her something practical to do first thing in the morning.

She jumped out of bed and filled the tank above the shower from the boiler. She jumped under the water, soaped and rinsed as fast as she could. A skill learned in childhood with more people here sharing the water. A pause, under the spray. Massaged by the mild stream of hot water, she allowed the erotic daydream to slip back in. She gazed at herself, craned her head around. Like she would shop for a sofa, she surveyed her body. For forty-two, it was more than okay. The legs tight, no flab. She'd always believed her knees bony, and her feet. Too bad the feet were long and thin, and the toes so prehensile. She twisted about, to catch the curve from her waist into her still-charming ass. No poochy tummy, rib cage just visible. Here lived the issue, above. She traced the scars, white against her pink flesh, with a fingertip. She placed her hands flat, where her skin covered only her pectoral muscles. What was she now, without a woman's breasts? A boy's chest, underdeveloped musculature and no hair. A hermaphrodite with scars. Because she was afraid of the knife. And angry at William. Because she owned the scars.

"Truth is, as long as you don't have tits, Bec, you can keep everyone at arm's length. Including Michael."

Coward. She slammed the shower off, dried herself with furious scrubbing. In her bedroom she jerked on panties, jeans, socks, shoes. With her flannel shirt in hand, she bolted for the door. As she shrugged her arms into it, she threw open the door. Plummeted down the steps. She charged down the road towards the Vet camp.

A careening zigzag past the piles of scrap, the chop saw station, the stacks of OSB. As she reached the tent, the flap swung back and Jason ducked out into the sunshine.

"Where's Michael? I need to talk to him."

Jason turned the good side of his face towards her. "Sorry, Miss Bec. He headed out to Tierra Amarilla with Tony. They'll haul back a dozen windows someone has gifted to us."

She turned her back on him, poised with her shoulders working and her breath a rasp. Of all the times for Michael to be away. She looked like a fool. And she might cry. "Double God damn it!" With four steps forward, she threw her foot against a sheet of plywood resting on two sawhorses. She kicked it over and stomped off across the pasture to hide in her cabin.

At noon, Bec glanced out the front window and spotted Jason on the porch. He waited as still as ice, humpbacked with his hands curled around the porch lip. She whipped back and forth in the living room, as fast as her thoughts. Why was he here? How long had he been perched there?

She eased the door open, waited behind the screen. She didn't breathe, for fear of making a noise. Reluctant to begin.

He didn't turn his head. "I brought you a ham sandwich."

She said nothing.

"Maybe we can sit here and have lunch."

She said, "Would you like some ice tea?"

He gazed out across the pasture. "Sure." Across the way on the meadow edge, the aspens showed off pitiful remnants of their golden blaze. Winter's dominion crept in on them.

"I could slice a tomato." She felt displaced, as if a dizzy spell assailed her.

"That would be nice."

She brought it out on a tray: two teas, a plate with tomato and pickles. She set it between them, eased to the boards beside him. She glanced at him – on the wrong side, the side with a sagging tattered eyelid and all the scar tissue. Leaned on her hand, dragged a foot up under her to stand.

He said, "That's okay. You've stared at it before. I don't mind if you don't."

But of course he did mind. "You want to tell me about it?"

"Not why I hiked over here."

"What can it hurt?"

"I already said how it came to be. Nothing more to say, beyond I didn't die and others did."

"No. I meant... I meant her."

He spoke only after consideration and after he twisted around so he could see her. "I guess I might have intended to speak of her. Sooner or later."

Bec bowed her head, determined. "Why not sooner? Today."

He remained mute.

They both stripped off Saran wrap from around their sandwiches. Bit in and chewed. Bec reached down between them and held out the plate with the pickles, the tomato.

His head twitched around to her so he could catch sight of it, and he reached for a pickle. "She visited me early, once in the MTF – that's a hospital – and then when I hit the Battalion at Quantico. I knew I wasn't going back to a regular unit, but it gave me two months to transition and to apply for my discharge. Back then I wore a lot of bandage which hid the worst, but she was quiet."

"Bound to have been a shock to her too."

"When I came home – it wasn't her fault. She... couldn't bear it. She forced herself, for a week. Better when we lay in the dark, in the bed, because she could pretend it was before. But the sun rose each day and I'd be lying beside her, with my wrecked face. She tried not to draw back."

Bec shook her head. She reached up to her own chest. "She'd eventually get used to it."

"No – no, I don't think so. I'd walk into the room and she'd flinch like I had slapped her. I could hardly abide watching her suffer that way and know I caused it."

Bec reached out and clasped his hand. No counselor should ever do that.

Jason twitched his hand out from under hers. "No, best not."

"Why not?" Because it demonstrated pity.

"You're nice. Maybe nicer than her. But it's a reminder."

That was a grievous tragedy.

"At any rate, the marriage was all burnt to ashes within a week, the last five years lost. She packed and left a note. It was laying on the kitchen counter when I stumbled back in from physical therapy."

Bec cleared her throat. "What happened?"

"Why, I tried to kill myself. Messed that up too. My brother discovered me before I died."

"Jason, you're a good man. You say your face is wrecked, but you're not."

"Feels like it."

"You've been the nicest to me of all, and I appreciate it. I want to be your friend, if you'd let me."

His turn to be silent.

"It won't always be this bad."

He said, "I know. Now when I shave, I don't even see myself in the mirror. I'm only aware when I meet someone new. Strangers drop that remembrance on me – the acknowledgment of what a strip mine of a face it is."

"Is that why you haven't talked to me?"

"Yes. No. It's more complicated than that. I'm just not ready for polite company."

Bec bit her lip. "Okay. I won't push. When you want to talk, I'll be around. Not all women will flinch – least of all me."

He dropped his head. "That would be nice to believe."

"I have scars too. Not inside, but real physical disfigurement."

His head jerked up.

"Take my word for it."

They ate, but the bread and meat tasted like chalk in her mouth. After a decent interval, he grunted his way onto his feet. He wheeled around to face her, his body at attention. "Anyway, what I marched over here to say needs to be heard. There'll be a day when you and Michael – when things aren't right. You'll need help. If I'm here – when that

204

happens, you can count on me to do what needs doing. Big or small. You just have to ask."

Great. Emmet, Chuma, now Jason. All these people protecting her from Michael, acting out some big-brother-big sister thing. She didn't need protecting, did she?

She could handle it.

—⟋⟍⟋—

Fall 1979.

Phys Ed was the worst part of school. Eleven-year-old Rebecca hovered in front of the locker, jiggled the lock. She couldn't lie to Mrs. Dravitch again, say that she had forgotten the combination. Dravitch had it written down in her desk. She creaked the door open, fumbled at the buttons on her shirt. She wore a heavy wool shirt and sweated into it. The dampness caused the bandages to itch. She thrust the shirt into the locker bottom. She snatched a T-shirt out of the rackety metal bin at the top and whipped around, turned her back into the locker. Her fingers skittered over the camisole front, but she didn't slip it off. Instead she dragged the T-shirt on over it. An extra layer might keep the bandages from showing, block the seepage from staining the cotton where every-one would spot it. Not for them to know. Pa said he was sorry. And it had been her fault, mostly.

Followed by the crush at the door, the whistle shrieking. All the girls elbowed, jostled their way through. Some of them her friends. Some who sneered at her – the wrong church, the run-down house in the country. Today they'd play dodgeball. She was small, hard to hit, quick. And she had a power arm. For once she'd be chosen early for a team. As long as the bandages didn't show and the secret didn't emerge. She could do what needed doing.

—⟋⟍⟋—

Late October 2009.

Bec waited behind the screen door. Michael snapped to parade rest on the other side. She forced him into the first words.

"The guys told me you were looking for me." With that face, flawed only by a nose once broken, he was classic beauty. "They said you were pretty scary. Poor Jason may need crisis counseling."

A nod to barely acknowledge what he said.

"They warned me to inform my next of kin before I tramped over here." He shrugged. "Like my sister would care."

She edged the screen part open. "Since you had the courage to climb up on this porch, you better come in." She led the way into the kitchen. His metal feet thumped behind her. Hid them in boots – nonetheless they sounded different.

She plunked herself into the chair and he hauled out the seat opposite. Hands planted at the table edge, ready to thrust away. "Am I in trouble?"

Her anger kicked in. "Who are you? I don't know who the hell you are."

"I'm a guy with tin legs. Goddamn expensive legs, but tin."

"Cheap answer, Michael. You can't slide by with something that trivial."

He gazed at her. His forehead wrinkled, his mouth twitched into a frown. "Okay." He tipped his head. "Why do you want to know?"

"You're in my head, ever since you started buzzing around like a bee prowling for a flower. You've upset my equilibrium."

"Upset your equilibrium. Sounds like big vocabulary to duck what's real."

She slapped both hands on the table. "Why are you so difficult?"

His teeth flickered white, vanished. "I don't tell my story easy."

"You could tell it to me." He could let her in.

He twitched his head, "So far only Marines have heard it – and most of them are dead."

"Tell me." If he did, she had a chance. At what?

206

"Why are we even talking about this?"

"Because you irritate me and attract me, and I don't know why. It must have to do with who you are." She studied him. Gears were turning in there – would they close or open the barriers?

He held out his hand, placed it palm up on the table. The fingers curled, waited. She nestled her hand in his. He grasped her hand with both his, locked down on it. He squeezed too tight – it hurt.

He leaned over her hand and avoided her eyes. "I'm the worst thing that could happen to you. I've always been so fucked up, I didn't know what life was. But I know death." He shoved her hand away. Backed off, his face white under the tan.

"Keep going." Death. For the first time, she felt afraid.

Now he slid far away, stared out the window. His voice grated. "My whole life is a track of death. The Corps gave that trail some meaning, but I held on to the stink of death. Even now I smell it."

"I don't know what you mean."

A flat voice, devoid of humanity. "When I was ten. My parents were farmers, like yours. We all worked, most hours of the day, but still I was a kid. My brother and I were playing, in the loft. He and my sister, they were twins, a year younger than me.... "

What's this got to do with Death?

"My younger brother and me were rough-housing. He shoved me, I shoved him – out the loft door. He fell on the empty hay trailer. Two-by-fours stuck up, all around, to keep the hay bales from falling off. One of the stakes pounded up through his body, ripped out his guts. It must have hit him like a cannon ball. He bled to death before I could bring my father from the house."

"Jesus Christ!"

Not even his voice anymore, something mechanical. His jaw muscles like strings of knots beneath the skin. "He died alone, can you believe it?" A long pause. "But we all die alone."

He knotted his fists on the table. Some dam cracked open behind the quiet face. "And that's not all of it. In high school we all owned cars, we were all wild. We played chicken. We felt really alive, you know."

"And you were in a crash?"

"I drove off the road and piled into a tree. My best friend was in the passenger seat. He flew through the windshield. I couldn't even recognize him, afterwards."

"But those were both accidents. You didn't mean to kill them."

"Most Marines believe in luck, and in luck running out. I never had luck. The people around me didn't either. But the Corps saved me from the hole I was in."

"Didn't anybody help you after the car crash?"

"No. I bought all the pot and amphetamines I could lay my hands on. I jumped on big risks, all the time. Idiot stunts where I might die. But the Marine recruiters showed up."

"I'm glad the Corps was there for you." Christ, that sounded weak, patronizing even. She didn't know what else to say.

He ignored her. He peered at the ceiling. "I deployed as soon as I could arrange it. We call it 'going hot.' Dying is hot, not cold. From the beginning, the war outside was like the inside. Friends died. They die every tour, and it's hard but we all expect it. It couldn't be my fault. The war swallowed up my death track and it wasn't mine anymore."

She clasped his hands in hers and squeezed them.

He nailed her with a cold knife-like glare. Cruelty. He meant to hurt her.

"Other people were scared shitless of the IEDs. I waited for one, ready to be grateful. They can be big, you know, some bombs. They can throw a truck off the road. I've been close by once when one that big was triggered. The concussion makes your brain swell. You see double. You puke for days."

Ignoring her, talking to himself. As if she weren't in the room, not even a witness.

"The rag-heads shot me twice. Once a through-and-through in the thigh, once a rip in my neck here." He touched his neck under his ear. "All that blood in my throat – I reckoned I would drown. The medic saved me with a trach job. So I had to wait for my bomb. Turned out to be a small one. I stepped on the right spot at a canal edge. The IED blew me into the field, left shrapnel all through my torso and my left arm. And made my legs disappear."

She cried, slow, without sobbing. That was bad. It meant she loved him. "But they saved you. And you have legs now."

He glanced at her again, a sneer on his face. "I should have stayed in, worked hard enough to return to combat, at least into an FOB as support." He stopped dead. "I could have copped myself another bomb." His voice – a coldness. Or a strange anger.

"Oh God, Michael. Have you talked to anyone about this?" She ached – a pain in her chest like a hot stone. Snot was muddying her nostrils – she swabbed it with the back of her hand.

"Besides you?" He snorted. "You wanted to know who the hell I was. Not the bargain you expected, I bet."

Like a kick in the stomach.

"Listen, I'm not used to this confession shit. I'm leaving now. You think about all this, decide what you want to do." He hoisted himself to his feet. A blond man, with a blond stubble, light blue eyes – the darkest thing she had ever seen.

The screen door slammed. This was as bad as the cancer. She'd chosen wrong again.

—ɯ—

Chuma's cubbyhole in back, near the deep-fat frier. It popped, hissed, threw out that breeze of hot oil stink. The desk – too cluttered to hold her PC. She held the laptop on her knees, the laptop lid unfolded as far as it could go. She gazed down into William's face. His cheekbones stood proud – he must have lost weight.

They had talked for fifteen minutes. Felt like an hour.

She hunched over the screen, like gaping down a well, and his face shone up through the distance. Her resolve faltered, but she plunged on. "William, listen. I have something more, something not about us."

"Hmm." He probably hated her surprises.

"I need your advice, as a chaplain. You know what war does to people. Something I need to understand."

He flared his eyes, dropped his mouth open. "You're considering divorcing me and you want me to give you advice? You're kidding."

"Who else would I ask about soldiers."

"Maybe you should ask other soldiers. Besides me."

She'd considered that. Kevin. Tony. Jason. "Won't work. Please, William."

A shake, a tremble of his head. He flipped the switch in his brain, turned on the professional, turned off the husband. Earnest attention, dedication. "Okay. What war does to you. Nobody understands what the war does, even the soldiers. Nobody has been able to write it down, because it doesn't have words. Not true words."

"One of the men here thinks he carries only death inside. He believes the people around him die."

He said, "Which guy? Or don't you want to say?"

"It's Michael. The marine with no legs."

"I never met him. He was nominated by another chaplain."

"But have you run across this belief before?"

He tipped his head. This was the pastor they had all loved in Dallas. "Some of the guys on the line, they turn too quiet and you figure – they've forgotten how to live. They only have the killing. Is that what you mean?"

She held the screen edges in her hands, their old gesture. "Not really. This man, he believes either he.... I don't know, it's twisted. He thinks he actually causes death to his friends and his family. He

210

also thinks his bad luck murders the people around him. But not him."

William scratched his blocky face. She picked out a couple days of stubble, silver in the lamplight. "Like a Jonah?"

From the swivel chair, she could study Chuma out in the kitchen throwing hamburger patties on the grill. "More like a carrier of death."

His mouth pursed, lengthened out into a frown. "All kinds of possibilities, and probably no single answer. This sounds very serious."

"Feels serious to me too."

"Your man could be suicidal, or dangerous to people around him."

That was what she didn't want to hear. "What can I do?"

His mouth drew taut, certain. "Check him into the VA in Albuquerque. Get him some real help."

"Yes. I'm way out of my depth here." If you only knew.

"Welcome to my world." They both gazed at each other.

"I guess this is my first test, if I'm to manage this center. It'll get easier." That was a lie, but she trolled it by anyway.

"I think each crisis will help prepare you for the next one. God doesn't ask you to do things you can't do."

Horse shit. She didn't believe that, but she kept quiet. She'd kept her secret for a long time.

CHAPTER TWENTY-TWO – OTHER PLANET

November 1, 2009.

Bec stopped the truck at the edge of her road and the dirt highway, in the shadow of the spruces and corkbark fir. Winter already swept in on them. The road led left or right – to turn right would carry her into the wilderness. She dreamed of the lushness of summer in the back country. A summer day on the mountain, clear up on Mogote Ridge – a gift so intense, it was like her momma's hug. A bottle of water, a tank of gas, all she needed. She would have been happy to turn right. But not in November.

To the left, the swale and the dip down a switchback into Santa Eulalia. The pokey outbuildings, the metal-roofed houses, the battered trucks and cars, the house trailers scattered. Fences to keep in cattle and block out neighbors laced the hills, clotted in dead yellow grass and weeds. Dirt roads like brown scars. She knew. "We deface the thing that brought us here. The place we live, our land, our love, cluttered by our possessions, our failure, till we're just another ugly town."

Which way? The wheels bumped onto the dirt highway, all of their own accord. The tires' hissing carried through floorboards. She let the truck coast and loop down the road on gravity's string. On the way, she passed Tony and Michael as they climbed out of the village in the battered Nissan. Her whole frame gave a wrench, her shoulders a shudder.

Through the Village and towards the Rio Chama. She drove into

Santa Fe, to the lawyer, to finalize the papers. What her mother should have done.

—⁓—

Summer, 1978.

Ten-year-old Rebecca wanted the summer so bad it burned inside her, smoldered away all year long. For six years she and her momma had fit themselves into whatever truck her father allowed them, slammed the doors and closed him out like a bad dream, traveled the hours to reach the New Mexico cabin. They clambered out of the truck – she ran up the steps. Stiff and tired, her mother shuffled behind her into the cabin.

And the cabin came stocked with cousins, who were friends by nature. By choice too. More friends than she had back in Texas for sure. Her best friend was named Nina, a red-headed girl whose father was Rebecca's grandma's sister's son. At least that's what Rebecca supposed she understood. Nina's father was called Cousin Rafe.

Nina and Rebecca lay in the barn loft, stretched out on an old canvas tarp head-to-head. The thin abandoned hay strewn beneath the tarp had decayed soft and gray, but it kept their sharp knees and elbows from bruises on the hard boards.

They had been whispering to each other. Nina was full of stories of her school, of the teacher she admired. Rebecca believed it sounded like a crush. She didn't have anything exciting to tell, so she lied about a boy named Joey.

Nina's eyes shone as vast white circles, with blue in the center. Rebecca gazed into them as she said, "And he kissed me."

Nina whispered, hoarse, "Really?"

Face to face like this but upside down, Nina appeared magical, alien to Rebecca, her mouth in a frown when she smiled, her eyebrows inverted. Rebecca laced her fingers into the fingers of her friend. Locked together. "No. Not really. I made it all up. Nothing good ever happens to me."

Nina reached out her free hand and traced Rebecca's lips. She whispered, "Your mouth looks funny, upside down. Your front teeth are your giant bottom teeth."

Rebecca giggled. "No funnier than yours." They drifted closer, their heads a brushing whisper on the old canvas.

Just as they touched lips, the barn door creaked its sorrowful moan and light swung into the rafters. Rebecca jerked back. "Shh."

Her momma's voice. "Shut the door, quick."

A murmur, a man's voice, low, deep.

"No," said Bec's mother. "I don't think anyone spotted us."

"Back here. In one of the old stalls."

The two girls hid their mouths with their hands, breathed so shallow they hardly breathed at all.

A rustle, and a plastic tarp bunching up. Rebecca's momma said, "Hurry. It's been so long."

The tarp crackled, a grunt, a brushing sound, a sigh. Bec's mother trembled out a long "oh," a whimper.

The deep voice said, "So good." He groaned, as if he were hurt. Next, a slow rhythm, a strange beat Rebecca had never heard before.

Nina eased up on one elbow, leaned down into Bec's ear. Nina's heavy hair trailed across Bec's face, like smooth cloth. "That's my daddy. And your momma."

—⁂—

November 2, 2009.

Wrapping it up with William. Once the envelope of dry legal language was eased into her hand, she had to talk to him right away. To share and diminish the violence the law's words would do to them. To shift it somewhere else. Not her fault.

After swinging by the Santa Eulalia Post Office, she dialed up the war from the diner, expected an instant answer.

214

War was the same now as with Napoleon. Some minor changes. IEDs had replaced artillery fire, and men survived, though maimed, where they would have died on the field two-hundred years before. But war stayed loyal to its foundations. The infantry fought, the infantry died.

What had changed was the surreal communication between the war zone and the peaceful, anesthetized country that financed the war. But when the links were severed, families boiled into anxiety.

Skype didn't answer. His last email was three days old, and her message was unanswered. She emailed two of his Army friends, typed out the words, "Have him call me. Tell him I'll wait in the café." She slumped in the diner's corner, in a waft of bacon and beans, raw onion and garlic. She tried not to catch people's eyes, fluttered a feeble wave when they forced a greeting.

Skype chimed.

William yawned, a gate-mouth open like a trap. A bare bulb blazed behind him, turned him into a grayish silhouette. Of course – very late on the other side of the world. "What is it, Rebecca? Something wrong?"

"I have to wrap up something with you. Hold on while I lock myself away in Chuma's office." She charged off across the room, dumped the laptop on the desk.

"What's this about about, baby?" A touch late to "baby" her.

"Where the hell have you been?"

"Just back. Most COPs don't have Internet. And I can't tell you when or where we patrol."

She hummed out a tiny answer, a chord of disapproval.

"I'm sorry I worried you."

Worried her? No, slowed her down. "I collected the papers. I mailed them today. You need to sign them and send them back." Just blurted it out – her voice sounded high, anxious to her.

He didn't ask what papers. He expected this. "Are you sure?"

"No more talk. We've talked until I'm sick of it and nothing has changed."

His face hid in the shadow. Unreadable. "I don't want this."

"But you don't mind it all that much. You have your new career, and I've become a complete bitch."

He toted his laptop over to a cot. The light shone on him and she could set eyes on his face. His eyes were fogged, disguised with tears.

"William, it's for the best. I'm dead to you."

A long tear snaked out of his eye, ran down his face to his lip and into the edge of his mouth. "You'd divorce a man in a war zone, thousands of miles away."

"I didn't claim I was a good person."

"I can't believe you have no regrets. This – this, I can't – Give me a minute, I'll call back." He eased the laptop lid shut, the way he would close a casket.

He ate up five minutes before he called. His eyes were lined in red. "I'll wait for the papers. I'm not saying I'll sign them. I have to pray hard about it."

She felt like a major shit. She brushed her fingers across the screen, knowing the camera above the glass couldn't detect her gesture.

He shook his head like a dog slings off water. "We've come this far, only to have you break us up."

Skype froze, turned him in to a nest of pixels. When it cleared, his face appeared calmer, set, as if he had decided to tough it out. He said, "Several days for the post to arrive here. I'm sure we'll talk before that." He made no move to end the call.

This false togetherness, a video call across two worlds, two foreign places linked by some hypothesis of image and sound. "I didn't mean to call so late. I was upset and I forgot to count the hours. So it's nearly three there?" Why wasn't she letting go? Why didn't she hang up?

"It's okay. We're not out of the FOB till day after tomorrow; plenty of

216

time to rest up. Besides, you should call anytime and if I'm here, we'll talk. I want you in my life, even if you don't reciprocate."

One of them needy, one cold. "Thanks, for helping me on my crazy veteran last week."

William leaned in close to his camera. It bloated his nose, a giant out-of-focus ball. "Even if you dump me, we're partners in this project, the Retreat. The vets, they're bigger than either of us. I pick them and ship them out to you. You fix them up and send them back – to the Service, or to their families. Partners again."

"Partners again?" What the hell was he talking about?

"Maybe that's the way we can, you know, get back together, the way we were."

God. "False hope, William. We're who we are, and we can't escape that." Even now, she was too hard on him. Even now, Michael's specter was in the room.

—⁓—

November 14, 2009

Saturday's dawn went missing in a white, lacerating wind. A wind that scooped up the scant snow and hurtled it forward like a charge of frozen ghosts. December should have owned this storm, not November. The previous weeks of Indian Summer were scrubbed away by moaning wind.

As if fear and longing for Michael wasn't enough, Bec had to manufacture another panic – the dorm wouldn't finish in time, the real snows would hit, and the Center die. The four vets would scatter across America.

But she hadn't known how tough the vets could be. This first snow, blown in two weeks after she mailed the papers – before the insulation had been installed, and before the roof was complete. The dorm was freckled with missing windows. But the Army and the Marine Corps didn't care – they ditched tent living as soon as they had a single room

217

closed off inside. They lived with all the dust and clutter of a construction site, as they built their shell like a Nautilus, one chamber at a time. That week they struggled against the wind while they screwed down the last four metal panels. They must have been frozen as they installed windows. She doubted they'd mention it much.

The honking scraped across her senses. She swallowed her profanity like cold tea and strode to the front door. The black Nissan shivered out front, in a wallow of slush. A hand in a work glove waved out the window. Tony wanted her to march out into the flaying wind.

She jerked the creaking car door open. Inside he smiled away, complained about the weather as if it was some joke on him that even he viewed as funny. "Wow, don't hang around out there, jump in and close the door. My gay balls just fell off."

She tucked into the front seat. The heater roared, blew flakes of snow around the interior that lit sporadically and transformed to irksome beads of moisture. She locked her jaw and said, "And the reason you called me out here is.... ?"

"I can't climb out of the car. If I lift my foot off the gas, the car dies and I'm pretty sure I can't restart it."

She glanced around the interior. The dash was scratched and dented as if a club had hammered it. The door to the glovebox had disappeared. A set of dog tags hung from the rear view mirror. The radio was turned low and its message masked by the heater. "I guess that's excuse enough."

"Don't worry, things warm up quick. Five minutes max."

She gazed at him, at the scruffy goatee plastered onto the young, strong face. Tony wore a stocking cap, drawn down to his eyebrows, hiding his ears. "Five minutes is a long time when you're freezing."

He handed her a white envelope – return address labeled Dallas. "I commandeered your mail at the post office. I threw away the junk. This one was from your brother-in-law."

"They gave you my mail? That's a Federal offense."

He shrugged. "It's a small village. Miss Junie likes me."

She ripped off the envelope end, shook out a sheet of paper and a photo. "This is bad. Normally Ted would never write a letter."

Tony snatched the photo and glanced at it. "Hot babe, even though she's not my type. She's bound to be why he wrote, the trouble at hand."

"Probably Mara, from Ireland. Let me read this." She scanned it. "They've made up... she's leaving Texas to do post-doc research in California at San Diego. He knows a friend who sells yachts in Catalina... thinking about asking for a job, wants to join her in California."

He grinned. "Good news then."

Her face dripped melted snow onto the letter. "No. Ted sells cars, not boats. And he can't even swim." She folded the letter back and wadded it in the front of her coat. "You didn't drive over here to give me the mail. What's up?"

"Wanted to check on you while I could – some of us are running down to Española tomorrow to load up rolls of fiberglass insulation."

She chuckled. "Can't stuff many rolls in here."

He grinned. "No problemo. I've borrowed a bobtail truck from Rubio's grandson."

"Rubio has a grandson?"

"Six, I think. I work with the oldest. His name is Francesco, but everyone calls him Little Rubio."

"Can you close in the building? Keep the weather out?"

"Done. One empty window left – but Kevin nailed a sheet of OSB over the hole. It'll do."

She poked around with one finger in the junk collected in the center console. "I've been meaning to ask you about this gay thing."

"This gay thing."

"Not really about you, but more about Michael. Do you think he would talk to you because you're not a threat?"

His gaze ranged out the windshield to the bluster. "I said I was gay, not a pansy."

This was not going well. Both of his hands gripped the steering wheel. She had hurt his feelings. "I didn't mean to be rude. I just wanted to know if he talked to you."

He turned his head, peered through her, spaced out his words. "I don't know him. Nobody knows him. We can't even figure out how many versions of him are locked inside."

She gave a long sigh.

"What's this about?"

"He needs to talk to the people at the VA. William believes he needs help. I called and booked the appointment, but I don't think he'll keep it."

"Did you ask?"

"Once last week, once this week." She flashed back on Michael's blue eyes, staring at her. When she had asked, he was on the edge of striking her. It was the second time she had been afraid of him.

Tony grinned. His world held no dark shadows. "You'll think of something."

"Help me out here."

"I'm the construction boss. You're the Center manager. I got my job and you got Michael."

Sometimes he could really piss her off. But perhaps this was payback.

—⚄—

November 15, 2009.

As yet only a windstorm, it scraped drifts along, worked up four inches of drift snow. Two or three gone from camp. Maybe Michael had ridden off on the supply mission. In her insulated suit and with a muffler wound round her head and face, Bec trudged the hundred yards to the dorm. She wriggled through the door and yanked it shut behind her. They had stapled up drop cloths as an airlock to block the drafts. She pawed at the plastic with her hands. Like a mime in the invisible box.

Kevin drifted across the far end of the room, stopped, gaped at her as she goggled at him. The plastic allowed her to patch together his outline, but everything about him was overlain by a wash of gray. She shouted, "Kevin, I'm trapped here."

His laughter echoed as he clumped all the way over to her. He flipped his hand – a thin triangle opened in front of her. She slipped through.

He laughed again. "Glad you didn't go bananas and rip your way through. Now you know the secret – search for where two sheets overlap."

"What a cool idea!"

"We make do. So what brings you here? Nobody would struggle across that field in this weather without a good reason."

"Hmm. Who's here, Kevin?"

"Me and Jason. Michael and Davy rode along with the boss Tony. Gonna visit the huge city, eat at Wendy's, shop at the big box stores."

"I did have a reason to hike over, and you're the one I came to visit."

He surveyed her up and down, folded his massive forearms over his chest. "Huh."

"Is there somewhere we can sit?"

"Coffee?"

The tastebuds in her mouth soured. "That would be nice."

He escorted her across the drab, jumbled room, pointed out details to-be. They maneuvered around stacks of Sheetrock, two-by-four studs, buckets, tools. He stopped to shout up a hatch past the ladder that guarded it, "Jason, I'll be ten minutes." He said to Bec, "Jason's in the attic running wire for the overhead lights. That goes in before we unroll the insulation."

One of the future bedrooms had been tricked out as a temporary kitchen, fitted with hot plates, a toaster, a microwave. Extension cords snaked across the floor. The room center held a rickety card table. The outside walls were bare studs in front of OSB. Kevin said, "No gypsum board till the insulation goes up." He turned to the coffee pot and some mugs.

The temperature was perhaps fifty degrees. She eased herself onto a metal chair – the cold metal bite nibbled into her legs and butt, even though she wore coveralls. The coffee smelled like burned caramel. "Sugar?"

Kevin said, "We not only have sugar, we got creamer that looks like rat poison."

"I'll pass on the rat poison."

He settled the cup of coffee in front of her. Its vapor rose around her face, a teasing humidity. He dropped into his chair like it was a foot lower than he expected. He folded his hands, waited.

He had male-pattern baldness, his kinky hair longer on top, razored short on the sides of his head. She said, "We haven't talked."

"We haven't talked when other people weren't around."

She bowed in agreement.

He kept his hands folded, as if not to spook her. "But you hiked over here today to talk. To me."

The flush that ran up her neck, the tickling behind her ears. "Um. Tell me your story, Kevin."

"That's not why you're here." He grinned, scratched his chin with the latte-colored false hand. "But I'll let you work up to it. My story. I was born a barefoot child in the Appalachian hills, destined to become either a bootlegger or President of the United States."

"Really?"

"Hell no. I grew up in Jersey. My dad was a pipe fitter, one of the few negroes allowed in the local union back then." His fingers flashed quote marks, his mechanical hand an eighth-beat behind the flesh-and-blood version. "My mom stayed home and raised five of us. I joined the Army because the recruiter made a compelling case for it. A place where I couldn't be tempted by booze and other people's cars. It stuck. I was bad at being a teenager. I was real good at being Army."

It trolled out so glib. He'd told this story before. "But you're out?"

"I think I could have been okay staying in with one real hand. They woulda tried to stick me with a desk job, but I could have weaseled my way back to the front. The trouble? Squeezing off a shot."

"Huh?"

"Takes too long, that microsecond of hesitation. But I could've learned to shoot left-handed."

"I believe I understand."

"I'm considering one of those tech schools, and later going back over as a contractor. Or maybe I'll open a bar somewhere warm. Do tricks like bending quarters for the patrons." He held up his hand. His thumb, with the faintest of whirring sounds, traveled like a piston down between his index and middle fingers. He probably could bend a quarter.

She needed to sneak sideways up to what she wanted. "You handle it well. I mean, losing your career. And your hand."

He gazed at her, straight into her eyes. "Couldn't last forever, could it? Though I imagined it would."

Those eyes, the whites brilliant in the black face, with tiny red veins etched across them.

"It must have been awful."

"Shit happens. You can't carry it around with you forever. Get over it, or get dead."

She cocked her head, tried for a casual expression. "Will Michael get over it?"

"I wouldn't know that. He don't know that."

"I hoped – you being friends and all."

He cocked his head, chuckled at her stupidity. "Michael and me, friends? Sure, we're soldiers. But even then, I'm an Army grunt and he's a Marine jarhead."

She waited silent.

"I did reflect some about it. It seems to me, either I'll save his life or he'll save mine. Or.... "

"Or?"

"If he keeps needling me, one of us will end broken up on the floor. Maybe he can't quit. It's something jammed back behind his forehead. Some days that something hides way back, like a headache. Some days, it jerks him around like he's a puppet."

"But you know what he's up to. You don't have to play his game."

"We're all puppets." His black face set into a wall, one maybe with secrets behind it.

They bowed their heads over the coffee. She sipped, full of trepidation. It tasted as awful as she expected, dark and like tree roots, simmered down to bitterness.

Overhead scrapes and bumps – Jason continued to do mysterious things overhead in the darkness. She wondered if the limited light bothered him, or if darkness was a natural state. No, he'd have a flashlight.

She said, "I believe Michael needs help."

Kevin snorted. "The boy needs some help all right."

"I'm serious about this, Kevin."

"Shit, I know you are. What type of help you thinking?"

"The VA in Albuquerque provides counseling services, doctors specializing in PTSD."

"The shrinks. About time."

"I can't convince him to go."

"How hard you try?"

"I talked to him in the middle of last week. Nothing. I booked the appointment and talked to him on Tuesday this week. It was like that night of the party, when he wanted to fight you."

"He wouldn't hit a woman."

She wasn't convinced. "How would you know? You just said he was broken."

He rotated his coffee cup in his hands, one flesh, one vinyl. He inspected it, slipping his words out casually. "You going to give him what he wants, so you can pressure him? You gonna be with him, figure out if sleeping with him signifies?"

She stiffened, jerked her head back as if he'd slapped her. Faked it. "I'm married."

He kept his head down, gazed at the coffee cup. "Ah. But that doesn't answer the question."

"I know what he wants."

"No you don't. None of us do. Sex is just a way to pass the time for him until he figures it out."

Tight, tight as a drumhead. "You an expert at this?"

"Christ no."

She said, as carefully as she would have fingered a loaded gun, "Maybe you would have a conflict of interest here, a bit of competitiveness? Word is, you think I'm hot."

He snickered, jostled the card table till it shook like it would collapse. "Bless me no, Miss Bec. You're real nice and all, but I got to tell you, I like women with big asses. You're so far from that, you're from another planet."

He continued to snigger and her ears burned with the rebuff. She said, "I'm glad I amuse you."

He reached over and patted the top of her head like she was a child. "I tell you what, Miss Bec. I'll badmouth shrinks and VA doctors. If that doesn't park him in the truck to Albuquerque, nothing will."

CHAPTER TWENTY-THREE – QUAVER

NOVEMBER 17, 2009.

Bec caught sight of Michael through the window and paced out onto the porch. She had wrapped herself in a blanket, a cocoon, just as she had pictured for this meeting. His head bobbed as he marched the lane across faint drifts of snow, his gait not that different from a man with real legs. The light from a setting sun threw his shadow out behind him and the shadow rippled, a long black cape across a gray-blue world.

Ten feet away, in the drive before the house, he halted. A blue parka ripped open at one elbow, a brown pair of coveralls, boots. Sunglasses perched on his head, nestled into the stubble of his standard-issue buzz cut. The late afternoon light cut his face with black creases, each wrinkle and seam a trench. He squinted into the setting sun as he stared at her, tried to pick out detail. To read her. She hovered in the porch shadow; the dimness shielded her, wrapped her in ambiguity. It wasn't decided yet. She could yet be saved. Faith and fidelity remained possible. Her face flushed hot, like a sunburn.

Another few steps forward, the wolf stalking. He was beneath her, scuffing a boot against a ridge of ice. "I noticed you this morning, on this porch. I was cutting a hole for the stovepipe. On the roof, what I saw... I don't know. Like I was locked inside a TV. Every time I reached for a tool or a strip of flashing, I'd see you watching us. Watching me. So still, like you were frozen." Each syllable, tone, clear as if he whispered in her ear.

She said, "I was watching. And thinking."

"I wanted to believe you were out here because of me."

Two feet away. Already in her head. "Maybe I was turning it over what you told me, days ago."

He jerked his head. "That's part of it, isn't it? But I was sure enough you wanted me to march over here that I broke my promise. Here I am to bother you."

She waved him past her, a gesture fluttering, a bird. "Come on in. We have something to talk about again."

—⚊—

Michael's mouth locked in a frown, the denial clear. Facing each other, on opposite ends of the sofa. She perched cross-legged, leaned forward. He wedged into his corner, slumped, his arm splayed across the old brown leather back. The couch where they first touched, where they sat hip to hip.

He waved her off, a hand that flicked out. "I don't follow your point." Angry wasn't quite the word. More bottled up. Walled in.

"The point is, you need to tell this story to someone else. Someone who can help you."

He drew his lip up. "I told you. Maybe you're already one person too many."

"I was.... " She held her hands out, ready to clasp his. "I was honored when you told me."

He didn't buy it – every line in his face said so. "You trapped me into it. It was a bad idea."

She disagreed. "Can't have been a bad thing. You're moving forward."

"Moving forward. I don't call this forward. To curl up in a ball on some shrink's couch. Not my idea of a good time." He shifted his weight and the old sofa complained underneath him.

She said, "It's necessary. You need it. Don't you see, you're still waiting to step on that bomb."

Surly, he crossed his arms. "What the shit do you know about me?"

"That's right. What the shit do I know? I know something is wrong. I'm afraid for you, and I want you to seek some help."

"You believe it's something fixable. I think it's who I am. If it was just a broken bit that they could reach into my head and tweak, I wouldn't be real. The afternoon I... that my brother died. That was the real me."

"The hurt was real. But you need to let it go, admit it was an accident."

"Death, that's my core. I won't let go of the one thing that's actual. What would I have left?"

Real. An excuse, a refrain, a doubt. She unfolded out of her end of the couch and crawled across the old cushions towards him. When she reached his lap, she unlaced his crossed arms and held his palm to the side of her face. She kissed it. "Try, Michael. We'll go together. Please." She nuzzled her lips into a hand stiff and hard. He was as unbending as the metal in his legs. "For me." Tears rushed into her eyes. Why was she perpetually crying?

His fingers curled around, touched her jaw line, nestled back behind her ear. They laced into her hair. "For you?" He willed her forward with a gentle pressure, brought her face to his, and touched his lips to hers.

It was good. Hell, it was great. That first gentle brush was as wonderful as anything in her life. She slipped into dizziness with it, as dizzy as if he whirled her around.

But the secret. In the moment of giving and taking the kiss, she had forgotten she wasn't complete. Here it was, swept up on her and she wasn't prepared.

She had to tell. Had to take a chance. Stupid. Frightening.

She rocked back on her heels. "Michael, you need to hear something. I had cancer. They cut me up. I don't have any breasts." Her arms were clasped across her chest.

228

"Bec, I know that."

"You do?"

He touched her her face with his fingertips, grazed her cheek. "The signs are there for anyone who wants to figure it out."

She flushed. "I'm that obvious?"

"You're kind of flat chested, and your hair – it's pretty feminine but it's as short as an officer's." He grinned. "And remember the day I sewed you up and you locked yourself in the bedroom? I snooped through all those pill bottles in the kitchen cabinet. Leftover drugs to help with chemo and radiation, I bet."

"You bastard." He acted pretty satisfied with his detective skills.

"That's not the point, Bec. I know, and I have known, and I don't care."

—⁓—

Bec had propped the single small window open – a faint draft of air glided in. She didn't turn on the light as they entered the room – through the window they could spot the deep purple as sunset surrendered across the snow. She lit a tiny tea candle on the bureau, slipped toward the bed in flame's benediction.

She came to rest on the bed on her side, and Michael eased down beside her, on William's side. William's side.

In a moment her jeans lay over a chair and Michael's coveralls puddled on the floor. She tucked her leg under her and leaned back on the pillow, facing him. She unbuttoned her blouse and as she shrugged one shoulder, it dropped to the side. He unbuttoned his flannel shirt. They caught each other's eyes, dropped their gazes further. He whipped his T-shirt over his head and she dropped her blouse on the chair. She curled her hands around her neck so her forearms protected her chest, stared at her shining, white knee. Shy, but already her body responded, awash in a blazing need.

Michael said, "This next part, please don't look. I want to wiggle

229

out of my legs. I have to peel off the socket, and a sock, and a liner. It's a pain." He grunted as he yanked the stumps of his legs out of silicon sockets and packing. The legs dropped onto the floor, one after the other. The clonking echoed across the room, jolted her. A nerved-up little girl.

They leaned in to each other and met in the middle of the bed. He loomed so close to her that his face broke into planes, pieces. His face strange. Compelling. He stole her hand and bending his elbow, cradled it to his collar bone.

It was electric; she flushed from head to toe. Their first time and she was in a rush. She slipped her hand free, reached down. "Hurry, Michael, hurry. I've waited so long."

He swept her hand away. "No."

"No?" She was ready and any delay – what if she changed her mind?

"We have time. Make it last."

"Now," she said. "It has to be now."

They struggled with underwear, the final ignobility before they could be naked. There in the queen-sized bed, in a room lit by the last of dusk from an uncurtained window. The new moon, a mere two days old, a sliver of hope, would set very soon.

—⁂—

Bec drove him like a team of horses thundering across the fields. No tenderness at all – more of a race. Would they finish first or would the earth split and swallow her in her wickedness? She fell forward onto his neck, felt the slick of sweat on her face, whether from him or her she couldn't tell. She rolled off him and collapsed into the bed. Sheets and the quilt puddled around her. They swallowed her, like a pond.

His breath rasped out, a sough nearly like pain. "Sweet Jesus."

"Yes. Jesus."

He twisted up on one elbow, his face hidden from her in the dark.

His fingers brushed out, sought out her face, traced her lower lip. "You know how to treat a boy right."

"Welcome home, soldier." They had – what? Consummated the drama? Given in? Strange, she felt empty. Maybe a mild relief. Perhaps a ghosting regret ran through her; possibly just the shudder of muscles unkinking.

His hand traced into the hollow of her throat, lay on her collarbone. She said, "Now we share something."

"Sharing bodies, that's not the big thing. You said you knew me, but you don't."

Couldn't he leave this death voodoo alone? "Here's the big thing." Taking his hand, she drew him to her chest. His palm touched her, his fingers began to search her. Across the middle of her chest he traced her scar, left none of it unexplored. His hand dipped and he explored the other scar. "No nipples, Bec? I hoped for your sake you kept your nipples."

"They cut away those too. But the nerves are in there somewhere, and I feel my nipples sometimes." She sighed, a sound that surprised her as he stroked her chest. She wanted desperately to glimpse his face. "Is this... is it bad?"

"No, not at all." He whispered the words. "I'm not running away. Smooth, sleek Bec, with a tiny zipper of a scar."

She tensed so much her hands and arms trembled. "And you? I want to know how you've been hurt. Show me, let me touch it."

He hiked himself backwards on the bed away from her. He raised his leg, lifted the knee above her. The remains of his upper calf hung above them. "It's not painful for me. It's healed and strong. I didn't suffer from those balled-up cut-off nerves – neuromas."

Her hand reached out to the stump. She ran her fingers over the folded flaps of skin. Her fingertips were just aware of the scarring. It felt warm to the touch and smooth, not knotted and lumpy as she had feared.

231

With a final circular rub, she nudged his leg behind her, wriggled in towards him. He dropped his heavy thigh over her hip. Her lips grazed his. She breathed out the words. "I'm not running away either."

He dropped his head onto the pillow, rolled onto his back. "Next time, my way, slow. This is the only thing I do slow." He wriggled like a badger hiding itself in a swale of grass and settled deep into the bed. As he drew her back on top of him, he kissed her forehead, dropped his forearm across her flank. He cradled her butt with his hand.

She cupped the back of his neck, massaged it. Beneath all that muscle, she could distinguish each vertebra. He breathed slower, settled into a rhythm that carried him into sleep. She rolled back, stared at the dark ceiling. Were men incapable of staying awake afterwards?

—⁙—

November 19, 2009.

Alone. Where had Michael gone? The candle struggled, sending out minute flecks of light and dark. The corners of the room were blackness itself. Bec's heartbeat accelerated, but she didn't know why. Rolling to the bed edge, she fished around on the floor – his coveralls lay there crumpled. She fished up one of the metal legs, leaned it on the night table. Hitching herself up, she propped up against the headboard and drew the sheet around her.

The sound of the back door. Her bedroom door opened and closed. Thumps approached hollowly across the boards. Michael appeared in the ghost of the diminished candle, by the bed, reaching out to her. He stood only four and a half feet tall. Her mouth dropped, her heart thudded.

Her apparition said, "I didn't mean to wake you. Just taking a pee off the back porch. Are you going to let me back in bed?"

"I decided you had ditched me." She surprised herself – her voice quavered.

"No such luck. You're stuck with me." He clambered onto the bed, edged the sheet from her. "Come here, you. I need someone to warm me up."

CHAPTER TWENTY-FOUR – IN COMMON

NOVEMBER 21, 2009.

Bec stashed herself in Chuma's office and picked up the phone. She hated to wait while phones rang and she counted each jingle – she always wanted to change her mind and hang up. She remembered to breathe.

"Ted Robertson here." That big voice, all salesman.

"It's Bec. I opened your email. It sounded pretty bad."

"It is." Chord of discouragement, like he threw a switch from jolly to miserable.

Bec leaned forward, her elbows on the desk, her mouth hovered over the receiver. "What happened?"

"I packed four bags and flew to California. I rented a car and drove to her department at the University. She totally blew up when I strolled in. Called me stupid for coming, called me an idiot for not warning her. Evidently our goodbye had been perfect and here I showed up unannounced."

"Wow."

"It grows worse. I tell her about the job in Catalina with my buddy. She throws things at me. She tells me she's only temporary in California, before she reports back to Trinity and pursues her career. And a life in Ireland. I should fly back to Dallas and sell cars, she says."

Bec's eyes scrolled across Chuma's paperwork under her elbows, not really reading. "Where are you now?"

"In Dallas. With some begging I landed my old job back."

"Ted, I'm so sorry. I don't know what to tell you."

"Tell me how to fix it."

It flashed through Bec's head – divorce papers in William's room in Kandahar, a man nearly half her age in her bed here. Fix it. "I really don't know what to tell you. Call her, apologize."

"And say what?"

"Tell her you weren't taking her for granted, that you care a lot for her. Tell her you want to see her and say you won't do anything again before you consult with her."

"Really? That would work? No wonder William thinks the sun rises and sets because of you."

Ted was clueless about them.

—⁓—

November 27, 2009.

Never again the same. Thanksgiving celebrated on Friday for the vets and her this year. Wrong day, wrong foot.

Friday night gathered its cast of characters into her cabin, a giant pot of chili on the stove. Most of the guys crowded around the kitchen table, but Michael lolled on the sofa in the living room, Emmet guarding him. Bec toted a cutting board with bowls of onion and cheese and a stack of tortillas in to them, ensured Emmet and Michael garnished their chili with what toppings they wanted. As she treaded back into the kitchen, she grasped the new reality. Voices broke off. Kevin dipped his head and Jason rolled the salt shaker in his hand as if he had never seen one. Tony turned to her with a sweeping gaze that measured her, surveyed her slight frame from head to toe. Only Davy remained unchanged, the lost boy – he swept a tortilla around his bowl, mopped it clean but forgot he should eat the tortilla. She set the cutting board on the counter, felt their eyes on her back. She drew a deep breath, turned and tried a smile on them.

235

It wasn't the same.

—ɷ—

November 28, 2009.

The same man but different, the man that changed into darkness. Bec discovered Michael at the sink in the kitchen – he stared out the small window at the dawn light. She slipped behind him, reached under his arms to hug his chest, and molded her body to the contours of his back. He let it go on for a few seconds. His shoulders twitched. "Please don't. Not now."

He shuffled a half step to the side, rolled out of her grasp and clicked his way to the stove top to pour coffee. When he faced her, she discovered that face again. Blank. He gazed at her, but without seeing.

She asked straight up. "Moody this morning?"

"Things on my mind." He bit the words off, let them drop into the space between them.

"Anything you can share?"

He shook his head. Sipping the coffee, he said, "Full day today. Tony has us pulling more wiring." His voice rolled out flat, with no inflection at all.

"When will I see you?"

"After work. Maybe after dinner. I don't know."

She tried to fit herself into the emptiness in his tone. "We'll play it by ear. You know where I live." He lived here too, his clothes in her grandfather's trunk against the bedroom wall.

"Sure," he said. He pivoted, headed to the door. The thump of his artificial heels on the boards and the sound of the front door. She grabbed the coffee pot. She poured it down the sink, fired up the kettle for tea.

—ɷ—

November 30, 2009.

VA day. Bec jerked to a stop at the new dorm, waited behind the

236

wheel. She had imagined the worksite would be littered with materials and scrap scattered under those few inches of snow. More like Camp Lejeune – the Marine Corps must have brought its standards to bear and demanded order from winter's chaos. Jason, in the dorm's door, spotted her. He crouched, popped out like the groundhog to drop to the ground. She leaned out the window. "Good morning, Jason."

He bobbed his head, turned his bad side away, and pretended to watch the dorm. "Michael'll be out in a minute. If he comes."

"Has he been bad over the last couple of days? He has, with me."

"Maybe even moodier than usual. I had to break Kevin and him up before they started whomping on each other."

"Did he provoke it?"

He threw her a glance, jerked his face back towards the building. "Does it matter? You know how he can set it up, even if he's not first to the fight."

She drummed her fingers on the steering wheel. "I had hoped things might improve. With me in the picture."

Jason shrugged. He drifted in closer, dropped his head towards her. "I can't figure him out. Or you."

Keep it neutral. "Me?"

"Yes, you. But mostly him. Like why isn't he living at your place full time –" He jerked his chin at her cabin, "Instead of showing up in camp every other night?"

"You'd have to ask him." Something close to anger, or despair, circled through her like a dust devil. What if she said, you believe I'm running things here? That I want my adultery announced to the whole world? Shack up, or sneak around? Which would suit you, Jason?

"Anyway, who knows if you're good for him. Miss Bec?"

"You can call me Bec, you know."

He wobbled his head. "I'm a sight uncomfortable with that. What I wanted to ask –"

She meant to sting him. "Something else you're uncomfortable with, Jason?"

"I hate to tangle in your business, but do you think Michael is good for you?"

She gawped.

"I mean in the Corps, fraternization is illegal. It sneaks its way in, but it always ends bad. Michael isn't exactly Sergeant Sunshine. And your husband an officer and all."

Her own fault, having given away all her privacy. "Jason, I need you to be my friend on this, to help me through the mess. I've landed myself in it, and it might be awhile to wiggle back out."

He turned to face her, oblivious for once of the burns and scarring. "I'll try like I promised, but I'm a bit lost here. You and I should visit a bit, in what time I have left."

"Time left?"

"I'm journeying out to California soon, have the VA do some work on me. I might not be back until spring. I might go on to something else."

Great. Peachy. "I'm glad for you. But aren't you from Wisconsin? Why not use the VA there? Or in Albuquerque?"

She watched him remember Wisconsin. He twisted his face away from her. "Couldn't be much comfort for me there. California should be nice during the winter – but here's Michael."

Michael marched through the tarp over the door. He stomped towards the truck, a canvas shoulder bag hung to the side. As Michael flicked those tin legs past the front of the pickup, Jason slapped the window frame. "Plumbing work calls out to me. And Miss Bec?"

"Yes, Jason."

He dropped his voice. "Thanks for... pulling his head out of the sand, maybe."

The creaking door, the grunt as Michael dropped into the seat beside her and swung his legs in. He slammed it, sat to attention with the messenger bag in his lap. "Okay. If we're going to do this thing, let's do it."

"What's in the bag?"

He fastened his seatbelt, jerked his head forward. "Remains of the departed."

She fired up the truck and drove into one of those New Mexico days, the sky gray one minute and full of snow, and in a blink so bright blue and transparent the firs appeared black. She said, "Not too long before the next storm blows in." Lame, reduced to chat about the weather.

He grunted.

No joy today. The other Michael. She counted stands of spruce as they drove, counted the curves down into Santa Eulalia. It would be a long day – longer yet if she slid off the road.

—m—

The VA in Albuquerque: the main building's lobby crawled with people, many sick and broken-down, progressing slower than treacle. The volunteers at the information desk tried to force coffee with an acid, bitter smell on Bec. Yes, they knew where Mental Health was – down the long hall here, out the doors and two buildings over. Building Number One.

Number One stunned her – her head rang. This wasn't right. Mental health issues had piled up to such a mountain in the Armed Forces that Behavioral Health should be damn important. She expected better, not this 30's lump of a building. She tugged at the old door with its ten lights – its battered handle and chipped paint. As she trudged a few steps inside, she glanced back. Michael was out there, in the dwarfish courtyard created by aged juniper trees and the building's tan stucco. Rooted to the concrete, he craned his neck back to sweep eyes across the four floors.

Bec slowly spun, took in the lobby. A dark ceiling, black varnished beams with frightening animal faces as corbels. Horrible broad-ass

1950's chairs, stuffed with ancient foam and covered in a light blue vinyl. Three patient windows behind glass, separated by wooden and steel panels for privacy, two cubbyholes darkened and their computers turned off. Behind the glass, a tired male Latino face ready to pretend compassion to the next vet he would log in.

She plunged outside, gripped Michael by the elbow and guided him in across fake wood-plank floors. At the front desk, they checked Michael in for his appointment. She did the talking, presented the relevant ID out of his messenger bag. The counter crouched so low Bec felt the undersized passthrough was at her crotch. Bullet-proof glass to protect the receptionist. From whom? She was marshaled before the battlements; she lay siege to the system. Michael braced at attention, his hands rigid at his side. The man behind the desk, a man with dark bags like smashed plums under his eyes, spoke only to Bec. "He'll need to fill these forms out – sorry, there are always forms. When he's done, you bring them back here. We're running an hour and forty minutes behind, but it shouldn't get much worse."

"What happens after the forms?"

"I'll send them up to the second floor to go in the file for the medicos, and you can ride the elevator up to wait there."

She cocked her head. "Will the Doctor talk to me, after? Can I be in the room?"

"Are you family?"

She shot a glance up at Michael's face. Family wasn't the right word. "Friend, I guess. He doesn't have family in New Mexico." And he's dead to his sister.

"I'm afraid the Sergeant here would have to request it."

The Sergeant. That was Michael.

"But I will leave a note for the Doc. Waiting area is to your left, toilets are behind the elevators. No concession machines except in the main building."

240

They lost themselves in the blue chairs, rejects out of an airport lounge from the turboprop era. Bec sank into a hole where the foam had given up – she felt all right about this, with less of her actually in the room. Rigid, Michael waited with few words.

As she filled out the paperwork – she dug through Michael's bag and asked him questions now and again – the man across from them wanted to talk. Loudly. An unlit cigarette danced in his lips. "First time here? D'ja have ta drive in or d'ya live in Albuquerque?" He yammered on and on, until a vet in distress shambled in and broke their wait into shards.

The man looked so ordinary – his hair cut, his clothes nice, his hands clutched together, a look on his face like his liver was being ripped out of him. His muttering to the receptionist, fast, spiky, cracking.

Reception immediately rang back, the locked double doors banged open, and a female nurse appeared. Triage, a series of pointed questions fired at the hunch-backed man who could have been thirty or fifty. She persisted, even after the fellow began to weep in anguish. All this in the lobby, open vivisection of the man in front of everyone else. Bec wanted to shout, "Take him back to a room, help him. Fix him, make him happy again."

—∭—

The second floor was better. The walls were a brighter cream yellow: banks of fluorescent lights ensured the banishment of shadows. Same bullet-proof glass, a batch of receptionists, double doors that closed the lobby off from the wings. As they waited, Bec inspected the facility for any clues of success or hope.

Rigid in the plastic chair, Michael endured as he had for hours. His stare straight ahead a rejection. She clasped his forearm, leaned in to him. "Thanks for this, Michael."

He grunted.

"What will you tell the Doctor?"

His lips drew back in a rictus, a derisive grin. "Enough to keep my promise to you. Let's check out how good they are."

"They're not the enemy. The VA is here to support the Armed Forces."

"But they're not Marines, are they?"

The Corps answer for everything. Us versus them. Belonging versus not. "I have to use the restroom. I'll be right back." She slipped back her hand, the caress he had ignored.

He didn't give her a glance. "Don't worry. I'll be here when you get back."

After an hour going-on-a-day, a male nurse scuffed out of the wing to announce Michael's name. He unlocked the door with a key hanging on his wrist– no swipe or keypad lock here – and waved him back. They passed, then, into the guts of the system.

—ww—

The blandness, the standardization of the waiting area – cookie-cutter. These places ended up identical – the plastic chairs, the squatty table covered in a swath of old magazines. The room held no surprises, had seen it all. Maybe it had seen another Michael or two.

She could sneak out, flee into the parking lot. She could drive away. It had flitted through her mind, a hope that ignited before flaming out. She'd be there when he got back.

On the wall in the waiting room, a piece of paper in a plastic sleeve, taped up. The VA apologized for the lack of WiFi. WiFi would interfere with the medical equipment. Phones were to be turned off.

Bec approached the windows, chose a woman receptionist. "I'm sorry, but the sign says there isn't any WiFi. I had promised to call my husband on Skype just about now."

The clerk stared over her half-glasses. She was one of those Anglas who had spent too many years in the sun. Her hair roached up with mousse above a forehead checker-boarded like alligator skin. "I'm the one who's sorry. I can't help you – the sign is right and we don't have WiFi."

The receptionist's name tag identified her as "Helen." "Helen, my husband is in Kandahar, in Afghanistan. Isn't there something that you can do?"

The woman checked her up and down. "Hunh." She twitched her head right and left, checked out her coworkers. Leaned forward, muted her voice. "Meet me at the door over there." Helen slipped out of her chair and disappeared from her booth.

―∞―

Bec scurried behind Helen, their shoes squeaking on a floor that smelled of Lysol.

"C'mon, c'mon. We need to hurry. I should be at my desk." The receptionist threw open an office door and shoved Bec in. "This is my supervisor's office. She's off today. Gimme your laptop."

Bec rocked back while Helen jerked the ethernet cord out of a desk PC and jacked it into Bec's small machine.

"I can't thank you enough. This means so much to me."

Helen plunked Bec's laptop on a flock of files, and it teetered on the mound. "I'm glad to help. Let me know when you're done."

"This is so kind of you."

"I won't tell if you won't."

Bec flashed her best smile at her.

"And besides, just between you and me – my supervisor is a bitch. Use anything of hers you want. Hell, eat all her damn breath mints." Helen clicked the door shut behind her.

Bec opened the laptop – middle of the night in Kandahar, but William had said to call anytime. She counted the rings.

He picked up. Behind him, an immense mess hall with a low ceiling, lit like a basketball gym. He leaned in to the camera, changing a square, tanned forehead into a roundish blob.

"Rebecca, what a nice surprise. Let me say goodnight to the guys here and I'll be right with you."

The lid of his PC half closed. Muttering.

"Okay, I'm back."

"William, where are you?"

"Base outside Kabul. I was ordered back from the hot zone for a few days, for R&R and detox. Doesn't mean I'm off duty though. Visiting with a corporal and some privates just in from Helmand." He laughed, a put-on chuckle. "Nobody sleeps well over here."

He fiddled with the laptop to set up distance and angle. This revealed his left arm hid in a surgery-green sling.

"William, you've been hurt!"

"Believe me, Rebecca, I was the first to know."

"William, you promised you'd be careful. What happened? How bad is it?"

"Hey, I like this. You're actually concerned."

"Of course I am." Cocky shithead. Even with everything fallen apart between them, she'd have to be a monster not to be concerned.

"It's trivial, I assure you. I caught a piece of shrapnel in the forearm. It cracked the bone and ruined a good shirt, but it's really nothing."

"Nothing? You've been shot!"

"Whoa, slow down. I caught a spent chunk of grenade, not a bullet. It happened two days ago and I lose the sling tomorrow – pretty small-time. Besides, it gives me some credibility with the troops."

"I wish you'd earn your credibility some other way." She glanced down to see she had seized the keyboard in a death grip. The fear manifest, that he would die out there where she had driven him.

He waved his hand. "Not to worry, not to worry. You're in some kind of office, not the café?"

"VA hospital in Albuquerque. I brought one of my vets – one of your vets – for an appointment."

"Why, can't he drive?"

"You know, I never asked. He's mastered his artificial legs and he can do most things.... " Didn't need legs for some things. She blushed without any warning.

Something in the mess hall distracted William – he twitched his head away from the camera and his eyes tracked off-screen. "Which one is he?"

"Michael. The marine we talked about." So this is what whoring around was all about, thinking about sex with another man while talking to your husband.

"The one with emotional problems."

"True of all the vets, but for Michael much worse. His first appointment, too."

"How's it going?"

"Just bullying him through the door was a battle. Denial. Hostility. Silent hours in the truck."

He yawned, tried to stifle it. "Keep me updated. I might be able to help, or at least consult."

"What time is it?"

"About one."

"Why don't you go off to bed. I can call you tomorrow or email and let you know the results."

"Sounds good to me. Let me mention one thing. How about we meet in Greece in about a month?" His eyes were the size of saucers. "Just consider it."

"William, you know that won't happen. How about signing those papers?"

The corners of his mouth drooped. A bleak face, frosted with disappointment. "Not yet. Goodnight, Rebecca."

—◦◦◦—

In the truck, icy like a freezer, Bec keyed the ignition. "How'd it go?" She hadn't been offered the chance to talk to the doctor.

Michael leaned on the window, tipped away from her. His voice eked out thin, distant. "Decent. Guy wasn't an asshole. Of course, he wasn't Corps or Navy. Air Force Academy he said – earned his degrees at their expense after his eyes crapped out and he couldn't fly."

She left it alone, waited her moment. As they drove, she pointed things out, made small talk. Tried to interest him in dinner at a restaurant on the way home. Nothing.

In Española he stabbed his forefinger at a bunch of young men at a fast food joint. They huddled under a metal awning, hunkered down at a picnic table. Their breath and their cigarettes spoiled the air, a scumbled hazy cloud that hung like poison. "Catch the cars, the clothes? Gang, you can bet."

"They say the town has improved. Police control the gangs pretty well."

"Just spreads them out. The lucky ones… ," and he nodded towards the boys. "The ones without a criminal record. They'll join the military and light on a reason to live. The others, they'll die on the street."

"You sound like you despise them."

"Not at all, Bec. I share too much in common with them to despise them."

"You joined up after high school?"

"I didn't mean back then. I meant now."

CHAPTER TWENTY-FIVE – MARRIED TO THE ARMY

Decmber 1.
One night later, a whole new universe. The other Michael knocked at the back door. Bec jerked it open, hoping against hope. He held a hand to the door frame, leaned casual as pride itself. "I wondered if I could come in. I brought wine."

Dry as dust, she said, "You can use the front door, you know. The guys all know about us. Except maybe Arthur." She waved her hand from the door on into the hall, the graceful gesture of a matador.

He jerked erect, strode that one step forward. He leaned down, tilted his head, and brought his lips to hers. Soft, brushing, turning more urgent. She opened her mouth – his tongue teased her.

He leaned back and placed his finger on her lips. "No need to chastise me. I know I've been a shit." He shrugged out of the ripped parka, let it fall to the worn hall boards.

"Admitting the problem is the first step to curing it."

He flipped his eyebrows – he thought that was funny. "I'll snag two glasses from the kitchen. Meet me in the bedroom."

He stepped past her and she remained frozen in the door, listened to whispers of dread rising above the thump of his feet, like sphinx moths out pollinating roadside primroses. She gazed sightless into the the dim of the evening outside.

The slap of a cabinet door brought her to and she closed the back door.

He had already circled back to her bedroom. She shuffled the three steps to him and he dropped his hand with the glasses across her shoulders.

He murmured. "Thank you for driving me to Albuquerque. Things are going to work out. I'll be right as rain, you'll see. Hold the bottle." He scooped her up, carried her backwards into the bedroom.

She jerked her head up to stare at him. No light in the room. She couldn't read his face. Even so, she'd opt for this Michael.

He dropped her on the bed. She hit like a kid on a trampoline. She reached up for him and wrapped her arm around his waist. Delusional, both of them.

"Can we have a light?" He fumbled around on the nightstand. The shade rattled. A dim golden glow flooded out.

She leaned towards him as he straightened. She wanted a gesture, some intimacy, something.

"Here," he said. He handed her the two glasses. After he dug at his belt buckle, he dropped his pants. He collapsed back onto the bed, compelled it to creak. He fumbled with his legs, rolled down the stiff silicon sockets halfway before he tugged.

They drank the wine cross-legged on the bed, the bottle propped inside her legs. Thank God he'd brought a white, the way they splashed it about. Pressed knee to knee. Her head began to hum with the wine.

When the time arrived, he caressed her neck below her ear, elicited a shiver. His hand trailed across her collar bone, unbuttoned the four buttons of her blouse. She shook as he brushed his fingernails across her scar. Two bruised people, cloaked in a dim, yellowed room – they fit like two parts of a broken mirror.

—⁂—

He did linger over each touch, every moment, as he had boasted. She didn't remark much tenderness afterwards. He lay her back into the nest, propped his head on the old wooden headboard. "Peanut butter

248

and jelly? You can slap together sandwiches and we can eat in bed. I'll tell you about my day on the job. You can tell me about the latest paperback you read."

In the morning the male side of the bed lay rumpled and empty. The room stank of sweat and semen, wine and pheromones. Infidelity smelled so mundane. She already craved last night's Michael. She dragged herself up, opened the window, and stripped the bed.

—⁓—

December 2, 2009.

Tony spraddled in a backwards chair as he played cards with Emmet in Chuma's café. He grinned when Bec entered, punched Emmet in the arm. "I told you so!"

She wiggled between the tables and slipped into a chair at their elbows. "Boys."

"I told him so. Chuma said once that you bought Arthur a cake every Wednesday. I knew you'd be in this morning and save us a trip out to your cabin."

Emmet said, "It was I who informed Tony of the opportunity. Don't forget I have ridden with him before. The road struck me as long, the trip perilous."

Bec laughed. "My, Emmet, I do like how you talk. Tony, what's so important you can waste all morning with cards while you wait for me?"

He glanced at Emmet. "Now let's see if you're right or I am."

She asked, "Right about what?"

"The news. I've been accepted into the writing program in San Diego – they've given me a waiver to begin in January on my prerequisites, but I want to drive out early."

"Oh."

"San Diego! Drinking on the beach, hot dates, finest literary minds in the nation. I'm off to become the next Pierre Salinger."

"Tony, that's great news. But I think you meant J.D. Salinger."

He snorted, not at all embarrassed. "I mix up all those eggheads. How do you feel about my news?"

Bec grinned. "I guess if your roommate can tolerate losing you, I can too."

Emmet held up a finger. "Wait for it. He has more to disclose."

Bec tipped her head, raised her eyebrows.

Tony leaned on his forearms, angled his face towards hers. "Did I tell you how I like your hair now it's grown out mostly? The raven-black, the startling white here and there? And on a woman so young. Compelling, I call it."

She waved the flattery off. "Tony, you liar. You're stalling."

"We've got money and expertise for getting more. Roland and Celestino are great at fundraising."

"That's nice." Was she about to be conned?

He rushed it like a bull at a fence. "I set everything up so you'll be off to a fast start. I've rounded up donated materials and cash enough to finish the build-out. We've stockpiled operating money in the bank. Kevin can run the show on the ground. You'll have no trouble as Chief."

"Chief?"

Emmet muttered, "Now you're in for it."

"The Charity Board elected you Chairman. The Center falls to you."

She dropped back against her chair. "What? I'm not on the Board. You're trying to recruit me as manager. How can I be Chairman too?"

Tony coughed. "You've always been on the Board. I've kind of been voting your proxy for you. Your name slipped onto the incorporation papers, right below mine."

"Anthony. Why haven't I heard about this? Why haven't I been at the meetings?"

Tony hemmed. "We held the meetings in the bar over at Buffalo Thunder Casino. I knew you'd be bored."

"Really."

Tony and Emmet caught each other's eye. Emmet said, "I win."

Bec pressed both palms on the table to keep her from throttling him. Her fingers arched, tense. "Let me restate – and please correct me if I get anything wrong. You've come out of nowhere – "

"Afghanistan. That's not nowhere."

"Conned me into giving you my land. Talked me into the manager's job of a recuperation center. And you expect me to take charge while you skip out to get on with your life?"

Tony beamed. "I knew you'd understand. Let's do a handover soon. Spring term begins January twentieth."

—⁓—

December 4, 2009.

Chuma's office, clotted with the smell of caramelized onion. Chuma had decided that soup-of-the-day would be French Onion, but with Monterey Jack cheese. Bec patched the call through.

Ted adjusted the screen and the camera on his end of the call, all fiddly. Bec perched in Chuma's chair, waited for him to settle. Ted stared at her image on his screen – it dropped his chin and brought his eyebrows down. "William said you used this Skype thing all the time. If he can do it, so can I."

"Piece of cake, Ted. You'll do fine."

The screen disappeared in a cloud of pixels, like a bomb, cleared to show his shocked face. "Whoa. What the hell was that?"

"Just the commercial. I muted it for you."

"Really?" He said that a lot.

"No, it was a glitch. It happens some times. Also, the internet builds in a delay, like on a bad mobile connection, so don't rush."

"Okay."

"Your dime, buddy."

251

"I'm just test-driving this new thing here. But we could talk about Mara." His face sagged.

"I imagined we would. Didn't my advice work?"

A sheepish quirk in the corner of his mouth. "Like a charm. She stopped off here over the weekend. She was on her way home for the holidays with her family."

"And?"

"Wow, it was great. The best sex we've ever –"

"Ted!"

"Okay, okay. Didn't change things. We have this long distance chemistry, but... but she's going to have a career and plans to teach at Trinity. She said the Irish scholar and the Texas playboy wouldn't make a good match."

"Teddy, I'm sorry."

"Maybe I could sell cars in Dublin? At any rate, I think I'll try to fly over to visit her, two, maybe three times a year."

"Make sure that's what she wants."

He grinned, turned into the old Teddy for a flash. "Sure, Sis. I learned my lesson last time."

She was in stitches. "What? You've reformed? I don't believe it."

—w—

December 5, 2009.

Bec had been spiraling in on this job for months, long looping turns as she descended. She was close to a "yes." No matter how things stumbled along in her life now, it was better than the clammy solitude she had wrapped herself in months ago.

But like a little girl she wanted to hear it from somebody else. First she talked to Miss Junie, who praised her for stepping up. "Atta girl. Women rule the world."

She wanted to talk to Michael, but the right version of him wasn't around. Instead the surly, moping beast prowled through the daylight

252

hours, hammer in hand. At night he didn't want to talk. Food, sleep, sometimes sex. Clear that he wasn't taking the meds.

She caught Jason outside the dorm. "What do you think?"

"It's a good fit. I reckon you ought to do it. Since you're in charge, can you ask the chaplains to send my replacement out? I'm due to rotate out in four weeks. I wanted to break the new guy in myself."

Fat help, that. She talked to Arthur.

"Miss Bec, could I have a job?"

Like most decisions, she listened to her instinct. As she drove back from Arthur's – two icy patches where she nearly slid off the road and one hole where the creek had burst out and run its ice dam over the road – she paused at the break from the trees into the Center's meadow. Fifty feet away the dorm shone its green roof into the sky. A vast snowy churn in front where trucks had driven in and out. Intensely colored by a midday sun.

Wheelchair ramps snaked down from each door and a backhoe hunkered in for the winter. She knew the community center would be just on the other side, and another dorm after that, like a siege line extended towards her cabin.

She could do it, she knew. She visited with Chuma. "I already handled the tough part when I gave up my privacy. Let them all in. Tony's done the initial fundraising, the construction. From here it's the day-to-day. Four men at first and later sixteen men at a time, sixteen men to support each other, ask my help only when they want an outsider to step in. Hire some staff – like a grant writer. Arrange for the food, the bookkeeping, the cleaning, the laundry. Bound to be some crisis every week. But I can do this."

"You think? I think so too. But you going to jump off the cliff? Do you want it?"

"A hell of a lot more than being married to the Army."

"I figure it's a piece of cake," Chuma said, "Compared to that Michael of yours. But I bet he doesn't like it."

"Why wouldn't he?"

"Changes things for him, doesn't it?" Chuma tapped her temple with her fingers. "They all hide small boys in there. Little boys who want what they want."

Chapter Twenty-Six – The Hell Away

DECEMBER 7, 2009.

The banging on Bec's screen door sounded a chatter like teeth. She grasped the knob and threw the door open. Michael kicked his boots against the log walls to knock off the snow. Already half-peeled out of his coat. Why did he still knock?

She backed up, none-too-fast. He nearly stepped on her as he strode in. Icy slush dripped off his feet. He dropped the parka to the side, bent at the waist to unlace his boots.

She said, "I expected you sooner." Wrong approach.

He flicked that black expression at her, straightened and stepped out of the first boot. "I missed you too."

"I waited dinner. Green chili stew."

The second boot dealt him trouble. A couple of antic hops, the effort not to fall over sideways.

She braced him, supported all that weight. The smell of bourbon hung in his clothes. That and something sweet, herbal.

He said, "I ate with the guys." His fixed stare bored into her, dared her. He shook the leg. The boot clattered to the floor, dragged the latex foot with it, and revealed the two long black toes.

"If you're still hungry – ."

"Long day. I'm off to bed."

She watched his back head across the floor and into the hall.

Shoulders hunched clear to his ears. What had she signed up for?

He would want sex. And she would give it. The only good time they shared now.

—॥॥—

December 8, 2009.

Tony's Nissan, a solid three inches of snow on its roof, edged across the pasture down the lane that Rubio plowed for her. Strange, he and Emmet normally drove out in the morning, not late afternoon. Lately they used Little Rubio's bobtail truck, not this towny excuse for a vehicle. Where was Emmet?

Probably here to dump something new on her. Tony climbed out. He clumped up the steps, stopped one below her. The corners of his mouth cut sharply down, his eyebrows tented in the middle. Grim – unnatural for him.

"Afternoon, Tony. Charity business?"

"I'm afraid not. Bec, I met some guys in town asking directions to your place. I've brought them out after they contacted the Sheriff. I want you to brace yourself. They're right behind me."

From the tree line, past the dorm, the Sheriff's SUV lurched, shadowed by a Suburban. At that second of recognition – men in a car escorted to her door – in a flick she knew. There in her head, it tried to worm into her consciousness – she blocked it, ground it down as hard as a person could. By the time they reached the cabin, she hung off Tony's arm. As they stopped before the steps, she was weeping.

Sheriff Martinez clambered out of his car. He closed the door quietly, watched the governmental SUV over his roof. As the Suburban emptied itself of men, he shuffled around to her, swayed to the porch edge with a heavy exhale. He scooped off his cowboy hat, cradled it across his chest. Bec gazed through her tears on his bald head; he glanced at her, stone-faced. "Mrs. Robertson. Tony. The Army's here." He held his hand out to

256

the men as if presenting them. He dropped it back to his side – nothing left that he could say.

The man in the plainest uniform said, "Mrs. Robertson, I'm Chaplain Gutierrez. This is Major Simon. These are Sergeants Ames and Chandler."

Her breath heaved in and out of her – she was suffocating. But she kept her eyes open, and she turned from one to the other as they were introduced.

The Major, whose name had already flown out of her mind, stepped onto the porch and gripped her hand. "Mrs. Robertson, I am sorry to inform you that your husband Chaplain William Robertson has been killed in action."

The tears burned her cheeks but turned icy where they dripped off her chin into her shirt.

Tony said, "Gentlemen, will you please come in?"

They all shuffled into the living room, silent as Trappists. By hand gestures they directed each other to seats, removed their berets and service caps. All four sat starkly upright, spines like steel. Sheriff Martinez propped himself against the post between the kitchen and the living room, as if he wanted to be close to the door.

She fell into a kitchen chair by the wood stove. She asked the first simple question. "How was he killed?"

The major answered. "It was a large IED. They exploded it in the middle of a convoy, and it destroyed the Chaplain's armored vehicle. No one inside survived."

Tony bobbed his head. "Was it a double A?"

One of the sergeants answered. "Probably." He leaned towards Bec. "He means was it ammonium chloride and aluminum powder. The report says that we swept the road that morning, but fertilizer bombs don't show on the metal detectors."

Tony asked the next big thing that needed an answer, "Did the Chaplain suffer?"

"The report we have says he died instantly. No chance he would have known."

Again Tony, "Do we know when he died?"

"About twelve hours ago. One p.m. on December 8th."

She couldn't stay seated like a rock in that chair – she rose out of it grating its legs on the floor. Between all their feet, she shuffled about in the small space. She clutched her hands together under her chin. She hunched over.

Tony asked, "Can you tell us who died with him?"

The Chaplain inclined his head. "No, I'm afraid we can't release any names. It's possible that other families haven't been informed yet."

Her tears blinded her. They all hovered in their seats as witnesses, tracked her with their eyes as she dragged herself round and round. She tripped over military boots – the soldiers scuffed their feet back and butted their heels against the chairs and couch.

The Major held his hand out to Bec as she circled around to him. "Mrs. Robertson, please sit down. Do you have any questions?"

Her whole face hurt. Her lower jaw clamped in a rigid bite. Her eyes burned. She stopped short in front of him. "Yes, I do have a question."

"Whatever I can answer."

She leaned toward him. "Will you requisition another one?"

"I don't understand."

She snapped at him. "Will you line up another preacher and send him out?"

The Chaplain said, "Perhaps I should answer that."

Her head whipped around towards him.

"The chaplains go where they're needed, to support the troops. Your husband did his duty gladly, worked tirelessly with our servicemen and servicewomen. He was good at what he did, and well-respected."

She glared at him through the murk of tears. "You can't know that. You didn't know him. You weren't in the field with him."

The Major said, "We've talked to the commander of his Forward Operating Base, so we do know some things. Over the next few days, Chaplain Robertson's immediate superior and some of his comrades will contact you. You'll hear more from the people who were with him."

She said, "Small comfort. William is dead, isn't he? And you'll send out another chaplain to replace him, to die in his turn." The pitch of her voice rose. Strange. She knew what poor behavior this was.

The Chaplain said, "It's a vocation, Mrs. Robertson. Our chaplains answer a calling like other ministers, but for this one you wear a uniform. Chaplain Robertson understood that, I'm sure."

Tony asked, "Please, Bec, won't you sit down?"

She backed away instead. "Would that make it more comfortable for you, Tony? For you all? God damn it!" She threw her hand out, smacked the clock on the shelf. The hundred-year-old wind-up pendulum clock tumbled to the floor, the glass door broke, the works flew out of the broken case. Jagged splinters reflected the light.

She dropped to her knees. Tony knelt beside her, wrapped his arm around her shoulder.

"Bec. It'll be all right. It'll work out."

That was meaningless crap to say. She scooped parts together, drew her family's clock into a pile. The glass cut her hand. Blood oozed out. Good. Maybe in a minute another kind of pain would kick in.

"Leave it, Bec. It's only a clock. Come back to the sofa." He picked her up like a child, set her on her feet.

His artificial hand lay heavy on her shoulder. A hand from the war itself. She turned to him, allowed his embrace. Into his neck, she grizzled. She whispered, "Tony, I betrayed him. I was in bed with Michael when he died."

This miasma of hysteria. She slowed into a continuous quiet lament. Leaning against Tony on the couch with a box of Kleenex in her lap, she allowed the quiet, intermittent talk to flow on around her. Why didn't they leave?

They had things left to say to each other. Command structure in New Mexico. A name to contact – of course there would be military benefits. No mention of the remains.

William in a body bag, in a metal coffin, a flag over the top.

The Chaplain rose, inclined his head to her. To the widow. "We're so sorry for your loss, ma'am." The soldiers leapt to their feet. Tony trailed out after them onto the porch, left the front door open, the cold pouring in. Maybe she would freeze.

She melted into the couch, her hands curled into her lap under the manilla envelope they had handed her. Through the open door, she listened to them dissecting her life, tiptoeing around her guilt.

Tony again. "You drove in from where?"

"White Sands."

"Long drive."

Sergeant Ames asked Tony, his voice trickling into the room. "Does she have anyone to stay with her?" Why hadn't he asked her?

"She's close to a woman in town. We'll check if she can come out – she can stay maybe a day or two."

"What happens after? Family?"

"Parents passed away and she's an only child. Not sure how close she is to her husband's people. She does have four veterans, on the other side of the pasture. But that might work out better than you expect. They all understand what happened, and what happens now."

All scarred by the war. A demonstration of loss, but not her's.

—៣—

December 10, 2009.

Chuma lay in the bed on William's side, snored in and out. Nearly as big as William, but not nearly as long – even so, Bec couldn't shrug off the shiver it gave her. She stretched out rigid beside Chuma, contemplated the dark of the ceiling – it appeared to shift like inky clouds, magic. The moon, waning and a third full, hung low on the horizon. It beamed its weak coldness in on them, painted the bedclothes in the palest yellow, with deep blue shadow in the rumples and folds.

Sleep denied her. She had spent the previous nights and the day rolled into a ball in this bed. Now exhausted, she alternately dozed and cried. She could smell the stink of tears, an odor of salt and mucus.

—ʍ—

According to Chuma, Emmet sat by the bed while she slept, but fled the awakening. The vets left her much alone. Shoveled her snow, asked if she needed anything, faded away back across the field.

All of the women paid their condolence calls. Miss Junie, Karen... all except Marcella who had flown off to South Africa for the warmth. Thank God. Bec could have done without any of them. They perched on the edge of their seats, crooned out comforting noises, talked over her head in soft voices. Like she wasn't in the room.

I never met him, did you? – It will work out. – She's busy with the Center, that will distract her. – I wish she lived in town near us. – Maybe we can set up regular dinners, girls-night-out. – Pity about the clock. – Pity about everything.

They brought casseroles. They cleaned the kitchen Chuma had already cleaned. Chuma folded up in a chair against the bedroom wall, disgruntled.

In the morning, she'd send Chuma back to the café. She would change the sheets. After that, she'd see.

—ʍ—

December 12, 2009.

The cabin was only a box. No comfort, no warmth. The dusty walls folded all around, the half-light and the creaking board floors, all felt stark, inanimate. It occurred to her that for sparse instants she forgot William was dead. Amazed at herself, a shattered blink of shame.

The knock, when it arrived as Bec knew it would – echoed in the wooden back hall. Neither timid, nor demanding. It was only a knock, not a monster.

She shambled her way to the door, dressed in a flannel nightgown and a white bedraggled robe with a tea stain across its front. When she opened it – she discovered what she had expected. After knocking, Michael had backed to the porch edge, that half space away. Behind him lay a foot of snow, spread beneath the stars. She hadn't noticed it sift down, while she grieved in this house.

She placed her palm on the screen.

He let out a long ragged breath. "Does that mean stop?" he asked.

"I don't know. Maybe it means help. Maybe it means I stuck my hand up." She kicked the door open and he stepped forward with his thump. Which Michael would this be? She couldn't tolerate the dark, bloodied Michael. Could she endure a consoling, affectionate Michael either?

He held the screen, paused at the threshold. "Is it too late?"

"It's only eight."

"No, I meant.... "

She said, "Yes, you waited awhile. Four days. Come on through to the living room." She led the way through the dimness, to where a single lamp burned. She slipped into an easy chair, its worn cloth arms wrapped around her, and hugged her knees. He dumped down on the couch, his knees kicked out left and right.

He craned his head around, as if checking for other people in the room. He dropped his chin on his chest, gazed at the floor. "I couldn't figure out if four days was too long or too short."

"Me either. You're here now. Would you like some tea?" She unfolded herself from the chair, set off to the kitchen past him.

He lurched to his feet and blocked her way. He dropped a hand on her shoulder. "Have you thought about us? And him?"

"Please, Michael, not tonight. I'm not ready, not even to talk."

He scowled. "That's not why I'm here. I needed to warn you."

"Warn me?" Her stupid parrot voice.

"The Chaplain is dead. I told you death curled up inside me."

How could she shut off this obscene drivel? "You only think you're full of death. That's just your own delusion."

He overrode her. "Now it's killing people around you."

She shrugged out from under his hand. "Michael, please don't be crazy. At least not right now. Just be quiet. As a matter of fact, go away."

He edged towards her – his boots scuffled on the boards. "It's anyone I touch."

What bullshit. She turned her back on him. "You'd like that, wouldn't you? But it's not true."

"I'm poison."

She bundled her robe tight around her. "I need you to go away, Michael. Please go away." She hadn't believed herself capable of it, but she began to cry again. A tear spilled out in a surprised flight down her face.

"I don't want to kill you, Bec."

She whipped back around. The lunatic had sunk his face in his hands; he swayed back and forth. "Kill me? You're not even going to touch me."

"That's not how it works." He dropped his arms to his sides, his shoulders rounded.

Her voice, loud, high and shrill. "Will you please, please get the hell away from me!"

CHAPTER TWENTY-SEVEN – CLOCKWORKS

D ECEMBER 16, 2009.
Locked on course, the Department of Defense strove to help Bec, forced their way into her attention not on the day after William died as they wanted, but when she allowed it days later – she drove down the mountain to use Chuma's phone. His voice sounded ludicrously young. He said, "This is Lieutenant Rodney Deltar. I'm your Casualty Assistance Officer here in Albuquerque. Thanks so much for calling me back. My purpose with this phone call is to arrange a visit with you at any location you want here in New Mexico."

She didn't want this visit. She wanted numb.

He confirmed her identity – did she even have an identity right now? He let her know the transport plans already in progress, the arrival date, the earliest day that the deceased could be delivered into civilian care at the funeral home of her choice. They spoke of the type of internment she would want – VA cemetery or civilian? William had chosen the Army over Dallas. She ceded him to the Santa Fe National Cemetery.

Lieutenant Deltar helped her select a funeral home in Santa Fe, chose it for her, really. He affirmed she could request a local minister in Santa Fe who was a retired military chaplain. He called that minister. The Chaplain and he chose a date for the service, and obtained her fazed compliance. He asked her, "Is there anything else I can do for you?" He asked this again and again. What could this young man do for her? She had done enough already, to herself and to William.

She began the phone calls to William's remaining family. She needed to apply to the National Cemetery. Her cousins would need to know.

—ⱳ—

December 23, 2009.

Now, two days from Christmas. Disguised as a minister's wife, she journeyed out of the high country into Santa Fe. There would be a civilian service in a chapel. Short of St. Francis Drive she slid off on the exit and wound round the green rolling spread of the military cemetery. Here, the place where she could leave him safe in the columbarium. She'd chosen cremation. Each casket ate valuable space as war and time filled the cemetery. But she had already chosen the fire. Because she didn't believe she could bear to look upon him again.

The civilians first. In the lobby outside a professional chapel for death, she met Ted and a flock of distant Robertsons she couldn't even place, plummeted in from Texas and Kansas and Oklahoma. They all queued to sign the book. None of her cousins could attend – the remnants of her mother's people, the Staffords, were in New York and California. Her family – an illusion. Her vets – she had asked them to stay in Santa Eulalia.

A woman in funereal black opened the double doors – Bec led the way inside, into the heart of her plight. The chapel, a half dozen pews on each side – floral sprays clogged the air with the sweet smell of embalmers. Beige carpet, white tile ceiling, somber chintz pads in the seats. The walls were paneled in the gloom of dark wood, lit by medieval brass sconces.

She could hear every single sound in the small room, every needling whisper. A loose assemblage of people, muted but catching up on family news. They were brought together as kinfolk are for weddings and funerals to somehow reknit the texture of bloodlines. Only she represented her side – and why shouldn't she witness for William and for the Grassics end at the same time? A terrible debilitation lapped around her ankles, swept up into her lap, burrowed in behind her aching ribs. Ted hovered beside her, held her hand, pressed her with his sponge of a paw. She extracted her hand; he seized it. She dropped her head – she might even appear to be grieving rather than turned to stone.

She glanced over at Ted, registered his rigid wounded face staring at the minister. The chaplain told the stories of William's childhood, narrated how Ted and his parents had shared special moments, jokes, activities with William. Ted's face told all. Tears glistered into his eyes.

The Chaplain wrapped up the first part of the story, the Robertsons and their William. She inspected her shoes, blue, open-toed. The dampness on the funeral home's grass had seeped into her stockings – cold everywhere.

She allowed no real stories about her and William. The last of the sermon focused on William's calling, about his service to the Army's children. She had mentioned only the good to the chaplain, not the faults, the failures – between them they mythified William. She held her betrayal close, along with the secret that she had fallen out of love and that she chose his way to death for him. She caught a gritty, sand-papery sound. Was she shuffling her feet – had they tracked in sand? Her teeth ground away like they would pulverize fate.

—⁓—

The funeral home provided a hearse, even though it transported only mourners and an urn. In a cold overcast day that inflicted sporadic rain and a bit of sleet, they paced solemn through the necropolis, up the sidewalk to the place where William would be sanctified by the military. Five chairs in a single row at the Committal Shelter, an open structure on a hillside that faced the snow-covered mountains. Dim mountains perceived through the mist. Four couples balanced on their feet respectfully behind her. She slumped front and center, a cloth-shrouded urn in her lap. William, that tall, balding man, so proud to wear the uniform, reduced to a dull weight on her thighs. Maybe he had deserved better than her. Maybe this had all been set in motion the moment she had chosen him.

Ted tried once again to hold her hand. He snuffled. Tears shone in his eyes, jeweled from the gray softened light. The back of her hand, wet from the drizzle outside, cold like death. Or just winter.

She couldn't blink. Her eyes dry and crusted. She had tilted her face to the wet sky before she ducked in out of the weather – maybe they would all think it her tears.

A flag. On behalf of the United States Army, and a grateful Nation, please accept this flag as a symbol of our appreciation for your loved one's honorable and faithful service. The warriors ritual, military honors. She handed the flag to Ted. The bugle, warbling, with a threat of missed notes, more of a griever than she. It was unendurable.

Final words – all the right words – a prayer from her retired chaplain. Ted nudged her. It was time. She rose, the bundle clutched to her. Cloth around an urn, around a sealed bag that contained the ashes, the bone chips, and William's service for his country. Four steps forward – a tall man in Army green accepted the urn, turned and handed William to a Cemetery employee. From here he would be carried to the grayness of that funerary wall. He would be placed in a military container, a one-foot tall box emblazoned with the American flag. They would deposit him within the niche. They would seal the marble door with four stainless steel rosettes.

—⚏—

A half hour wait and they could visit the columbarium. The cemetery held three columbaria in all, eight foot walls, crowned with a concrete pediment painted a Southwest adobe orange, framed in native stone at each end. The solemn walls staged up the slope, set into the hillside, stared out at a rich neighborhood across deep gulches choked in desert plants. Carefully separate, the war and the nation.

The wall ran to the left and right, inset with inscribed doors. Each place occupied held a cross or a Star of David, a name, a rank, dates of birth and death, a message. The bottom of William's marble portal held the chiseled words "You Are Not Forgotten" cut deep. She knelt on the wet walkway, touched the carving with her hand. This inscription the worst burden she could inflict upon herself.

As they drove her back to the funeral home for her pickup, Bec couldn't dwell any longer on William, left in the niche, the warehouse of the dead. Instead she remembered her momma's death.

—m—

Mid November 1999.

Lying in the bed, its head tilted up and the pillows half burying her, her momma said, "You can't spend all night here, honey. Go on back to your motel."

Bec submerged herself in a chair that hunkered three inches too close to the floor and was cut wide for overweight visitors. "Okay, I'll go in a bit. I can stay till you drop off to sleep." Lubbock's hospital offered its best – a semi-private room, painted a sickly green color. At least William's giant church and the good living had that payoff – a trifling privacy for her momma.

"Lord, don't wait for that. I don't sleep much anymore, unless the drugs kick in." She appeared worn, a faded rag.

This is what the long night stretches were for, in the end. The questions unasked. "Momma, we haven't talked about it, not yet."

"Rebecca, honey, you've never been one to dance around tough questions. Just ask."

268

"I want to know about the melanoma."

"Lord, child. It's something farmers come down with. I'm forty-eight and that means forty-seven years in the sun."

"No, I meant when did you detect it?"

Her mother appeared so tired, but not frightened. "About five years back. Honey, could you press the button for me? I'm a bit uncomfortable."

Bec glanced over at the pump. "I'm sorry, Momma. The yellow light's on, so it won't give you a drip yet."

Her mother's eyes flicked out, towards the window sheathed in three-inch-wide venetian blinds. "We'll have to wait then, won't we?"

"Five years. That's a long time."

"Not so much. My old-age spots showed up even when I was young. Five years ago these basal cell things began showing up. They cut a couple of them out two years ago, but it cost a lot."

"You didn't tell me. I could have helped." Yes, she could have, if she had been there.

Her momma frowned, lips thin. The grayness in her face, the wrinkles, the flannel scarf wrapped around her neck. "I know, Rebecca, I know. Maybe it was pride. We've always done for ourselves."

"Basal cells aren't melanoma, though."

"No, that was last year. The first melanoma – I couldn't see it. It began as a mole on the back of my neck. I didn't notice it until the soreness kicked in. The latest is this purple one on my collarbone." She twitched down the hospital gown – her neck, her upper chest withered and skin drooping. They'd taped on a square dressing, and previous tape had torn her skin, left it bloody and bruised around the edges.

Bec leaned forward from the chair depths. Hesitant, afraid to hurt or shock, she reached over and touched the bandage with her finger. "It's not very big."

"Oh, little one. It's not this teeny patch. It's where the cancer freed itself and ran through me everywhere." Unless their poison worked, Bec would lose her mother.

Bec dropped back into the chair, as defeated as her mother's body. She glanced at the pump. "The light's green, Momma. I can give you a dose."

—⚋—

December 23, 2009.

The hearse took them back across Santa Fe to the civilian funeral home. In the office of the director, Bec made arrangements to pay off the funeral over a three-year period, and in return, received a barracks locker with William's rank and name in white stencil on the lid. Later she would discover the divorce papers. The poor soul had signed half his name, but quit before the end. A signature that trailed off, like their marriage. They put the locker in her truck for her.

Ted gripped her arm as they paced from the funeral home to where their cars waited. "Hey, little sister. What will you do? Move back to Dallas?" His eyes shone red as the flag's stripes.

Her smile felt like a sad baby twitch of the lips. "I'm sure you'd drive out to New Mexico to help me pack, too. But no, not Dallas."

"Closer to family. Plenty of things to keep you busy."

Yes, William's family, the only family left to her – except for Santa Eulalia. "No, Ted. I'll go home. The Center won't run itself. A real job, even though it doesn't pay much."

He flapped his hands, waved her words away. Or maybe flapped at his own distress. "We've planned a big dinner tonight, before we all go home for Christmas. We reserved a room in the back of a restaurant."

"I'm driving right back, Ted. My only reason to be in Santa Fe is this cemetery." She knew that must sound cold, but she couldn't sit and share grief like wine around a restaurant table.

He said, "It'll be like a wake. We'll talk about… him."

God no. "I'm sorry, little brother. I couldn't endure it."

They paced quiet a dozen steps, his hunched shoulders a plea. "I had hoped – that is, I need time to talk some. I wanted to ask you something about Mara."

She fobbed him off. Reaching up and caressing his shoulder, she said, "Email me about her. Maybe we'll Skype. Don't do anything stupid in the meantime."

—◊—

She detoured north on Guadalupe through Santa Fe's core so she could pass the Cemetery again. She gazed back over the lawns blurred with the fog. The wave of the hill cascaded down towards St. Francis Drive. Only here could the battlefield chaos be tamed and brought into a regular grid of the dead. The fallen and the deceased would continue arriving, four or five a day until they used all the land, and all the plots possible had accepted their dead. They could build more columbaria. They would acquire more land.

—◊—

Late November 1999.

As Bec shuffled down her momma's long hospital hall, hushed in the midnight hour, she chewed over why she had forbidden William to come. He had been busy, a conference coming where he would speak, plus the usual Church holiday season – but that wasn't her reason. She didn't want him to be here with her momma. She wanted this to be for the two of them.

She didn't want to use the bathroom in her mother's room either. Something about it gave her a shudder. No logic to it – the other half of her mother's room lay empty and her mother no longer left her bed. But Bec trekked down the hall, to the visitor's industrial-strength restroom, where she bathed her face and examined it in the mirror. Right between her ear and her cheekbone, the first brown old-age spot, the first one.

271

The nurses had pinned back the door of her momma's room – they'd flipped on all the lights, a cacophony of brightness. Two hovered over the bedside, another leaned over on the other side, removing the IV. She forced her way forward, tried to shove past them. "What... what?"

A tiny nurse, Asian or maybe Philippine, said in a flat Texas accent, "She's passed, dear. The monitor told us a couple of minutes ago."

Bec wasn't ready at all. She wormed her way past the nurses and seized her mother's hand. She dropped into the chair and peered into her mother's slack face. Death didn't look like that. Her mother's face – waxy, abandoned. Done.

The nurse patted her shoulder, like she was a child. "You take all the time you need, dear. We don't have to wheel her away for a bit." The three retreated, eased the door shut behind them.

The dull refrain she would repeat for years. She hadn't been there.

—ᵐ—

December 23, 2009.

She arrived at the cabin late in the evening. The dorm's windows glimmered across the pasture – eyes watching. She couldn't face the vets yet. She didn't need to be confronted by anyone who had worn a uniform, who came from the war.

She hadn't ever been there when it happened. Not for Uncle Howie, not for her father thank God, not for her mother. Or William.

Pretense kept her functioning – she pretended life continued, that trivial things could displace death and betrayal. The New Mexico sky opened above her as she drove out from under the trees. Her pasture shifted away from her at the speed of light as she lurched over the lane. A sky filled with huge white cumulus, white in the slivered moon against a black so deep it struck her as fake. She dropped her eyes to the treeline.

So crisp and sharp. All the world in focus, but not her. Somewhere in her head, she knelt in that living room, swept together the broken clockworks. Dreamt about burning the cabin. Angry.

And Michael – she slipped into the bedroom, opened the trunk against the wall. His clothes had disappeared. Thank God.

CHAPTER TWENTY-EIGHT – DREAMING A GOOD DREAM

D ECEMBER 30, 2009.
      Snow sifted slow, steady, created the same white-out as in Bec's mind. She couldn't park near the café. SUVs and a bus clogged the street, all focused on Chuma's place. Timid, she circled the block twice. Busy in the café. The locals would know about William.

She hid the truck in the alley by the dumpster. For the first time ever, she slinked in the back door. The shiny yellow-enamel walls hung close; fluorescents pelted down a shadowless light. Stainless metal crowded every wall and ran through the center as an island. She could smell the grease trap and a huge storm of odor from the food – bacon, onion, spices from a cauldron of soup, toast from the Panini press. Two youngsters split duties – one washed a mountain of dishes and another attacked vegetables on a counter with a knife. One old woman plated sandwiches – Bec recognized her as a cashier at the Mini-Mart. Chuma whirled like a tornado before the griddle, the prep station, the counter behind her, added cheese and green chili to four round fat burgers and kicked off six more. The sizzle was alarming, the banging and clatter in the kitchen a shock.

"Bec, what the hell you doing back here? You need a job? I never seen the place like this before!"

"What is it, Chuma? Who are these people?"

"Albuquerque touring club. On the way north to ride that damn narrow-gauge train. Some New Years Eve party shit."

"I realize you're busy." She'd better slide out gracefully.

"Here, strap on this apron. Run this order out to table four. That's the one by the pie counter. No, grab a tray – Honey, you don't have time to make two trips."

—៕—

In the mid afternoon light, the children and their grandmother slumped exhausted at a table in the empty café, picking at burgers and sandwiches. Across the room Chuma sprawled in her chair at Bec's table. A dishtowel clotted with green chili hung over her shoulder. Her round face was scrubbed gray under the brown and her eyelids drooped more than usual. "Hoo-wee. I'm whupped. If it hadn't been for Lisa and her grandchildren – and you – I'd be passed out on the floor in the kitchen."

"You don't look that whipped." Treat the truth kindly.

"A few more days like today and I'll retire to the Rez."

Bec trickled out a thin smile. "That had to be the most intense three hours of my life."

"That's the restaurant business. Slammed or empty. Look around – not a single customer."

"Thank God."

Chuma eyed her. "We missed you for Christmas. They all asked for you. And how did you show up today just in time? Drive in to email?"

"No one to email. William's brother Ted, I suppose, but not today."

"Right. Just to visit with me? It's been a while."

"Actually," Bec leaned on her elbows. "I wonder if I could borrow your revolver again."

Chuma knotted her eyebrows. "Borrow a gun?"

"If you would."

"Need a reason, girl. This isn't about William passing, is it? You're not thinking –"

"No, no, nothing like that. And I don't want to talk about William yet. I want the gun around because of – well, because of Michael."

"Your vet gone rogue?" Chuma's eyes flashed wide – Bec had finally surprised her.

"I don't know. He did something that hit me as wrong. Something drove me to conclude he might be dangerous, not just depressed."

"You're not serious."

Bec gazed at Chuma, willed her to get it. "I watched him and a deer in the meadow. The deer's leg was broken. He put it down by breaking its neck."

Chuma grimaced. "Sounds like a kindness. A bit macho, but a kindness."

"Michael carried a knife, so why did he break its neck? He cut its belly open and stuck his hands in. It was creepy. And he knelt with the doe's blood all over him, for maybe five minutes."

Chuma's eyes were startled wide. "Whoa, what kind of sick ritual is that?"

"How the hell should I know?"

"Let me fetch that gun for you. It's only a thirty-two – maybe not be big enough."

—⚊—

January 6, 2010.

In the mountains of New Mexico from October through December, the winds howl round wooden buildings sprinkled through the trees or across the grasslands. The aspens are stripped of their leaves, firs topple to the ground, and pines snap off to leave poles as wind monuments. The freezes hit one after the other, bone hard, and the late-coming snow finally flurries in as a soft relief. All during January, snow piles in. The northern counties fold themselves in and wait.

The pasture wasn't any easier to drive with the ground frozen than when the ruts were full of mud, even though old man Rubio had plowed the road out. Snow bracketed the lane with four or five foot walls. Little Rubio's truck occupied the place of privilege in front of Bec's cabin as she arrived back from the village. What did Tony want this time?

He packed her into his commandeered vehicle. "Let me drive you over to the dorm. No need to hike through frozen shit."

At the Center, he clutched her elbow and marched her up the wheelchair ramp. They ducked under the tarp that sealed off the entrance. "I begin classes in ten days and the show will be yours. I want to take off for California tomorrow."

"Damn." She had avoided this till now.

"Time had to come."

She touched his forearm. "So what's the secret to keeping this place in the air?"

"I recommend a walkthrough every day and a consult with Kevin. Otherwise, make it up as you go along. I left all my paperwork inside your front door, neatly categorized."

A young woman perched on a ladder wired a light fixture. Bec pointed. "Someone new?"

"That's Allie. Lost her hand like me and uses an old-fashioned hook. No time delays like myoelectrics."

"Five vets are living and working onsite?"

Tony stopped in the middle of the room and gripped her shoulder. "No. I thought you knew. You're not reading your email. Jason is gone, off to California to rebuild his face. Allie is his backfill."

She dropped her head. "Without a word? That pisses me off. Or makes me sad." Tears seeped into her eyes. Silly burning sensation.

"Sucks, doesn't it? He left a letter for you – it's in the truck. He said he'd drop by in the spring, on his way back through."

"I don't know if we can run this place without him. The way he kept Kevin and Michael apart and in their corners.... "

Tony lifted her chin, tilted it up with the plastic shiny hand. "Hey, he deserves his own life. Jason's going offshore, onto the oil platforms. He wants a job with hard work in a remote place. Come meet Allie."

They paced up behind Allie on her ladder and watched her work. Four wires dangled out of a square box in the ceiling. With her hook she twisted a ground wire around a terminal. She crimped it, clipped the wire off with her pliers. The bare piece of copper whizzed back and missed Bec by a foot.

Allie snapped a look over her shoulder. "Incoming! Sorry about that."

Tony said, "Let me introduce you to our Chair Person and Manager. Allie Houston, Rebecca Robertson."

Bec stuck out her hand, "Call me Bec, please."

Allie kept her hand and hook up over her head. "Nice to meet you. Now, if you don't mind, ma'am, Kev has me on the clock here."

"We'll spend some time together Friday when you come over for dinner, okay?"

Allie blew her off, turned back to the work. The cold wait-and-see. This is the way it would be – arrivals, departures, beginning each relationship from scratch.

Tony steered her away. "Kevin is installing cabinets in one of the bathrooms. Michael is floating Sheetrock. And Davy, he's our tile man."

Across the room, she spotted Michael at a wall, a board and a taping knife in his hands, joint compound spattered across his clothes. He regarded her levelly. She dipped her head at him and let Tony drag her the other way.

Davy knelt in a shower and spread quickset. Dust from the saw covered his dark hair, gray quickset caked his hands. Bec crouched beside him, watched him lay a twelve-by-twelve of tile, true it, and tamp it with the handle of his trowel. "Lovely work, Davy. You know what you're doing."

He turned his face to hers, gave her a loopy grin. "Tile and I get along."

Bec wandered away with Tony. "Did I just see what I think I did?"

"If you mean Davy, you did. He's coming out of it some. At least he's benefitting from the Center."

"And Michael?"

"I ran him down to the VA for his regular appointment while you were unavailable. I dunno." Tony's frown rippled out his doubt.

"Don't know what?"

"On the way to Albuquerque I drove Sergeant Sunshine. On the way back – a different matter. It's Jekyll and Hyde."

They threaded their way across the floor through all the construction. Near the front door, Michael strode by with a five gallon can of compound. He shot her a dazzling grin. "Great to have you back. You're looking good." He thumped on across the room, not waiting for an answer.

Tony grunted. "Told you."

—៣—

January 19, 2010.

A hard snap squall – a storm blew in from the west, dropped five inches of white, and stalled on top of them. It hovered around them with unsettled cold wind and patches of white gathered in the corners, lurking on the porch. Planted at the front window, wrapped in a quilt to cut the chill, Bec pursued her own addiction. As she held the cup of oolong, she breathed into the mug. Steam wafted across her face. A tiny tease of air ghosted across her hands, a leak in the old window frame. Sunset, and day's gray overcast slid into a blue even colder.

A figure left the dorm, tramped straight towards her. She knew it

279

would be Michael. Dressed all in black, with a stocking cap low over his face. Hands in his pockets, he rounded the cabin and headed for the back door. Black, like a carrion crow. She clacked the tea down, strode to the back door to be in time for his knock. Her breath, shallow and fast.

No knock. The door banged open – he was in – he slammed it against the wind. He shuffled in far enough to settle his back onto the wall. He hauled off the stocking cap and balled it up in his two hands. "It's been awhile."

What kind of mood would he dump on her? "Thanks for giving me some time." Why the hell did she thank him? The gun was in the bedroom.

"I needed it too. In Albuquerque they're telling me things that make some of this easier."

So it would be about him tonight. "Easier for you? I just left my husband in a military cemetery. I'm glad it's easier for you, but.... "

He thrust his cap into his pocket, stepped forward and cradled her face. "I'm sorry. Let's start again."

She shook her face loose of his hands. "Is that such a good idea?"

"Lady, you let me in. You need to know as much as I do."

"Know what?"

"This." He reached his arms under the quilt and around her waist, even as she flinched. The quilt cascaded off her shoulders onto the floor. He hoisted her up against his chest. Her feet dangled – he stared into her face. She couldn't read his eyes. "Let's find out." He stepped over the quilt and carried her into her bedroom, laid her out like a doll on the sheets.

Not at all like the lover she knew. Not gentle, but in a hurry. He hurled his clothes into the corner by the bedside. She rammed her palm in the middle of his chest and shoved him back – a big mistake. A snarl, deep in his throat. He tugged her jeans off as he would skin an animal. He grasped the tail of her shirt in both hands and ripped, popped buttons. With his fingers he shredded her underwear and tossed them away. He crawled onto her, pried her knees apart with his torso.

She curled her upper body around his head. "No. Wait, Michael, wait! Let me warm up to.... "

He grunted. "Now we'll find out."

"Stop it! Get off me!" It burned like scalding water.

He pounded her, as fast as he could grind. At the top of his moment, he sucked in a breath and shuddered. When he finished, when he lay on her wheezing, she realized two things. His silicon sockets pinned her legs to the sheet – he had left them on. And he was crying. Crying? Tears and mucus collected on her neck, ran into the sheet below. What right did he have to cry?

—⁓—

January 20, 2010.

She wouldn't prosecute. No one would ever believe her side. Bec was sore, bruised and torn. That toughened her resolve. She would drop him back into the hell he had grubbed up for himself. He had to leave the Center, today.

The snow from their stalled front sifted down, with a wind fretful, confused. It shoved and prodded at her, first one way then the other. She stumbled, locked inside her head. All during the hike across the pasture, she never saw it. At the Center, she paused, her hand on the door.

Something was skewed, not right. What was she missing? Was this what the day after rape felt like?

Inside Bec discovered her team milling about in the entrance. Angry, she stared past them all for Michael. Not there. Something boiled in the air – the soldiers were tight. "What's up? Normally you're all at it by this time of day."

281

Allie, her face drawn in a scowl, said, "That dumb-ass Michael's disappeared."

Good. Problem solved. "Moved on?"

"No. His gear is still here."

No joy – she'd have to deal with him. "Why the concern? He goes off and broods all the time."

Kevin flapped his good hand. "He mostly comes home by daylight, even when he... when you and he –"

Bec cut him off. "Okay, I get it. Out all night. With weather like this, he could freeze to death."

Kevin added, "Allie discovered something else. Your truck's missing. She did a recon. We have to assume Michael's driven off in it."

Christ. Michael, what are you doing?

Lights blue and red, flashed in the window. They all piled outside. A County pickup parked in their snow-choked lot, police color cascading from the light bar on the roof. A tall man dressed in a car coat with sheriff patches clambered out. Paralyzed, all four of them on the porch watched him stride towards them.

"Mrs. Robertson, I'm Deputy Sheriff Jerry Block. We met about a year ago."

Bec stuck her hand out and advanced a step. "More like eight, nine months. Good to see you again." He didn't reach for her hand.

"Mrs. Robertson, do you drive a white 1972 Ford pickup, license plate...." He glanced at his notebook. "New Mexico KCK544?"

"Yes. But I'm not sure of the license. My truck's gone." Should she say anything about Michael? What did he that know she didn't?

"We have your truck, Mrs. Robertson. Could you accompany me to identify it and maybe the man inside?"

Man inside. Numbness, and a roaring in her head that drowned out the wind's whistle. Her job to handle. She turned to the crew. "You all go back to work. I'll send you news as fast as I can."

Kevin leaned to her, "We're okay here. You take care of yourself, Miss Bec."

—ɯ—

The sun lay in wait behind the low clouds, the light paltry, the air like a gray paste. Mannie's in Santa Eulalia. The snowfall had eased off for the moment – she spotted the truck wedged among the mounds of plowed-out white. Two cop cars angled close to it. Their lights strobed the scene, but a half dozen people wandered about slow and calm. They clumped together in small groups, or poked about the pickup. No reason for hurry. As she and the deputy sheriff climbed out of the cruiser, an ambulance and a civilian auto turned in behind them, blocked them in. She couldn't catch her breath.

A short man in a white cowboy hat and a calf-length coat – Sheriff Martinez – abandoned a small ring of his people and hustled towards her. He seized her by the upper arm. "Mrs. Robertson, we meet again. Is that your truck?"

She gazed over his shoulder. The dent in the tailgate – hers. "Looks like it from here. I'll check." She lurched one step to get around him.

He pinned her elbow. "Wait. We have to process the scene. Even then I'm not sure we should let you back there."

She scanned his face. Locked in eye contact. "Sheriff, one of our men has gone missing out at the Center. He's a veteran. And he's unstable. I believe he's the man in the truck, and so do you."

"We see it the same. He doesn't seem to have any ID.... "

"He's my employee. Do you want me to confirm it's him?"

The Sheriff sucked on one of his incisors. "Yes. Yes I do. It's not pretty – it chalks up to be suicide. Looks like he was punishing himself – he shot himself multiple times before he finished it. Are you sure you're up to this?"

She gazed into his Chicano face. Funny, she had never noticed all

283

the gray in his mustache. Her head spun, she staggered a half step side-ways. "I'll try."

Clutching her elbow, he steered her down the side of Mannie's, wove through the people and around the back of the pickup. A gray-haired Anglo in a knee-length coat blocked the door. The Sheriff said, "This's our Coroner, Doctor Dumas. Hey, Doc, can I slide in for a minute? We can make a positive ID."

The Coroner turned, revealing a lined, pale face. Thick glasses rimmed in tortoise shell illuminated watery, aging eyes.

The Sheriff added, "Now, don't touch anything, Mrs. Robertson."

Space opened up for Bec – people shifted out of the way. The truck stretched out wide and tall, many yards long. Black dots pinwheeled across her vision.

Voices filled her ears. Small caliber. Corpse not that torn up. Guy must have hated himself, all those holes. Dead how long? Rigor mortis at its peak, so fifteen hours. Liver temp might narrow that. Who's the woman?

She stepped forward, a bitter taste on her tongue. Shuffling into the triangle between the door and the cab. She smacked her shin into the running board. A broken window to her left – crusted on the inside with something like fireplace ash. Why didn't she turn her eyes on the man? Her neck felt locked like a steel rod. She stared first at the boots and the pants. Those pants would cover carbon fiber and silicon and titanium. Two gouges in the fabric above the knees. They blossomed with black gore. He wore no coat, only a T-shirt. Black stained his left bicep, a small puncture. Behind, his tricep torn away where the bullet had plunged through. His arm lay across his chest, had bled into his lap. A small clotted pool. She craned her head past and stared at his right hand. On the seat beside him, Chuma's revolver, from her dresser drawer.

His head had fallen back on the seat, his face turned towards her, nestled on his shoulder. On the right side of his head, a blackened ring at his temple. The left side was turned under – just as well. Serene, his eyes closed, his face relaxed. He appeared as he had on his best nights, dreaming a good dream in her bed. Beatific, the crippling animal in her bed.

A keening sound. It welled out of her throat. The Sheriff tugged at her shoulder, saying, "No, Mrs. Robertson, don't do that."

She clasped Michael's face in her hands, kissed his forehead.

Bec's Storm

CHAPTER TWENTY-NINE – SNOW

THE HIGH COUNTRY DIDN'T CARE. Bec leaned against the truck hood, bundled in coat, gloves, knit cap. The morning light knifed sidewise, gold and hurtful to the eyes. She considered the land she had chosen, its forces crushing together, its own needs that rolled over dwarfish human enterprise. The land persisted, no matter how much mankind scabbed it over with temporary structures that squatted on the earth.

She could catch sight of the Jemez crater to the south, primal and awful in its indifference. To the north and west, Mogote Ridge rose above 9400 feet. Close up, the trees plunged down the valley tracking the wild stream.

She hovered on the cliff edge, where they had bullied the gravel highway through, and the wind called across the rock face to her.

Wind had stripped the aspens months ago, but a few leaves hung as witness, tawny against the firs' darkness. From the west, weather rolled in, brought by the Pacific train of storms that lined up one after the other. Huge clouds painted a dervish, cast out of the black and subsumed back into the front. Dry lightning cracked at the leading edge, a sure sign of the sky's violence. This would be a punishing blizzard that could last a couple of days. Up here, she existed as a small and perishable outsider, not a piece of the sweeping fabric. If she waited too long, she wouldn't come down from the high country at all, but be discovered frozen dead in her truck.

The hood burned hot against her back. The truck was impossible. Even the ride up here was too much, surrounded by the stink of suicide. She didn't care if Davy and Kevin had spent hours cleaning out all the spatter, the flecks of a human being. Scrubbing the vinyl with bleach. She could smell the gunshots. She swore she could.

The reverberation of her voice settled her down, like the throbbing of a chord on an organ. " 'Whatever does not kill us compels us to be stronger' – that's such a lie. No heroes here."

Those hard things that drive us close to death leave their marks. Year after year, sorrow after sorrow. The physical scars are easier. "The hidden scars crust over, bind our minds into traps." She grinned, but it felt like a mask. A drama queen, she knew.

She crossed her arms, sensed the flat chest buried beneath layers, her two hot stripes of mutilation. She imagined the scars glowing like embers in the fire, heating her hands through the shirt, the sweater, the fleece coat. "Live day to day, embrace life. That's what all us cancer patients say, isn't it? But what day do I want?"

The sky foamed black, tremendous bubble-like cells where the wind raced around and skirted back through itself, worked into havoc and wrath. A bastard of a blizzard, a mirror of her heart. People who live alone go crazy. People who wrap themselves in the world are driven insane. She was as crazy as they come.

She could buy an acre up here with William's death money and build again. Spend another winter alone in a darkling log sanctuary. She could stay in her mother's cabin below, where she had helped two men spin themselves out into their deaths. With all her heart, she wanted to move on. To be someone else.

"The moment of longing, that's what defines us." Her own voice sounded idiotic in her ears. But she had seized on an idea that the meadow and her family's cabin – her mother's refuge – was finished for her. Longing had trickled away, had dried up.

Lightning struck nearby – she jumped clear out of her skin as the thunder shocked past her. Over on the next ridge, a fire – gray smoke whipped sideways to the east. The snow would snuff it out soon enough. She faced the truck's hood, dropped her hands onto the metal.

Her consciousness was a layer of paint slapped on top of her sub-conscious. She understood what consciousness did. It invented reasons for what happened. But the inner self hummed and ticked, raged and boiled. Wanted to survive.

She jerked the truck door open, clambered in behind the plastic faded wheel. She wondered what her decision was, now that she was ready for it. She stared out the window for a last clear view of the river buried in snow and ice below, indifferent submerged music.

She drove down the mountain, shoved forward by the first snow-flakes crazy in their frenzy. The sharp morning light disappeared into a wall of gray. The wipers beat a steady time and the defroster roared. For a half-hour, blind curve after snow-obscured straight, the weather slowed her as it swept past and on down.

She paused at the turnoff to her family's pasture, engine idling. Jesus, there could be no going back into that cabin. She jammed the truck in gear. The pickup switch-backed on down to the village. A family of sorts, below in the valley.

About the Author

Scott Archer Jones is currently living and working on his sixth novel and first novella in northern New Mexico, after stints in the Netherlands, Scotland and Norway plus less exotic locations. He's worked for a power company, grocers, a lumberyard, an energy company (for a very long time), and a winery. He has launched three books: *Jupiter and Gilgamesh, a Novel of Sumeria and Texas, The Big Wheel,* and *a rising tide of people swept away.*

https://www.facebook.com/ScottArcherJones
www.scottarcherjones.com

About Fomite

A fomite is a medium capable of transmitting infectious organisms from one individual to another.

"The activity of art is based on the capacity of people to be infected by the feelings of others." Tolstoy, *What Is Art?*

Writing a review on Amazon, Good Reads, Shelfari, Library Thing or other social media sites for readers will help the progress of independent publishing. To submit a review, go to the book page on any of the sites and follow the links for reviews. Books from independent presses rely on reader- to-reader communications.

For more information or to order any of our books, visit
http://www.fomitepress.com/FOMITE/Our_Books.html

More Titles from Fomite...

Novels
Joshua Amses — *During This, Our Nadir*
Joshua Amses — *Ghatsr*
Joshua Amses — *Raven or Crow*
Joshua Amses — *The Moment Before an Injury*
Jaysinh Birjepatel — *Nothing Beside Remains*
Jaysinh Birjepatel — *The Good Muslim of Jackson Heights*
David Brizer — *Victor Rand*
Paula Closson Buck — *Summer on the Cold War Planet*
Dan Chodorkoff — *Loisaida*
David Adams Cleveland — *Time's Betrayal*
Jaimee Wriston Colbert — *Vanishing Acts*
Roger Coleman — *Skywreck Afternoons*
Marc Estrin — *Hyde*
Marc Estrin — *Kafka's Roach*
Marc Estrin — *Speckled Vanities*

Fomite

Zdravka Evtimova — *In the Town of Joy and Peace*
Zdravka Evtimova — *Sinfonia Bulgarica*
Daniel Forbes — *Derail This Train Wreck*
Greg Guma — *Dons of Time*
Richard Hawley — *The Three Lives of Jonathan Force*
Lamar Herrin — *Father Figure*
Michael Horner — *Damage Control*
Ron Jacobs — *All the Sinners Saints*
Ron Jacobs — *Short Order Frame Up*
Ron Jacobs — *The Co-conspirator's Tale*
Scott Archer Jones — *And Throw Away the Skins*
Scott Archer Jones — *A Rising Tide of People Swept Away*
Julie Justicz — *Degrees of Difficulty*
Maggie Kast — *A Free Unsullied Land*
Darrell Kastin — *Shadowboxing with Bukowski*
Coleen Kearon — *#triggerwarning*
Coleen Kearon — *Feminist on Fire*
Jan English Leary — *Thicker Than Blood*
Diane Lefer — *Confessions of a Carnivore*
Rob Lenihan — *Born Speaking Lies*
Douglas Milliken — *Our Shadow's Voice*
Colin Mitchell — *Roadman*
Ilan Mochari — *Zinsky the Obscure*
Peter Nash — *Parsimony*
Peter Nash — *The Perfection of Things*
George Ovitt — Stillpoint
George Ovitt — Tribunal
Gregory Papadoyiannis — *The Baby Jazz*
Pelham — *The Walking Poor*
Andy Potok — *My Father's Keeper*
Frederick Ramey — *Comes A Time*
Joseph Rathgeber — *Mixedbloods*
Kathryn Roberts — *Companion Plants*
Robert Rosenberg — *Isles of the Blind*
Fred Russell — *Rafi's World*
Ron Savage — *Voyeur in Tangier*

Fomite

David Schein — *The Adoption*
Lynn Sloan — *Principles of Navigation*
L.E. Smith — *The Consequence of Gesture*
L.E. Smith — *Travers' Inferno*
L.E. Smith — *Untimely RIPped*
Bob Sommer — *A Great Fullness*
Tom Walker — *A Day in the Life*
Susan V. Weiss —*My God, What Have We Done?*
Peter M. Wheelwright — *As It Is On Earth*
Suzie Wizowaty — *The Return of Jason Green*

Poetry

Anna Blackmer — *Hexagrams*
Antonello Borra — *Alfabestiario*
Antonello Borra — *AlphaBetaBestiaro*
Antonello Borra — *Fabbrica delle idee/The Factory of Ideas*
L. Brown — *Loopholes*
Sue D. Burton — *Little Steel*
David Cavanagh— *Cycling in Plato's Cave*
James Connolly — *Picking Up the Bodies*
Greg Delanty — *Loosestrife*
Mason Drukman — *Drawing on Life*
J. C. Ellefson — *Foreign Tales of Exemplum and Woe*
Tina Escaja/Mark Eisner — *Caida Libre/Free Fall*
Anna Faktorovich — *Improvisational Arguments*
Barry Goldensohn — *Snake in the Spine, Wolf in the Heart*
Barry Goldensohn — *The Hundred Yard Dash Man*
Barry Goldensohn — *The Listener Aspires to the Condition of Music*
R. L. Green — *When You Remember Deir Yassin*
Gail Holst-Warhaft — *Lucky Country*
Raymond Luczak — *A Babble of Objects*
Kate Magill — *Roadworthy Creature, Roadworthy Craft*
Tony Magistrale — *Entanglements*
Gary Mesick — *General Discharge*
Andreas Nolte — *Mascha: The Poems of Mascha Kaléko*

Fomite

Sherry Olson — *Four-Way Stop*
Brett Ortler — *Lessons of the Dead*
Aristea Papalexandrou/Philip Ramp — *Μας προσπερνά/It's Overtaking Us*
Janice Miller Potter — *Meanwell*
Janice Miller Potter — *Thoreau's Umbrella*
Philip Ramp — *The Melancholy of a Life as the Joy of Living It Slowly Chills*
Joseph D. Reich — *A Case Study of Werewolves*
Joseph D. Reich — *Connecting the Dots to Shangrila*
Joseph D. Reich — *The Derivation of Cowboys and Indians*
Joseph D. Reich — *The Hole That Runs Through Utopia*
Joseph D. Reich — *The Housing Market*
Kenneth Rosen and Richard Wilson — *Gomorrah*
Fred Rosenblum — *Vietnumb*
David Schein — *My Murder and Other Local News*
Harold Schweizer — *Miriam's Book*
Scott T. Starbuck — *Carbonfish Blues*
Scott T. Starbuck — *Hawk on Wire*
Scott T. Starbuck — *Industrial Oz*
Seth Steinzor — *Among the Lost*
Seth Steinzor — *To Join the Lost*
Susan Thomas — *In the Sadness Museum*
Susan Thomas — *The Empty Notebook Interrogates Itself*
Paolo Valesio/Todd Portnowitz — *La Mezzanotte di Spoleto/Midnight in Spoleto*
Sharon Webster — *Everyone Lives Here*
Tony Whedon — *The Tres Riches Heures*
Tony Whedon — *The Falkland Quartet*
Claire Zoghb — *Dispatches from Everest*

Stories
Jay Boyer — *Flight*
L. M Brown — *Treading the Uneven Road*
Michael Cocchiarale — *Here Is Ware*
Michael Cocchiarale — *Still Time*
Neil Connelly — *In the Wake of Our Vows*
Catherine Zobal Dent — *Unfinished Stories of Girls*

Fomite

Zdravka Evtimova —*Carts and Other Stories*
John Michael Flynn — *Off to the Next Wherever*
Derek Furr — *Semitones*
Derek Furr — *Suite for Three Voices*
Elizabeth Genovise — *Where There Are Two or More*
Andrei Guriuanu — *Body of Work*
Zeke Jarvis — *In A Family Way*
Arya Jenkins — *Blue Songs in an Open Key*
Jan English Leary — *Skating on the Vertical*
Marjorie Maddox — *What She Was Saying*
William Marquess — *Boom-shacka-lacka*
Gary Miller — *Museum of the Americas*
Jennifer Anne Moses — *Visiting Hours*
Martin Ott — *Interrogations*
Christopher Peterson — *Amoebic Simulacra*
Jack Pulaski — *Love's Labours*
Charles Rafferty — *Saturday Night at Magellan's*
Ron Savage — *What We Do For Love*
Fred Skolnik— *Americans and Other Stories*
Lynn Sloan — *This Far Is Not Far Enough*
L.E. Smith — *Views Cost Extra*
Caitlin Hamilton Summie — *To Lay To Rest Our Ghosts*
Susan Thomas — *Among Angelic Orders*
Tom Walker — *Signed Confessions*
Silas Dent Zobal — *The Inconvenience of the Wings*

Odd Birds

William Benton — *Eye Contact: Writing on Art*
Micheal Breiner — *the way none of this happened*
J. C. Ellefson — *Under the Influence: Shouting Out to Walt*
David Ross Gunn — *Cautionary Chronicles*
Andrei Guriuanu and Teknari — *The Darkest City*
Gail Holst-Warhaft — *The Fall of Athens*
Roger Lebovitz — *A Guide to the Western Slopes and the Outlying Area*
Roger Lebovitz — *Twenty-two Instructions for Near Survival*

Fomite

dug Nap— *Artsy Fartsy*
Delia Bell Robinson — *A Shirtwaist Story*
Peter Schumann — *Belligerent & Not So Belligerent Slogans from the Possibilitarian Arsenal*
Peter Schumann — *Bread & Sentences*
Peter Schumann — *Charlotte Salomon*
Peter Schumann — *Faust 3*
Peter Schumann — *Planet Kasper, Volumes One and Two*
Peter Schumann — *We*

Plays

Stephen Goldberg — *Screwed and Other Plays*
Michele Markarian — *Unborn Children of America*

Essays

Robert Sommer — *Losing Francis: Essays on the Wars at Home*

CPSIA information can be obtained
at www.ICGtesting.com
Printed in the USA
LVHW050511160919
631107LV00002B/35